Advance praise for *The Butcher's Hook*

'Ellis has created something marvellous in the character of
Anne Jaccob – her voice is strange, dark and utterly mesmeric.
This is historical fiction as I've never encountered it before:
full of viscera, snarling humour and obsessive desire. I loved it'
Hannah Kent, bestselling author of *Burial Rites*

'Beautifully crafted. Janet Ellis is a masterful storyteller'
Clare Mackintosh, bestselling author of *I Let You Go*

'*The Butcher's Hook* is bewitching: Anne Jaccob is a dark and
dangerous heroine and her story is gripping and full of surprises.
This is an exciting and hugely impressive debut from Janet Ellis'
Antonia Hodgson, bestselling author of *The Devil In The
Marshalsea*

'A triumph; dark, shocking and funny. The voice is perfect and
the words glitter like little black jewels'
Erin Kelly, bestselling author of *The Poison Tree*

'Terrific . . . Anne is no 18th-century milquetoast heroine in
love. Her savagely witty observations of those around her
reveal a sharp and cunning mind . . . Every word of it is really
very good'
Bookseller

THE
BUTCHER'S
HOOK

THE BUTCHER'S HOOK

JANET ELLIS

www.tworoadsbooks.com
First published in Great Britain in 2016 by Two Roads

An imprint of John Murray Press
An Hachette UK company

1

Copyright © Janet Ellis 2016

A CIP catalogue record for this title is available from the British Library

Hardback ISBN 9781473625112
Trade Paperback ISBN 9781473625129
Ebook ISBN 9781473625136
Audio Digital Download ISBN 9781473625143

Printed and bound by Clays Ltd, St Ives plc

Hodder & Stoughton policy is to use papers that are natural, renewable and recyclable products and made from wood grown in sustainable forests. The logging and manufacturing processes are expected to conform to the environmental regulations of the country of origin.

Hodder & Stoughton Ltd
Carmelite House
50 Victoria Embankment
London EC4Y 0DZ
www.hodder.co.uk

To my darlings.
And for my mother.

'It is not from the benevolence of the butcher, the brewer or the baker that we expect our meal, but from their regard to their own interest.'

Adam Smith, *The Wealth of Nations, Book 1*

THE
BUTCHER'S
HOOK

Part One

'I am a little world, made cunningly.'

John Donne, *Holy Sonnets*

Chapter 1

London, 1763 – Summer

When my mother lay down to birth that last baby, she was so tired of everything that I thought I could have sold her shoes; surely she'd not get up and need them anymore.

I go to her now only because I should. My glass is full to the brim with sorrow and there is no room for another drop, whether sweet or sour. This is my nineteenth summer, but I have known only thirteen happy years to this date. And that is only if I include my early childhood in the reckoning, back when, in all honesty, I owned no accountable state of mind. Without that, it is a very poor tally.

Her room is heavy with a milky fug, close and thick; the curtains are drawn so that they fold over each other and there is only one lamp lit. It is not the time for visitors or street sellers; carriages go quickly past without stopping. These tall buildings stand opposite their identical counterparts in neat rows, matching window for window and door for door. Castle Street is a dull, brick corridor for any traffic to pass along without distraction. Even if there were people walking outside, they would not cast more than a glance at this unprepossessing house or wonder what is within.

I do not take much notice of the scrap in the cot – it seems a waste of fine linen and lace to me – but I put my hand on my mother's forehead and marvel at the cheery pink of my skin next to her cloudy grey face.

Do not think me harsh that I do not coo at this new-born infant, but I had done much loving with that boy my brother, and he had coughed his last just before his third birthday two years ago, so a lot of good all that loving did *him*. So many affections and songs and jolly games I'd put into him yet they could not keep his breath in his body. I am done with being light towards babies, and had thought my mother the same. After she saw him dead, she got dry and thin, like those cases of the honesty plant – do you know them? – that become crisp as paper, with all the seeds rattling inside.

But she was got again with child, before six months were gone. 'Perhaps another brother is coming!' she said, not meeting my eye. Her stomach had scarcely swelled before that baby had shrivelled and died there.

Only the doctor's coming and going marked her subsequent confinements. Their optimistic beginnings and bitter endings were not mentioned. The possibility of a sibling was no longer discussed. I never saw her sew a single stitch on a tiny garment or prepare the crib.

Once, though, she took my hand and held it to the round, curved front of her dress. A baby's movement pushed the cloth against my palm.

'The quickening!' she said. I pulled away – surely it would not live very much longer and I thought I might feel the very moment of its death if I kept my fingers there.

That baby had died as soon as it breathed air. Perhaps I had felt a fish swimming instead.

But this infant rattled around inside till she was spat out, with her nose in the air to sniff out love. I am cried too empty to hold her or do more than merely glance in the crib. I turned off my tears tight like a tap after my brother's small body was buried, and she will have to put her snout elsewhere for her games and rhymes.

My mother only stares at the ceiling, but she trails one hand over the rail of the child's bed. If I was to think of the mite, it would be to pity it: so new in the world and with only a cold sister turned away and a bony, limp hand dangled above it for company and comfort. Scarcely a week before, despite her full belly, my mother had held me to her and whispered some small sweet words close to my ear. I am woman enough now to carry my own infant, but I am still my mother's child, too. Let's see who is the better fighter for her favours. I'd been tested with such sadness as would try a martyr, and I'd stood straight. This new piglet won't get much room at the trough.

'Annie . . .' There is too much breath in my mother's voice, and yet not enough of it. She dozes, her lids half-closed. She will not remember this moment, I think.

When I was small, my nurse would hold my dark hair from my face and look at me carefully. 'You are not like your mother at all,' she'd say, 'but you are your father's child.' I do not have the flaxen hair of my mother, nor her bright beauty. It is faded now, like a rose, but not with the full-blown heaviness of the flower, but of a bud which was picked too soon and never bloomed.

My mother used to stand with her warm back pressed to

mine, to see where I reached against her. By the time I had grown above her head, she was seldom upright. 'Your eyes are the same colour as my sister's were,' she had told me once. My aunt had died when I was too young to be sad, but I hoped that my brown eyes did not upset my mother. They sat wide apart in my round face and looked at her with love, as her sister's once did. I had wanted to ask if I resembled her or anyone else in the family in other ways, but the moment passed. It was left to me to peruse my appearance and decide that my features were acceptable if not startling, and to note the narrowing span of my waist as I got taller.

The sash is closed tight. There seems hardly enough air in the room for the three of us to share. If my father could brick up all the windows he would – not to put money in his pocket, but because he has no use for light within or the sounds without his house. The curtains and wall coverings are all of a piece: a sprigged, floral pattern that my mother chose many years before. It has darkened with age and neglect, a barren field where once was a cheerful garden.

Her bedroom aches with my mother's weariness. If she is weary now, it is as much with what's in her heart as with the struggle of birth. I'd sat in the room below while she laboured, watching my father's face, while above us there were sounds that made me blush. He didn't flinch at my mother's grunts and low groans, neither did he smile at the small cry that followed. He only met my eye when the nurse, Grace (though why is she called that when she has none?) a silly red-faced girl not much older than I, tapped at the door and opened it wide as her fingers were still knocking.

'You have a daughter, Sir,' she said, important with news.

'I have two daughters then,' my father said, looking at me all the while. She laughed as though this was wit of the highest order, but I'll tell you why he didn't smile. Two daughters living and one son dead! What use is that to him? Why does this pig-faced idiot clap her pudgy hands together to applaud his achievement? He must rise from his chair and climb the stairs to hold a wife he doesn't love and admire a baby he doesn't want. My father has never exchanged a single private thought with me, yet I know what I know as surely as if he'd written a treatise.

I almost wished the nurse were a friend to me, so that we could share some confidence about his failings, while he was adding up ours. But then I looked at her face and thought myself better alone. No one but a fool could look so happy in a miserable house, could they? The mice here probably throw themselves on the traps for a quicker end.

The baby stirs and cries, and my mother rouses herself a little and picks the infant up from the crib. They are all white cotton and ribbon together, my mother unlacing her nightgown to free her dug. I look away. I do not want to watch this intimacy and the thought of it makes me squeamish. Tiptoeing to the door, I turn to see my mother's head bent over her task. I do not bid her farewell, only stop the door's slam with my arm so I do not attract her attention. In truth, the tableau disturbs me. The sounds of nursing and the sight of my mother's bare skin make all my thoughts complicated. For a moment I cannot tell which of them I envy more, but this envy makes my blood run hot.

The nurse stands on the landing, her face set as usual in a smirk. 'Evelyn,' she says. 'That's pretty, isn't it?' I don't answer, which she takes for ignorance. She is right. 'The baby's name,' she simpers. 'After her grandmother, your mother tells me.'

If I didn't think it would cause more trouble than it was worth, I'd box her ears for that. Cuff! for knowing the child's name before I did. Cuff! that I didn't think to ask what my sister was to be called. Cuff! for even mentioning my grandmother to me. I could cope with her tears, and watch the red weals rise on her face all right, indeed I would relish the sight, but if she prattled to my father or stormed out of the house I'd suffer for it worse than she her short smacking.

So I say nothing. From downstairs comes a hoarse 'Dinner!' and the nurse nods her head to me a little, remembering at last that she is in our employ, and pushes open my mother's door.

'Let me take her when you are done.' She sings the words almost, adding 'ohs' and 'ahs' and 'nows' as she goes about her business. Then there is rustling and murmuring, the mingled noises of these women and that child and I go away from what troubles me.

My father is already seated at the dining table, a large wodge of linen at his throat, a glass of wine in his hand. I suppose we cannot afford another maid, or my father will not pay more likely, so the cook serves on. Which is a shame for her, as she must listen to my father's nightly abuse of her offerings. She is supposed to take off her apron before bringing in plates and bowls, as if to mark her transition between stove and table, but oftentimes forgets and it amuses me to see her try and turn her apron behind her back with one hand, as she balances her load with the other. Tonight she has realised once more that she still wears the thing and attempts to roll all the fabric up and tuck it in to the waist of her skirt while aiming to distribute the plates between us.

My father regards her with contempt. 'Just bring the food, Jane.' He doesn't rise to help her, or include me in what might be a shared amusement.

'Oh, Mr Jaccob,' Jane says, 'this baby arrived safely, thank the Lord. Does she resemble her mother?'

'Does this resemble meat?' My father grunts his words, pushing at the meal in front of him with his knife. 'What grey beast died for this, eh, Jane? And how long it must have suffered, for no amount of good living would lead to this quantity of gristle in death. And you have added to its misery with poor gravy and sad potatoes.'

Jane bobs, and tucks and pulls at her wretched apron, and altogether makes such a complete show of being a miserable woman that I don't like to look at her. Bright spots of shame paint livid colour on her cheeks, and her voice trembles.

'I swear I cooked it as usual, Mr Jaccob, but I'll tell the butcher's boy of your displeasure.'

'You are a gang together, a pair of idiots: one who can't sell good meat, the other who can't prepare it.' He continues in this vein for a long time, all the while shovelling in and chewing at the accursed stuff. The linen at his throat turns brown with gravy, he sometimes grabs at the folds of material and swipes them over his chin and cheeks. I wonder, if Jane were to leave the room, might he subside like a pricked bladder and grow quiet? But she stays and stands and falters and apologises and tries to change the subject. The one probably needs the other, I think: this nightly ritual, their ridiculous conversation.

I stare at the floor. The painted petals and leaves have worn thin under my feet to reveal a dull, dark green beneath. In the church the stone stairs bow under the footsteps of the pious, as they all take the same path to prayer. I am very far from good thoughts and proper observance as I sit here, scuffing the floor cloth into a smear, day after day. The heavy furniture seems to close in. I think it must creep towards the middle of the room when I'm not looking, like the child's game.

Do not imagine that I have lived only in this endless winter. The sky above my head was not always the colour of an old man's snot. There was a time of such bright light you would have to shield your eyes and, until you were accustomed to the glare, you would be only able to make out shapes. But then you'd surely look twice to make sure you were seeing what you thought you saw. That man bending to swing a little boy onto his shoulders then imitating a whole farmyard to make him laugh? That was my father. That woman singing as she went about her day or making a dolly walk and talk and say nonsense to entertain a child? Not her twin, but my mother . . .

* * *

My mother was so often confined to her bed when I was a child that I barely remembered her being well. The cause of her indisposition was never mentioned to me, although I heard whispered clues and decided the reason for myself. *'Poor woman, another one died.' 'Will she ever carry to term?' 'Burn that little shawl, she won't want to see it again.'*

The changing for the better happened slowly. My mother's swelling stomach was mildly interesting and I stood in front of my glass with a cushion under my petticoat to see how it suited me. But I did not imagine it would mean a new person in the world. When he arrived, the baby was swaddled not only with blankets and quilts, but with his own mucky binding. The crusted rime at his ears, the posseting puke that dried rancid and hard, his caterwauling insistence on attention and comfort all reminded me more of young animals than people. I asked when he would talk or play and was met with patronising answers. 'All in good time, Anne,' or, 'Nature will decide.'

There was an energy in the house, though, which was all the more surprising as its little instigator did nothing. He only fed and slept and followed each large face with his new eyes as they bent over his cot to greet him. But I saw my father stand aside to let Jane pass instead of colliding with and then rebuking her. I watched him touch my mother's arm lightly and deliberately as he asked after her day. I noticed her glance at him when in company and how warmly he returned her look. I was not jealous of the effect the infant had, but only curious as to how this little body, that could only lie flat on his back, could cause it.

'Give him this toy,' my mother held out a little dog made of soft cloth. I turned it round to inspect it. I knew it to be a thing I had played with. It had two cross-stitch eyes and a small bell hung from its ribbon collar. I shook it to hear the familiar little jangle. My mother watched me, pensive. 'My Anne. You are fourteen, you're nearly a grown woman. It seems only moments since this was your toy and you crawled to fetch it.' My mother went to take it back, but I turned to the cot and waggled it about over the baby. My brother did not look at this offering, but instead fixed his lidless stare on me. And smiled. As if his mouth instructed his whole body, he poured his good feeling from the length of him. His toes pointed in joy and he curled and waved his fists with happiness. I could not help but smile back, which only increased his response. Like idiots, we gazed at each other and prolonged this wordless exchange.

'He smiles at you!' I did not need my mother's confirmation. I put my fingers to my brother's little hand and he gripped as hard as his untested muscles allowed, which was strong enough to squeeze my heart, too.

After that I could not wait, on waking each day, to go to him. I propped pillows behind his back before he could sit alone, to show him more of the world. I made sounds in his ear until he could copy them. I held his arms as he sat on my lap and clapped them together to hear him laugh as his pudgy palms met. I was moved to tears by the beauty of the place where his neck joined his back. I marvelled at the unworldly softness of his skin. I curled the immature tresses of his downy hair till they stood from his head like a halo. 'Where is Anne?' I played peekaboo with him, hiding my face behind a scarf. 'Am!' he said confidently when I reappeared. I crouched in front of him to encourage his steps and applauded even when he toppled. I will not catalogue all his achievements but you can be sure they followed the path of any such infant. He learnt steadily and rejected or accepted what he needed to build him. He was probably no cleverer and no more beautiful than others. I have seen wrists as plump and heard sounds as sweetly gurgling since. But he filled me as completely and lightly as feathers in a quilt.

If my mother seldom vouchsafed a confidence or asked me my thoughts, I forgave her for this boy was more than reparation.

I could not imagine the world would ever change and indeed, on the day that it did, the sun rose as always, in mocking imitation of a better morning.

My father stood outside the nursery like a guard and put his hand across to prevent me passing. 'The doctor comes,' he said, keeping his eyes to the floor.

Panic laid cold hands on my skin as if I stood there naked. I had hardly enough wind in me to speak. 'What is wrong?' I whispered.

'A fever. Your mother found him ailing,' he said, still looking away.

'Did he not cry out?' I said. If my brother had spoken 'Anni!' in his quietest voice, I would have heard him and scampered to his side.

'He was very brave and waited till she came,' my father said. I thought this elision of illness and courage very stupid. When he was well, I would teach him to fear every sniffle.

'Let me past,' I pushed at my father's barring arm.

'There may be a contagion,' he hissed, but he let me win the contest.

The room within was muted with fear. My mother sat by his bed and Jane was pressing a flannel in a basin. I could hardly focus on him when I looked to see. His eyes were closed but when I called his name, he opened them to reveal a glassy stare.

'He sees angels already,' said Jane. I struck her hard on the arm. She winced, but did not make a sound. My fingers were still sore with the blow when I put them to his forehead. It was ridiculously hot.

'Where is the doctor?' I said, not taking my hand away though I hated what I felt.

'He comes, he is sent for,' my mother said, her voice high with anxiety.

The doctor's arrival caused the curtains to flutter and the

candle flame to shake, but I stayed immobile as a statue. He bent over him and rubbed at his chest and put a tincture under his tongue, but my brother slipped further from my desperate arms.

'He sleeps,' the doctor pronounced, though there was no discernible change in him. 'You should rest, too,' he turned to my mother. She shut her eyes at once, as though he hypnotised her with this instruction.

Jane led her from the room. 'Tell us if . . .' she left her sentence unfinished, but the words she didn't say reverberated as if she had shouted them.

The doctor began to unscrew yet another vial of liquid. 'Leave!' I said to him. He did not question the command. His very obedience demonstrated what little more he could do. When we were alone, I began to speak to my brother but my voice trembled and I stopped. I did not want him to hear me falter and then feel afraid. His breathing was so shallow I could not see any movement in the bedding. I put a fingertip to his nose. If I pinched his nostrils even lightly together, he would fade like a shadow exposed to light. His suffering would cease. His eyes snapped open and he read my intent. I snatched my hand away. I began to make promises to the empty air if he could live. Before I could even say *Amen*, his last breath failed to reach his tiny heart.

I would not leave his side. Though my mother begged and my father admonished, while the doctor left me medicine and Jane brought food that I did not touch, I stayed. It was not until the vicar arrived, kissing his jewellery and making signs that I got to my feet. He blessed the small body, muttering of heaven and pure souls. He wrapped him in a linen shroud that would cling more diligently than his clothes ever did, for he wriggled and kicked in life. My mother and father knelt with clasped hands and closed eyes to pray to their God, but I only watched a man tend a corpse.

The day after he was buried, although I lay with a pillow to my head to muffle my thoughts of him in the earth, I could not help but hear my mother and father raise their voices to each other.

'There is still love.' My mother was pleading. She sounded like a little girl. 'There will be other children.'

'I wanted my son,' my father said. I hugged the pillow tighter but his words leaked in.

'And we still have Anne. We still have each other,' the child-woman said. 'You still have me.'

He roared his answer. I would never be deaf to it. 'You are not enough!' And again, '*You are not enough*.'

Chapter 2

Her ordeal almost over ('Stop clattering and spattering, woman!'), Jane collects up the plates and leaves the room.

The clock has an echo within the case, and every tick-k-k tock-k-k reverberates in the room. Perhaps I shall count the minutes as the clock chops the silence about. My father tugs the napkin free from his neck, wipes around his mouth strenuously with it then bares his teeth to rub his gums. I hope he will not turn his gaze to me. I must neither catch his eye nor seem to evade him. There might be some topic he wants to address and he will sermonise and lecture till he is done, without interruption. He will not take too long about it, at least: he always tires swiftly both of his own voice and my face.

It was not ever thus. When I was a child of perhaps ten or so years, he seemed suddenly to find me diverting. I was a bright little thing, eager to ask questions and learn facts. 'Listen to her recite!' he would say to my mother, and I would entertain them both with a song, or recitation, even some Latin, that my father had put in my head. My father's old friend Dr Edwards stayed with us a while during this brief period of my father's affection and, being a scholar and seeing my appetite, he persuaded my father to let me sit at lessons with him.

*   *   *

Ah, Dr Edwards. If I had thought the world an amazing place before now, with Dr Edwards to guide me I understood, vividly and for the first time, what you might carry in your head about the things you could see. The people he told me of and the strange words he knew!

'My friend Onions has told me about a delicious Zoffany,' he said one day, laughing with me at the strange conjunction of names but then describing a painting so clearly to me that I could imagine I smelled the paint.

He unlocked the secret code of the Latin I'd chanted in ignorance, to reveal its meaning. *'Da mi basia mille, deinde centum,'* he recited, sliding a little Catullus onto my lap. *'Give me a thousand kisses, then a hundred.* See how he declares himself.'

He taught me the names of plants. He showed me maps of foreign lands and spoke to me in their tongues. He read me the plays of William Shakespeare, he took all the parts himself and played each enchantingly well. Even at the piano he excelled and we sang together – I was uninhibited then – and it made us laugh to harmonise and warble.

Dr Edwards' eyes were rheumy and dim; he was rather alarmingly whiskered and (though I was not offended by it, for I loved him) he was even a little unpalatable to be near: he carried a great deal of his luncheon in his beard and often it was not even the luncheon of the day, but of several days before. His coarse coat scratched him at the collar, where he rubbed his neck raw, and although his two front teeth top and bottom were sturdy, their fellows were absent or black. But he was handsome to me, as he was the key to learning, the gatekeeper of the wider world.

He visited only once weekly, but in the days between I pored over the books that he left, I memorised every word he ordered and more besides. If he had told me to learn all Shakespeare's works, I'd have attempted it for certain – but he was a reasonable man, and only asked what I could properly do.

And so we sat, side by side, on a hard settle (my father not lending us his study, we had no desk and were forced to make a schoolroom out of a scarcely used anteroom) and to each of my questions Dr Edwards had a reply. 'Why does a caterpillar move as it does?' 'Why should it make a cocoon?' 'Tell me about the sizes of the moon.' 'Explain to me how the sun shines!' I had so many questions, it was as if everything I'd wondered at had been held tightly wound in my head and now it unspooled, to my teacher's obvious delight, and he proffered his learning with a lightness I still miss.

'What does London look like?' I said. 'I can only see a little way in front of us from my window.'

He reached into his bag for a book, but then stayed his hand. 'A practical demonstration,' he said, getting to his feet. 'Come.'

We had to step round Jane, she was on the floor in the hall cutting a large spread of moreen in two. She and Dr Edwards pretended to be in a kind of dance as he passed her, joining their red hands together. She came just to his waist in height as she was on her knees and so could only sway to and fro.

Dr Edwards left the house at a brisk pace. I had not been out in the streets with him before and he seemed to forget that I did not know the way. He did not always remember that I was with him, either. He kept up a constant dialogue aloud with himself as we went, punctuated by wheezes and coughs. 'Must *not* pass on the left hand side here, Huggins might see me through the window and it would be: *"Where's the money? A debt is a debt."* He's stuck with those words now, isn't he, till I pay up and free him. Which I shall not. Eh, Huggins? Ah, no, NOT that way, no, Sir, no, Marylebone Gardens are out of bounds. Too much temptation and not enough pleasure after. Old Davenport, isn't that where he fell? Righted quickly but still limping. Though I swear I've seen him dip down on both legs forgetting which was lame. Number 21! I could eat that sweet stuff she served there at every meal. What was her name? She told me how many eggs but I cannot recall much else. What was she called? Ten eggs. Ten!'

I wasn't listening, I was more concerned with avoiding collision with the other pedestrians. I tried to observe where we walked, too, but what with Dr Edwards hastening and chuntering and the crowded streets, I only caught brief glimpses of doorways and railings and the beginnings of flights of stairs whose ends I could not see.

When we came to open ground, with a high hill before us, Dr Edwards appeared to notice me as if for the first time. 'Anne! Here we are.' It was a scrubby place, dotted with some ramshackle cottages and lacklustre vegetation. 'We shall not linger,' Dr Edwards said, seeing that I was puzzled about why we had gone there at all. He breathed in with relish, as though the atmosphere had markedly improved in quality. 'Fresh air!' he declared. I could still smell the fumes and vapours as before, but I agreed to humour him, inhaling deeply through my open mouth. 'Take some lungs full, you will need plenty for the climb.' I knew, as did he, that you could not store air inside you but that you must repeat and replenish your breath every moment. I hoped the exertion of our walk had not knocked all knowledge from his body. He reassured me by taking up our lesson as we proceeded, pointing out flowers and trees. He tested me on the names of blooms I'd hitherto seen only in illustration and hurrahed when I was correct. His words came with more difficulty as we ascended and by the time we neared the top any botany was beyond him. It was an effort for me to climb, too, my head was bent over with concentration. There were little rocks and hillocks on the path and I didn't want to stumble.

We stood facing each other on the summit, panting and blinking. Wiping away tears of effort, Dr Edwards put his hands heavily on my shoulders. 'Close your eyes,' he instructed. He propelled me round to face away from him. 'Open,' he said, still breathing hard close to my ear and spattering me with hot air.

In front of me, precise as a tapestry, was a spectacular, great, open spread of fields and distant buildings. The river snaked and looped, careless of what had to be built around and over it. The sky above us seemed wider here than when we stood on the ground, as though we needed a greater space above us to marvel at the panorama below. At first Dr Edwards pointed out landmarks that I was familiar with and then proceeded to indicate places as foreign to me as were any abroad. I began to make sense of the living geography he illustrated.

'And there you live,' Dr Edwards pointed to the right. The houses were too far away to be distinct, but I could imagine the neat rows and the ordered streets. From our viewpoint, the trees and green spaces held sway, mocking any attempt to restrain them. They could easily overpower the man-made landscape if they chose, forcing roots through the floorboards and sending thorny brambles to reclaim the alleyways.

The vast sky and the high hill should have made me feel closer to heaven than earth, but lately I had begun to have doubts about the Almighty. I was winded by the huge responsibility of God's tasks. He seemed to punish or reward indiscriminately, presumably as he was overwhelmed by the magnitude of His responsibilities. How could He keep His all-seeing eye on all of us at once, for instance, even from this most convenient spot? If He had watched Dr Edwards and me walking here just now, how could He have minded my mother and father, too? And Jane was often out of sight in the kitchen. Did He really trust her to be alone?

'Dr Edwards,' I said, noticing that his jacket was torn at the pocket where he had caught it on some errant branch, 'where is God and how can He be everywhere? I am not sure,' I said, regarding the chaos of human creation below us, 'that He is anywhere at all.'

Dr Edwards puffed out his cheeks. This forewarned me that his answer would either be lengthy or obscure. When he divulged a simple fact, he jumped on it like a boy into a river. 'Well, I do not think He is *up there*,' he pointed over his head. 'Or in any building.' We could both see St Paul's, which seemed to stand for all churches. 'It is pleasant to attend a place of worship, though. And some of the language in the Bible is very fine. But who knows what awaits us after all this is done? In this world we, not an invisible deity, are the architects of our lives.' He waited to see what I would say, bouncing his fingers against his lips. I said nothing.

'I doubt, too,' he went on, 'that we are created innocent and become filled up with desires and vices, evils that we can avoid only by devotion to prayer.' He lowered his voice as though we were overheard. 'To my mind, we carry all that we need to survive, indeed to live well, in our heads and our hearts from birth. We must decide our own paths accordingly and individually. There is precious little other instruction available.'

'Who cares for us, then?' I said, thinking of my nightly petitions on behalf of my whole family to this effect.

'Each for the other. Or not,' he replied. He watched me weigh up this new idea. 'You should continue to attend services,' he said brightly, 'I find one can use the time for a great deal of inspiring private thought and examination.' Dr Edwards' hair spiralled in the wind that buffeted us from all directions. The scudding clouds behind his head made it seem as if he was falling towards me. I thought that if God had manifested beside him then, they might be taken for twins.

I stretched my hand out in front of me and pinched my fingers together where my house stood, as though I was a giant who could destroy the building with one squeeze. I raised my hand and imagined my family tumbling against the walls as I lifted it up, making them cling fearfully to the furniture and slide, helpless, across the floors. I set it back down gently. I felt tender towards the household then, a sentiment I have since found impossible to summon.

'When your father and I first went to Castle Street, there was only brown earth. We watched it grow brick by brick.' He glanced at me. 'I expect you imagine us looking then much as we do now.' It was true, I could only picture them both overseeing the work and examining plans together as the portly and broad-shouldered men that I saw each day. 'We were young,' he said. Try as I might, I could not shrink their bellies or lighten their steps in my mind's eye. On the way home, Dr Edwards seemed melancholy, as though he had only recently exchanged coats with his younger self and wanted his youthful one back.

We didn't speak of the Almighty again. I was satisfied that Dr Edwards had drawn our discussion to a proper conclusion. But now that we had touched so easily on this grave subject, surely any other question I raised could be as swiftly and simply answered.

*　　*　　*

One day I asked him about the differences in a man and woman's body – I had been regarding myself carefully of late, gazing down at my body and feeling all of its shapes with my hands and fingers. I'd only the briefest acquaintance with the form of a man and mostly, I confess, from paintings. I remember one most vividly; it hung on the wall at my aunt's house. It was a depiction of a saint: naked, doubtless persecuted, carrying a large wooden cross, his body bent over away from the painter. This back view showed a round behind and a long back studded with bones. The buttocks were large and taut, the painter had gilded everything with the fierce rays of a high bright sun and this light burnished his flesh as the figure strained. Looking at this image stirred something in me that could not be explained, and I felt on the cusp of some great revelation. Dr Edwards, with his kindly gaze and great learning, must be the person to help.

I described the scene to him as best I could – the angle of the man's body, his muscles engorged as he gripped and grappled with his burden.

'Why did the sainted man have such a wideness to him?' I asked. Dr Edwards smiled, he pawed at his neck and the skin there stretched under his nails. 'It seems to me that a woman could not be made that way, that she must be narrow.' I continued in this sorry fashion; I did not have the words to find out properly what I wanted to know.

Did Dr Edwards pause, did he question how he might proceed and discard caution? I see myself, barely nine, looking up at him, all infant brightness and keen anticipation, and then I see him regarding me with, perhaps, a different gaze. Did he clear his throat? I think he cleared his throat.

'It is a complicated thing, this difference of which you speak,' he began. 'It is mainly regarding the matter of new life. Did your aunt just recently bear you a cousin?'

'She did. A squalling thing, too. Must we speak of babies?'

'Inspect him closely, before we speak again.'

'Inspect him? In what way?'

'The virile difference, child. The way he's shaped.'

How I wished I had only asked about the umlaut and why it bent the vowels in its charge. Or why spices made me sneeze. But I had posed a question and Dr Edwards would answer it. I had no need to peer closely at a baby boy, I understood what Dr Edwards hinted at – the nobbly flesh sac between the legs of a male. It was its *purpose* I'd wondered at, not its *existence*. I blush now to think how I'd asked him such a thing outright, and I blush even more at what happened next.

*   *   *

You cannot say my teacher wasn't eager to impart what he knew, and you must marvel at how practical the lessons became. The next week Dr Edwards arrived with sheaves of paper, each illustrated with representations of men and women together. Fear not, they were not in any way demonstrative of what I'd enquired: the reason for their differences. They were depictions only of men and women posed in pairs, as if they were courting. Chastely, his painted examples gazed at each other, they held hands at most, and only their eyes met.

'Do you see how these two types of person, the opposite of each other in many ways, must cleave together?' Dr Edwards shuffled his pages to show yet more pairs at play or conversation.

'Must they?' I'd given up thinking about what I'd asked. Since our last lesson, I'd heard a song in French that amused me, eaten a berry I'd never tasted before and watched a spider spin a web. I had much to ask about each, but here was Dr Edwards still wandering doggedly in the cul de sac of last week's enquiry, not out on the open road of this week's fascinations.

Dr Edwards got up from his seat, walked to the doorway and stood there listening, his gaze on me the while. 'Are we alone?' he asked. 'For this instruction is a private one, and we mustn't be disturbed.'

I nodded. The household seemed uninterested in what Dr Edwards and I talked about in our lesson, and left us alone for its duration. Obediently, I fell silent too. We listened together: the house was still.

Dr Edwards began to unbutton his coat. His britches were tight about his waist and his shirt billowed above them. Sitting back down beside me, he wrestled the fabric from its tucking and draped it with some care over his lap. He continued to fret and worry his hands underneath this shroud. Why didn't he speak? This extraordinary action surely needed a commentary. He only breathed heavily, his face working as if he were chewing hard bread.

'There!' He turned his head sideways to me, and freed one hand to take mine.

In hindsight, I like to think that I was reluctant, that I pulled back a little from his grip, but I think I let him guide me all too easily to where he wished my hand to go. My fingers were placed around what I fancied felt like a child's small arm, tense and warm to my touch. All the while, Dr Edwards looked me in the eyes, his expression triumphant, as if he had performed a magic trick I should admire. I moved my hand away a little, which had a startling effect on Dr Edwards, who till then – although serious – had stayed calm.

'No!' Was he angry? I began to retract my hand. 'No!' he cried again, and placed my hand back on the object. 'This a man has,' he said, in a hoarse whisper, 'and the woman must make a little space between her legs to let it enter her. Thus, a baby is born.'

We had only studied the merest Latin till then, and briefly dallied with a little French and German. There was some Italian, too. Now I felt as if he talked in another language altogether, and puzzlingly fast, too. Enter a space between a woman's legs to make a child? The man was clearly mad, and I began to feel a little frightened. Not of his strange claims – I could cast those off as soon as he left, I had obviously reached the very edges of his learning and he was consequently resorting to invention – no, I was afraid of his demeanour, of his reddening face and tense gait. He sat bolt upright, all his energies going into that one place, to the thing I held, that I was barely able to keep my fingers around even as he bid me keep them there. It seemed to grow and swell, it fought against my grip while Dr Edwards exhorted me to hold on.

You know what happened next, I think. How his hard muscle erupted in a terrible hot mess then softened in my grasp, how his breath laboured then calmed. You can imagine how he took my hand tenderly and wiped my fingers with his handkerchief. I recall I blanched at this, because to add to the indignity of my suddenly sticky hand, his kerchief had recently attended to his nose and I had a vivid image of its contents smeared onto my open palm. I felt as dizzy as when you leave a carousel, and the spinning world in your head adjusts slowly to the stationary ground under your feet.

I did not feel afraid, but I knew all was changed between Dr Edwards and me. I once kept a mouse for a few days in a wooden box in my bedroom. I had found it small and sickly in the middle of the floor; it had made no attempt to escape when I lifted it – its body so light I could only tell that I held it by keeping my eyes fixed on its little form – and I fancied I could tame it and restore it to full mouse health. Of course, it did not live long and when I found its tiny corpse, I felt as sad as if I had loved it for all my life. I had wanted a playmate pet; I had imagined making miniature beds and toys for it, and it had died and none of this was possible. Such plans I had for it, all now dead, too, and how my little heart grieved.

I had similarly conjured a world where Dr Edwards and I would continue to study together. Why should we not? We had both enjoyed our meetings, after all. Until this time, he was the fount of all wisdom to me and I imagined I would never tire of his teaching. Perhaps we would progress to the practical, not in the grotesque way Dr Edwards had done, mind, but with a little botany in the open countryside, some geography in travel, much conversation *in situ*. We had created a schoolroom in an unloved part of the house, we could just as easily build a classroom in a field or foreign town.

Fount of wisdom? Oh there was a *fount* all right. His personal geyser had fairly flooded the land of my ignorance and wiped out my innocence, too, as it spilled its gelatinous matter. I was crudely shot to the study of advanced physiology in one lesson and could not unlearn what I knew.

What happened next? There must have been an adjustment of his clothing, a gathering of his papers, I don't recall. Did he pause at the door to turn and talk to me? I don't remember what was said. I do know that Dr Edwards did not exhort me to keep my counsel about the events of the afternoon, neither did I weep when he left, though I was miserable.

'Do you leave now, Ted?' My father stopped him in the hallway. There was a scrabbling noise as Dr Edwards pulled on his cape; next I heard his boots scuffing the floor. Around me, the portraits on the wall met my gaze. We all knew more now than we knew a moment since.

'On my way, Sir.' Dr Edwards coughed a reply.

'And is her head more full of matter now?' Said with a smirk in his voice. The painted faces around me leered.

'Indeed it is. You will find her much enhanced.'

There was some more muffled conversation with my father as he left – no wonder he hurried away – and shortly after, my father called to me. He stood in the hallway as I came downstairs, taking each step as slowly as a toddler. He saw nothing different about me, I'm sure, though I felt transfigured. In a clear voice, I told my father I had had enough of learning. He was delighted. He fancied a girl's head could not hold much, anyway, and although he'd found my recitations and the like diverting, it never occurred to him it might have any value to me. My wishing to retreat was proof positive that, had I continued, it would all have come to nothing in time.

It was not that I was repulsed by Dr Edwards' member or its unexpected contents. If he had promised never to behave in such a way again, if he had chastised himself to me for this aberration and sworn he had not intended it to happen, I still could not have studied with him afterwards. It was for *this* reason: when I held him and worked my hand around him, I saw that I was making a thing happen to him that I was completely in charge of. His expression of desire had waxed and waned according to the grip of my fingers. His urgency unmanned him and made him weak.

How foolish he looked! If ever I think of Dr Edwards now, it amuses me to remember his round eyes and lolling tongue.

* * *

'Why do you laugh, you foolish girl?' My father addresses me now as I sit at the table with him: I swear I had quite forgotten he was there. I don't think he has heard me speak in a good long while, much less say his name.

'I was imagining the sweet games I might play with my new sister,' I reply, knowing this answer would silence him. He has no time for the pretty thoughts of women. Any of their thoughts, come to that.

He makes a sound in his throat as he stands and pushes back his chair. Without another glance in my direction, he leaves. The air in the room ripples a little as he swings the door wide.

Chapter 3

How were the days punctuated after Dr Edwards left me so abruptly? In the great world beyond our doors, the world turned as it ever does. I suppose that the sun rose and set and the seasons changed. As usual, buds swelled and blossomed. Rain washed away leaves. I imagine that snow replaced frost. Water would have hardened to ice then melted. These things happen regularly, whether we are aware of them or not. There was a pattern to our habits, too, but it was a dull one, devoid of colour. My father farted at nine o'clock in the morning as he performed his ablutions; the church clock chimed in his malodorous wake. The clamour of the house rose toward noon, while tradesmen called and those with household duties bumped heads or clinked crockery, then subsided towards dusk. We had a few visitors; sometimes they sat with my mother and, once, I heard her laugh. I waited till her companions left and when I peeped over the banister, I saw her tug her cap back to the middle of her head where she'd skittered it happily askew.

My mother was mostly to be found in her bed, though: either keeping her insides still to hold a baby there, or to rest them after they had expelled another unformed infant. There were always copious sheets and linens hung to dry in the yard. The flapping of them as they caught in the wind made me think of ships and sails. But I was marooned. Dr Edwards had cast me off from boredom and let me fish in new waters. Until his ridiculous behaviours struck rock and wrecked us both.

All the knowledge that Dr Edwards had put in my head sat there unmoving, a petrified forest whose branches would never send out leaves. I truly believed that I had learnt everything I would ever know. No one spoke to me at length any more. I was enduring a grotesque hibernation; it was not a delicious oblivion but a waking torpor. I am describing the passage of some two years, I suppose, but there were few anniversaries to punctuate the passing months.

From only one room in the house did I hear anything like the exchange of information, beyond women's voices giving instruction about stewing food or starching laundry. My father conducted some of his morning business in his room and, more often than not, I found myself pausing as I passed to listen to what was being said.

Before long I was deliberately waiting at the window of the drawing room to see if my father had visitors. From this upper vantage point, they were a collection of wigs and hats. Sometimes a protuberant nose was visible or a cloak flowed behind them. Some dawdled and strolled, others flapped and rushed. They never raised their eyes, so no one ever noticed me and I was keen to remain unseen. As soon as I thought they were ensconced in his study and after the first pleasantries had been exchanged (for I learnt to avoid the preamble about health or the weather), I would creep as near as I could and, having opened my little book of fables to seem occupied with reading it, I would sit on the stairs and eavesdrop.

If you were to pull my fingernails from their roots with sharp pliers, I could not recall a single useful sentence from that time. It was all to do with monies and weights and foremen. They spoke of forecasts. They argued about timetables and transactions. It was not of course the content that I craved, but the delightful ebb and flow of conversation. With each slight altercation or shared amusement, my skin tingled with pleasure. Although I did not understand their meaning, the words thrilled me, too. I wrote them afterwards on a blank page at the back of my book, spitting in my inkwell to revive it. I could make only a poor attempt at the spellings.

My father would signal the end of these episodes with a rise in volume, and a bluff 'Well, then!' or 'We shall see!' as he brought things to a conclusion. This was my cue to scurry away.

One day, though, I was so genuinely distracted by the tale of the 'Wolf in Sheep's Clothing' that it was only when my father and his companion stood in front of me in the hallway, their boots close together on the tiles, two brown and two black, that I looked up.

'What's this?' said the other fellow, taking the book from me without my permission and bending it to read the cover.

'This one always reads,' my father said, as though he was apologising for a fault.

'I have such a child at home,' the man returned the book to me with a wink. 'It is like a thirst, isn't it, so I suppose a little book from time to time will quench it.' He winked again. I kept my two eyes on him without blinking.

By now I had risen to my feet and was going backwards up the stairs away from them, feeling for each tread with my heel.

'Perhaps,' the man continued, 'I should bring my daughter here, to sit with her, next time we meet.'

My father's eyebrows rose in query. 'If you think it a good idea,' he said, without enthusiasm. His visitor must be valuable to him, I supposed, otherwise he would have squashed that notion flat. My heart sank at the prospect of a companion, particularly one I hadn't chosen. This man was a great long coil of a person, his face was a thin stripe of flesh with features squeezed on, even his hands were stretched and narrow. I imagined his daughter perched beside me, so tall that her hair would catch the breeze, like a pennant on a ship's mast.

'She is a little older, I think.' He regarded me carefully as if he could determine my years by staring. 'What age are you? Ten?'

'Twelve,' I said, peeved that he thought me so childish.

'Ah, Keziah is fourteen. Not so much your senior.' Enough to create a chasm, I thought, already convinced that she was an old maid.

Satisfied, the two men went to the door where I could hear them slapping hands and backs in farewell.

All the taste and flavour had gone out of my spying. My father set off alone the next day anyway, but I didn't watch him go.

*   *   *

A few weeks later, when I was despairing of any distractions, he told me at dinner that Mr Heath had called in the morning and he was bringing his child. 'You might look out some books,' he said. Unmoved by his instruction, I did not reply. I was not about to oil the wheels of his business by entertaining sundry offspring. I resolved to keep my counsel and to make the girl feel entirely unwelcome on her first visit and thus she would wish to abstain from another. By habit, I stood at the window to watch them arrive. Heath was loping, bent slightly forward to show me the curve of his back. His stride was as long as his height and, beside him, reaching only to his shoulder, bounced an unbonneted head of yellow hair.

I do not know why my heart quickened at the sight of her, because I had not seen Keziah's face then and her little hands were hidden in a muff. Perhaps it was the keen vigour of her gait, or the way her feet pointed out from her skirt that excited me. When I think of her now, in spite of everything that happened, I can still summon that sharp thrill at her arrival.

We stood awkwardly beside our fathers as they introduced us. She gazed up at hers with affection as he announced her name to me: 'Keziah!' But I only stared at her. She kept her hands in her silk muff and I thought they must be warm there. I longed to feel inside it. Once the men had closed the door behind them, she looked enquiringly at me.

'Where shall we sit?' she said, looking about. There was no chair in the hall. The stairs looked coarse and inhospitable – she wore a pale costume and wouldn't want it marked.

'Shall we go to your room?' she asked. That startled me: when I thought of that most private space, the walls seemed to bulge and swell and the furniture grew sharp. How would this girl manage without snagging her dress?

'Do you keep your books there?' She was already going upstairs. She must have thought I slept in a library.

'There are only a few,' I panted as I tried to keep up. She was taller than I and took the stairs easily. My own legs felt stunted in comparison. With each step, she appeared stronger and more graceful while I shrunk and thickened. On the landing, she had to pause to let me lead the way. The ranks of closed doors offered no clue as to which was mine. I went ahead of her down the corridor and had to stop myself knocking before I went into my own room, as if to warn it that we had company.

I doubt that I would have arranged anything differently if I had known that she might inspect here, but I noted with relief that my pot was tucked away and my coverlet pressed flat. There were no items of clothing left about and only a poke of lace from the dresser drawer betrayed any intimacy.

'Oh!' said Keziah, looking forlornly at this monkish cell. 'You are a little Spartan.' I bridled.

People had a habit of describing me as a 'little something-or-other'. 'Our little Columbus', my mother once said, taking me on a rare visit. 'My little Linnaeus!' Dr Edwards announced with glee as I pulled a stem apart. I did not feel little at all, indeed parts of me were growing very fast and I could no longer run my hands over my body without encountering new hills. 'There is not much on display,' I agreed.

'Ah! But much is hidden?' Keziah said. I did not like being teased, it usually made me itch to retaliate, but hers had a light quality. It was as if she opened her arms wide to me, to show nothing was concealed. 'Where are your dresses?' She opened the door of my wardrobe as she said this and brushed one hand lightly against the fabric hanging there. She cannot have been expecting to find a great many treats. 'Do you have a length of ribbon?' she asked, closing the door again without any comment on the contents. I fetched her a piece from the drawer below and she held it wide apart. 'Come here,' she said. I tensed with embarrassment as she circled my waist with the ribbon, joining her hands behind my back to mark the circumference. 'There! Now mine.' Raising her arms above her head, she stood still as

I encircled her narrow frame. She noted the discrepancy with a happy squeak. 'Mine is smaller,' she said, a scientist proved right. 'But I am taller than you,' she added, as though I should be disappointed. I wanted to ask her to repeat the experiment for the unexpected joy of the embrace, but I said nothing.

She picked one of my only two books from the shelf and sat on the bed. There was nowhere else to sit. I could have squatted on the small stool I used as a step to reach upper shelves, but that would have positioned me ludicrously low. 'Aesop's Fables', Keziah read, leafing through it swiftly. At once, a flower that had been pressed between two pages fell out onto her lap. 'Do you have a sweetheart?'

'No.' I went to take the flower from her, but she held it from me.

'No? Why do you have this little keepsake if it isn't a love token?'

*　　*　　*

Dr Edwards had handed the bud to me 'Pasque flower. I visited my cousin in Cambridge. They grow more easily there.'

Long out of earth and water, it was limp and dull.

'Can I revive it?' I had said.

He had shaken his woolly head. 'Alas, no. But you may press it.' I had done so obediently and – except for occasionally having to avoid those pages as I read – I had forgotten it was placed there.

'Medicinal and beautiful,' Dr Edwards had said. 'Of great relief for the treatment of . . .' He had mumbled something.

'For what?' I had asked, nagging at him like a fly at a horse's head.

'For that *uncomfortable* time.' His answer had left me none the wiser. He would have done a great deal better to teach me a useful herbal remedy than an incomplete anatomy.

*   *   *

'You blush!' Keziah said in triumph. 'It *is* a token, after all.'

'It is,' I lied, I didn't want her to grow impatient with me. I wanted to keep her held before me, her face towards mine, wanting to see what I'd say. Her two years of seniority must account for her insistence on continuing this uninteresting subject. I would indulge her. 'A man gave it to me.'

'A *man*?' Keziah said. 'Don't you mean a boy?'

'I will tell you one day who I mean.' I felt taller than her now. 'Let's read, as our fathers think we do.'

She snorted, looking at me as though she were impressed. 'A-anne!' she said, making two syllables of my name. She sighed when I did not offer more information, frustrated by her stubborn playmate. 'Which is your favourite, then ?' She indicated the book.

I had no ready answer, it would be like choosing a favourite toe on my foot to favour one fable above another, all of them supported each. 'The Lion and the Mouse,' I said, to keep her happy.

She ran her finger down the list of contents and her eyes widened with delight when she found the one I had named. 'The Lion and the Mouse,' she said, wriggling further back on the bed. 'Under the shade of a spreading tree, a lion dozed, his mighty head resting on his paws . . .'

I had not thought that she might read aloud to me. I'm afraid I did not listen to a word, instead I fixed my eyes on her face as if she were a poem I must commit to memory. I would happily have been tested on her blue eyes and her smooth mouth. As she spoke, her cheeks were gradually washed in a gentle pink, as though a painter had thinned red colour with water there.

'"And so," said the mouse, "you were right to save me, Sir."'

'Anne!' My father shouted loud enough to be heard several houses away. In this one, there were doors opened and closed on each floor in answer and Keziah snapped the book shut.

'Is he angry?' she asked.

'He is always angry,' I said, and she giggled as though I had spoken in jest.

Heath and my father stood like sentries in the hall, one on either side of the staircase.

'Did you read together?' Heath asked brightly. Keziah nodded and took his arm.

As if goaded by this filial display, my father rounded on me. 'Where were you?' His face was red. It was only moments before that I had noted the charming flush on Keziah's cheeks. This had quite the opposite effect. *He* was the victim of a careless artist. Even his eyebrows were mottled with crimson spots.

'In my room, Father.' I looked sideways and upwards at my accomplice. She stared ahead. He drew his breath in to condemn me, but Heath cut across him.

'It is a girlish pleasure, to be gossiping together while they read.' His stretched frame undulated with pleasure at the thought, as if he had rather been sat side by side with us talking of pressed flowers than knee to knee with my father. 'What did you read?'

'The Fables of Aesop,' Keziah said. 'Anne has a rather *special* edition.'

I frowned. Surely she didn't mean that she might betray a

38

confidence, even if it was not quite the secret she thought? I looked at her in question but she only smiled in return.

'They will be reading together long past our business, Jaccob. That Aesop fellow was very busy with himself.' Heath slithered toward the door. 'Tuesday?' he hissed to my father. 'Tuesday,' he whispered again to me.

My father's ears were vermilion with fury by the time the door had closed behind them. What could he do? He must keep in Heath's favour until contracts were signed and he had no proper reason to object to my keeping company with Keziah. He chased his anger like escaped bees all the rest of the evening, swatting it with curses and sharp words.

I could not eat at dinner. When I went to bed, I could not sleep. My thoughts were all of Keziah, her sharp eyes and soft lips, her teasing and her questions. Everything in my room seemed at once the better and the worse for her having been there. How coarse my bedcover felt, yet how special my books seemed now she had held them.

*　　*　　*

Keziah did not come with Heath the next time he visited. I felt choked and dizzy with despair when I realised he was alone. No bright hair kept his hat company and although I screwed up my eyes to peer down the street, in case she lagged behind him, I could not make her appear. Upstairs, the precious objects I had assembled to show her waited untouched. I wanted to run downstairs and fling myself at Heath, demanding an explanation. Instead, I waited on the stairs. I pretended to be caught unawares when the men emerged at the end of their business.

'Anne!' Heath said, genuinely surprised to see me. 'Ah, yes.'

He remembered why I might be there. 'Keziah is, alas, unwell and confined to bed.' At the thought of her ailing, my eyes filled with tears. Heath showed he had noticed this with a tiny upwards movement of his chin. 'She is not dying,' he said, a little too heartily. 'Indeed, she will accompany me on my next visit.' He straightened his mouth. It was not quite a smile. 'She has her cousin to nurse her,' he said.

Jealousy clapped hard hands over my ears and squeezed my throat so that I could not hear clearly or breathe easily.

'You wish to see her soon?' Heath laid a hand on my shoulder, his voice full of sympathy at what he imagined the cause of my distress. 'You must,' he ventured, 'be very fond of reading.'

'Yes!' The word rushed out as quickly as a fish over a waterfall.

I tried to visualise Keziah at home, alone, in rooms I had never visited and amongst people I had never met. This was impossible, my image of her wobbled like unset jelly and wouldn't stay put. So I placed a vision of her next to me. She walked alongside me as I ate or washed; she lay on my bed, curling her thin fingers over my knuckles as I stretched out my hand. She responded with gleaming praise after I read aloud. When my father belched at dinner, she caught my eye and giggled.

Frequently, I imagined her meeting some sort of accident. The heroine of the hour, I would rescue and then nurse her. Her gratitude would, I thought, be lifelong and fulsome. Although I was a pixie to her Amazon, I felt protective of her. My Aunt Elizabeth had a small dead bird, preserved as in life, its feathers shining, with only its glass eyes giving the game away. I would keep Keziah under such a glass dome if I could. How could Dr

Edwards not have felt the same about me? I did not want to sully her with my desires.

* * *

She was not with her father at the next visit either. My heart sank so low it hindered my walking. I did not wait in the hall, I could not bear how bleak the place was without her. Instead, I was summoned there.

'Anne,' Heath held out a slip of paper to me. 'Keziah asked me to give you this.'

As I went to take it from him, I tried to remember how I would extend my arm if nothing mattered, how my breath would come naturally if I did not think I might expire with happiness. My actions were as jerky as if a violent puppeteer pulled my strings.

Heath noticed nothing amiss. 'What does she write?' he said. 'She held her arm over the page so that I might not see.' He turned to my father. 'These girls . . .' he rippled like a worm on water, 'they love to have their secrets!'

'What does she write?' my father asked in chilly echo. I unfolded the paper, dreading that its contents might make me tremble or faint, or fall in twitching apoplexy with grief or joy.

The letters swam; for a moment I forgot how words were made. 'My favourite fable is "The Tiger and the Crane".' Nothing more.

Both men said 'Ah' and 'Oh' together.

'Prepare it for the next time,' Heath said, waving his flexible hand.

* * *

When I heard Keziah's voice in the hall, I had to put my hands over my mouth to prevent shrieking my joy. She came to my room without waiting for me to collect her. She seemed to bring extra air with her and I felt light-headed when I stood up. For a moment, the acquiescent, adoring companion of my imagination argued with reality. She was somehow less visible than before, yet more solid. I shrugged in greeting.

She appeared momentarily dismayed. She cast her eyes about my bleak room, looking as though she had expected bunting or some other decoration to welcome her. Then she put her shoulders back, bracing herself to be polite. 'Today you must tell me about the flower,' she instructed, positioning herself on the bed. 'You are a dark one, Anne. Who knew you might have an admirer?'

This tack irritated me. I had many important things to share with her but we'd be tiresomely delayed if I had to invent an amour. 'First, I want to show you some treasure,' I said.

'More tokens?' She bit her lip in anticipation. 'From more *men?*'

'This,' I said, taking a little tin box from under my bed.

She tipped her head on one side, as a dog does when you whistle. I fumbled as I opened it, for I had never done so in company before. She leaned closer, so near to me that one wayward curl caught on my mouth.

'What's in it?' she said, holding her hair from me, though I would have left it there, tickling till my lips tingled. 'What's that?' She peered inside and pointed.

The mouse's skull glowed pale white.

'Anne!' Keziah sat up, straightening her spine. 'I don't care to look too well, but I can see that there are still morsels of flesh on it.'

The mouse had not been dead long, you would hardly have expected it to be clean bone yet. I lifted the tin up, thinking that she might yet be intrigued if she gave its contents more careful examination.

She recoiled, sniffing melodramatically. 'Why do you keep it?' she said.

'I think it is beautiful,' I said, but even as I spoke the object seemed to lose its lustre under her squeamish gaze. I could not risk showing her anything else, her scrutiny might diminish everything else I had collected. I could not think how best to explain to her the charm of the decayed or withered. We sat in silence for a while, and the responsibility of not disappointing her further weighed heavy on me.

I decided that I would give her something I had only, until now, made for my own pleasure. 'Watch!' I said, delighted with my idea. 'I will fashion you a necklace!' I tugged at my hair and selected the longest strand from those that I had pulled free.

Putting the hair to my mouth, I spat copiously at regular intervals along its length till a bead of saliva hung suspended at each point, a neat inch apart. I had practised before and this was going to be the most perfect example yet. I did not look up until I was finished when, in triumph, I held the natural necklace aloft. The wet, translucent pearls twinkled briefly then some slowly dropped, elongating into ribbons of spittle as they fell. Keziah was transfixed. I was about to suggest that she attempt the feat herself, as a gift to me, when I realised her expression was not one of admiration, but horror.

'Oh!' She said. She put both hands to her mouth as if she was about to retch. 'Oh!' she said again, taking in lungfuls of air and expelling them loudly. 'That is quite—' she shook her head as if choosing just the right word, '—disgusting!' she finished, which I thought a poor choice after such careful consideration. She rolled her eyes and clutched her throat for some time before subsiding.

I watched this display dispassionately. I thought how odd it was that she had so recently entered my room gilded, but would leave tarnished and dull. I had laid secrets at her feet but she had kicked them aside. Until that moment, I had wished I might extend each minute of every hour to have more time to relish her company, now I wondered how much longer I could stand to have her near. Wearily, I closed my eyes.

'A-anne!' Again she made two notes where there should be only one. 'Wake up!' As this was the last time I would have to do her bidding, I obeyed.

'I did not sleep,' I said. 'I was merely waiting till your performance had ended.'

'Indeed?' Her voice sharpened with spite. 'My *performance* bored you? Better to be bored than repulsed, I can tell you.'

'I cannot help it if you are not curious about the natural world.'

With a sudden instinct, I looked to where my little tin sat beside her and thought I should pick it up, but I was too late. Keziah followed my gaze then reached for it and held it in front of her. Then, with elaborate care, she turned it upside down.

The things I had collected over many months lay spread out on the floor, vulnerable and exposed.

Keziah examined them with distaste. 'A morbid tableau,' she pronounced. Holding her finger and thumb like tongs, she picked up first one item, then another. 'A dead spider! A piece of wood! A fingernail!' she said, as though completing an inventory. 'A snail shell with a dead snail inside! A baby bird!' She turned to me with the solemnity of an advocate. 'You are quite insane.'

Then she spied something else. As if holding a lit torch aloft to better light her way, she went straight to the coil of paper among the ruins of my treasury. 'Oh, you kept this?' she said, retrieving it with relish. She read aloud to me, but I had learned what it said. '*My favourite fable is "The Tiger and the Crane".*' Then she looked afraid, as though it were a spell reversed. 'Why did you keep this, Anne?'

Because your hands had touched it, I thought. Because I imagined that those words came from your head to my heart.

My father's shouting my name was a relief to us both. She was nearer the door than I and as she rose to leave, she suddenly swooped like a bird of prey to the shelf and seized the book of fables. 'Shall I show your father your *flower?*' she sang, her talons holding tight. You could show him a whole bouquet and he wouldn't care, I thought, but I did not want her to have my book and tried to snatch it back. She held it above her head and her useful stature kept it far away from me.

Galloping down the stairs, she arrived laughing in front of the men and started to open her prize. I waited for her to hold out the shrivelled bloom for inspection, but instead she began to turn the pages.

'What is all this?' I heard her say. As if my feet were nailed to the floor, I was unable to move. I understood what she was looking at.

'Miscellaneous.' Keziah read. 'Debt. Budget. Constituency. Ensign. Carnet. Freight. Abaft. Disbursement. Chock. Demurrage.' My father pushed out his lips in bewilderment as he recognised the terms.

They were words that I had not understood, words that I had captured listening outside his room, and I had written them down to examine them later. She would have gone on, but Keziah's father took her hand and removed the book. He regarded my list with solemn deliberation. 'They are not spelled thus,' he said, handing it to me. Very slowly, he closed one eye in a last, kind wink.

Keziah stood in the doorway. Directly above her was a large stone curlicue, one of a pair that needlessly decorated the lintel. If it cracked and fell, it would flatten her like linen under a smoother. I wanted this to happen so much that my teeth felt loose in my gums. Had I been tall enough, I would have stretched my fingers to its edge and pushed. The notion that she would not then enjoy herself any more was both pleasing and sensible. Her punishment would be in my prayers that night – with an extra plea that I might witness it.

*　　*　　*

'Can you not keep a friend without it souring?' my father said later. He did not ask why I had recorded what I did.

I will choose more carefully henceforth, I thought. I will not be swayed by dainty feet or rosy faces. I will wait until I meet the other side of my coin before holding out my hand.

Chapter 4

Tic-k-k-k toc-k-k-k. The clock and I are alone. Very gently, in riposte to my father's gusty exit, I ease back my chair and stand away from it, then set it carefully against the table. During my mother's confinement the house stayed close to itself. She had had many babies die inside her, and after my brother was lost it was as if we all walked about as quietly as possible so as to keep this baby safe till its time. Any sudden noise still seems rude and coarse. Except to my father, whose life runs on unchanged.

Jane stands now in the hall, her mouth open as she lets some thought or other keep her busy. She starts when she sees me.

'Mistress!' She tugs at the strings of her apron. This woman cannot be still in my company, she twists and fidgets so. There is a stray lock of hair on her forehead that would be usefully tucked away, instead she busies herself with her clothing.

'Missy Jane?' The little nurse is there. 'Oh, Mistress!' bobbing when she sees me. 'Oh, Mistress, I have a message for Jane.'

'Take your message, Jane. Oh, deliver it to her, Grace.' Do these silly women need me to interpret for them?

'The butcher's boy, Warner, is here, Jane, he wishes you to inspect.' The nurse bobs again and looks at the floor.

47

'He is late to our house. It is nearly six, we have already dined.'

'He has a reason. Mistress. To do with his uncle. Shall I send him away?'

I think of my father's ire at the food he ate tonight and imagine Jane continually choosing fat over flesh for him, tough rather than tender. Shall I watch the transaction to make sure Jane takes the proper care? My mother lies abed; I will stand where she would.

'Where is this boy? I will look at what he brings.' The two women look startled at my sudden interest in matters of the home. They exchange a long glance. Perhaps if I banged their heads together, they would stop this shilly-shallying. Instead, I say, 'I shall come with you, Jane. Let me oversee your choice. Neither of us needs to encourage my father's bad humour.'

We go together to the kitchen. As a little child, I used to spend much time there: it was cosy amongst the warm ovens and homely smells of stock and bread. My nurse would heat milk for me, or sit me at the table while she folded cloths or somesuch. I had not visited for a long while, but here is the unchanged smell of it and the familiar pans and pots.

At the door, leaning on the jamb, stands the butcher's boy. At his feet, a basket. In his hands, a joint of beef. I have never seen him before, but it is as if I recognise him. I stop in my tracks, because otherwise I might run to him. He looks as if he would speak but cannot remember how. We stare as intensely as if we're about to jump together from a great height. The world gives a great lurch then resumes its customary spinning.

'Mistress Jaccob,' Jane announces. We both start, as if we're surprised to find her still there.

'Mistress Jaccob.' I look at his mouth as he says my name. There is a faint line of dark hair above it. I do not want to look away. Everything I have done today till now seems pointless. I have wasted hours not looking at him.

He is taller than I am, but not so tall I must look up. I guess that he is older, but that may be because I am suddenly childish and gauche. Which way should my feet go to keep me upright? Where should I put my hands? I clasp them together, then let them fall by my side. I'm sure they hang lower down than usual. His hair grows long about his ears, but is a little pushed back off his face, and in the centre of his forehead it comes to a point in a widow's peak. The brows are straight and dark, set a little in from the corner of his eyes which makes the line of his nose strong and straight. Below it, a full mouth. He smiles. His face is the only answer to any question I ask.

'Do *you* choose now?' He regards me with cool appraisal. He holds the meat closer to me; there are tracks of bright blood on the raw flesh, and it smells of iron and earth. The size of what he holds is the width of my waist, and I want his hands there. If he didn't wash away the blood, I'd not mind.

'Do you approve?' His voice is deep. I imagine him saying my name. Then I think I would like to hear him whisper or howl it.

'Let me see it, Fub.' Jane comes up close behind me, her hands outstretched, but while he proffers the beef to her he keeps his eyes on me.

I have the curious sensation of being observed from all angles. I am aware of the lace at the bosom of my dress and the small buttons at the nape of my neck. He continues to stare and I feel the colour rise in my cheeks. I wonder if he likes what he sees. His gaze strips me and slices at the world. I fear that if I turn round, I will face a sheer drop behind me, and tense my feet in my shoes so I don't fall. At the very least, I cannot be sure my dress still has a back to it.

Jane is twisting the beef this way and that. She sniffs at it, then puts it on the counter and turns her attention to the basket. As she holds up each piece, she prods and pokes at them and I am reminded of living flesh. Of the skin on soft arms or stout legs, of the smooth warmth of bellies and thighs. I shiver as if something touched me, as if his fingers stroked.

'Will you,' says the boy at last, 'will you always come to the door now, do you think? Shall I teach you to examine what Jane will cook?' He speaks softly, his words innocent enough, but I know there is no mistaking what he means. *Be here again. Let me look at you. Look at me.*

'Yes, I shall.' But I hear my voice tremble a little and see from his face that he knows why I falter. I should not be so quick to agree. 'When it is convenient for me,' I add, then: 'When I have no other business.'

Oh, hush! I am ashamed of my prattling.

'See to it now, Jane,' I say as I retreat, not catching his eye, although catching myself a glancing blow against the counter with my hip, which makes me want to gasp in pain – though I suppress it.

*   *   *

Later, in my bed, after I have blown the candle out and lie in darkness, I find I cannot summon his face. A curl of hair about his forehead, perhaps, and that steady amused stare, but his features elude me. As my hand steals beneath my nightdress and seeks to find my place of quick wet softness, it is my mother's breast I see, as she places the pink tip of it in my sister's mouth. And with this vision, I speed my hand about its business to a completion of spinning stars.

Chapter 5

My room is full of the aroma of roasting beef. It will be cooked to the exact measurement of my father's disapproval by the time it is served. And as soon as I smell it, my mind is full of that boy Fub, the width and the weight of him. I was buried under thick frosts, till he woke me. There is nothing soft or sweet about my feelings for him – they throb like a heart cut living from a beast and I am as ravenous as a bird of prey. I must see him, but I cannot wait to catch him by chance at our door. Days may pass before his next visit; I could fade and die of hunger before he comes. I will find him myself. I will have to ask Jane where he stays, of course, and my cheeks burn to imagine what I might say to her to extract this information without arousing her suspicions.

I'd thought that Keziah and I held either end of a ribbon and would skip towards each other in full sunshine, until I found out that I held both ends myself. Perhaps it is better now that I dig, secretly, blind as a mole, to meet Fub in darkness.

I feel the little bruise on my hip, pushing at it to a satisfying point of pain. My insides contract to remember his looking at me, how he'd stopped me with his stare. My exhaled breath is white in the room's cold air, though the light outside the window is bright with the late summer sun. From the room below, I hear the cat-like cry of my new sister. It snags and catches against my ear, urgent and insistent. She will get attended to with swiftness, that is certain. I sit awhile, waiting until I think her needs have been met. I have no desire to witness her care. None at all. But I still want my mother's embrace. There is something for her where my heart used to be, but it isn't as warm as love.

I pause outside her door till I am sure I can hear no crying infant or any whispered words. I knock softly and enter the room without waiting for a reply. My mother's face is pale still, and drawn, but she smiles at me, and pats the bedcover beside her for me to sit there.

'Anne,' she holds my hand, her fingers curl round mine. A little squeeze. 'Shall you hold your sister while she sleeps?' The hairs on my arms rise with chill, but I nod in answer.

She disengages her hand and turns to the crib, bending over to slide her arms beneath the bundle of baby. I remember how often I had cuddled my brother. I would wake him from his nap simply for the pleasure of smelling his soft neck and nuzzling his tiny ears, holding him up close to have his hot breath on my cheek. But the love I had for him is atrophied and shrunken inside me, and this plump skin and wet cry cannot revive it. Still, I open my arms as my mother lays her small daughter gently into them, and I peer at the little doll face and beam as if I mean it.

'Has my father attended?' I say.

'*Attended?*' My mother leaves a little space round the word, to show she thinks it an odd choice. 'Yes, he has *attended.*' She holds my gaze, looking amused the while. 'It would be an odd father who did not want to inspect his new child.'

I reflect briefly on the number of ways my father is odd, but it's best not to include her in this musing. She has long ago absented herself from his doings – certainly she seems not to care if he blethers at Jane or ignores me. They move around each other without grace, scarcely exchanging words beyond the essential. Once, as we sewed together, I asked her about love, how should we know if we feel it and did God's love feel the same? She coloured beetroot red and told me not to be so demanding, that it was not for any of us to fashion such queries and greater minds than ours could not provide an answer.

I stare at the baby. Fortunately, gazing down for longer than is necessary is expected when you hold an infant. Her eyes are shut tight, while her mouth sucks empty air, hoping to be filled. She is as heavy as a dead cat. I shift her to spread the weight on my lap and she starts, flinging her arms and legs outwards, her limbs pointing to all four corners of the room. She quivers but doesn't wake.

'Say your welcome to Evelyn,' she says now, and I put on a good show of following the instruction.

*   *   *

When I leave the room, holding my fingers to my nose, I can still smell the baby's scent. I hurry back to my room, pour water from the ewer into the basin and keep my hands immersed till it is gone.

'Anne!' My father calls from the hall. The house holds its breath to listen as my feet tap tap down the stairs to find him – we are both wondering what he might say.

'Come!' He is at his study door and indicates I should follow him in. I lift my skirts a little as I enter the room as if crossing shallow water. It is the moat of my father's constant disapproval that I try and avoid, for it wets so much and stinks when it dries.

'Sit!' There must be a tax on words, that he uses them so sparingly. Well, this conversation has not cost him much yet. He sits at his desk, pushing aside some papers and books to place his arms there.

He gestures at the chair set at an angle to him, the only other sitting place in the room. This is where he comforted me when my first tooth fell. I recall it now, just as if I still had to look up at him. At six years old, I had thought I was dying – crumbling away mouth first – and he had laughed and reassured me, then conjured my tooth gone from his hand to replace it with a shiny coin.

I look at him square on and it is hard to do, for I know that I have much the same face. The same wide eyes and high fore-head, the same rounded cheeks and straight mouth. His mouth, though, is held now in an expression of irritation, all pulled up at the edges, and between his brows there are two dark, straight lines of concentration.

'Will you go—?' As he speaks, he searches through the piles of papers in front of him. 'Letter, letter, letter,' he mutters to himself, moving them into different configurations. He shifts left and right on his chair, unwittingly polishing its leather. One less job for Jane to do, though if he knew that he spared her a task with his action he would stop and sit as still as a basilisk.

Around us there are shelves of books that have not been disturbed in a good long while. A thick rime on top of each volume, the idle browser would sneeze and cough. All those words locked up there! They should be strung up like bunting, lines of them fluttering in a breeze. It is marvellous how re-arranging their order can completely transform their meaning. I long to take a book down, blow the dust away and begin it. 'Shall we read together, Father?' I do not say. 'Which is your favourite book?' I will not enquire.

I still keep two precious books that Dr Edwards had lent to me, forgotten in his haste, one a dictionary and the other full of fables. They are opened and read so constantly I almost know them off by heart and they are soft and translucent with use, unlike these that are all hard and closed tight shut.

'Letter!' He holds a single slip of paper, closely written on, and folds it small.

'Take this to the priest at the Marylebone Chapel. It requests a christening. Which must be done,' he adds, but there is no joy in this, no promise of celebration.

'Yes, Father.' Is this to be our exchange? Will he make no more conversation with me than this perfunctory example? I pause, as if to prompt him to fill the silence, but he is already busy with something on his desk, and does not even look up.

I do not go.

'Where is my tooth, Father?'

'Eh?' He raises his head. His tough grey hair sways and settles. It is the only wild thing about him. His simple thoughts are ordered, there is no frivolity in his conduct.

'My tooth. When I was a little girl, when I lost my first baby tooth, I was frightened. You—' I pause. I do not want to become sentimental or vulnerable, or he would find me easy to dismiss. I keep my tone even and calm. 'You comforted me, and magicked my tooth away. You gave me a coin for it. It was in this room, do you remember? Did you keep it afterwards?'

He stares to the left of him, to the unhelpful volumes. 'Your tooth?' He shakes his head, looks back at me.

'It was still bloody, fresh out of my mouth.'

He exhales. 'I don't remember, Anne,' he says. There is no softness in his tone, it is only hard fact he delivers. 'I don't keep such things,' he says. 'Why would I keep such things?' He throws his arms wide to the crowded shelves, as if to suggest even one more tiny object would overfill them and bring them crashing down.

We examine the silence between us. I cannot think of a reply, save 'Because it was of me.' Unbidden, even as I have this unspoken thought, I feel tears spring in my eyes. He must not see this! I turn around to the door and feel for its handle as my sight blurs. A rustle of papers behind me and he has turned his attention to his desk again.

From the kitchen, a low clattering murmur suggests Jane is ordering things about in there. I pause at the door, rehearsing in my head a reason to step inside. Before I can, Jane flings the door wide. As ever, she is startled to see me and her genuflection takes the form of a quick, urgent cross of her legs, as if she were in need of a pot.

'Jane,' I don't let her see me smile as she untangles herself, 'I must go to the church with a missive from my father, and if there is any merchant we have outstanding business with, then tell me so that I can combine my errand with that office.'

A little frown. Jane's eyes and mouth are small, they cluster close together as if to keep her nose company. And her nose turns up sharply at the end in a bid to escape them, revealing her nostrils, wide and red.

'No, thank you, Mistress Anne.' I can see she is flummoxed by my enquiry. 'All is in order.'

'I would like to pay visits to our suppliers in turn, as my mother will be abed a while yet.'

At the mention of my mother, Jane casts her eyes to the ceiling and smiles as if there were a little window there, revealing to her a delightful picture: the mother and her child. It is strange how the presence of a baby softens everyone all at once. Perhaps if those in danger at the hands of others cried 'Baby!', they would avert the crisis. Instantly, the dagger would be sheathed and the strangling rope loosened.

She catches *me* smiling this time, and assumes I share her sagging, soft feelings. 'You are good to think of it, but your mother left us well informed before her confinement.'

'Nevertheless . . .' Oh, I only need one bit of information from this silly dolt. I will go about it another way. 'I am minded to visit them. I mean you no injury, Jane' (for I can see she is beginning to interpret my queries as correction, her little eyes are becoming moist), 'I wish only to practise my household duties, all of which I shall most certainly need when I am wed.'

And as swiftly as the mention of an infant melted her, so too does the notion of me as a bride.

'Oh, indeed!' She claps her hands together, inclining her head and grinning as if she already sees me at the altar. 'It will stand you in good stead.' She is practically choosing flowers for a bouquet.

'So, where is our butcher found?' I had meant to delay this question, but my mouth is so full of it now it must be spat out.

'Mr Levener?' (Yes! A name!) 'Oh! I do not think you should go there, his shop is hard by Smithfield but it is not . . .' She searches for a word. 'Not . . . *comfortable.*' She is trying to convey just how out of place she thinks I would be.

'Le-ve-ner.' I ignore her opinion and note the name with due seriousness. I'm in no danger of forgetting, it is already engraved on my skin. I leave a measured pause, so she cannot read my haste. I want to run, but I must preserve propriety. 'Thank you. I shall not visit him today, of course.' (Of course I shall!) 'But, when the opportunity arises, I may make his acquaintance.'

Another little smile. She sees me now as her pupil in house-keeping. I will fill her up with this sort of talk to put her off the scent and keep her happy. There is only a small space in her head for her thoughts, it will be easy to keep it stuffed and satisfied.

'Perhaps you would take me with you when you next go about your business? I could do no better than observe you.' I have gone too far. Jane overflows with pleasure. She curtsies so low I have to help her up. She goes off to the kitchen, a quick conspiratorial glance over her shoulder at me, wiping her hands on her apron, full of purpose and intent.

And I am now condemned to spend the next little while finding excuses not to accompany her anywhere at all.

Chapter 6

I had to consult the household ledger for Levener's address; it was tucked in with Jane's receipts and invoices. She has a large looped hand, spread indiscriminately over each page. I suspected she looked at a boiling pot as she wrote and only guessed at where her pen went. But I found it eventually and slid the information into my head. For my map, I have only my standing beside Dr Edwards on Primrose Hill. If I become lost, I will close my eyes and imagine the view we saw together. Dr Edwards looms up in that vision if I'm not careful, so I must concentrate. That will not be difficult. I cannot think of anything else much but reaching Fub.

As I walk, I rehearse my exchange with him, to be ready when we meet. In my mind's eye, he raises his eyebrows in question when I appear and I need to be ready to explain myself.

'*I need to understand your business,*' I might begin. What would he say to that? The Fub of my imagination is no fool. '*My business?*' he would retort. Of course, he is only apprenticed and therefore quite a way from understanding it himself, I should think. There must be a better way to begin.

'*My mother is confined, I will conduct her affairs.*' Quickly, he would come back with: '*And did she not instruct her housekeeper and cook before retiring?* What sort of a scrappy household would he think the Jaccob woman keeps? Better to speak my mind, if I can be brave enough. *'I want to stand near you, smell the very skin of you, know your face as your glass does.'* That is the truth of the matter.

And somewhere he waits, though Fub does not know he waits, and I am closer with every step to his shoulders, his arms, his belly, his hands. My fellow pedestrians, observing me as I hold my flowered skirt above the street's muck and keep my eyes modestly averted, would not guess my thoughts. They cannot tell I am propelled by a longing I cannot describe, something huge that chokes me, that covers me like a heavy quilt, making me dizzy and too warm. It makes me hold my breath, lest I pant like a dog.

Why did I think I could set out from my house with so little idea of how to proceed? My excursions from the house have always been short and familiar, little outings with my mother, small errands run. I am ill-prepared for this foray. The streets quickly follow no pattern I understand, this one leads nowhere I recognise, that one ends unexpectedly with a stop of houses. The crush of people, the din of horses' hooves and the jangle of livery do not help my concentration. I have not brought any money, or else I could have got in a coach. Jane must walk this way on household errands, mustn't she? She'd not summon a coach and yet she puffs loudly and rests her legs when she even steps up a stair, so I can surely manage a few more paces.

I must find a place where I can see St Paul's fat head of a dome, keeping always north of it. I had intended to call at St Peter's on my way home (my father's missive must be delivered) but at this rate I'll still be going at nightfall. The jostle of the crowded street chafes at me like a pinching shoe. Have you seen a pack after their prey? These dog-brained folk follow and nip at each other with no thought except forward motion. They do not know they have a fox in their midst; I am keeping low to the ground and masking my scent well.

'Woah!' A hand grabs at my sleeve. I wheel round and almost collide with a man, who holds me still to stop me going further.

'Look! There!' He points to a heap of steaming dung where some nag has recently voided. If I'd walked unseeing into it, I would hardly have been able to bear my own company on the journey home, let alone pay any visits.

He grins, slowly releasing his grip till he's sure I won't topple over. I shake my arm from his grip, not so much to be free of him as to steady myself. I rejoice in his intervention, though he's an odd kind of guardian angel.

'All hurry and haste and no sense,' he says. There's a soft addition to the 'r' and 's' as he says the words, prolonging the sounds. He is not much taller than me, though a deal older, and his face is pitted all over as if little feet had stamped there while it was still soft. He has pale blue eyes and coarse russet hair, springy as hay. He wears a Scottish skirt over his breeks and a coat fashioned oddly from black woollen felt; the sleeves are attached by tow threaded through gaping holes which appear to have been made by a blunt knife or dagger. The tow must have been pushed through with thumbs. It is as far from delicate sewing as I've ever seen. There's a tatty beret of sorts on his head. It might be fixed there with nails it clings so tightly. He nods his head at me and the hat doesn't move.

'Thank you, Sir.' I make to go on, but he keeps looking at me

– perhaps he hasn't seen me grateful enough. 'I would have cursed my folly if I'd stepped there!' I laugh and move away as if foolishness itself speeds me on. 'I am so very fortunate that you caught my arm.'

'Where do you go?' Again that 'r' is rolled and long, even the 'go' is luxuriant.

'Near Smithfield.' No harm in saying that, is there? He isn't a spy for my father. I feel a sudden chill at the idea of being watched or followed, but when I meet his eyes his gaze is kindly.

'Smithfield?' He looks askance, weighing my journey. 'That's a fair way. A long way.' And his way of saying 'long' extends to match. 'You have friends there, or other matters?' He only asks with interest, I'm sure he's not intending harm or spite.

'My mother is confined with child. I go about her business.' I had thought I would say all this first to Fub, now I am telling his strange understudy.

'A little mother *manquée*,' he says. He is amused at this and although I don't know what he means I smile back at him. His teasing is light and gentle; it tickles rather than pricks at me. 'And where does this task take you, then? Do you know the whole route?'

I am winded by his concern – it knocks all the passion and purpose out of me. I have been walking far and long enough to be weary and easily disconcerted.

'No.' He waits, and does not prompt me. 'I am going to Meeks Passage.' There is a magic in saying it aloud, as if the words are a spell to conjure Fub. 'Titus Levener, the butcher, has his shop there.'

'Indeed he does.' He nods. 'He does indeed. And your family does well to give him trade – he is all *honour* about his slaughter

63

and his slicing.' The sly way he says this suggests it might be otherwise with the butcher, but I am not going to pursue that notion. The fact he knows exactly where I am bound is astonishing. All the world conspires to get me to Fub; so proper is my intent that fate even puts horse muck in my path to help it happen.

'Soooo.' A great roll of the word, several vowels long. 'Shall I take you there? Modom?' He purports to bow and holds his felted arm out for me to take. I have to warn him of one circumstance, though, perhaps to prevent him from doing me harm otherwise.

'I have no money to give you for your trouble.' It sounds false, as if I secretly carry gold weights in my stays. He raises a stiff eyebrow.

'No money, eh?' He purses his lips, considering how he must now act with charity alone. 'I did not look at you and think you would make me rich. I only thought that while there are many I would like to see face forward in dung, you are not one of them.'

We laugh together; the shared humour is a very pleasant glue. But are we now a pair? He acted as any kindly stranger, saving me from a disgusting fate, but that does not make him trustworthy. I weigh up my choices. The streets are throng enough to have someone come to my aid if needs be. And if he tries to divert me to a lonely place, I'll shout loud enough to save myself. I have long thought my senses were alert, ready as a cat for a mouse, ready as a mouse to flee. I trust my instincts about him as I do with Fub – quick and sure. 'Show me the way, please.' I take his arm. Under the stiff fabric, I think I can feel the bone.

I steal glances at him, sideways as we walk briskly along. His chin curls up and his nose points down, while his dimpled cheek rises like a hillock. Sparse red hair springs from his chin in single strands, as if he had decided to grow a beard but could not persuade every follicle to join the endeavour. He is a crude drawing of a man and I suspect that he sleeps outside, for he has not the finish of one who rises from a soft bed and washes with fresh water. I can see little of any youth in him either; he has been aged and sorrowful too long and it has all been covered over.

He starts to sing, his voice low and tuneful. The song is full of battles, of kings, of Charlie this and James that and all at once I understand his speech, his garments. Of course, my skirted companion must be a Jacobite. A vanquished soldier! He warbles of heather and moors, but that's not what takes my fancy. I have heard so many stories of slaughtered Highlanders: I recall pictures of ripped flags of red silk, and tales of punished chieftains and prisoners killed or confined. I think of several questions to ask him but do not utter them lest I seem callous or cruel. I badly want to know about battles and fighting. I have never stood so close to a warrior before. Can he tell me how close *he* stood to his pretender prince? Did he see any blood shed?

He chews his lip over some of the words; he lingers over the rhymes, draws in his cheeks and whistles between the verses, then keens in imitation of the pipes. Overall there is such sadness in his music that we might be going to a funeral. Not that I have attended any, of course, but I cannot imagine they contain a wealth of jolly songs.

When he finishes his tune, I say 'What was that ditty about?' I do not want to upset him now – he might lead me up all the wrong paths and abandon me there.

He detects the guile of my tone, however, for he turns his head to me quickly with a frown. 'My girl, I think you know. There's a wit to you that you cannot disguise. It's no help with your *geography* . . .' he lays great stress on this and holds his arms wide to the streets about us, 'but I'll warrant your *history* is sound.' Again a mocking accent on that word.

'It's true,' I acknowledge. 'But I do not want to enquire about things that might cause you sorrow. If that's the case, I'll hold my tongue and you may resume your concert.' He shrugs at this, but turns to me with all the sorrow that was in his singing on his face.

'What's your name?'

He deserves a truthful answer. He is a good companion and a useful one besides, that's in no doubt. 'Anne Jaccob.'

'Ha! Another Jaccobite of sorts. Angus.' He salutes, speeding his hand to his temples and clicking his heels together. 'Well, Miss Jaccob. Anne.' He makes my name rhyme with 'done', the 'a' hardened to 'u'. He waits a moment, without comment. I glance at him, to catch his mood. His features stay immobile. He does not break his stride but quickens, if anything. I increase my pace to match, but my legs are not so long as his and I must step in double-quick time with a skip every third or fourth step to keep up with him.

'My mother warned me not to fall in line with the Camerons,' he says, ignoring my awkward gait. 'She guessed I'd not be a soldier easily. When I was a boy we'd sheep then: not so many we were overworked but enough to keep us. My brother was newly married and she wanted to keep me home awhile, to aid her, and then I'd stay on where I'd one day inherit.'

I should be sitting at his feet for this, not hurrying alongside him, catching what I can above the noisy streets we walk. I press myself to his side.

'But the cause was a hook to me and it reeled me in. Why would I sit on a stone in a field watching wool grow when I could fire a gun in a regiment instead? My uniform was the smartest and warmest clothing I'd ever owned, and I looked up to my sergeant as we stood in ranks. Till I watched how we proceeded, of course, and realised those in charge were soft as sheep. Softer! That winter I had no idea of how our plans were progressing; it seemed to me we marched about in a cruel and random way. Back and forth over the border we went. Our dog rounded up the flock with more precision. Gah!' He punches his two fists together – if a man's head were there in the middle of them, it would feel very sore after.

'Where were you born?' I ask.

'Fort William.'

'Oh! Is that a castle?' If I sound surprised, it's only that I didn't take him for high born.

'No, no, no. It is far from that.' He narrows his eyes for a moment. 'Look over to that church.' He points and I squint to see. In the far distance is a spire. 'Then look behind you to that coffee house.' It is the same long way away. 'In Fort William, all that is grass, then rising to high mountains. When I was a boy, I thought that all the world must look like my home, for I could run to lakes or hills or trees or open places all in the same day.'

He closes his eyes, and I think he is a child again in his head, not heeding his mother's 'Come home!' cry as he sprints, barefoot, over places lost to him now.

His eyes open. 'Through bog!' He sounds angry and his pockmarked face is closing up with bitterness. What bog?

'We'd no chance!' He shouts now, and several people round us look quickly at him then away. That is how they look at the queer and damaged, isn't it? I cannot quite see how we got so swiftly from grassy plain to bog in his recounting; he has squeezed his story up like a concertina.

'*Stuck like pigs!*' he bellows. This has all taken a most unsatisfactory turn. One moment, I am listening to his memories, enjoying the cadence of his voice, next I am shushing him while trying to get him to walk straight. He is wriggling about like a worm on a stick.

'Butcher!' My butcher? Are we arrived?

'That bastard Cumberland.' Not my butcher, then. He has grown quieter, hissing the name. He spits. He stares at the gob where it lands, then at me. His expression shifts, as if he is trying to remember who I am. I smile brightly.

'Tell me more of your home,' I say, in an effort to pull him back to the place we were before his temper flared and keep him on our path.

'Home. Aye, aye, that's what *he* said. Sir, *I AM come home*. But then he's beggared off to France and me thrown into a cell and look who's pissing in the palace now.' The beret clings hard to its perch as he flings his head about.

He has snapped shut now, like a book. His final chapter is not a happy ending, of course, but he must tell it; his recounting is speeding his steps and that is a good outcome.

'How did you come to be here?'

He slows down at this, draws in to himself, his voice not much above a whisper.

'I was traded, as a prisoner. Then chucked from my cell with the clothes I stood up in. And they were rags, almost. No home to go to, and if my mother wasn't already dead she'd be dead of fright if she saw me so changed. They'd punched the teeth from me, and twisted me about so I couldn't tell who was king and who a pauper. I'd no trade and no ambition. This is all I have.'

He stands stock still, his arms spread out, forcing several passers-by to give him a wide berth. After three people have urged him angrily to move or hurry up, he comes to his senses. We walk on in silence.

I am weary of his story now, with its rapid trajectory from boy to eager soldier to this chastened individual, all the guts of him reduced to a soup of self-pity. Still, it has lasted through our journey. It did not take much to wind him up like a clock and set him ticking.

'We are almost there.' He turns in a circle where he stands, scanning the crowds as if he's looking for a friend or an enemy. He whistles to a boy who looks half asleep, leaning in a doorway with his hair over his eyes and his arms folded. The boy wakes and starts and comes to him like a loyal dog. 'Where is the man Levener?' he says. The boy points to our right, then offers the same hand, palm flat, for a reward. It's a single, graceful gesture.

'Do you know him?' I say, as our guide disappears into the throng. 'No, only his type. Too docile to lie.' But there is the lane marked 'Meeks'. My heart jumps. All so fast!

'I thought *you* knew the way.' He stares hard at me. 'It's all meat here,' he says. 'I knew we'd find him.' I am impressed at his guile. And now I am indebted, too, as he pays the boy for his pointing.

'Here is my price, Anne.' I look carefully at him. I do not

speak but he answers as if I had. Did I misjudge his true intention toward me?

'A while more of your company, is all. I will leave you at the shop. After half an hour – no more – I will come for you. Where do you go next?'

'To St Peter's in Vere Street. That is the last place I must call.' I cannot help but be truthful. It seems he brings out the worst in me, for being honest is not my best suit. 'And I am so grateful for your kind—'

'Enough!' He cuts me short. 'Never mind your gracious thank yous. Your mind is fixed to another post now, I see. I know that I bore you with my meanderings. And that you suspect me.' Is my head made of glass? Otherwise how can he tell what I am thinking? 'You shine with purpose.' He plucked me from the crowd like a man panning for gold.

'What brings you here, Anne?' He raises his eyebrows in question. 'Love,' he answers himself. 'Love. Ah, love. Love is like water. You need it, but too much and you'll drown.'

When I loved my brother, my feelings were like the steady flow of the clearest stream. I am standing under a torrent now, splashed on all sides.

'You can leave me here. I'll not pine.' He sits on the ground, puts his back to the bricks and pulls his tatty hat over his face. At once there is a steady snoring.

The butcher's sign is propped by the wall, the fixings that once held it above still swing and chinkle as they hang empty. A few lumps of red meat stuff lie in the deep window, and the door is closed. I push at it, just to test if I can open it and it swings wide before I can regret my hasty action.

Fub stands there, behind the wooden counter. He wears a leather apron, shiny in patches where it is slicked with wet, but it is too dark-coloured to be sure what the dampness is. All around and above him hang the amputated legs and bodies of numerous beasts, each in their caul of fat. Creatures that could never in life have shared the same field, for they would have fought or cowered, have had no choice but to jostle close together in sullen deathly silence. The smell is so strong that it is almost visible, a great sour reek pricked with a sharp tang. Gobbets of blood stick to the sawdust on the floor; they look solid enough to thread on a ribbon like beads. Fub cuts up a small piece of meat, concentrating on his task, so that his head is tilted down and the top of his head is visible. The dark hair swirls outwards in two whorls from a double crown. The sight is so affecting to me that I gasp. I want to stroke him there, or pull hard. The impulse is the same. He looks up.

'Do you need any gloves, Miss Jaccob?' He gestures along the chopping block to a small mound of empty fur that was once around a rabbit. The little paws are flung wide apart and the head lolls. That is the stuff he slices, then, his small prey. He speaks as if we were mid-conversation, unruffled.

'It is too warm for gloves,' I say, trying to match his light tone. Not very successfully, for I am breathless.

'I don't deliver to your house today. Not till—' He pauses, considering his appointments. 'Next Tuesday. But you may check the order, if that's why you are come.' He lays the little knife down by the raw flesh and wipes his hands over his apron. He gathers the pile of diced meat together and lays it on a square of cloth, then folds it carefully. I watch his hands, thinking of them on my clothes, unpeeling them in the same neat way. He washes off the blood in a pail. There is no sound but the water splashing.

'Is that why you are come?' He looks at me so directly I feel as if I am on trial. I have not sworn on any bible to be truthful, so I can say what I like.

'Yes.' My collar feels tight, but I stop my hands from going to my neck, pressing my arms to my sides though it takes a huge effort to be still. 'My father is most particular about his cuts.'

'And you are not? Any old gristle for you?'

That does it. A great blush starts at my feet, ice cold at first then warming as it rises. I am suffused with colour when the heat reaches my cheeks, and if I can't see my bright shade reflected in his eyes, I can certainly tell how much he enjoys my discomfort. Even my breath comes out hot.

'Do you know what this is?' He holds a short twist of thick metal, in the shape of the letter 'S', sharpened at both ends. I shake my head. 'A butcher's hook,' he says, testing the tip of his finger against each point. 'A perfect design. Whichever way up you use it, it's always ready. One end to hook, the other to hang. It has only one simple purpose.' He stands on a stool and fixes it over the bar above him. It waits there, empty. He climbs down. 'Pleasing, isn't it?'

'And who is this young veal?' A man, monstrous in size, looms in the doorway behind Fub. He is as vast as two men joined together, and each of them very large. Great slabs of flesh swell beneath his shoulders and his forearms are broad spreads of pale skin. His neck circles hugely round to his back and balloons in the front where it joins his many chins. Small red-rimmed eyes – I am reminded of a pig – are closer to his ears than each other, set wide apart and leaving all the freckles on the speckled pink expanses between and above his brows to fend for themselves. He wears a vast leather apron, but where Fub's would have taken the skin of one cow to sew, his must have demanded a whole herd. Despite his bulk, his voice has no strength or depth; he wheezes out his words in a high-pitched tone.

'Not much meat there.' He wrinkles his pudgy nose. 'But the liver and lights would be all pearly pink and sweet.'

Fub laughs, and says: 'Thomas Jaccob's daughter.'

'Ah, Thomas Jaccob,' the man mountain repeats. My blush is fading. He does not react to my father's name nor show me any deference.

'Fine veal. Not hung enough yet.' The ape continues to cast his eyes over me as if he really were about to take me to market. 'Shall we fatten you in darkness, then?' He winks. I am keeping still.

'I am here to peruse our order, Sir,' I say. Does he hear my haughty tone? I hope so. I do not intend that 'sir' to confer any status.

'Then I shall fetch our ledger, *Mistress.'* He fully intends me to hear the slight mockery in his voice. 'Accounts and orders for the Jaccob household for your *perusal.'* He giggles. It is a shrill and silly sound from a grown man.

'Enough, Titus. Don't mind him.' This is said to me. He waves a hand at each of us, indicating one to the other. 'This is the master butcher, Titus Levener.'

The Levener fellow squeezes back through the passageway behind him, still snickering to himself. I'd like to suggest he puts animal grease on the door frame, so he could slide more easily through.

There is a pause. Fub looks at me again with amusement.

'Do you continue your education in the baker's next, or the farrier's?' Fub undoes his apron, hauls it over his head, hangs it on a hook on the wall then comes around the counter towards me. All the while, I feel as though I have my hands cupped over my ears, there's such a rushing sound in my head. Just as soft hot wax gives to the touch, so I would yield now to take any shape he fashioned. He picks up two small stools, swinging them in either hand, and places them on the floor next to the counter.

'Here.' He sits on one and gestures to the other. It is set close by him. 'Something to play with.' He picks up the little knife he'd been dicing the rabbit with, wipes the blade on his leg then twirls it quickly around.

'Watch.' Then he places his left hand, fingers splayed, on the wooden block. He begins to stab the point of the knife, quick and darting, first in the gap between thumb and forefinger, then forefinger and middle, next middle and ring finger, lastly in the small space between his ring and little fingers. There's a little 'pock' as the tip connects to the wood.

I cannot take my eyes from him, but Fub looks only at the knife's journey as it speeds and blurs. I blow air into my cheeks in a noisy sigh, laughing with delight at how clever and how deft he is. When the knife can go no faster, he raises it high above his head, his arm extended, then slams it down with a flourish. Stuck upright by its tip, the knife trembles. I make to clap my hands at him, but he seizes them both in his.

'Miss Jaccob,' Fub says. My name in his mouth is the sweetest sound I have ever heard. Let me sit here, on this stool on the sawdust floor in this place and keep my hands in yours for ever. His eyes are blue, but in the right one there is a dash of dark brown on the iris. A perfect flaw.

He takes my left hand now, and spreads my fingers on the

block as his were. Thus opened I wait, tense. The blade flashes, pricks wood, lands safely. When he is done, Fub leans closer in to me. He bends over my hand then nicks with the knife's tip at the taut skin next to my smallest finger. The sudden pain is an affront, a shock. I breathe in through my nose, hard, but I do not flinch. I clench my other hand into a tight fist, chafing at a hangnail on my thumb to distract from the hurting. Only when he releases my hand does it fly to my mouth, unbidden, and I suck at the blood that flows where he cut.

'That is what would happen if I didn't have the skill.' He takes my hand to examine the small wound.

'Did you come to harm from his party piece?'

I did not see this woman come in. She has appeared in the same doorway as the giant went out, but she takes up a scant sliver of it. For the first time, Fub is discomfited. He shies like a horse at a gate, flings my hand back to me, wipes his sleeve over his mouth and stands up, the stool falling over behind him.

The woman is so thin that she seems flat, her dress hanging from her bony frame as if there's no body beneath to give it shape. Perhaps Titus rolls on to her as they lie in their bed, pressing her like cider apples. White hair escapes from underneath her cap, each strand following a different path to its fellows so that it sticks out from her head like a frill. She has very small eyes, set so far back in her head that she appears to squint.

'Does it need a tincture? Ayee.' This last sound is not a question, it is a jarring tune that starts with great emphasis on the first note then sweeps the full length of the stave from the lowest to the highest. It is like an elaborate bow that ties up the end of her sentences. I suspect if I spent much time in her company,

I might catch her habit of 'ayeeing' too. I do not intend to spend much time in her company.

'Bet, this is Mistress Jaccob.' Fub straightens the stool, recovers himself.

'Thomas Jaccob's child?' She looks me up and down, gathering her skirts into a bunch in each hand and bending both knees together, as you do when you begin a dance. 'Mistress.' She bows her head to the floor. I think she looks at me when she rises, though her hidden eyes make it hard to tell.

She turns to Fub, then clips him lightly about the ear. 'If you persuaded her to sit while you jumped your knife near her little mitts, Fub, it's no wonder she came to harm. Ayee.'

The mother tiger will wield her sharp claws trying to protect her cub and, seeing her lay hand on Fub so casually, I wish I were a beast and could strike at her. There'd be four tracks down both cheeks where each claw pierced. Off she'd scurry, clutching her bloody face, and leaving us in peace.

'I am not very hurt, Ma'am.' I hold out my hand and show her where the blood begins to set.

'Good.' She peers at the wound as much as her tiny peepers will allow. No wonder she is dressed in poor gabardine spotted with black marks and two of the buttons on her blouse are unfastened. There must be much effort in looking at things properly if you see the world from such a narrow point. 'What will you show her next, Fub, if you've begun with your greatest talent?'

Again, he looks awkward and embarrassed. She messes at his hair, catching it in clumps and tugging. The tiger growls.

He ducks his head away, smooths his hair down and smiles at her. 'Bet! There's more to me than that!'

Her eyes become little straight lines as she smiles back. If she were a cat, she'd purr. But I would slit her open with my tiger strength.

'Now, hold these, my darling.' Titus is returned. The ledger has sheaves of paper tucked inside higgledy piggledy and she has to push the covers together to keep everything inside as she takes it from him. Several pages land on the floor and she picks them up with haste, shaking the sawdust from them. She looks at me, raising her eyes to heaven to share her irritation at his slovenliness.

'Don't bring these here, Levener,' she says. 'There's muckment about might get on the pages. Ayee.'

He tips his head to indicate me, as if I couldn't see him. 'The mistress wants to check our accounts.'

'Why, Miss?' She looks nervous. 'Is anything wrong?'

That is not my purpose at all – I hardly want to look at lines of numbers. 'No,' I tell them, 'I want to understand about—' They look expectant and nervous, like children caught taking apples. 'I am interested in household matters. In ALL matters of cooking, or preparing—'

They both lean towards me. They are like puppets on my hands, both bending to left or right as I choose. If I look one way or the other, their eyes will follow. Titus has the groggy stare of someone newly awoken, while Bet is hunched attentively. I have to suppress a desire to clap my hands or shout aloud, to watch them start back in perfect symmetry.

'Miss Jaccob is ordering for the household while her mother is confined.' Fub looks at me while he says this.

'Oh, I had heard your mother was delivered. But not of a boy . . .' says Bet, her voice full of sympathy. 'A lovely daughter!' she adds, to soften her message. 'Another fine girl. Ayee.'

77

There might be more in this vein, all beautifuls and preciouses, if I don't stop her. 'We are blessed,' I say curtly.

She folds her arms. 'Indeed,' she says, thoughtfully. 'Well, let us begin then.'

Titus Levener appears behind her shoulder. He is anxious. 'Begin what, love?' he squeaks.

'If you wish to see all the preparation of your meat,' Bet goes to the counter, pulling a small crate towards her as she speaks, 'then you should bring an apron or suchlike. You cannot avoid blood here and I regret I have none to spare for you. Ayee.'

'I shall borrow one from our cook.' She can't imagine I have many in my wardrobe, surely?

'You will have to wrap Jane's apron many times around you,' Fub says. 'She is outside a great many pie suppers, that one.' He holds his hands apart.

'But there is a quick thing I can teach you.' Bet opens the crate, setting its lid carefully on the counter, and reaches inside. She holds out an egg. It is still stuck with chicken mess and dirt; sticks of straw cling, too. She brushes it clean with great care, and motions me to take it.

'Put your lips to the larger end,' she says. The egg looks equally sized each end to me. I look to her for guidance. She turns it gently in my cupped palm, rubs at one end tenderly with the point of a finger and then I can see there is one end slightly bigger and flatter. I do as she bids me, putting the hard shell against my mouth and feeling the swell and warmth underneath. It smells of manure and fresh air, in that order.

'What do you sense?' Bet raises her sparse eyebrows, her small eyes unblinking.

The egg is smooth against my skin, its heat almost a heartbeat.

'It is alive,' I say, seeing Fub in sharp focus in front of me.

'If it's cold there, don't buy it.' Bet takes the egg from me and places it back in the crate with slow movements. 'It must be bought and cooked as close to the laying as possible, and some heat stays awhile. Your next lesson might require more stomach. Ayee. Do you faint at the sight of blood, Miss?'

I don't know as I haven't been tested, but I'm not about to admit that to her. 'No,' I lie. 'I am not given to vapours. I have a stout constitution.'

'Then when you're next come, we will show you some processes.' She turns to her husband. Titus no longer looks nervous, indeed they both seem to have grown in confidence. I know they think I am the sort to fail or fade, while they are always unsqueamish and robust. I doubt I will pass out, but Fub will be there to catch me if I should become light-headed and so I cannot see that I lose either way.

'I should take my leave,' I say, and Fub says: 'Do you go alone? It is a fair way.'

I had almost forgotten my unlikely escort, but when I look to the door he is already there.

'Hey!' Titus lunges at him. 'Be off with you, Scotsman!'

'Mr Levener, Angus showed me the way here.' I'd better defend him, though he looks shabbier than ever.

Titus recoils. He glares at the man, then at me. 'These types are not allowed on our streets, Miss Jaccob.' He is gruff, put out at having to keep his fists to himself. 'This garb is illegal.' He grabs a handful and shakes the thin tartan about Angus' legs.

The soldier swings away from him, with all the dignity he can muster. 'I'll thank you to keep your hands to yourself, butcher.' He almost growls like a dog.

'Do you have a tiny dirk to threaten me with?' Titus advances on him, waggling his little finger suggestively in the soldier's face, his bulk dwarfing the man. 'Where is your sporran?' He grabs at his own crotch, thrusting and taunting. 'Where, indeed, are your precious highlands?' He pretends to cry, pushing his pudgy fingers to his piggy eyes. 'Oh woe for the king over the water and his throne!'

'I'll go, I'll go.' The wretched man walks clumsily backwards towards the door and his escape, Titus lumbering at him all the while.

'Titus.' Fub speaks low. 'I'll see him off. And Miss Jaccob, too. I'll see her safe along her way.'

Levener slows to a wobbling halt. 'Och aye,' he whines, not giving up on his prey. 'Fare ye well, then, you scrag. I would throw you a bone if I'd any to spare, but I let the dogs have 'em first and that is the right order.' His squeaky giggle shakes his body from top to toe.

We make to go, a ragtag trio, but Bet calls 'Fub!' and he turns to her. 'Do not be too long on this errand.' It is a sharp little instruction. He goes back and stands close to her and while he speaks, he fastens the two buttons on her blouse that she had left undone.

'I'll not be long, Bet. Our friend must be directed away and Miss Jaccob shown the route to take. That's all.'

'Oh, was I undone, Fub?' She looks coyly at him, her hand over the place where he neatened her clothes.

'A good thing in a woman!' he says. And her hand goes to his neck, stroking. Jealousy winds through me like a snake and twists tight coils round my heart. Her eyes are set too far back to see them, but I bet they sparkle at him like jewels under water.

The soldier skulks outside, his eyes on the ground. I touch his arm gently and when his eyes meet mine he looks so sad and tired I fear he is not long for this life. All the sleep and all the good food in the world could not restore him. He is heart-sick and broken.

'I'll take my leave, Anne,' he says, pushing a hand to his head and screwing his beret in place.

I don't know what to say. I don't want him here, not now, not with the prospect of Fub all to myself, but he deserves some generosity. 'Will you find a bed tonight?' I ask.

'Shall I share yours?' he says, but when he sees this makes me flinch, he shakes his head. 'When you lie on your pillow tonight, don't have any thoughts about me or where I rest. I'll hold you to our bargain at some other time.' He smiles, still kind. 'But, Sir –' This to Fub, who is with us now, 'a nip of gin might make the hard ground more of a feather bed.' He holds one hand out and uncurls his fingers to reveal his palm.

Fub feels in his pocket and brings out a coin. You probably don't have much to spare, I think, but when Fub catches my eye and winks, I realise he is paying the man off and thus out of our company. I want to cheer aloud at the pleasure of knowing this. I am excited to be complicit. Never mind his fastening Bet's buttons or my enduring Titus' teasing. I know that we must part when we reach our destination, but I am full of anticipation simply for our walking side by side.

'Farewell, then, you two.' The Scotsman waves his fist at us, closed tightly over the money, then raises it to his temple in salute.

You two! That was his benediction. He joined us like a strange priest in a swift union. Anyone seeing us for the next little while will think us a pair, then. For the second time that day, I will walk with a man I do not know.

Fub points the way and we set off together and I am so excited that, if our journey were a thousand miles long, I swear I'd have the energy for it. I wish that it was, I wish that we could walk on and on through days and across great spaces together.

Chapter 7

'Did he call you Anne?' Fub has been watching me. I nod. 'Do you wish to take the longer or the shorter route home then, Anne?' He has said my name. I wish it had more syllables to keep it in his mouth for longer.

'The longer.' I answer too quickly; I cannot help myself. 'I have no need to be home for a while.' His expression is one of amused curiosity. 'They are not expecting me back till nightfall. We dine late.' I had better not carry on trying to make all this sound convincing, for the more I say, the more false it sounds.

'The longer,' he repeats. 'Miss Anne Jaccob wishes the longer route.'

For a while, we walk without speaking. I glance at him from time to time, taking in as much of him as I can before he sees me. Several times our eyes meet as I do this, so I imagine he must be stealing looks at me, too. He has a bouncing gait, as if he has just been given good news and wants to share it. The sheer pleasure of being by his side makes me feel as if I am on the verge of laughing aloud. We share the world about us. We see everything together, the same light meets our eyes. If rain fell, we would both get wet.

'Why do they call you Fub?' I ask, wishing I could link my arm through his.

'I could not say my name when I was a little boy. Or so I'm told. I thought they'd christened me Fub as I never heard anyone call me anything else.'

The image of him as a small boy is unbearably moving. 'What is your real name, then?'

'Perhaps I shouldn't say. You might start using it, then I'd not recognise myself.'

'You are Fub to me,' I say, glad he can't see me reddening, because I am thinking of a circumstance where I might say his name with pleasure and it is a fully intimate one. 'It suits you, for no one shares it, do they?'

'Whereas many are called "Frederick", I expect. You think I am one of a kind, do you?'

'You are,' I reply.

'So are you, too,' he says quickly.

The silence that follows is busy with our thoughts. Then I remember his hand on Bet's costume, her giggle. 'Who is she to you?' I say with as much innocence as I can manage.

'Who?'

'Bet.' I say it with a little shudder.

'Bet? You ask "Who is *Bet* to me?" She is my mother's cousin.'

I hadn't thought of Fub with a family.

'Titus offered me apprenticeship.'

'Where is your family?'

'Somerset.' He kicks at a stone on the road. 'Do you know it?' He looks slyly at me, daring me to say I do.

'I do not. Is it fine?'

'Very fine. Full of fine things. But not "fine" enough to keep me there. No "fine" work except breaking my back on a farm for tuppence a year and freezing all winter waiting for crops to grow. No "fine" girls, but those who fetch milk and are simple as the cows they tend.'

'Do you want only fine girls, then? Have you known many others, to judge them by?' This is a dangerous question. Too late, I have asked it. I do not want to think of him with any woman but me and I do not want his thoughts dwelling there, either.

No answer. I bite my lip, considering what else to ask. He finds the stone again with his foot and sends it further along the path. 'I do not know exactly where I am.' As if I had been blindfolded till now, I cannot recognise the street we have reached.

'That way,' he points down a side street, 'that way is to the river.' I imagine the broad sweep of it, the deep dark water. 'My uncle has a boat there,' he says.

'Titus?' It must be a mighty boat to keep him afloat.

'No, not Titus. He's not my only uncle!'

'Do your family sprinkle themselves all over London?'

'As much as your family spreads their money round it.'

'I don't care for my family's money.' I shrug my shoulders, to show how no load of wealth rests there, weighing me down.

'You can say that easily as you've never been without it.' He is serious. I look quickly at him but he is not angry with me, only patient, like a parent with a child slow at their lessons. 'Anne, don't talk of money. It will divide us quicker than a fault in the earth.'

'We must not be divided.'

'We must not.'

We sound playful. We are not playing.

'Tell me about your day, Anne.'

'You know about most of my day, I think.'

'Not today!' he laughs. 'I don't suppose you spend every day strolling along with old soldiers in tartan rags and kissing eggs. No, your most ordinary day. Where do you wake? Which way does your bed face?'

'It is a small, narrow bed.' I have to think hard to describe my room to him. It is so familiar to me that I don't see it any more. 'Away from the window, which faces east. Yellow curtains hang there. On the wall opposite there is a little sampler I made as a child.'

'What does it say?'

'It says: *Honour thy father and thy mother.*'

'And do you?'

I wait a moment, then: 'I do not.'

'My parents have to fend without my honour, too,' Fub says. 'I think they'd rather I gave them one hundred pounds than that.'

'Are they good people?'

'Sturdy, God-fearing, causing no sorrow. Is that good?'

'It'll do. Do they enjoy good health?'

'My father shakes off illness like a dog, he chucks it out of him and carries on. My mother has a cough all the time as would empty churches, but she doesn't complain. What wakes you, then?'

'These days, the baby. With its crying.'

'Ah, the baby. A boy?'

'A girl.'

' Your little sister.' He glances at me, to see how I respond. I am silent. 'What sort of baby is she?'

86

'Dull. Sleeps or cries. I don't know.'

'Pink nails and fat thumbs?'

'As babies have.'

'Smelling sweet as vanilla?'

'I expect so, I do not know.'

'Do you not tend to her, then?'

'No, I do not. She takes up the place where my little brother should be. He was the sweetest boy who only made everything happy in the house. And my father is angry that she was born a girl, so his mood has darkened worse than ever. And she has taken my mother from me, too; where once we sat together, or visited, or sewed, now she is pale and wretched, with hardly the strength to say my name, let alone ask how I do. And all the while, this infant leeches the very heart from her, and its every need must be answered with all speed, its every appetite quenched. I do not tend to her. I don't even want her near me.'

'Do you hate her?'

'Yes!' I did not know it until I said it, but at once I know it is true. I hardly dare look at Fub. Surely he begins to be shocked – repulsed, even – by my coldness. He looks at me with an expression I can't read, but it is not disgust.

'Well!' he says, giving great force to the word. 'I know one thing: if you can hate with such passion, Anne, then you can love with great passion, too.' The look he gives me does not remind me of love. I think he cannot decide whether to consume or caress me.

As we round a corner there is a smell of roast meat and a woman shouts 'Hot!' and 'Fresh!'

'Are you hungry?' Fub says, and I am. He buys two pies, almost too hot to hold, and we stand near a wall to shelter from the throng and eat them without being jostled. If one of the passing carriages held someone I knew, they would see me with a pie to my mouth and a boy by my side. Although I think I do not care if they did, I turn my back to the road.

'Come here, you careless child, you have spilled gravy.' Fub puts his thumb to one side of my mouth and wipes across it, then he puts it in his mouth and licks it clean. Everything inside me is focussed at the very point of the triangle between my legs, urgent as an itch that needs scratching and heavy as lead. I want to put my hand there, to put Fub's hand there. I fear I will dissolve. I am like glass; surely he can see to the very centre of me. He takes my arm.

I once saw an aerial display in a circus. A girl climbed a tall ladder to a small bar under long ropes and dangled from it as she swung in wide sweeps of the marquee. When her partner let go of his swing, she too released her grip on her own, then dived, dizzyingly high above the ground, in a perfect arc to reach the other. For a moment, she was in the air, free, flying. And standing with Fub, his arm through mine, I am suspended, exhilarated, not heeding how far I might fall.

'You have a good shiny pelt,' Fub says. 'And dog's eyes.' He laughs, seeing my startled expression. 'I am unpractised in flattery, I'm just saying what I see. I like the look of you and you remind me of a proper hound that looks at me nicely.'

'Just say *"I like the look of you"*.' I don't look at him when I speak.

'I like the look of you. I like your brown hair and your yellow eyes. I like the height of you and your small hands. There is a proper space in your face for your features and they're all of an even size.'

'You can leave aside describing me as an animal, then,' I say, my voice sounding higher than usual. 'Besides, it's getting late and don't all women look the same in the dark?'

'I would know you,' he says and I shiver, although I am warm. 'Nightfall or not, if I get you home too late I can whistle for your father Jaccob's business.' He lets my arm go, but I can still feel the warmth and pressure of his fingers. He stops suddenly, listens for a moment then turns round sharply. 'Oy!' he says.

There's a small boy on the path behind us. I cannot see the child clearly as, although he is close, he is crouching down. He scuttles away. There is no one else about.

'Little spy!' Fub says after him. 'I'll leave you here. I don't go to the front door.'

The house looms up, ready to divide us. We hold back a while near the gate. How shall we part? How can we?

'So,' Fub reaches to a little bush on the path, picking at the leaves, keeping his hands busy. 'You will be the next Levener apprentice, then? You will come and see what we do?' He shreds the blooms as if it matters that he does it very carefully and with no hurry, letting the tiny neat pieces fall to the ground, one by one.

'I will come.' I watch his fingers and the scattering pieces. I do not want to meet his eyes. 'I need some more lessons from you if I am to learn how to manage a household.' My voice is high and bright; I am spinning out these matters to keep him here. I do not want to say the words that will set him free.

'Come tomorrow, if you will.' Fub is trying to sound at ease, but he's not looking at me either.

'If I can,' I say. Tomorrow? I will have to look for another reason to leave home. 'If I can,' I say again.

He picks a little flower from the bush. 'Here.' He holds it out to me. Then, because I do not take it at once, takes my hand and opens my fingers, curling them over it.

He does not say goodbye, but turns on his heel and walks off with that jaunty step of his. I wait, but there is no backward glance.

Too late, I remember the note, the church, the real purpose of my setting out. Leaving the house this morning seems a lifetime away. I am surprised that I still wear the same clothes. I am very tired.

The little flower in my hand wilts already.

Part Two

I am two fools, I know
For loving, and saying so

John Donne, *The Triple Fool*

Chapter 8

Pushing the front door wide, I can see straight into my father's study. That door is, unusually, ajar. My father is bent over his desk, examining some book laid open there. Next to him, but with his back to me, is the figure of another man. A silvery tail of hair, caught with a velvet ribbon, winds down his back. He wears a purple frock coat of some soft stuff, pale brown britches and little black shoes with large buckles and he is talking in a low tone while my father listens. As the door closes behind me, my father lifts his eyes and, on seeing me, smiles. This is most strange. I suspect he must be about to reprimand me and therefore he smiles with pleasure at the promise of my punishment, but instead he says 'Anne!' sounding very jolly, as though he were really pleased to see me.

He taps the other fellow lightly on the shoulder and he looks up, then at me. He is holding the book my father studied and as I get nearer I can see the pages have no words, but instead are covered with bright shapes and colours. He closes it and secures it under one arm.

'Anne!' Again my father speaks with beaming pleasure. Perhaps he is full of wine. 'This is Simeon Onions!'

The man turns and bows low, he even sweeps one arm across

his body, a full courtly gesture. A lock of hair, as pale as the rest, falls over one eye and he winds it back off his face with long thin fingers. The gesture is youthful, even a little girlish, though his dark eyes – as brown as pitch – do not smile and his face is gaunt. His skin is pale, ash white with grey craters in the hollow of his cheeks. It is like looking at the surface of the full moon. Underneath his eyes, his bones protrude sharply. From one sleeve there falls a kerchief of crisp lace, and he pulls this free and mops his brow in a dainty feint of exertion. Onions. I seem to know his name, but I am sure we have never met before. I can dimly hear it in my head, said in another's voice. A man's voice. It is a memory I cannot quite pin down.

Onions turns fully towards me until he faces me square on. His black gaze is steady, unhesitant. He seems to be confirming something to himself, examining me thoroughly and taking his time. There might be no one else in the room. When he addresses me, I try not to flinch.

'Ah, your father spoke to me of your gentle beauty, your graceful demeanour, your noble carriage. But he failed to do you justice!'

I am taken aback – not by his wittering, that washes over me easily – but because the sound of him does not match the sight. I expected him to simper in a high falsetto but instead he has a rich baritone voice. He enunciates carefully and rather too loudly, as if he declaims from a written page to a crowded hall and wants to be heard at the very back of it.

'How Venus must weep to know such a creature exists!' He uses his free hand to make sweeping motions in the air as he speaks; he would probably like to give the book to one of us to leave both hands free. 'Aphrodite must declare herself ugly in comparison! Thomas—' He turns to my father, who has been listening to all this with a daft grin fixed to his face. 'Thomas, I know your wife to be a beauteous woman, and you are fine featured, but still how *remarkable* and how *fortunate* that you have produced such a vision.' His oration over, he dabs his handkerchief at his forehead again.

I wait for my father to send him packing, or at least to grunt his displeasure at this copious flood of nonsense. He does neither. He takes the book from Onions and holds it out to me.

'Simeon is something of an artist.' Onions simpers at this, looks to the floor and mutters 'Too kind, too kind.' Even with this little aside he clips the words neatly and sends them out into the world very separate from each other. My father opens the book to reveal some hectic yellow blossom.

'He is decorating our drawing room, ready for when your mother joins us again. I want the house fully ordered when she comes down.' When was this decided? All the papers and hangings and curtains in the house date from my parents' marriage. They are so aged and worn as to be invisible and that has suited us all very well. Long ago, she held swatches up for him to agree to, or he bought furniture she had chosen, but they are different people now. They have long since forfeited any interest in their surroundings or made any joint decisions, let alone any as frivolous as these.

'She has given me a healthy baby girl and Simeon is going to transform her domain in some, um, small recompense for her labours.' I cannot help snorting through my nose at this. If I believed in spells, I would think my father was under one that rendered him completely changed. No more the surly, frowning grump but a sparkling aesthete, in love both with his surroundings and all mankind. I look down at the book. Its pages are all stiff paper covered with rich colourful patterns, some with birds perching or great flowers entwined.

'New wall coverings will greatly benefit what is already a charming room.' Onions takes the book from me and begins to leaf through it. 'I am trying to persuade your father that a rich yellow-gold will be like waking to a bright sun every day.' Though his words are florid and his cadence musical, his cold dark eyes give nothing away. It is disconcerting how intricate his web is, while he sits spider-like in the centre. My father is already rolled up tight as a fly.

'I have no eye for such things, I'm afraid.' I bob a little curtsey in his direction but avoid his eyes. 'Forgive me, Mr Onions, I have to see to supper preparations.'

'Oh!' He positively brays. 'No, Miss Jaccob, I cannot let you leave without even glancing at my poor offering.' His fingers trail over the book, stroking the patterned page as a snail marks its path with slime. He holds it out to me again.

'This one is particularly delicious, is it not?' He is lowering his voice now and getting closer to me. I try not to flinch. 'I think,' he whispers, 'though the gods will smite me if I am wrong to attempt to sway you, that this is my favourite.' I glance at the swirls and loops in front of me. I smell ether and cologne on his breath. The dense pattern and his odour both suffocate me.

'Very fine,' I say.

'Very fine? Very fine? Thomas, I am NOT wrong to declare that your daughter is possessed of so clear a judgement, so acute an eye, that I wonder you have not consulted with her over the arrangement of the entire house!' He is declaiming again, and I take the opportunity to step back. He steps forward to match and if it were not for the fact that the door is closed behind me, I would turn and run away.

'Mr Onions will dine with us tonight, Anne,' my father announces. 'Make yourself tidy while we discuss these matters further.'

Dine with us! I am suddenly longing for only my father's silent company later. It requires nothing from me. Its very familiarity is comforting and as a beaten dog seeks out his cruel master, I want his presence. I meet my father's gaze. He looks blankly back. I am suddenly aware of what his intention might be. Mr Onions will dine with us! We have not entertained anyone at our table in a good long while, much less included me in the hospitality, but I remember a conversation my father had (over my head) with my mother.

'A good husband,' he had said, 'is both Anne's right and our loving gift to her.' He must have learned these words, he meant no kindness. He scarcely dreads being parted from me and I have no apparent worth. He would rather I were a coin he could bite to tell its value. 'When the time is right, and after I have investigated their suit, I shall ask any gentleman I think might provide her with a good home to eat here, with us, so that we may see how he comports himself. Observe how they match. And note how she behaves.'

I recall thinking that he might as well have been talking about taking a dog to whelp. Onions is much closer to my father's age than mine, more suitable in years as a colleague of his than as a suitor to me. But my father would never be so fawning and craven in his business affairs. This confirms my suspicions. What else can be the reason for this sudden, strange alliance? He must intend Onions to be my wedding present. He would make an oddly shaped parcel. I should not be able to keep from shrieking in horror when I undid the ribbons and discovered him inside.

It will take a great deal of effort for my father to remain gracious for the duration of a meal, particularly if he has the task of including me, too. At least watching him try to act the host will be diverting, or it would be if it weren't for the fact that he will be attempting to pair us up.

If Fub stood here, at my side, I could turn to him.

'Let us leave these two old, odd men to their evening, shall we?' He takes my hand. I lean my head on his shoulder as we leave the room. We stay close together as we go out of the house.

Onions places his sample book on the table, placing a ribbon elaborately to mark the chosen page. He stands in front of me and takes both my hands and although I try to pull away, he is too quick and surprisingly strong. He turns my left hand over and unpeels my curled fingers where I am holding the little flower Fub picked for me.

'To add to your many undoubted talents, Miss Jaccob, we must add "lover of nature".' He gives me a quick look, sharp as a needle. If I didn't know he had been standing here a while, persuading my father to part with his money for fripperies, I might suspect he had spied on me earlier, hidden in the shadows like a ghost. He lets my hands drop, but I feel as if he still holds them, they are scarred by his touch.

'Later, then.' He smiles the words.

In my room, I put the little blossom between the pages of Aesop's fables. It is truly my first lover's token. How Keziah would have loved this story! It is exactly what she had hoped for, as she held Dr Edwards' offering out to me, her face lit with curiosity. I sit by the window, watching the gathering gloom. My heart has followed a tortuous path today, by turns fearful and then exalted and is now heavy as lead. What does Fub do now? If I close my eyes, I can see him as he washes away the bloody day and prepares for the evening. It will be spent in the alehouse, I suspect. I want to sit by him as he swigs at his bottle and jokes with his friends. Titus Levener might be there; he'll get drunk quickly and loudly, then Fub will have to help him home, almost rolling his vast heaviness along the road. There they'll go together, Titus singing a ribald song, raucous and off-key and Fub laughing, indulging his uncle's pleasure. How does his heart fare? Does he think of me? I spread my fingers at the memory of his flashing knife and sigh aloud at the thought of his hands on mine. Outside, the lamplighter rattles at our lantern to spark the flame and downstairs I can hear Jane loudly getting plates on to the table. The night gathers in the corners of the room, concealing the lines of the furniture and muffling the sounds around me. I put my hand to the cold window glass and push against it: if it gave now, I swear I would climb out and jump into the street.

When the call to dinner comes, it wakes me from a doze. I had lain back on the bed and closed my eyes as I had thought I would rest a little, but now it is pitch black, so much time must have passed. It is too late to change my dress. I hope both that my father does not notice – for it would irritate him – and that Onions does: I should like him to interpret this small thing as an indication of my antipathy towards him.

As I reach the hallway, my father and Onions emerge from the study. They have evidently been lubricating their discussion, or at least my father has, for he's a little unsteady and stumbles. He reaches for Onions' arm to stay upright. I catch an expression of distaste, a little purse of his lips, as Onions feels my father's hand on his velvet sleeve. But then he sees me, readjusts his face to a pinched smile of greeting and waves.

'Your father keeps a fine cellar, Miss Jaccob.' I saw his look though, I know his true feelings. 'Dear girl, the hospitality of this house is positively gargantuan.'

'Not "dear girl" yet, Shimeon.' My father wags a finger at him, in mock admonition. 'Although it is mosht pleashant to hear you say it.'

This evening will be interminable. How will I survive it? By trying to catch Onions out, I decide, watching the fault line between his utterances and his feelings grow steadily wider. As we go into the dining room, my father makes great show of seating Onions first, standing behind his chair to ensure that his tiny bottom has made full contact, offering him a square of linen for his neck. He sits beside him and begins to pour water from some height into Onions' glass. Just as Jane is coming in with her first burden of victuals, I am horrified to see my mother in the doorway behind her. Is she ill? There is no place set.

Her appearance galvanises everyone. My father leaps up, splashing water as he sets the jug down with a thump. Jane shrieks and her bowl sways from side to side in a pantomime of trembling. I stay seated, rigid. Only Onions stays calm, rising to his feet and extending one skeletal hand.

'Is this vision the lady of the house? What an honour!' He goes to her, taking her right hand from her side where it hangs limply, and bends over it. She looks blankly at him, her hand in his like a dead fish. I study her face; she is herself but not fully herself, as if she were sleepwalking. He rights himself, retrieves his hand and splays his thin fingers against the ruffle of lace at his neck like a fan.

'Your place is here, Mistress.' He indicates the seat he left for her to sit there, and stands where there are no waiting irons and crockery. In turn, my father seizes his guest's arm a little too hard and pulls Onions towards his own vacated seat. Jane is trying to follow this charade, taking little steps in all directions and, when it seems as if it is my father left at the empty seat, she puts her brimming bowl down and scuttles off to find the things he needs. The room settles like the sea after a storm.

Onions beams and addresses my mother. 'How very fortuitous that you join us tonight.' He turns to my father, who is assisting Jane with her placement by roughly grabbing from her every item she proffers.

'Yes!' He takes a glass from her. 'Yes!' Then a napkin. 'Yes!' Now he clatters knife and fork onto the table. His voice is too loud, his movements too brutal and I see my mother wince.

Ignoring this, Onions leans towards her, as if they were alone.

'Another daughter, I hear. And if she grows to be as beautiful as your elder, then the world will be truly dazzled. But seeing you, Madam, I can fully understand how such loveliness came about. I am no poet but, when I need to, I draw on the rich panoply of verse already created by the masters of our tongue. Now is such a moment.'

He stands. From the corner of my eye, I see Jane look nervous. Does she need to take something from the table? Guests getting up by themselves are an unnerving thing, against the laws of etiquette. She looks at my father, who is in turn looking at Onions with his mouth agape. My mother stares ahead. The man pushes back his chair a fraction, to afford himself room to take position, one hand on his hip, the other held in the air with his palm upwards. He joins the tip of his index finger to the end of his thumb. Clearing his throat, he tips his head back and recites to the ceiling:

> *'Come, little infant, love me now,*
> *While thine unsuspected years*
> *Clear thine agèd father's brow*
> *From cold jealousy and fears.'*

And on he goes, drunk with his own voice, oblivious to our expressions, regardless of the text.

> *'So, to make all rivals vain,*
> *Now I crown thee with my love:*
> *Crown me with thy love again,*
> *And we both shall monarchs prove.'*

There is silence and with a tweak of cramp I realise my toes have been curled up tight in my shoes. Then Jane claps her hands together, and the mood is broken. Onions seems almost grateful as he acknowledges her applause. My father merely taps the table once with one hand, he cannot bring himself to do more.

'Very fine,' says my mother, the first words she has uttered tonight.

I say nothing. Onions catches my eye, and he is angry that I don't praise him. But because he cannot show his displeasure, he turns to Jane with great energy and swagger.

'Dear lady! Do you admire the work of Marvell? I think, if I may be so bold, that he is, quite simply, the finest poet. I hope I do him justice.'

She looks at the floor and mutters: 'Sir, it was—' But she cannot find a word.

'Tell me, Madam, what is your name?' He holds his head on one side, and speaks in a soft, emollient tone, as if she were a child.

Jane looks nervously at my father, anxious to know if she may speak to this man without getting into trouble. My father is flummoxed, though, and only shrugs his shoulders at her.

'Jane.'

'Jane. Your full name, Jane?'

Jane swallows. This is becoming a little too much of an interrogation for comfort. 'Jane Bradshaw.'

I am startled. I don't think I've ever heard her name as more than a simple, plain 'Jane'.

'And how does Mr Bradshaw do, may I enquire?'

There is a pause. Jane opens and close her mouth twice before answering.

'He is dead, Sir.'

'Ah.' Onions offers no sympathy, he is just taking notes.

'He died twenty years before, Sir.' She clasps her hands in front of her and twists them together. Her voice has dropped, so she almost whispers. She breathes in deeply, steadying herself.

It is as if she is taking shape before me. I had not known she was a widow. I have never even thought of her before as a woman, much less a wife. She has hitherto been a deliverer of plates, a boiler of meat. I did not know she was ever loved. That she had once loved someone. That she had risen from her bed with the thought of her lover, wanted and waited for him all day and slept with dreams of him. My stomach knots with a mixture of sadness and frustration. We should let her go now, dismiss her to her room to remember her loss, to mourn. I cannot meet my mother's eye in case I see tears shining there.

'We must all bear some sorrow.' Onions looks piously round the room at us all, appointing himself minister and sage. It is a lucky thing that he does, because it has the effect of a bucket of freezing water – his sentimental posturing wakes us abruptly. We stiffen to attention like soldiers called to battle. Jane is first to speak.

'It is a long time since,' she says, and pats at her apron with brisk hands. 'Some meat, Sir?' She bustles to the table and reaches for a platter, knocking the glasses into a tremble as she leans. With relief, I see her restored to both bustle and clumsiness.

'Mr Onions,' my mother turns to him. She is calm. Solemn, even. 'Do you conduct business in London?'

Onions brushes the air in front of him, to indicate that while he has some poetry in him, there are serious matters to attend to, besides. He leans one elbow on the table.

'I won't go into detail, Mistress Jaccob, as I have bored your husband with my enterprises and while he has listened tolerantly –' he smiles indulgently at my father, who harrumphs in return, 'suffice it to say that the running of the estate should be easy enough but the getting of good staff is hard.' He raises his eyes heavenwards. 'Goodness only knows why the common man does not understand that regular employment is a boon to him, and he will do no better than to find himself a regular, menial task, apply himself daily and thus get a little money for it. But they drink or fornicate themselves out of work, and have not the wit to stay sober and chaste. They are hardly going to fill their idle hours with such occupations as *thinking*, are they? They had better get on with hard graft and be grateful.'

Not a moment since, he had encouraged Jane to join in the conversation, now he dismisses her kind with one swipe.

'What employment do you offer, then?' My mother's tone is sweet, but I detect a little sharpness.

Onions pauses. I think he can feel a prickle, too.

'I have the *good fortune* to have inherited a large chunk of Derbyshire.' He stresses the words, implying that it is in fact a careful strategy rather than an accident of birth on his part. 'That is the correct measurement for the place, is it not? Derbyshire is counted in chunks, isn't it, I think?' He sniggers, but no one joins in.

'A cousin minds it for me,' he continues, 'so I do not have to concern myself with the day to day events. Too much talk of accounts and inventories and I feel quite faint.'

Jane is beside him now, placing his food on the table.

He glares at the plate in front of him. 'Ah, forgive me,' he pushes it away with both hands, 'but I cannot tolerate meat.' He pulls his mouth into an expression of distaste. 'Do you have any milk or a little bread?'

Jane looks as if she has been beaten. Her head shrinks to her shoulders. My father, who has been listening to all this with a deepening frown, now takes charge. He slaps Onions across the back – it is meant playfully, but Onions is too slight to stay fully upright and sways forwards with the blow.

'No meat!' my father bellows, regarding Onions with amused curiosity. 'Then fetch what we have, Jane. But I will continue to eat the stuff. Avert your gaze, if you must.' He spears a slice of meat from Onions' plate and slams it on his own.

'I am sorry our dinner disappoints, Mr Onions.' My mother smiles at him. 'I hope Jane can find something else to tempt you.'

Onions smiles back, shaking his head ruefully. 'I should have thought to warn you, Madam. But if I eat meat, delicious though it might be,' – it is obvious he doesn't believe any meat, particularly our offering, to be delicious – 'then I suffer for it.' He pats at his chest, then strokes there. His insides must be purring with all this affection. 'My mother used to say I have inherited a certain delicacy.' He holds my mother's gaze, inviting agreement.

Her expression is one of faint pity, perhaps, nothing more.

Jane returns with a platter of bread, a little cheese and a pear. They sit apart with naked acres of china between them. It hardly looks like a feast. Onions nods wordlessly at her, giving her a tiny, brave smile to show he forgives what she offers.

My father laughs, though, not caring that he might offend. 'You'll hardly grow fat on that!' He chews at a tough mouthful as he speaks and there is more than a glimpse of revolving meat on view.

'This is excellent!' Onions attempts to join in with good humour, but he cuts the pear into small portions in a way that suggests he might like to slice at something that would feel pain.

I am delighted by all of this. With every simper and flounce, every utterance and recitation, Onions must surely be putting himself further from the role of suitor. The idea of him courting me is risible and ridiculous. I am convinced that his performance tonight must have sounded a loud death knell to any such suggestion.

Conversation fades. Onions scissors pieces of bread with sharp front teeth, then brushes his dry fingers together to remove invisible crumbs. He chews each mouthful at the very front of his mouth so there are only tiny movements in his cheeks. My father bends lower and lower over his plate, as if it were a trough. It is like dining with two low species of animal: Onions is the little rat beside my father's ox.

I go carefully at my portion; it is a precious offering, having most probably been touched by Fub's hands. Only my mother does not eat. Her head is inclined forward over her untouched food. The candlelight throws our shadows against the wall. You cannot tell from my soft dark shape how my black mind plots and plans.

Jane brings a platter of stewed fruit. It is a mush the colour of mulberries, but no single fruit is visible. No one takes a portion. Onions cranes his head to look behind her – I suspect he thinks there is a chance he might see a sudden surprising army of staff bearing more plates. We have long since abandoned any sort of feasting.

'Now, Miss Jaccob.' Hearing him speak is like stepping barefoot on a slug. Onions touches his napkin delicately at the corners of his mouth, then folds it into a neat square.

'Anne,' my father corrects him, grinning.

'Anne.' He looks at me for a full minute as though he's been instructed to convey adoring admiration. At any rate, it is an uncomfortably long time and I stare back. It is as if we play that childish game of refusing to blink or look away. I will be the winner. He will be afraid of my cold eyes before too long.

Sure enough, Onions' eyes eventually slide sideways.

'Such beauty,' he mutters.

This nonsense again! I glance at my father. Perhaps now he will tire of this posturing and say something, even defend me against it.

'What do you reply, Anne?' he says instead. 'Surely you have some polite answer to such praise?'

I look to my mother, trying to plead wordlessly with her to intervene. Her eyes are cloudy now, and she looks away and down – anywhere but at me. Her little awakening, the way she questioned Onions and did not engage with him, is over.

'Anne?' My father's tone is cold, peppered with annoyance. There may be three other people in the room, save Onions, but I feel entirely alone. Perhaps I should spring up, grab Jane's hands and demand she shelter me? What would I say? *I am in love, Jane! Let me tell you about him! Talk to me of—*' Here I falter. I don't know her dead husband's name and my imagination baulks at saying *Mr Bradshaw*. I could not speak to her like that anyway, it would only frighten her.

'Mr Onions,' I say aloud, instead. 'Your words are very kind.'

'Kind? I am not meaning to be kind, Anne.' He is rebuking me. He looks to my father for confirmation of my improper conduct.

'I regret I have not instructed her to take praise. Forgive me, Simeon.' My father puts his hands together as if in prayer, and pretends to offer himself up in supplication.

'She will have to learn, there will surely be so much of it to come, with all her attributes.' Onions does not look at me. 'Oh!' He looks to my mother as she rises then leans forward on the table to support herself. The act has made her dizzy.

'Please, stay seated,' she says, catching Onions in the act of getting up so that he remains comically halfway between sitting and standing.

'For God's sake, man!' My father, finally exasperated, pulls at his arm to lower him down.

Ruffled, Onions adjusts his jacket and brushes at the sleeves. 'Your kind hospitality is overwhelming,' he says.

My mother fixes him with a look. 'Mr Onions, we did not provide you with a proper meal and I'm sorry. If you dine here again, I shall make sure there is something heartier on your plate. Do you prefer—?'

'*When* you dine again,' my father interrupts her and his meaning is clear: *I am in charge of who is and who is not invited.* 'I'll put a strong fish down, not a poncey pear.'

'Too kind,' Onions is muttering again. He steeples his fingertips together, and I notice that the nails on both forefingers are longer than the rest and curled like claws. 'I enjoy fish of the water. I can even tolerate a little fowl of the air. It is just, alas, alas, the beast of the field that disagrees with me.'

I am reminded of the great corpses hung in Levener's shop: decapitated, sinewy and skinned. I imagine them bearing down on Onions, roaring a terrible roar while he shrieks that they might disagree with his dainty digestion and tries to run away. They'd trample him without even noticing him underfoot.

'You smile, Anne, and what light shines.' Onions pours more oily words from his mouth.

My father slips in them. 'Do you have a plan, Simeon?' He raises his eyebrows enquiringly, prompting him. He wants Onions to say something they rehearsed. 'Might you have a *plan*?'

'Indeed.' He nods to my departing mother. 'Madam.' She doesn't look back. 'I wish to invite you to accompany me to a small exhibition, Anne. I have it on good authority that it is most enjoyable.' His conspiratorial tone implies that he has heard this from the tongues of kings or the lips of nobility.

What can I do? My father answers for me. 'Fortunate girl, of course you'll go.' He stands up, stretching his arms above his head. 'Gah!' he shouts. I know that he is bored with sitting so long at the table. 'I have a little fortified wine in my study, Simeon. I want your opinion of it.'

'Just a thimbleful, dear man. I begin to tire. Not of your company, Anne,' he says hastily, and looks sideways at my father to see if he has caused offence. But my father is already thinking of sweet wine in a warm room and isn't listening to Onions. 'I travelled from deepest Derbyshire this week and I fear the jolting of the coach has quite displaced me.'

Behind him, the little blade of the knife he cut his fruit with twinkles in the candlelight. It is a short distance from the table to my hand, and only a little way from my hand to his heart. One movement would do it – there! Even if it didn't kill him, it would stop all his blathering. The two of them are standing still, waiting for me to leave.

'Mr Onions, I bid you good night. Father.' I go to leave, but my father catches my arm.

'Say thank you for your kind invitation,' he hisses in to my ear and turns me to face Onions. I repeat the words, just as he said them, trying to sound light and unafraid.

'And "I look forward to our outing",' my father hisses again. He waits for me to repeat this, then pushes me away. 'I apologise *again* for her rudeness. I suspect she is a little unpractised, that is all. You can teach her!'

Onions laughs with my father but he is obedient, not amused. He is almost plump with glee at this possibility. It must be a great effort for him not to rub his hands together.

It is a wonder I can put one foot in front of the other, I am so heavy. Behind me, I leave two unloving men who together will design the most unhappy of futures for me. My breathing is laboured; climbing the stairs is like scaling cliffs. I am not safe here. The very banister feels colder than usual, the familiar paintings reproachful.

I am almost at my door when my mother steps from the shadows.

'Anne.' She lays one hand on my arm. It is a timid gesture but I am grateful for it. 'Your father has your best interests at heart.'

This is so trite and so untrue I feel a surge of anger. I have to hold my arms tightly by my sides to stop me from seizing her by the shoulders. If she seeks to console me, there are better ways to do it. She could say: *'We are both in thrall to your father, you and I; my daughter, I cannot help you, except to confess that I do not love him any more and you must not expect love from your chosen husband either. It is not our due.'*

Or: *'Run, while you can. Let me hide you while you leave the house. Follow your heart's desire. Don't look back.'*

'How can you say that?' is all I can manage, and I sound childish and petulant.

'Annie,' she squeezes my arm. 'You know you must make a good marriage, and it is about time.'

'But with *him?*' I am too loud; she shushes me.

'He may not have made the best impression, but I expect he was nervous. He has been a bachelor for many years. He may have a good heart . . .'

Nervous! That's not the word for that snivelling, snide fop. And his heart is a long way from good, with all those expressions of distaste when he thought no one could see. The only way I can think of his heart without crying aloud is to imagine it impaled on a fruit knife and that lace shirt of his getting redder by the minute.

'I wish you safe,' she continues. 'Happiness can come later.'

'Is that how it was for you?' I cannot imagine my mother as a young girl, tripping over her feet in her hurry to be beside my father. The darkness around us lets me speak. If I could see her eyes, I would not be able to question her.

'With me, it was the other way about. Oh, we were happy once, Annie. We each thought the other held our happiness tight. When we let go it fell and shattered.' Her voice sinks to a whisper. 'But I am safe now.'

The baby wails nearby, and my mother is lost to me at once. The cry is a blanket thrown over her head, smothering her and obliterating everything else. Absently, her hands go to her tender breasts. The nurse appears on the landing, the child bundled up in her arms.

'Mistress, she is hungry. Do you come?' I see my mother torn between her two daughters for an instant, but that child's tugging cry snares her and she cannot resist it. Shall I wail, too? If I started, I might not stop. With a hurried, 'We will speak again soon, good night,' she is gone.

When I reach my room, I throw myself on the bed and bury my face in the cover. I want to scream, but I must not make a sound. I may not cry out, or fight, or protect myself. I hold my bolster tight and, when it is warm with my embracing it, I can imagine it is Fub, close to me. Close enough to kiss. I put my lips to its calico cover and whisper, 'Oh my dearest, my darling.' And the Fub-pillow answers, *Shh, I am here.* My own right hand stands for him, embracing me, stroking my shoulder, my hip, my breast. I wipe away my tears as he would and I promise myself that in time, soon, it will be his true hand caressing me and his real voice in my ear.

There is little comfort in this, but I am a prisoner now in this cold house and must find warmth where I can.

Chapter 9

I dreamt that I was happy. On waking, though, I cannot remember why and when I try to retrieve the dream, it slips away as water leaks through your fingers, however tightly you hold them together. And just as quickly as those pleasant feelings fade, so the memories of last night's events crowd in to my head. It is like watching a tragic play unfold and I do not like my part.

As I dress, the little slip of paper for the priest falls to the floor. All that snaring of Onions so that he might pay court to me had put that errand from my father's thoughts. I snatch it up. I have another reason to pass Levener's door! And as I'm now sure of the route, I'll not need an old soldier as my guide. I recall with a pang his look of sadness at Levener's teasing and how he slunk away into the gloom when Fub and I stood together. There was kindness in his actions, he sought no recompense. If I lived in a different household I might tell my father of our adventures, then beg him to find my helpmeet and give him a reward. But if this was a different household, I would not be going as carefully as I am down the creaking staircase, anxious not to be discovered.

As I get to the safe stone floor, I realise that each step of my exaggerated journey has been observed. Grace, the little nurse, is not confined to my mother's room at my sister's cot as she should be, but she stands in the hall, waiting for me. I am flustered, but turn, with as much purpose as I can muster, to the hooks by the door to fetch my bonnet. With my back to her, I take a deep breath so that I can turn back to face her with a calm demeanour. She in turn looks at me with some defiance. If we were playing cards, she would think she held the winning hand.

'It is early, Mistress,' she says, stepping forward. 'Shall I fetch some bread for you?'

She is a pretty girl. Without her usual preoccupying bundle I see her clearly. Under her little cap, her hair is gold and shining – some of it curls round her face – and her eyes are very blue. Her neat lips are pushed forward, as if they are about to speak or to kiss. There must be a queue of suitors waiting to take her from here and get her with her own child.

'I am going to St Peter's.' I need not tell her more. In whom would she confide, anyway? Jane is too many years her senior and the servants in the next house come and go too much to gossip. Fub would pass the time with her, though. She is just the sort of girl to sit beside him for an evening, then kiss him too easily and for a little too long on the way home. His fingers could thread themselves in that shining hair, while her small hands stroked his dark head. I wish I could tell her to stay upstairs, or banish her altogether. When I am mistress of my house, I shall employ the ugliest servants I can find.

'Ah, yes, the christening!' Someone speaks to her and tells her what is happening in the household, then. Her life is not all handing over a baby to be fed, then mopping and wiping it after. I suppose during the long hours when the child sleeps, this girl must listen to my mother. 'Yes, Grace,' my mother would say, 'Mr Onions is a possible suitor for Anne. In fact, he is the only suitor!' They would laugh at this. 'She is a difficult girl, isn't she? Too cunning for her own good. Too unsettled. Having to manage a household in remote Derbyshire should quieten her, don't you think? But now, let's attend to little Evelyn, her sweet nature is already obvious. Look how she begins to smile!'

I go to the door. It is still bolted and I fumble at the locks and keys. On her tiptoes, Grace unlocks the highest bolt, which sends her off balance and she falls against me. I can smell the starch of her petticoat and a tiny sourness from her pits. I stand stiffly while she recovers. She laughs nervously, then, seeing that I do not respond, she becomes serious.

'Shall I say when you'll return, if they ask?'

It would only be my father asking, and I curse myself for not being kinder and softer to her just now. I don't want my father wondering how I spent the long hours yesterday and why I was too tired to change my costume before dinner.

'No need. I would rather you didn't say you had seen me leave.' A tiny raise of her yellow eyebrows. 'I had intended to go to the priest yesterday, but I became very lost. Foolishly lost!' I laugh at this, but it is too late for her to join in; she doesn't trust me.

'Do you know the way now?' Her tone is a little arch. She must realise that the church is not far – she might even attend herself. She could be on her knees there thrice weekly for all I know.

'I discovered the way when it was almost dark, so I thought I should return today. In daylight.' This is enough explanation – if I carry on, I might reveal more than I mean to do. For a moment, I long to tell her everything. This is why girls go to their friends, I suppose, because it is hard to keep all this excitement to oneself. *Oh, Grace, I went to Fub! He held my hand and gave me a flower! He danced a knife between my fingers with speed and skill, then cut me – here is the scar – to test my courage. Do you love a boy, Grace? Do your very organs contract at the thought of him? Will you walk over broken glass or crawl through fire to reach him?* But her little face is sly; she is as wily as I am. We would not play like kittens together but square up like vixens, and our screams would alarm the neighbours. I shall not let her have anything of me that she cannot see.

'It is light enough now.' I swing the door wide. 'There is no need to speak of this. My father would be vexed at my stupidity.'

'Ma'am.' She doesn't believe me, I can tell. She has seen my father scowl at me and preach his worst and I did not cower, so she knows that I am not afraid of him. There must be some other reason why I want to leave unseen. She is still curious and unsatisfied; she'd like to pick more at this sore.

'You may close the door behind me.' My instruction is cold. She gives a tiny shake of her head then curtsies. But she keeps her eyes on my face as I leave, hoping I give myself away. The hem of her dress is wet, she must have been out already in the early dew. She'll not see much daylight again today.

The route to the church is a straight enough one, and I remember it, although I had gone there only reluctantly before. On my last visit, I was mired in such grief for my brother that my eyes were almost closed with crying. I can see the road clearly now.

Despite this breakfast hour, there are plenty of folk about, crowding round the coffee shops and chattering at the stalls.

Their numbers thin as I approach the church, and by the time I tread the path to the door, I am alone. The huge heavy door is only slightly ajar, and it's quite a struggle to push it further. A smell of wax, incense, dust and something floral is so thick in the air it's almost visible. Not so any other person, for my footsteps sound loudly on the floor and even my skirt's swish is distinctly audible. There are no candles lit, doubtless to save money, for, even though it is morning and daylight outside, within is fusty darkness and shadows. When one of these shadows becomes solid and speaks, I jump with alarm.

'Ah, I startled you, I am sorry.' The man in front of me is tall, dressed all in brown but with a priest's white collar at his neck. I do not recognise him: in the time since that last most miserable attendance, my brother's funeral, the keeper of the parish must have changed. He has been sitting on a nearby pew, but he was not praying there – unless it was to say grace. He has a large slice of cake in his hands. It is hard to manage and he cannot keep it in one piece; it splits softly in two. Cupping one hand beneath the other, he attempts to catch the crumbs, but the thing disintegrates with great speed, with most of it failing to reach his open mouth despite him lifting his hands up to get it there.

'Please finish your . . . meal,' I tell him, wishing I was still five minutes down the road and he could stuff his snack into his face without an audience. I gesture to the seats beside me. 'I will sit or, rather, kneel here for a minute.' I hope I am making the face of someone who genuinely wishes to do this.

He nods in agreement and I assume a position of piety and try to ignore the noise of mastication from behind me. I have no prayer to offer up for, even if I believed in a helpful god, I would surely be trying his patience with my list of needs. Perhaps

I should petition for my mother, that her health be restored and her strength renewed, that she might take up her full place in the house? For her greatest happiness, though, I suspect my father must die and leave her a widow, but to ask for that in this place would be more like witchcraft than religion.

I look up to the vaulted ceiling. Come, then, I think, punish my wicked thoughts. But no lightning strikes. The pale stone is blank. Of course, I reason, this is because I have right on my side and any just deity worth their salt would approve of my request and act on my behalf. Perhaps, when I get home, there will be only a smouldering pile of ash where my father stood. A large pile, as He might as well burn Onions too, while He's at it.

A little cough behind me and I remember the vicar is there. I stay kneeling a moment longer, as though I am finishing off an especially lengthy prayer, then I get to my feet. Edging to the aisle, I put my hand out to the polished wooden orb at the pew end. The vicar mistakes this for a greeting and takes my hand, so that I am pulled towards him while stuck by my skirts in the row of seats. His hand still has crumbs on it, several more garland his neckpiece. I pull my hand back. He pats at his unwigged hair with his messy hand. The man will be so covered in foodstuff as to be almost edible himself by nightfall. He waits awkwardly while I wriggle free.

'There!' I say, then I extend my hand to cheer him up.

He looks perplexed by all this social difficulty. He takes my hand gingerly, lest more awkwardness prevail.

'Mistress Jaccob. From Thomas Jaccob's house,' I say.

He puts his head on one side, like a bird. 'Ah, yes?' There is a question in his voice. Surely he knows my father? We might not be often in this place, but we are a long time in the parish.

'We are at Castle Street.'

'Of course.' He makes little soft fists of his hands and rubs his fingertips where the crumbs still stick and chafe. 'Shall we go to my study?'

He indicates the door behind me, but then squeezes past to lead the way. It seems he must do everything in the most uncomfortable way. He goes to the little side door, then holds it for me to go in. It is a narrow entrance, again, and quite hard to get my wide dress through. I cannot think of any conversation to fill the moment, so hold my breath as I manoeuvre myself. He says nothing, either. Inside the small room, there is a table with a lone chair behind it, which must serve as his desk. There are only a few books on top, along with a large solid Bible and the rest of the cake. It sits resplendent on white paper. We both regard it solemnly.

'The kindness of some parishioners . . .' He points at the cake – it is a great doorstop of a thing and although he took a considerable slice, there is plenty left. 'Would you . . .?' A vague opening of his hands.

'I am not hungry, thank you.' Nor do I want to manoeuvre any of the cake – I have witnessed how hard it is to consume it at all daintily.

He sits behind the table, then jumps up again as he realises I am still upright. 'Forgive me, Miss Jaccob. I don't seem to have had many visitors of late. I am out of the habit of entertaining.' He looks disconsolate, then casts about for a chair.

'I can stand here . . .' I begin, but he is out of the door again, saying 'Ah!' as he goes, then returning with a little folded stool.

'I had to stand on this to retrieve a dead bird,' he says, as he straightens the thing out. A print of his shoe is clearly visible on the flat surface. 'Ah!' he says again, then rubs at it with one sleeve. 'Ah,' he says sadly, for the shape is still there despite his cleaning. But nothing else can be done and we must proceed.

My stool is much lower than the chair he sits on, so I have to peer at him over the edge of the table.

'I confess that I have not yet made acquaintance with your household.' He looks down at me, as he might from the pulpit. 'I am quite new in this parish, of course. My predecessor unfortunately, ah, died not long ago.'

I would have thought dying was the highest achievement of any priest, putting him at last in the vicinity of the unseen realm that he had spoken of at such length.

'He has not left me very busy, Miss Jaccob. Not a very, ah, substantial flock. Hence I am not much called on. I rather think,' he leans forward, 'that there might have been a great exodus here to, ah, the Methodists.'

I might ask Grace if she now worships in the open air. In her Sunday-best clothes with those cornflower eyes raised heavenwards and her little bosom swelling to sing Wesley's plain hymns. If I cared to know where she aims her soul, which I probably do not.

'Jaccob.' He looks quizzically at me, then at the books, then opens one. It is a register, full of columns and detailed entries. 'What does your family require?'

I retrieve my father's note from my pocket and hand it over, which requires me to lift my arm quite high to reach him. He opens it, turns it about, then reads. He is a slow reader, and while he deciphers the message, I look at him carefully.

The surfaces of his face are curiously flat and they meet in straight lines and sharp angles – chin with cheek, brow with forehead. Where the light hits them, they darken beneath in rigid shadows without a curve. Only his nose is wayward – at the tip, it is round and purple as a grape. He is probably the same age as Dr Edwards, I think, and that thought gives me such a great pang of sorrow. If Dr Edwards had not behaved as he did, we might sit now in his study somewhere and discuss, oh, *everything*!

My gaze goes to the tabletop. Just as the books my father has in his study gather dust because they are unopened and unloved, so these, too, seem seldom used. They are at eye level to me, so I can clearly see a faint layer of grey dust on their covers. Squinting, I read the titles on their spines. There is a Greek primer, something about the birds and beasts of Wales and *Some Theological Musings From a Learned Source*. They are sideways on to me, so I have to crane my neck to read the lower titles. When my head is inclined at the furthest point, the vicar pushes the volumes aside to speak to me and, finding my face at an acute angle, he tilts his large head to match. As I right my head, so does he, like a figure in a mirror. I am tempted to tip my head over the other way to make him copy me.

'Do you like to read?' he asks, when we face each other upright again.

'I do, very much,' I reply.

'Ah.' He chews at his lip. 'I have a small library. Most of it collected during my time in Oxford.' He turns his head away, smiling wistfully to himself as if seeing a lovely vision. I have never been to Oxford; it might as well be the moon. Or Wales. Or Derbyshire. But I am sure Oxford is lovelier than any of those, for it seems to cheer him up a great deal to think of it.

'Yes!' he says brightly. 'I should like to share it. Do you have a particular preference?'

What should I say? I try and remember even one of the books Dr Edwards used to bring to our lessons. But they are all jumbled up together in the past and I cannot think of anything specific to mention. Then the image of Onions, reciting at dinner to Jane's mortification and my cold eye, flashes before me.

'Poetry!' I state.

The vicar frowns. 'Ah. I have tried,' he ventures, 'to assemble a collection of, ah, *improving* works. But a friend gave me a volume of the writings of, ah, John Donne, and many say he is quite adept. I have only glanced at it, but perhaps you, Miss Jaccob, might volunteer to be my reader?'

He leaves the room, and is gone a while. His scent – a mixture of camphor and incense – hangs in the room as if he were still here. When he returns, it will settle on him again like a cloak on its owner's shoulders. My father's note lies on the table. We have not yet properly addressed this business and I wish now to hasten, to go quickly to where Fub is, even to see him as he leaves on an errand. Any sight of him would be enough. I am suddenly irritated by the vicar's absence.

When he comes back in, I begin to get up. The stool is so low, I have to cling to the front of the table to aid me and it wobbles alarmingly. The vicar leaps forward to steady it, dropping the book he was holding and attempting to keep the contents of the desk safely in place. The books survive this earthquake. The cake does not.

'Never mind,' he says bravely and falsely, for I can tell as he stares at the destruction that it is nothing less than a calamity. He picks up *The Poems of John Donne*, retrieves a little bit of cake from its spine and puts it in his mouth. Too late, he catches me watching him do this. He gives me the book.

'Thank you,' I say. 'And perhaps you could write a reply to my father?'

'Of course.' He pats at his pockets, then goes to his table. 'Ah! No pen, no ink.'

I think I shall go mad with frustration. 'You could say it to me, I'm sure there would be no offence?' I offer, trying not to break in to a run to the door.

'Yes?' He looks quizzical. 'Then please convey to your father my very good wishes . . .'

'YES!' I almost shout now. 'I shall,' I say more softly.

He runs one long finger down the page of the ledger, straight as a rule, till he comes to a space. 'I shall organise events for tomorrow week and pay a visit to the house on . . .' he looks to the ledger again, ' . . . Friday, to discuss the order of things. Can you remember that?'

I would learn the works of Shakespeare backwards if it would speed me from this room. 'Of course, and I am grateful for the poems. Thank you!'

I fairly fling this last sentence at him, while reversing, encouraging him to remain where he is while I leave. He, though, is resolute in his intention to bid me a proper farewell. The distance between us is too great for him to reach me comfortably and we have to hold hands in an arc over the broken cake beneath us. It is a positive vignette of regret.

I am halfway down the path when I think that I did not ask his name and I would like to know it, the better to quote him to my father. When I put my head round the door, I see that he is on his hands and knees, tidying up the cake by eating it straight from the floor. I tiptoe away.

Chapter 10

If Bet and Levener are surprised to see me, they hide it well.

'Come for our business?' he says, smoothing the front of his apron as if he stroked his own skin.

'Have you brought a cover?' Bet asks, looking askance at my dress.

'Of course.' I took an apron of Jane's, a plain thing but serviceable.

'Better leave that there,' Bet indicates the book. She probably cannot see the need for it at any time, certainly not now.

Without explanation, they bid me follow to a doorway behind the shop. Beyond, a corridor goes into a high windowed room. Long ropes dangle from the beams above and there is a broad, low, wooden trestle, fit only for one purpose, to one side. I wait for my eyes to accustom to the gloom.

The little calf is tethered to a post in the middle of the room. Its hooves skitter on the floor but the restraining ropes leave it little freedom to move. Its bright eyes catch any available light.

'Where is Fub?' I ask. They exchange a look.

'Need him to hold your hand, ayee?' Bet says.

'I do not. But my business was with him and he should see I keep my word.'

'Here.' Fub steps from the shadows. 'I bring the weapons.'
He unrolls a cloth with an array of different knives inside. Great
blades jostle thin ones. 'Each has their purpose,' he speaks so
fondly, they might be his clever children.

'Right,' Levener instructs, but Fub is already next to him and
together they bind the creature's legs deftly and neatly. Levener
pulls on one of the ropes above him and grabs the hook that
descends. The calf has seen the world right ways up for the last
time. It now hangs suspended and the hook sways as the animal
twists uselessly on its line.

I do not see him stick the knife in, he stands so close to his
quarry they might be intimate. Then he pulls hard at the handle,
left and right, till an arc of blood gushes with such force that
some almost hits the ceiling and sprays a red shower outwards.
Fub has a bucket almost full in minutes.

'You want the heart beating strongly when they go,' Bet says.
She is next to my shoulder and I jump, but only with her presence,
not the slaughter. She snickers. 'Poor little thing, is that what
you think, ayee?'

I move away from her, nearer to the corpse. Its brown eyes
are still open but dull. The pupils are cloudy as if, instead of
looking out at the world, it turned its gaze inward to its slow,
visceral decline. I examine it carefully. How is it here, but gone?
I touch it and it swings, still warm.

Levener has begun to saw away its head. 'Take care, precious
stuff this,' he says, more to himself than me.

For a moment, there is only the sound of the blade through
hide, gristle and bone. Levener grunts occasionally and the effect
of all this together makes me blush, though I do not know why.
He turns the head upside down and carves out the tongue. Fub

hands over instruments like a doctor's companion: this little blade to skin it, this stout one to cut off the tail. There is so much fluid and mess that I am surprised to see my apron is still clean. As each part of the beast is detached, so more of the glistening innards are revealed, in layers, like the rings of a tree. The three work almost in silence, only sometimes saying perhaps 'Here!' or 'Hold!' They move carefully, with respect, as though at a funeral rather than a dismembering. They are like dancers, each knowing the steps without instruction. The music is a steady sawing with the occasional, percussive crack of bone.

They carry the body over to the trestle once its legs are off and, bracing themselves against its stomach, let the guts out. A rush of dark green liquid flows first, then they catch the looping intestine. Bet tends to the contents of each pail like a midwife, dousing the head with cold water in one then tenderly swirling the blood in another.

The place smells of iron and ordure, of sweat and straw. There is a sudden flutter above us as a bird flies through the narrow split of window and zigzags to and fro, seeking escape. It is so alive, so present, that I want to hold it, to feel its tiny heart beat. I remember the calf, how it looked at me in fear through long-lashed eyes. It has left only its meat ghost.

Levener and Fub are brisk now, their shoulders square with pride, their voices loud again. They slap each other on the back at a job well done.

Bet takes my right hand and turns it palm up, laying her index finger lightly against my wrist. 'Does your blood flow more quickly with all this?' she asks, looking to Levener conspiratorially, as if they both test me.

'I feel quite calm,' I say.

She smiles. 'Yes, you were not afraid. Ayee. You still have a good steady heartbeat.'

'The better for slaughter, then.' I turn to Fub. 'I think I learned my lesson well.'

He takes my wrist, too, but not to feel my pulse. Which is just as well, for my heart leaps in my chest at his touch. Instead, he leads me to the remains on the trestle. Dipping his thumb into the flesh of the beast, he then twists it against my forehead. 'Blooded,' he says.

Levener giggles and says, 'There's always blood the first time!'

The air on the skin between my eyes, where he wet me, feels cold.

*   *   *

As I return to Castle Street I spit on my hand and rub my forehead. The mark there has dried and I have to go at it several times until I can no longer taste iron. I wish I had a mirror to test my efforts. I would like to crouch and pull up my skirt at the hem then wipe my face with my petticoat, to ensure no trace remains. Instead, I cautiously use my sleeve ruffle. The cloth is white. There is no bloodstain. My father opens the door wide as I climb the steps. He has been waiting for me. Judging by the look on his face, he has been waiting for some time.

'Father, I come from the church,' I announce and make to pass him.

He stops me, his hand on my arm quite tightly. 'And where else?' *How does he know?* 'You were seen on the street nearby some two hours since.'

Who saw me? Who is my accuser, my traitor? 'I became . . . lost.'

He stares at me, his anger making his features livid and tense.

'LOST?' he thunders. 'You may have lost your wits, I can't vouch that you haven't, but you had better come up with a better tale than that.'

'I became lost . . . in this book.' I hold up the little volume of verse. 'The vicar lent it to me, he could see I had a taste for literature when I admired the books in his study. I sat on a wall and began to read and before I knew it, the day sped by.'

This is plausible. My father takes the book with suspicion, holding it as if it were poisonous. He may not be fond of reading himself, but he must allow the habit in others.

'You had better not read more, then, for your days are to be taken up and there'll be no time left over. Make yourself ready at ten tomorrow, Onions calls here for you.' He looks me up and down with distaste. 'Thank heavens I shall not be responsible for you for much longer. I only hope you can keep civil and obedient for long enough to ensure your smooth and speedy passage from this house.'

'The vicar will arrange the christening for tomorrow week and call here on Friday.' At least no one can accuse me of not delivering my message.

He stands to one side, allowing me to pass at last.

'My book?' I reach to take it.

He holds it close to his chest then above his head. 'You'll have no more need of it.' He pauses. Will he confiscate it? Instead, he hurls it into the fire. I gasp, watching helpless as the flames lick.

'What are you staring at?' he asks, giving me a little shove. 'Dinner will be on the table soon and you'll find you have only my company tonight. What's that?' He points to the skirt of my dress and when I follow his gaze, I see a spot of dried blood there: a perfect dark red circle. 'What have you been up to, you stupid girl?' He raises his arm again. I think he might strike me.

'I walked too close to a rough sort of beggar. He clutched at me, wanting money – he must have had blood on his hands.'

'It is not the print of a hand, is it?'

What else can I say? But before I can invent some other cause, my father's usual boredom with any subject discussed for too long comes to my rescue.

'Change out of your costume, that's all.' He goes towards his study.

As I leave, I see movement, a flash of skirts at the entrance to the kitchen, someone leaving in a hurry. Grace! She must have been listening. And it must have been her that betrayed me to him – who else knew of my errand? Well, she has got her reward. I am more captive than ever now. The damage has been done.

I didn't want my father to see me cry, but once I am alone it comes easily. How shall I visit Fub with the terrible Onions stuck to my side? I wipe my face with the sleeves of my dress – if I am thought as scruffy as a beggar I might as well adopt slovenly ways. Perhaps the fastidious Onions might be repelled by me if I sink into the gutter in my habits. Which would leave me alone with only my family, who do not care for me either. I am truly between a rock and a very hard place and when I concentrate my thoughts on my plight, it is as painful as stubbing my toe against stone. If they would all only vanish and leave me be.

Sudden as a lightning strike, I have the thought that if they all died, together, I would not mourn. My father, Evelyn, even my mother, every last one of them. I would see them set sail in a ship that I knew would sink or watch them fall into a hole that dropped them down to the earth's molten core and not mind. A plague could ravage or a stampede of mad bulls flatten them, it would be all the same to me. I wait for guilt to nibble at these thoughts and make me regret them, but it does not come.

There is a tapping on the door, faint as a mouse's scrabble. Grace stands there, pale and timid.

'What do you want?' If she has come to apologise, I am in no mood to hear it.

'The cover is a little charred, but some pages survive.' She holds Donne's verses, the little book my father sought to burn. 'I ran to get the tongs when I saw him throw it in the hearth. I thought it was a wicked thing to do, Miss.'

I cannot speak. Like a bucket full to the brim, I have been carrying myself carefully in front of her and now this little tip of me has caused a flood. My face is running wet with copious tears. She fishes in her apron pocket and hands me a square of rough cotton. Then she puts the book gently into my other hand.

'There is no window closed so tight it won't give a little, Miss. And Mr Donne's words are doubtless strong, too.'

I might as well embroider that homily on another sampler, for all the good it will do.

When Grace is gone, I open the scorched book and breathe in the faint acrid tang of the burnt pages. Her handkerchief is hemmed all round in large stitches and smells of lavender. I spread it flat on my pillow, to scent my dreams later.

Chapter II

At supper, my father had sat in silence, except to say 'Eat!' when he saw that I only pushed at the food on my plate without lifting it to my mouth. Jane had caught my eye several times and I fancied she'd smiled conspiratorially. Perhaps she and Grace had discussed my plight on the back stairs or over a steaming pan. I did not smile back. It seemed to me that those two women had more freedom than I would ever have, for all that they do my family's bidding.

This morning my stomach aches. It is a low insistent pain and, sure enough, when I squat over my pot there is a ribbon of red blood mixed in the waters. I prepare my little bundle of cloth and bind it up with wide strips round my waist. All the better to meet Onions, for I warrant that this state will repulse him mightily and I shall not attempt to hide it.

I wait in the hall, my bonnet already tied. Just as the dining room clock creaks out its chime, there is a knock on the door. I open it myself, I don't want to give Onions the pleasure of being announced. He is a little taken aback, for he is still smoothing his white locks into their ribbon and was probably admiring himself in the brass plate too.

'Miss Jaccob! Anne!' He bows, then holds out a little posy of flowers.

'They are all wild things, picked on my way.' He waggles his fingers at them. 'Such brave, fragile blooms.'

'Did they make you think of me, Mr Onions? Am I brave and fragile, too, do you think?'

'Anne, you have many, many fine qualities and if I was to present you with a floral tribute to match every one, I should be standing here behind a veritable hedge.'

His voice has a souring effect on me, like lemon juice in milk.

'Shall we be on our way?' I hope that the streets will be so busy and loud I'll hardly be able to hear him. 'Where do we go?'

He points left, and I set off at a trot, obliging him to scamper beside me in his neat black shoes.

'Where do you go?' he pants, catching me up. 'My carriage waits there.'

Of course! How foolish I had been to imagine we would walk anywhere, his feet are probably too soft to bear rough stone and his chest would most likely tighten with any exertion. But what a further punishment to have to sit with him in the confines of a carriage! The coachman holds the door for me, then takes my hand to help me up. This is the only man who'll touch me today, unless Fub manages to breach my prison walls. I've no intention of even the smallest intimacy with Onions. As he settles himself fussily opposite me, spreading the cloth of his coat and shaking his sleeves, I ponder on how odd it is that, while they are ostensibly both men, there are so many differences between Fub and this offering that they might be different species.

'Do you agree, Anne?' Onions has raised his brows, waiting for an answer to a question I did not hear.

'I beg your pardon, I was distracted.'

'Charming.' Onions smiles in his peculiar way; his wide mouth and his cold eyes do not join forces. 'How I wish I could spend a while in your head, to see what delicate images play there, what thoughts pervade.'

We both know it is just as well he cannot.

'I was merely opining that it is a fine day. You are very pale.' He leans close to me, his eyes narrow with suspicion. 'Have you applied blanc?'

'I am not in the habit of rubbing lead on my face,' I say. He continues to stare. 'You have a great resemblance to Maria Gunning,' he tuts. 'She, alas, was killed by vanity.'

He is closer to that death than I. 'That is unlikely to be my fate. Where do we go, Mr Onions?'

The streets roll by. He leans forward again. 'Could I request, dear girl, that you call me Simeon? I hope, although I know I am scarcely worthy of your company, to entertain you at some length over my stay in London and thus we can dispense with formalities, I think.' A little cough. 'I hope.'

I lean forward, too. 'Any time we spend together is not of my doing or is my wish. My father gives his permission for you to pay me court and I must do as he says. Let us be clear, though, that I have no desire to be with you now and absolutely no intention of being with you at any point in the future. Furthermore, I do not want anything from you.' And with this, I turn to the carriage's open window and fling the flowers out of it.

Onions braces himself against this onslaught, then takes stock. He leans back. 'Then all is indeed clear, *Miss* Jaccob.' He presses on the word. 'But I shall be clear, too. Your father has indicated, nay, has *insisted,* that you should become my wife. It suits his business if I am persuaded to invest in it and of course, as your *husband*, I would do so. It suits my standing if I am attached. I am in no particular hurry to marry, but I am aware that an estate such as mine requires heirs and suchlike.' He waves his hand in the air. 'My cousin minds it well enough but I could not go to my grave thinking that his low-born wife and children would end up inheriting it. It is my duty to marry someone. In terms of mating, Anne, you are good stock.' He looks away, sighing. 'And I do venture to hope that you may, in time, find me acceptable.' He sighs again. 'I keep myself in good order and am well-acquainted with those who matter. My mother spoke often of my beauty and nobody who heard her disagreed. I read a great deal and am something of an expert in music. My writings – though I hardly take any time over them, they come so easily – are much admired.'

He looks at me full in the face. 'I think, in all honesty, and please forgive my frankness, that you could not do better.'

His vanity is outrageous. I could point to almost any person going by and demonstrate the many ways in which they outshine this man. His scented breath makes me gag; his every movement makes me recoil.

He taps on the roof, 'Hurry, now, driver!' and sits back, satisfied, as the carriage sways and jolts and rumbles. My stomach tenses and the pain there pulses and throbs. I am glad of it. Like the arrows through the martyr's sides it is a physical reminder of all that I fear and all that I desire.

At length we pull up at the gates of a great building, with a wide avenue before it for carriages to enter.

'Where are we?' I ask. Onions pouts, petulant as a child. 'Ah, she speaks! I had not thought you could hold your tongue for so long. I am tempted not to reply, to see how you like it. But—'

he taps my arm, 'I have decided to treat you as a pupil and school you in the ways of wifely companionship.' He gestures outside. 'This is the foundling home. I have not the least interest in the fallen women who clutter its doorways, nor the children who need its services,' he shoots me an arrogant glance, 'for that is their doing, and they must pay the price. But it is a repository of art, in which I take great pleasure. And of which I naturally know a great deal. I shall be your teacher and your guide. It will be a positive Grand Tour!'

How have I been cursed in my tutors! They are instructing me in all the wrong ways: the one with his graphic illustrations, the other with his fawning and fakery. Teaching me how to be his wife! Lecturing me about paintings! Surely I have not been so sinful thus far in my life as to deserve all this punishment? Perhaps I pay in advance for my wickedness in the future. There can be plenty of it to come, in that case, to make up for this torture.

When we come to the door, it swings wide as if invisible hands tug at it. From behind its great bulk creeps a little man. He is bowing so low that he could easily inspect the floor while he's down there.

'Where is Legge?' says Onions, irritably, to the back of the jacket below him.

The man straightens upright in instalments as if each vertebra instructed the next to move. 'He sends his regrets,' he says. He has a curious manner of speaking as if he were about to break into laughter in the middle of his sentence.

Onions bridles. 'Most unfortunate.'

'Yes', agrees the man, still jocular. 'Shall I—?' He points up the staircase in front of us.

135

'I can find my way,' Onions cuts across his words and his amusement.

'As you wish,' the fellow chortles.

'Where are the children?' I ask.

The two men exchange a look.

'They do not come here,' Onions explains, as if to an idiot. 'They live at the back of the house.'

'As they first come in,' the man guffaws.

If he were to actually encounter humour, perhaps he might expire in a paroxysm of mirth since he finds such prosaic things so funny. I rather wish he could accompany us, nevertheless, as Onions obviously finds him tremendously annoying and I would relish the entertainment of the two of them in conflict. Instead, the vast space of the hallway echoes only to our footsteps as we cross it alone. 'Elliot's clock,' Onions says as we climb the stairs past a polished walnut casing. Its blank face marks the exact moment of my despair and its hands will turn impassively throughout my ordeal here.

Onions is inclined to greet the paintings as if they were servants who were suspected of stealing from him. He scurries past crossly, not wishing to make contact, flinging the names of the offending artists at me. 'Collett,' he hisses, 'Hogarth, Reynolds, Brooking.' I stop at this last, a study of huge ships under a darkening sky. Although they are all straight on the water, the waves around them threaten to tip and tilt them dangerously before too long. 'He is dead now,' says Onions, over my shoulder.

'This lives,' I say, under my breath.

We continue to hurtle through the rooms. There are no signs of any of the inmates here, or of their fabled education and entertainments. From time to time, Onions looks about him and listens keenly, like an animal scenting prey, but we are by ourselves and there are no sounds of life from elsewhere in the building.

'Do you look for something, Sir?' I ask when he next performs this ritual.

He starts as if he had forgotten I was with him. 'No, no,' he smoothes the ruffle at his neck.

In the next room, white cornicing as rich as cake decorates the ceiling. The paintings crowd onto the walls: it is a feast laid out for the famished.

'The finest exhibition,' he says, proudly, as if he had painted them all.

'Can we rest a while?' I sink on to a stone bench. I feel as full as if I had eaten a large meal, although nothing has passed my lips.

Onions looks puzzled. 'The female has a complicated constitution,' he pronounces. He stares at me as if I were an object behind glass in a display. We are in front of a vast picture of a woman, a child and an angel; they form a triangle of anxiety as each one seems on a different mission to the other. A gash of light behind the pointing angel indicates that all will not go well for the woman he gestures to. Certainly, her clothing is inadequate for the storm clouds above her. Her nose shines like a beacon.

'Casali,' breathes Onions, close by. He looks at me without sympathy as I sit. 'Shall I leave you a while?' He seems keen to do so and I, too, crave my own company.

'By all means,' I reply.

'I may seek out a little food,' he says. 'Will I bring you something?'

I shake my head and close my eyes, stopping any further conversation.

At last, I hear him leave. I might imagine it, but I think he has quite a spring in his step. It would appear that art is not quite as nourishing to him as he made out and he seeks to satisfy his appetite elsewhere. I open my eyes gingerly. I am alone. The room is quite silent. I regard the shiny woman and accusing angel with solemnity. The overgrown child beside them seems ignored. The room is cold, both with the lack of a fire and a chill in the atmosphere. Do the unhappy women who must leave their children at the secret door of this place breathe their grief into the atmosphere, where it collects in a mist? With each inhalation I take in their misery and mix it with my own.

After a while I wonder if Onions has forgotten me, or at least has forgotten where I am. Perhaps I should seek him out – the huge doors could close without anyone realising I am here. The key could turn in the lock and, even if I do not relish his company, I am afraid of being shut in. I go back the way we came. There is no one on the staircase and I cannot hear a sound from any of the rooms beside. I walk softly, to catch any noise. There are voices at last, someone is speaking so gently that I have to strain to discover where they are.

In an anteroom, in its far corner, almost hidden, Onions has his back to me and does not hear me come in. He is close to a boy, not far into his teens by the look of him, and the boy's hand is on Onions' arm. He wears the foundling uniform, dull brown and short-trousered, and he looks into Onions' face with a patent urgency. They speak in low and sibilant whispers. I screw up my eyes and lean forward, but I cannot make out what they are doing or hear what they are saying. The boy moves but

Onions stands still as a statue, his legs braced apart. I step back sharply, my heartbeat thumping in my ears and then I catch the boy's eye.

His look is one of conspiracy.

I wait as long as I dare to make sure Onions has not heard me, but he doesn't turn round. Then I retrace my steps, going backwards out of the room, walking on tiptoe lest I make a sound.

I sit down where Onions left me, my chest heaving in exertion. Otherwise I am quite still. I close my eyes.

'Are you rested now?' Onions is there, calm as a sleeping cat. 'You are a little flushed, Anne, are you unwell?'

'I bleed.'

'I beg your . . .?'

'It is my woman's time, Sir, I bleed. And my body aches with it. I am—'

'Enough!' He holds both his hands out in front of him, to silence me. The palms are yellow white and I can see the long nails curling like carved ivory over the tips of his forefingers. 'You do not need to explain further.' He waits for me to get up, then whispers next to my ear. 'And now I know you are capable of carrying a child, at least. That is a comfort.'

The laughing man swings the door wide for us. 'I trust you found everything you wanted to find?'

Onions ignores him, sweeping imperiously out without a farewell. He beams, happy as a man who has secured a prize pig for breeding. 'I am going to organise many such expeditions for you.' He puts his shoulders back, smooths his lank hair into place and offers me his arm. I fold my own arms at him instead.

'Shall we dine together later?' Onions asks, as we find the

carriage. 'I am satisfied for the moment, but you have had nothing to eat.'

'I am a little faint.' I pat my stomach. 'This wretched—'

'Madam!' He cuts me short again. 'I fear you overstep your feminine boundaries with this candour. I am one of the most sympathetic creatures on God's earth, indeed I am almost over-whelmed with fellow feeling on occasion, but you must understand I cannot hear of this particular misery without becoming . . .' he screws up his face '. . . a little vexed.'

'Please take me home,' I say. 'Whether we can discuss it or not, I am weary with good reason.'

He looks about to lecture me on a subject he has failed to bore me with thus far, and breathes deep into his chest to prepare his oration, so I pretend to become fascinated by something outside the window. Looking sideways at my companion I watch him as he picks at his nails, using the longest and sharpest as tools.

I am almost bowed over with pain now; it seems as dark red and angry as the blood itself and pulses like a heartbeat. I cannot be comfortable and inch this way and that on my seat. It will not ease no matter how I move. The journey feels like a round-the-world voyage it takes so long and, unhappy as I am to live there, I am relieved and quite lifted to see my house again.

'Do not see me indoors,' I instruct Onions, as he arranges his shirt ruffles to present himself. 'I shall give your good wishes to my father, shall I?'

'And tell him,' he is disappointed to be cheated of the encoun-ter, 'that I shall call . . .' he looks at me carefully, gauging the length of my recovery, 'in three days' time.'

Three days of respite! If I wasn't bent double in agony I might cheer. When Jane answers the door, I am obviously so pale that even she doesn't need to ask why I return early.

'What can I bring, Miss?' she says, her little features bunched up in concern.

'Nothing.'

The rags are wet through. I roll them up and put them on the washstand. There's no need to replace them, I don't intend to be upright for a while, and even the effort of rinsing them through is beyond me. I lie on the bed breathing as deeply as I can through the clenching pain, rocked by its cruel waves.

'Miss!' Jane is calling me. Why doesn't she leave me in peace? 'Mistress!' Outside my room now.

'What is it, Jane?' She can tell me her business through the door; I'm not opening it to her.

'The boy is here.'

'What boy?'

'Fub. The butcher's boy. He has some meat for you to inspect. He says—'

I am at the door before she can finish the sentence.

'Wait! Fub is here? Tell him to wait.' Knowing that he has come is a veritable panacea to my ills. 'I am coming.'

She pinches her lips together. 'Are you sure, Mistress? I can see to it today, if you—'

'Jane, I am coming.' I'm sure my face betrays my excitement. She looks as if she would like to say something to keep me away from him, but she cannot stop me.

He is turning over the contents of his basket when I get to the door, squatting on his haunches. As ever, Jane hovers behind me.

'Would you brew me an elixir? I think there is a little of the

Fraunches left.' She still stands there, an insistent chaperone. 'Go!' I clap my hands and she flaps her arms and flees like a startled bird.

Fub laughs, watching her retreating scuttle. 'Jane has the disposition of a chicken.'

'Without the usefulness. There are never any eggs from her.' I lean on the doorjamb. All my pent-up sorrow, all my self-pity at the ordeal of my day, cannot be stopped up any more. 'Fub, I am miserable.'

He picks up a joint of beef, squeezing it and pressing his fingers into the flesh.

'I am about to be promised in marriage. To an odious man.'

He holds the meat to his nose.

'Fub!' Why doesn't he answer?

He looks up. 'It would not matter if he were the sweetest man alive, would it? It would make no difference.'

'No. But this man is especially vile. He stinks like an apothecary's closet. He is a bore and a snob. And—' This is the worst. '—he lives in Derbyshire!'

Fub pretends that his heart stops at the news, replacing the meat with a thump and then clutching his chest. 'No!' he wheezes. 'Not that! There are only two places I was taught to fear: the bowels of Hell and Derbyshire.'

Can he never be serious? It is like trying to catch a butterfly, watching him dart and flit while I try and pin him down.

'Anne.' He stands up, wiping his hands on his britches. The wedding is not happening today, is it?'

I shake my head.

'Or tomorrow? Or any day next week? Not even next month. It is a dark prospect, I grant you, but it is only that – a prospect.

It is some way into the future. How long I cannot tell and neither can you. I won't let all that is to come, however dreary it might be, muddy the clear water now.'

'Is this clear water?' I indicate the little yard where we stand and the tall walls surrounding us.

He shrugs. 'Clear enough. Who knows what's going to happen in the next little while. Your man – what's his name?'

'He is not *my man*. It is Onions.'

'Onions?' Fub stamps his feet with glee. 'You would be Mistress Onions? You would go from sitting with me next to a tray of meat to enduring such a rotten vegetable diet?' He thrusts his tongue through his lips and squirts the air noisily. 'Anyway, this Onions!' More mirth – he'll never tire of finding his name, at least, a joke. 'This *Onions*: he might go under the wheels of a coach. Or fall from a cliff. Or die of the pox. Oh.' He stops, thinking he has offended me.

'Little chance of that, unless the poor boys of the parish infect him.'

That shuts him up. Sombre, we look at each other, measuring the space between us. Suddenly, I scream: shivering on the ground, its fur dark as oil and its maw and claws livid pink, is an enormous rat. It is close enough to me to pick up or to kick, but I do neither. Instead, I lift up my skirts and freeze, glued to the spot with fear. Fub looks me up and down, as if preserving my predicament for his edification, then kicks the creature with his boot. It scurries away, limping.

'Oh!' I let out my held breath with a gasp. 'It was so near! I thought it might bite or scratch and that we'd get the plague and be dead before we could—' I dare not say what I am thinking. He kneels in front of me and gently lifts at the hem of my dress.

His dark hair is close to my hand, but if I touched it now I would not let go. He is still raising my skirt, just as I did when the rat threatened.

'Here.' He points at my ankle. There is a thin line of blood dried there, snaking up my leg. It would reach to the top of my thigh if he followed its path. It has come out of me as I stood. He wets his finger and smudges the place where it begins to stain my skin.

'It is all blood with you, Anne.' He gets to his feet. The toes of his boots meet my pointed shoes and I can smell his breath. I look at the brown mark in his eye, at the coarse hair on his chin and the rise of his forehead and they blur as I try to see everything clearly enough to remember him later, in private, when we do not stand like this.

'I heard you scream.' Jane appears in the doorway, flustered. 'Is . . . are you . . . is anything amiss?'

Fub and I spring apart and speak over each other in our haste to explain. At least there is one word common to both our accounts.

'Rat!' exclaims Jane happily, seizing on the innocence of this explanation so that she does not have to fret over whatever else it might be that makes us blush. 'I'll get the poison to put down. There won't be just one, that's for sure.'

Fub positively saunters to his basket, as casual as if he'd just been caught whistling. 'This, then,' he picks up the first thing to hand, 'is a tender piece of pig. Our lesson was going well till Mr Rat attended.' He smiles at her, but Jane is solemn.

'The lesson is over, Fub. Mistress Anne has not been well today and ought to retire now.'

'Is that true? Oh, I am all concern for her,' Fub says to Jane, looking at me. 'I cannot think of anything worse than harm coming to her. Or to anyone else in this household, Jane. Including you. I shall be off, then, Mistress Jaccob.' He swings his basket and goes up to Jane, playfully.

She is not so easily persuaded. She may not have the mind of a scholar, but she is no fool. 'If you spend too long at this door, your other orders will be overdue.' There is the tiniest hint of a threat, sharp as a dart, and Fub feels it prick and nods his head.

'You are right, Jane.' His livelihood depends on her good word. My happiness depends on it, too.

Jane stands stockily in the doorway, her swollen middle wrapped in layers of cloth and her bonnet frayed like cabbage leaves, unaware that she holds us in her hands. She clutches a great flank of raw meat with affection. 'We'd not find a butcher as fine as your Levener easily. Good, good,' she says, patting it like a dog. She cuts a strange figure as a diviner of our fates.

'Mistress,' he bends his head as I pass him. What if I turn instead, cling on to him fast as a shipwrecked sailor to a floating branch, offer up my face to his? I know what would happen, Jane would shriek more loudly than I did when I saw the rat and Fub would be banished forever, that's the likely outcome. I am half resentful that we may not make plans as others do but half glad that we have been together at all.

'I have put the tincture by your bed.' Jane makes no reference to Fub as I leave and I dare not look back at him.

'Thank you, Jane. I am a little better, but I shall not sit at dinner.'

Chapter 12

I have not heard my mother speak above a whisper much recently, let alone shout, but her voice is raised now. There is another voice, this one heated, too, but lower in tone and slow to respond. It appears my father has no quick reply to my mother's questions.

'And why would you not come?' she is saying. I pause on the landing, pressing myself to the rail to stay steady and listen. 'My father and mother both ailing, and you would bundle the child and me off alone to visit them?'

A burbling response, some mention of 'necessary' and of 'custom' from him, but I cannot catch anything clearly.

Then she speaks again. 'I must go to them, Thomas. And since this house was my father's gift and you greatly enjoyed spending my dowry, it would ill-behove you to stay here. Your absence would suggest apathy or even disdain.'

'I would not intend either.' I can hear him now. 'Let us at least ration the days of my visit, so that I can inform my associates when I might be expected to return.'

'Associates! I go tomorrow, Grace will come with me and Jane can see to the house.'

And I? I think. *Who will see to me?* And quick as a flash I have the answer. *Fub!*

'Two days,' my father harrumphs, defeated. 'Then I must return.'

I cannot hear what she says, but that is an end to it.

'Anne!' My mother calls for me in a strong voice. She sits in the drawing room, sorting her needlework box, brisker than she has been for many months. 'Your dear grandparents are in poor health. We are to go to them tomorrow and of course I am taking Evelyn with me. I am sorry to leave you in an empty house, but I shan't be gone long and your father will return before I do.'

'Can I not come?' I had better seem willing.

'Your father suggests that Mr Onions calls on you here this week and must then depart. Your Aunt Elizabeth will receive him for us so that his suit is proper.'

I want to tell my mother that Onions and his visits would keep till her return. The further prospect of Aunt Elizabeth – a woman for whom the business of others is her life's work – overseeing this grim charade adds more wasps to the nest. I am stung over and over.

'Mother, you know that I am reluctant to see Mr Onions.' I am turning sideways hoping only she will catch my words. But she looks to my father before answering.

'Anne, you must.'

'You must.' My father joins his hands and flexes his fingers till the joints crack.

'Mr Onions is an extraordinary man.' I do not lie. 'But I am hardly ready for marriage.' I have walked into an open trap and my father snaps it shut.

'You're ready. Furthermore, it is not up to you to decide on when the time is right. Let us imagine I put it to you: *Anne, how do you like Mr Onions? He has asked for your hand in marriage. What do you think of that?'*

He leers and replies to himself in a high, whining, childish tone: *'Oh I am not ready! I would rather remain here an old maid till I get too aged to be anyone's bride.'* Would that be better, eh? Eh?'

'I understand, Father.' Better to cut this short than inflame him further or, worse, to have him decide to stay to make sure I comply.

Jane waits outside the door. She has her shawl on and carries a straw basket. It rustles like wheat in a field; her arm must be trembling. She has evidently been listening, for she pretends a sudden keen interest in a spot on the floor.

'Mistress Anne, I am going to the Leveners,' she says, scraping at the dirt with her shoe.

'Why should I know this?' I begin to go past her, but she stops me with a hand on my sleeve. I look hard at where she touches me till she takes her hand away.

'You had asked me to instruct you in domestic matters,' she says.

I was not quick enough to see where her announcement might take us. A thousand reasons not to go with her scatter in my head, inviting me to choose one. They are all either too insubstantial or might be argued against, even by someone as slow as Jane. She knows of my parents' plans and that they leave me free. I shiver to think of us lined up together at the Leveners' counter, Fub so close to me I could touch him, but as out of reach as if he were behind glass.

Perhaps he will be on an errand. Or I might feign fatigue and insist that I wait for her nearby. *'So good of you to take me with you,'* I would say, *'But I'm afraid I will have to forego your demonstration of good housekeeping.'*

Buoyant with her plan, Jane sails out of the house with me in her wake. She glances over her shoulder to make sure I am still there. I watch her halloo and wave to several people as she goes. From my vantage point, I can see them make only the tiniest greeting in return. Sometimes they do not acknowledge her at all. Blithely, she continues, looking this way and that for her next quarry. I drag my feet, the distance between us increasing. She may simply lose me by dint of getting too far ahead. She reaches a corner and stands stock still, aware, without investigating, that I am not with her. When she turns round, she puts her hands on her hips and smiles broadly at me.

'Mistress Anne, how can I be swifter than you? When I am carrying all this bulk and you are so many years younger?' We might have been playing a game of hide-and-go-seek, so thrilled is she that I have caught her. 'Have you ever walked this way before?' Jane says.

Is she trying to catch me out? What else is there on the route I might have visited? 'I do not believe so,' I say, cautiously, 'but I am not familiar with much beyond our house, and I might be mistaken. I do not recognise this place, anyway.' I blink as if I cannot see clearly. 'Do we even go East or West, Jane? I cannot say.'

'I will lead the way, you have no need to mark where we are. It all looks different from a carriage,' she says, satisfied that my breeding might explain my myopia. She tries a few times to engage me in conversation. She and I have never talked much before, but the fact that she is facing away from me yet keeping by my side makes her bold. She points out places of significance or notoriety, but I am so conscious of where we'll end up that I'm either curt or mute. This does not diminish Jane's enthusiasm. She trots as happily as a pony pulling a gig. Fortunately, she is just as blinkered with her purpose.

She pauses momentarily at a point where the road forks. She inclines her head, puzzling as to the way. I am about to suggest we take the wrong path, *'Shall we try here?'*, but she chooses correctly. She identifies some landmarks to confirm her choice and, satisfied, settles back into her babbling and bouncing. As we approach Meek Street, as I knew we must, I can make out a figure outside the butcher's. It is engaged in some task. It is Fub. 'No!' I say aloud.

'What's that?' Jane looks at me, then all around her in case I can see something she can't. A thief, perhaps or a pothole.

'I said, are we here? I saw the sign.' It is facing almost away from us.

'Did you?' Jane says, perhaps wondering how my vision has improved so much in the last mile. I walk forward more boldly than I feel, to halt this line of enquiry.

Fub is hammering a nail into the leg of a stool, holding it between his legs to keep it steady. His hair hangs down as his head bends over. He looks up as my dress swings in front of him. 'Anne!' he says, springing up and smiling broadly. Then – too late – he spies Jane.

She does not say anything, but her face is a mixture of rebuke and glee. Neither sits well. Beyond Fub in the shop, coming into focus as though they surface from a deep pool, Levener and Bet swim onto the street. They greet Jane, but their fish eyes look at Fub and me. The three of them circle us.

'Mistress Anne is come to see how things are done,' Jane says, clasping her basket to her chest.

'Again?' says Bet. The plug is pulled and I am left gasping.

'Eh?' says Jane.

Bet looks squarely at me. As if we are equals, she reads my expression carefully. I see the merest nod of her head, the trace of a smile. Her deep eyes glisten. '*You* are come again, Jane. We have not seen you here for a while.'

'There is a new baby in the house.' And Jane is off down the open road of little dimples and nightly colic, treading a familiar path.

I breathe more easily but I feel a sliver of resentment that my fate hangs, once again, in the hands of someone I would not otherwise cross the street to see. Bet listens to Jane's paean of praise to my mother – 'So brave!' – and the baby – 'So beautiful!' Her head tilts to one side and she punctuates with appropriate responses. But I can tell she is really thinking of me.

'Well,' says Jane, having eventually exhausted every detail of maternity, 'let us go in.'

'This is not the place for a young lady.' Levener swells up as if he'd been deflated till this point. Like Bet, he looks pointedly at me but, unlike her, his expression is only snide. 'If we had known that you were coming, we'd have swept and tidied.' He turns to Jane. 'We don't keep a shabby place, of course. But it's a messy business, butchery, and guts and gore are involved. As you might struggle to imagine, Mistress Jaccob.' He smirks at me, revelling in my enforced silence.

'Fub!' he bellows, as if Fub stood in the next town and not beside him. 'There are new puppies born next door.' He bares his brown teeth at me. 'Fub'll show 'em to you.' He squeezes his fat hands together. Fub puts down his hammer on the mended stool. He ignores the other three and beckons to me. As if he is the man and they the small children, they stand aside and let us pass.

'Girls will always follow boys to see puppies, aye,' Bet sings.

'This way.' Fub goes ahead of me. I suspect he is a little chastened by the errand. We go through the yard into a small lean-to beside it. I blink in the gloom. Fub takes my hand as if he always does, to lead me without stumbling. He pulls aside a shabby cloth over the window and reveals a mass of brown fur wedged into the corner. The mother and her puppies lie so close together that she seems a beast with many little legs, tails and heads.

'Hallo, girl,' he says. I envy the bitch his fond greeting. He has let go of my hand. I have a swift memory of the last time we met, a jumble of rats and bleeding and the scent of his breath. When I had lain down and thought of him last night, I had pictured our next meeting in a sweeter place.

'A midden, eh?' Fub sees my nose wrinkle, though I do not mind the smell. There is no sourness to it.

'Shall you hold one?' Fub indicates the animals at his feet.

I would rather hold you, I think. Or have you reach for me.

'Why is it always assumed that young things are catnip to girls?' I say.

'I do not think you are like all girls,' Fub says, looking at me as if he would like to investigate if I am, at least, the same shape as the others. He squats on his heels and frees one small fellow from his brothers. At this, they all stir and stretch as if connected. The mother lies immobile, her teats as fat as fungus. He takes another, one in each hand. They wave their legs as if trying to find another warm and sleepy body for comfort, even in mid-air.

'Why has she come to see us?' Fub adopts the voice of a sulky child, holding one puppy higher. 'When she has no fondness for we creatures?' The dogs in his hands sleep soundly now; the little crescents of their closed eyes do not respond. 'She wants to follow Fub,' he makes the other say in a squeak. 'She wants to be where he is and if we are there too, it is of no importance to her.' He turns the first one to face his brother. 'She is a pretty visitor, anyway. I shall look at her while she looks at him.' I laugh, the idea of these runts discussing me is deliciously foolish. 'She is indeed. Happy the dog who makes puppies with her!' he squeals.

'Fub is very brave when he has mouthpieces to speak for him.' I tell the puppies. 'One child would be bad enough, I should not want a litter!'

He shakes one dog gently. Its ears flap and it shivers as though in a draught. 'The *practice* without the *consequence* then,' he says for it.

'Give me one of them,' I say. 'I do not want to hear what else these naughty pups might say next.' I only want to know what he will say when we are alone, away from dogs and dank corners and far from the people that may be listening outside.

I kneel and take one of the puppies from him. It lies awkwardly on my lap, for it does not shape to me as a baby would. The pink stomach protrudes from dark hair, plump and round. The small mouth gapes and I put my finger there. At once its teeth clamp. They are sharp as needles. I cry out in pain, but I cannot shake myself free. Fub puts his little finger in where the jaw hinges, and prises it open. 'Learning to bite. You are practice for the rats he'll chase and kill. Or he mistook you for food.' He puts the pup down, then shifts more recumbent bodies away from the dozing bitch and strokes her head. She does not move. Motherhood seems to be equally exhausting for all living things. He squeezes one teat till a bead of milk appears. 'Offer him that,' he says. When I put my milky finger to the puppy, its tongue explores and then licks.

We do not need pretty rainbows, Fub and I. We will not brush hands at a dance or exchange covert glances in the back of a carriage. That is a sugary romance, collapsing in brittle shards when you bite. Ours is as chewy as glue. We have better settings than blossom paths. The air stinks of sodden straw. The puppy sighs and sleeps and sucks. Fub's patchwork eyes gleam. I would strike dark bargains to make this moment last.

'Mistress Anne!' Jane's shriek is like freezing air on my hot cheeks. I get to my feet, gripping the puppy too hard to avoid dropping it. It yelps in protest. She is at the doorway. 'Ugh!' she says. 'That dog needs to clear up after her pups!' She looks at my face then down at my skirt, pulling it towards her, brushing and tutting. 'Have you been kneeling on all this dirt? Fub, why did you let her clothes soil?'

We are the infants again as Jane scolds. Fub puts the pup back with the litter. They move to make room for it as if they were liquid.

'How many?' Jane says, peering at the pile.

'Seven,' Fub brushes his hands on his shirt. 'We'll keep one. They'll probably put the rest in a barrel if no one wants them.' When I look down at the dogs I cannot tell which one I held.

'That's a shame,' Jane says, without any particular sadness. 'Come, Madam. We had best walk the longer route to let that odour leave your dress. Or I shall be in trouble.' She sounds quite gay at the prospect. 'Fub, you are a bad boy.' He holds his hands to his head in a parody of a chastened child. These two are enjoying themselves.

'I chose to kneel where I did and hold the dog,' I say sharply. 'Fub is not to blame.'

'Fub will know what he is guilty of,' Jane says, as if I were merely petulant. 'Come along.'

I turn round once in the street, as we leave. But Fub is not there. Instead, a man I do not wish to acknowledge steps quicker when he spots me and waves. 'Mistress Anne!' he calls.

'Who is that?' Jane glares at him, batting him away as he approaches.

I am resigned to an explanation of sorts. 'A Scotsman,' I say. I wait till Angus draws level, so that he can hear my denial. 'I do not know him well, we had a passing acquaintance.' I meet his eyes and know he will not give me away.

'Only passing,' he agrees. 'It was at church, was it not?' He bows to Jane. I see her little features twist to work this new puzzle out.

'I am pleased to see you, Mistress Anne,' he says. 'Are you well?'

'I am,' I reply. 'I am at my lessons. Jane is teaching me how to keep house.'

'Did you receive instruction here?' he jerks his head towards the Levener's sign.

'The butcher's boy, Fub, knows that business well,' I say. 'And more besides. I am talking about the puppies, of course,' I tell Jane.

'Where is your tutor, the butcher's boy, now?' As he says this,

I feel Jane twitch. She is torn between hearing more of this odd exchange and hastening me home.

'We leave him behind. And we must say farewell to you.' I turn to leave but he comes very close to me, on the side away from Jane. 'Does he teach you to do without him?' He whispers this, so she cannot hear.

'That is a necessary instruction, is it not?' I whisper back.

'He had better not be too good a teacher in that regard.' The man is hard to hear, he is speaking so quietly. 'You are a keen student, Anne. You are very quick to learn, too.'

'Be off with you.' Jane swings her basket in front of me like a scythe.

He doesn't look at her, but bows again. 'I do not wish to offend, Madam.' He stands still, watching us go as if we are casting off and leaving him ashore.

Chapter 13

'The puppies put colour in your cheeks.' Jane scarcely looks where she is going as she strides, she is so eager to watch me while I answer her.

'You know it was not that. Do not pretend.'

'You are more your mother's child than you realise.' She relishes our intimacy. It will last only till our front door. 'I have seen her eyes sparkling like yours.'

'That sort of talk is silly.' I am not going to humour her with fripperies and giggling. 'My mother would not like to be discussed in this way, either.'

Jane's mouth curls downwards at the corners at this admonition. Her new role as keeper of my secrets fits awkwardly; it is not a garment made for her. It slips around her as if it's too large and unwieldy. But she cannot unfasten it now, even if it hinders her. She walks in silence, sulking. 'Do not imagine you are all grown up because you give a boy a stalk.'

I look at her in astonishment. Then I laugh. 'Well, Jane,' I say. 'You are very coarse with me all of a sudden. Are you sure I know enough of these things to speak as you do?'

'Quite sure.' She gives a little shake of her head. It is as if we have two steps before us and take turns to stand one higher than the other. She certainly thinks she looks down at me now.

'And were you this vulgar with my mother?' Jane was my mother's nurse, although neither of them indulge in fond reminiscing.

'When I had to be.' Jane wobbles on her perch.

'When her eyes were sparkling?' I say, pushing her off.

Jane draws her breath in noisily through her nose, then expels it in one long sigh. 'Oh,' she groans as her shoulders sink. 'Mistress Anne, what is started now cannot end well.' She purses her lips as though the words she speaks makes them sore. 'I should not have talked of your mother, her happiness was so brief.' I can hear tears in her voice. 'Every girl hopes to find love and situation neatly bundled. It is hardly ever so.'

Love. The word makes me queasy. Love claws at me. It spreads like hot oil.

Jane sighs again; she will run out of air soon. 'You cannot see him, Anne,' she says, solemn and low. 'You must deny yourself.'

'I cannot choose one way or the other.' I clasp my hands to emphasise the point. 'Love grows where it will and as it wants.'

'If you feed it, it does. It'll latch on like a parasite and be all the more difficult to remove.' Jane sounds so sour that I have to look at her to make sure she is not replaced by an impostor. 'I've said enough,' she says. 'You know the truth of what I say.'

'Did my mother understand this, too?'

Jane does not reply, but I see her brush underneath her eyes with the sides of her little fingers to catch the water there.

* * *

Aunt Elizabeth comes by nightfall. Her fussing begins at the doorstep and her questioning shortly after. She is my father's sister, but as unlike him in bearing and appearance as a bird to a bull. Even her voice is a trill, and she twitters and cheeps her instructions and queries. If we left the windows wide, I wonder if she might fly out. She is, at least, a diversion from all the talk of marriage.

At dinner my mother does not come and my father sits his sister in his wife's place. She responds by asking Jane about every morsel she brings in and by the end of the meal she is even lifting the lids of the dishes to examine their contents. She also affects to find my father the very soul of wit and treats his every utterance as though it was mined from the seam of comedy itself.

'Too much salt!' she repeats, chuckling and gazing at him fondly. 'What happened to the potatoes?' she crows, just after he's said it.

'This is all pips.' My father spits on to his plate.

'All pips!' She giggles in delight as we tackle the fruit.

He doesn't react to this constant quoting and admiration, although he invites her to take brandy with him in his study after, so it cannot annoy him too much. I hear his gruff remarks followed by her peals of laughter for a long time into the evening before there is silence.

*   *   *

I don't want to watch all the packing and packaging – it is enough that they will soon be gone – and, when my mother shouts to me to say farewell, I only lean down from the top floor and call back to her. The door closes, the house settles with a heavy sigh and I begin to wonder how to order my day.

I am not alone for long. Aunt Elizabeth takes the stairs at quite a pace to reach me. 'Don't be sorry, Anne, they'll all be home soon enough.' She takes my face in her two hands. 'Such a sweet daughter. And sister. And niece.' She kisses my forehead. 'Now, come sit with me and tell me about your suitor. I am agog to meet him.'

We face each other across the parlour. My aunt takes up some needlework from a small basket by her chair. 'Do you work on something?' she asks. I shake my head. She inspects her work of the previous day, picks the needle free then pulls the thread taut and begins to sew. The needle squeaks through the cloth.

'Thomas tells me Mr Onions has several improving outings planned for you.' She keeps the sewing close to her face and squints, her tongue beginning to protrude as she concentrates. When I do not reply, she looks up. She puts her head on one side. 'It is a demanding time in a young girl's life. Heaven knows I do not speak from experience, but I have been a keen observer.' And a gossip and pontificator, I think. 'And getting to know a gentleman is a new challenge for even the most well-rounded person.' She resumes her sewing. 'How do you find him thus far?'

I did not know I had a plan until I say 'I am frightened of Onions' so easily it might have been stored up for months.

She is puzzled. 'Frightened, why?'

'He . . . oh, he . . .' I look to the floor as if I am too pained to continue. I count to five in my head before I look up. 'He made attempts on my . . . modesty.'

Is that enough? She holds her hand to her mouth, looking anguished. Her sewing falls to the floor. It would seem to be enough, then.

'I told him I was an innocent.' She nods and bids me go on, a little excited by my confession. 'He would not hear it. He pressed himself on me. I cannot tell my father, but I must not see . . . that man again.'

She touches her hand to my knee. 'Did he . . . ?' She wants to know more. Every detail. I'll tell her more than she needs. I am like a maypole, watching as my ribbons weave prettily together without tangling while my lies dance.

I spin her an intricate tale of unwanted touches and crude words and underhand threats and illicit caresses. It is all so vivid I almost believe it myself.

'Please,' I entreat in scarcely a whisper, 'let me go daily to church in the times where I might have received him here, for although I don't believe I did anything to encourage him, I am sullied by what has happened and want to ask forgiveness.'

I worry I might have gone too far with this, but Elizabeth's eyes shine with tears of sympathy and she says, 'Of course, you must go. You have done nothing wrong, poor child, but the Lord will surely heal your heart.'

Before she can suggest we go to the church together and kneel side by side, I embrace her, catching her stiff bonnet with my cheek, and mutter about going alone – the better to under-stand and then forgive.

'And, dear Elizabeth, please oversee the kitchen. My mother's confinement has meant we have lacked leadership at the helm.'

That should keep her busy. She nods vigorously, full of energy at the prospect of stepping into my mother's shoes and doubtless even ready to find fault with their laces and buckles.

She begins her work at breakfast, subjecting Jane to such a barrage of enquiries I suspect the poor woman can hardly remember her own name by the end of it. These two will occupy each other like fighting cocks put in the same cage. I will be left to my own devices. I intend to go on sharpening their spurs and shaking the cage for some time.

*　　*　　*

After enduring a great many of my aunt's sympathetic sighs and lingering glances, I take my leave.

'I am going to the church.' I make my voice tremble a little.

'Of course.' One last sorrowing shake of her head.

'Thank you for your comfort,' I whisper, suggesting that I am at once fearful yet brave. In case she should be watching me go, I walk with my eyes downcast and shoulders drooped.

Once out of sight, I could almost fling my bonnet to the sky. A whole day with only myself to consider! It is like finding a jewel in the dirt. I think I cannot go again to the butcher's shop – even the dullard Leveners might be suspicious of my motives if I did – but I have taken the precaution of carrying some small coins for my purposes. If I go towards the Inns of Court, there should be company enough that I am safe, and plenty of those with little to do that I can employ.

I have not been there long when I see a girl of about twelve. She is shooshing and clapping to the birds that flock there, watching them fly up and land again at a short distance from her. She stops when she sees me.

'A pretty game,' I say. 'They are so foolish, aren't they? If they wanted to, they could fly to the rooftops and end your sport.'

She looks about her to see if there are others who have been watching her. She looks at me quizzically. 'Yes, Miss.' She makes to leave.

'Wait. Do you know your way about these streets?'

'Well enough.'

'Do you know Levener's at Meek Street?'

'Ye-es.' She answers with suspicion, thinking that she might have done a wrong thing to invite my questioning. I smile to reassure her.

'What is near the place, to prove what you say?'

She describes the alley to the left. Then the sign propped up.

'Good girl.' I hold up a penny. She goes to take it, but I snatch it back.

'This is for when you've earned it.'

She holds her head up primly, wanting to appear deserving. 'I am ready. What shall I do?'

'Take this to the boy there.' He won't be a boy to her. 'The young man,' I correct myself. 'He has dark hair. And a nice look. There is only the fat butcher and his thin wife there besides him, so you can't mistake him. But don't give it to anyone else and keep it secret from them, too.'

I give her a note for Fub. It tells him to meet me by St Peter's at noon. I have not signed it with love words, only 'Anne'.

'I'll stay here until you come back. I know the way and how long it takes, so don't get distracted or detour from your path. This waits.' I hold up the penny again. She runs off, scattering the birds more effectively this time.

Perhaps I should have brought my book of verses but, having no other diversion, I can only watch the street around me. The time hangs heavy. There is only so much entertainment in the doings of others. Sometimes a passing horse takes my eye, then one stops and messes nearby and I have to pinch my nose at the smell. I observe an old gentleman go so slowly and with so much effort that I want to offer him my arm, but I daren't move in case the child is quicker than I bargained for and returns to find me gone. Two fat babies, identical to each other, are pushed by their nurse in a vast contraption. They couldn't be told apart; they could be displayed at the fair as curiosities, they are so alike. I imagine the route to Levener's, to estimate how far she might have got, but I can't sustain this fancy and resort to singing snatches of song in my head, over and over, instead.

'Miss!' She is returned. She holds something out to me.

'What did he say?'

'He gave me this.'

'A button? Is there no note?' What has happened? Why has he given her this?

'He took your letter and gave me this, says so you'd know it was from him.'

'I had rather have it written,' I say under my breath. She still holds out her hand.

'My penny, please, Miss. Was I quick?'

'As the wind. Here.' She snatches it with a soft 'Yes!'

I roll the button about in my hand, curious. It does not seem like Fub to offer me a token, especially without any significance. I don't know what meaning a button conveys. I can ask him soon, though: a clock chimes and I count eleven strikes. In one hour, we can discuss buttons and plenty more.

* * *

At St Peter's, I'm tempted to go in and call on the vicar, but there is only a little time to wait when I arrive and anyway, I foresee complications – that man is too unwieldy for a short visit. I settle myself just inside the church wall, reading the stones on the graves while I wait.

I could be examined on the inscriptions, the dates and even the types of stone, I have to read the words so often. *Here Lies Jerome Stephens.* One quarter hour passes. *Dedicated to the Memory of Agnes Field,* marks another quarter. *Peter and Joan O'Reilly, In God We Trust.* He is nearly an hour late!

When the church clock strikes one, I have him dead and buried himself – surely there must have been an accident? That is why he does not come.

After fifteen long minutes more, I decide he is unfaithful. He had chosen not to come. He got my note and decided it was worth a button, that explains that. By the next chime, I am resolved to give him up, for today and for good. And I shall tell him so. One last visit to the butcher's – who cares if the Leveners find it odd, it'll be the last time I come. With such a set purpose, I hardly notice how stiff I've become sitting so long on the wall.

*　　*　　*

I peer at the shop from across the street. At first the sight of the place is dear to me: this is where he stays! Then I remember why I am here and the happy vision is corrupted. Much as I don't mind what that under-roasted man and gristly woman think, I'd rather not encounter them if possible. Is Fub there? Is he alone? It is difficult to see clearly into the depths of the shop, so I zigzag my way over to try and see inside. On my last pass, Fub appears in the doorway. He is smiling broadly.

'Anne! Have you adopted the habit of a donkey going up a hill?'

I am so angry I can barely speak. First, he fails to keep our rendezvous, now he mocks me. 'I have been waiting for you, stuck where I was like a scarecrow. Nearly two hours passed!' I hiss. 'Did you mean to make me look a fool? Then you have failed, for I am far from stupid and hardly need your estimation of my intellect for proof. I am certainly clever enough to know that I don't care much for you, either.'

'What?' He is taken aback. I study him carefully. I don't think he pretends. 'Anne, did you not get the button?'

'Oh yes, a valuable thing to send in reply.'

'Anne, I told that girl that you must come here, to tell me what you wrote yourself.'

'Why should I do that? She did not say any such thing to me. Only that you had given her this.' It is still in my hand. 'Never mind all that, even if you could not meet me, you should have replied to my note. I had written that I didn't want to come here, hadn't I?'

'Was I to meet you?' I can hardly hear him.

'At St Peter's. At noon.' Why can't he recall this?

'Anne, I . . .' He casts about, looking to the ground then to either side. It is most off-putting, that he doesn't defend himself.

'I cannot . . .' He mutters something.

'What do you say?'

'I cannot read.'

I blanch.

'I cannot read. Your note, *any* note.' He looks surly.

Oh, this is wonderful! Light-headed with relief, I embrace him. He staggers back as I fling my arms round him, then holds me for a moment, too.

'Why does that make you so happy?' He disentangles himself, looking towards the blank window-glass in case we're observed.

'I thought you were dead,' I gasp, still laughing. 'Or wounded. Or that you had decided not to see me again. This is a much better reason. You are safe!'

He watches me with his usual amused patience. 'Yes, I am safe. Such a little thing makes you so pleased.'

'Not a little thing, my waiting in broad daylight, where anyone could see.'

'Then tell me what you would have said, if I had kept our appointment.'

'I would have said . . . "Well, I was surrounded by the dead, we did not discuss much, so I would tease them for not living. For instance: there lies poor Jerome, who can never know the happiness we have. And there is dear departed Agnes, who cannot spend two whole days with *her* sweetheart, as *I* can, because *her* parents are not visiting in the country. And Peter and Joan there must be mourned twice over because they don't know that my suitor is banished for a while. None of them can share my good fortune!"'

'Two days? I'm trying to understand your babbling. We can spend two days together – is that what you mean?'

'It is!'

'Tomorrow I have to be with Levener. Then we – yes, then *you and I* – are going to St Bartholomew's Fair. The day after tomorrow it is! Titus shuts the shop and I have nowhere else to be.'

I have never been to the fair, it must be a riot of pleasure. My head fills up with images of jugglers and puppets, a parade of freaks and conjurors. In the centre of this gaudy vision, Fub and I run wildly, hand in hand.

'Fu-u-ub!' Bet's shout is a reedy thing.

'And if you can fetch some money with you . . .' He trails off.

'Fu-u-u-ub!'

'She will come looking in a minute.' He takes a step backwards, then steps to me again.

'And tomorrow?' I have to be bold, there isn't enough time to be polite.

'Tomorrow we can meet at St Peter's. At noon.'

'I can share my reading matter with you there.'

'With the ranks of the buried? I'm in good company, they all appear to be old friends to you.'

'I'll introduce you. They are the best sort of people: reliable and stout.'

'You certainly always know where they are. And they *lie* but they do not *lie*.'

'FU-U-U-UB!'

'She'll shatter the glass any minute. But, one thing before we part: am I worth only a button, do you think?'

'It came from my mother's wedding dress.' He shrugs. 'She gave it to me when I came up to London. She'd owned nothing else precious. Precious to her, that is – it's not worth anything.'

I hold it tight. Extending my hand, with my fist still closed tight about the trophy, I say, 'Best have it back then. Till you mean to give it.'

'I mean it.' He folds his hand over mine.

'Tomorrow!' I turn on my heel and leave, but ten steps on I turn around. He still stands there, watching me.

* * *

I think the way home has never looked lovelier, or the people more charming. I even smile broadly at my canary aunt, before I remember how heavy she thinks my heart. 'God is good, Aunt Elizabeth!' I say, to explain my expression.

'Yes,' she answers warily. 'He works wondrous quickly, to be sure. Do you feel his spirit already healing you?'

'I am just grateful to be setting out along the right and true path, with Him as my guide,' I tell her. 'But I have much comfort to find yet.'

'It cannot be done in a day.'

'His way is not easy,' I counter, 'but rewarding and uplifting.'

She raises her eyes. 'All praise be to Him.'

'How have you kept, Aunt?' We cannot keep quoting platitudes at each other.

'Mr Onions called, to enquire after you.'

This pinches me. I thought I had made it clear that he should stay away, in case my woman's blood got on him.

'I . . . I had not thought he would call so soon, after his . . . Did you tell him I was gone?'

'He enquired after your health. I was as civil as I could be, Anne. I said that he should not concern himself with you and that as long as I stayed here, he should not visit. I said that I had reason to be disappointed in him, but I did not elaborate. Of course,' she adds, 'I could not bring myself to accuse him of his . . . crimes. They are altogether too vile for any virtuous woman to speak aloud.'

'How did he take it?'

'He asked if it was my place to deny him.'

If I had scripted the exchange myself, it would not have

been better. How her breast would have swelled with ire at this slight.

'I informed him that I am mistress of the house until further notice and that your father would not be returning for some time.' She preens, smoothing her feathers.

'Did he leave directly?'

'He tried to persuade me to reconsider, but I was deaf to his entreaties.' She demonstrates how resolutely she stood her ground, placing her feet wide and her arms across her body.

'I am only sorry that you had to encounter him at all, Aunt Elizabeth. You must have thought, from how he behaved to me, that he would look like a monster but, as you now know, he is only a man.'

'He has the mark of sin on him,' my aunt says, confidently. 'Even if you had not described his *behaviour* to me,' she shudders with displeasure, 'I should have known him to be wicked. It *issues* from him, his wickedness.' She shivers again. 'While your goodness streams from you like a beam of pure, bright light.'

I take her hands in mine and squeeze them. Then I run up the stairs as quickly as I can, because if I stay in that pose a moment longer I will laugh till I burst.

Chapter 14

In the morning, Aunt Elizabeth waits for me. She wears a bonnet with a wide brim and it is trimmed, I am delighted to notice, with large feathers. She has put tied flower-bunches at intervals around the house. They give off the odour of pond water. She places yet another on the hall table.

'Dear child,' she parrots concern, 'have you slept well?'

I slept like a baby. 'Only a little,' I say, sadly. 'My dreams are very frightening and keep me awake.'

'They will pass. Do you go to the church today?'

I am truthful in my answer to this. In part, at least. 'I do.'

'I prayed for his soul, that undeserving creature.'

'He has both our prayers, then.' Mine that he should come to a painful end and meet up with the Devil and hers that he should bounce out of Hell when he falls. He'll have an uncomfortable Eternity waiting if both our prayers are answered.

'Do you go out, Aunt?'

'I must pay my visits.' She sighs. She would have me believe this is an onerous obligation, when I know full well she cannot wait to hint to anyone she speaks to of Onions' perfidy. In a few months' time, with this town crier spreading the news, he will be unwelcome in all of the good houses around.

'I shall rest here. Please give my regards to those you call on.'

She watches me go to the parlour, fixing this last image of me – solemn and dignified – as the one she will report. 'Despite everything,' she'll say, 'Anne is carrying herself properly. She will make a good marriage yet.' And her confidantes will click their tongues and shake their heads with enough force to effect a change in the weather.

From the parlour window, I watch her walk swiftly down the street, only her heavy skirt and stays weighing her down enough to stop her taking flight.

The house is still and, for a moment, I relish the silence. Jane is a floor beneath me, and Aunt Elizabeth has given her a recipe for a cake that sounds so elaborate to make that she'll hardly have time to sleep, let alone appear upstairs. Even so, when I cross to my father's study, I look about me carefully.

When I enter, I half expect to see him in his chair, or standing by the fire tapping his pipe against the mantleshelf. But he is not here and first I stand stock-still then turn a full, slow circle to take everything in. There are the papers on his desk weighted with a marble orb. There are the books that no one reads.

There's a small glass, spotted with dark mould at the edges, set above the fire. I catch sight of myself, thinking that the last time I stood here I was not waiting to spend a day with Fub. Neither was I about to steal from my father. Is the expression in my eyes changed now? Is my bad intention visible? I've been telling so many lies to so many people this last little while that I may well look different. I examine myself carefully. Apart from the fact that my cheeks are flushed – and this is becoming – I appear unchanged, and I smile at my reflection to reassure us both.

I assume he keeps some coins here, but where? I must leave everything as I find it, and so begin to touch things so carefully that nothing moves. Becoming bolder, I pick up a paper from under the weight then replace it carefully. It is covered with figures, added and subtracted; they are of no interest to me.

The desk itself is the most likely hiding place for anything precious. I ease myself into my father's chair set behind it, sit as he would and open the lowest drawer. More papers. No wonder my father is so often bored; all this stuff is enough to put anyone into a stupor.

The next drawer is no better: leather volumes and more reams. I put my arms on to the desk in front of me, as he does.

'Now, Thomas,' I say in his gruff voice, 'where do you keep your money? Here?'

I slide open another drawer. 'No. Not in this place. Then – here?'

The largest drawer, running the full length of the desk, is slimmer than its fellows. Inside I see his pipe, a small almanack and two little boxes, one enamel and the other made of wood. This one jangles with good news when I pick it up and inside are several coins of the realm. At first, I remove only a couple, then go back for the rest. I may as well take them all, and I imagine Fub will be pleased with my haul.

The enamel box has a bouquet of flowers painted delicately on its domed lid: a surprisingly pretty thing to find here. Perhaps a treasure of my mother's that has found its way here by mistake. When I open it, I almost drop it in surprise. My little tooth, that my father had said he did not remember, lies there, wrapped in a twist of silk.

Beside it, so soft to my touch that it might almost be warm, is a lock of blond hair. A tiny curl, gathered at one end with a ribbon. 'Oh!' I say aloud to the empty room, for I know it to have been my little brother's. I recall, with a catch in my throat, snipping it free from his head myself. I had used my smallest scissors and was tender and careful when I took it, although he was waxy with death by then and would not have felt any cut.

I cannot see clearly any more. Fresh tears spring but do not spill. I blink them back, and look quickly to the ceiling to keep them in my eyes. I have my same mournful trophy in a locket of mine. And here must be the one my mother kept. Two fat tears disobey me and snake down each cheek to meet beneath my chin. Putting the box back with tender care and closing the drawer softly, I wipe at my wet face with a sleeve. I exhale until there is no breath in my body and my stomach draws in tight.

'Come, Anne,' I say to myself, summoning a heartiness I do not feel. 'Get your swag and go.'

When I close the door behind me, I gulp for air as if I had been underwater.

*   *   *

I cannot settle after this. I pick up my book, but cannot read; the pages blur and I lose my place. I go to the front door, as if to leave, but do not go.

When Jane appears with a list, I am glad of the distraction as she bids me go through it with her, to approve her purchases. She worries over every detail, as usual.

'So many eggs. And so much beating.'

'Stand back from the bowl so you do not perspire into it, then, unless the receipt calls for salt.'

From time to time I go to the dining room and consult the

clock, but its hands hardly appear to move. When, at last, it approaches the half-hour, I set off in such haste that I am still pulling on my gloves and tying my bonnet strings as I walk.

There is no sign of him at first but, before I can fret, Fub saunters towards me.

'Long time since I was so close to a church,' he says. 'How do you do?' My earlier melancholy dissipates like puddles under sunshine now he's come.

At first, we walk through the graveyard as if we are visitors to an exhibition, courteous and restrained. We remark on the names on the stones or point out their sentimental verses. It is as if we must constantly talk of these trivial things to prevent ourselves saying what is really in our heads. At one moment, I trip over a wayward root and he catches me, then holds on too tightly to be just making sure I am upright. At another, I seize his arm to indicate another amusing epitaph, but I don't need to keep my hand there for such a long time after as I do. Our eyes meet for an age as we decide which way to walk next. Anyone observing us would think the only way we wished to go was straight towards each other.

'Miss Jaccob?'

Just as he did before in the church, the vicar seems to materialise out of thin air rather than walk solidly as other men do. He wears a heavy cloak over his priest's garb, but his collar still shows.

'Miss Jaccob? Is it you? Ah, yes!' He looks expectantly at Fub.

'This is Master Warner,' I say. We all look at each other.

'I had better take my leave, Miss Jaccob. Mind where you put your feet, now. She almost tripped and I saved her from the fall.' Fub is walking backwards as he says this, addressing the vicar the while and bowing.

'No!' I cannot help myself. He must not go! Both men look at me sharply.

'She protests at my kindness.' Fub bows quickly to me: 'It was only what anyone would do.'

Crestfallen, I watch his retreating back.

'A good Samaritan, then.' The vicar watches his departure, too. He reaches into his pocket and retrieves a handful of soft bread, studded with raisins. He examines it with affection, then holds it up and out to me. 'Would you like to share this? Newly delivered. Still warm.' I shake my head. 'Have you had any moment to peruse the verses?' He takes a large bite, then has to keep his mouth wide as the sticky bread resists his teeth.

'I have read some of them.' I think of the charred leather cover and blackened pages inside. 'Most edifying.'

'Opinion is divided,' he says, still chewing, 'but I find him realistically romantic, if such a thing is possible. He was a church man too. When you have read further, perhaps we may discuss them?' He is so disappointed that we may not talk of poetry now and yet so hopeful that we might do so in future that his expression shifts about like the moon behind clouds.

'I should like that,' I say, and mean it.

'I climbed to the top of the bell tower.' He points upwards and I follow where he indicates. The tip of the tower seems to move towards me against the scudding clouds.

'It is very tall,' I say, dizzy even from looking up at it.

'Many steps to climb,' he agrees, 'but the view is extraordinary. There is a little window from where you may see almost all of the city. Certainly, I could clearly note the extent of my parish.'

Can you observe your flock going everywhere and anywhere but into your church, I wonder?

'I should like to look out from there,' I tell him.

'Then bring a muffler. There is no glass and the wind blows right through.' He rubs his hands together, though whether in memory of the cold air or to remove sticky crumbs I could not say. 'I, ah, have commitments this afternoon, Miss Jaccob.' He pulls his wayward cloak onto his shoulders. 'Until we meet again, farewell.'

He cuts an almost dashing figure as he strides off. Once he is free of doorways and aisles and furniture and other man-made impediments, he is quite graceful.

I look about the empty churchyard and the silent companions beneath. I am still thoroughly frustrated by the manner of Fub's going. We have not even arranged tomorrow's rendezvous, and my heart sinks that I may once again have to trudge to the Leveners' shop to find him. I am almost wearing a groove in the road there, like a coach's wheel does, with my steps. Before I can summon my strength to set off, I hear a low hiss nearby.

'Psst!' It comes from the church doorway. 'Psssst!' again. Then Fub appears, beckoning me to him. He pulls me into the great porch, where we are concealed from the road and cannot see the passers-by, nor they us.

'Did you wait here?' I cannot conceal my delight.

'He seemed no threat to us, that priest type, nor to have any purpose other than church business.' Fub imitates the vicar, mocking his mouth coping with its contents and pretending to swirl his cloak and take great strides.

'He is a good man,' I say gently, surprising myself by wishing to defend the fellow.

'Here is another.' Fub takes a step towards me.

'Where do we meet tomorrow?' I keep him at bay, to postpone

what will follow, however earnestly I wish it to happen. Nervous excitement digs into my stomach with sharp spades.

'Westminster Bridge.'

There is no space between us worth measuring now. We breathe the same air. He puts his mouth to mine.

It is not a kiss that a mother might give a child or a priest's lips might give the sacred chalice. Nor is it the polite brushing of a lady's hand in greeting. It opens me from my head to my toes like a paring knife. Then he slides his tongue between my teeth and I leap back in horror. He cannot have meant to do such a thing! It must have been his eagerness made him clumsy.

'What's the matter?' he speaks thickly, as if he had just woken.

How can I explain his error kindly? I feel as if I have just broken something into so many pieces it cannot be mended. I am embarrassed for both of us.

'You put—' Oh, I cannot say it. 'I felt—' I pant, not wanting to meet his eye.

'Have you never been kissed before?' he asks, surprised. This is a riddle I cannot safely answer. One way, I am a wanton and the other, a child.

'I am not fruit, ripe for picking.'

'I am not after fruit.' He cups his hands to my cheeks and moves his mouth closer. 'If I do this . . .' he kisses me softly, his lips dry. 'You don't object to that?'

I shake my head. 'I do not.'

'And again?' Another kiss.

'No.'

He kisses me once more, pressing harder this time. I don't close my eyes completely, but peek through my lids to see that his are shut. He stops, looks at me and raises his eyebrows in enquiry. I nod.

'And, now, further . . . But if it doesn't please you—' He doesn't finish, instead kisses me once more, this time snaking his tongue in little by little till my mouth is full.

At first I feel wet softness then it hardens to muscle till I can hardly tell our mouths apart. It is no mistake. I am sure there must be places in the world where people fervently wish this very moment gone. But not I, not here, in this mossy porch, with this boy at my mouth. I do not want this time to end. I would be quite content to stay fixed here for all time, until I have no breath in my body and even till I rot into the ground where I stand.

He stops, then holds me away from him a little and inspects me.

'Oh, Fub. If I died now, I would make a happy skeleton.'

'Are you thinking of death, Anne? I've not felt so alive before.'

'Give me another lesson.' I lean to him.

'I cannot believe I am giving you instruction like this in the doorway of a church,' he says.

I kiss him myself, to show that I am a quick learner.

'Anne!' Fub says. 'Will you remember this lesson, then, do you think?'

'One more, to make sure.'

He kisses me again. 'You are an excellent student. Till tomorrow? Will you come to the fair?' He points to my feet. 'Tough boots and a purse, please, when we meet.'

'Tomorrow!' I say.

We move apart but keep our eyes fixed on each other, recording every small detail of our faces. I put both my hands against the cloth of my clothes and trace the shape of my body. I feel the curve that goes in at my waist and the swell of my hips below and marvel at the living warmth. I am a new-made miracle. Not since I yelled my way into the world at my birth have I been so loudly alive.

'Can we not kiss again?' I hold up my face and shut my eyes tight and wait to feel his lips on mine.

'Just this.' He lifts the strands of my hair and puts his open mouth to my neck. His teeth don't bite though he sucks hard. 'Another lesson,' he says when he stops.

'My turn.' I have to stand on tiptoe to reach him, but I do as he did. He tastes of soap but smells of sweat.

He rubs at his neck where I sucked. 'Go,' he says, 'or I'll keep you longer.' He is looking at me as if he'd just bought me and I was worth more than he paid.

'And then?'

'We address a different subject.' He is serious.

'Will you teach me?'

'I may have to. I may not be able to keep myself from teaching you.'

'I am ready for that.'

*　　*　　*

The house smells of rotten eggs. Aunt Elizabeth is nowhere to be seen, but there are urgent, raised voices from the kitchen.

Opening the door, I can hardly see across the room for acrid smoke. After my much calling her, Jane appears, her eyes pink from the haze. She is never calm, but now she is raised to an alarming level of agitation.

'Oh, Miss Jaccob,' she glances round in each direction as if someone had summoned the magistrate. 'Your aunt gave me a receipt for a strong cake that's to be served at dinner. And I followed the instruction to the letter, I'm sure I did. But it's a sorry thing – half burned and half raw. And it took so many eggs! There are shells all over the kitchen.'

'It can't be helped.' I have bigger concerns. In my mind's eye, I walk to Fub. I remember his wet mouth.

'Your aunt does not approve of waste.'

'Is there any hope of a rescue?'

'I might fashion the centre, where it's cooked through, into a flower, and add some candied peel for effect.'

'That's a good plan, Jane. And I have one, too. Tomorrow, as we are a small household, please take a half-day's holiday.'

'A holiday? Is someone hanged?'

'For half a day, that's all. My father won't return for two days yet and I'll inform my aunt of my instruction.'

She looks suspicious, as if I had given her a jewel which she expects any minute to turn into a turd.

'Jane!' I speak to her as though she is simple and deaf. 'Here are your instructions: Get to your work and present what you can of the cake tonight! Take a half-day holiday tomorrow, from noon! Is that all understood?'

The poor woman ties herself into her usual knot as she bends in answer. Her legs must be so tangled under her skirts that they'll cut off her circulation one day.

*　　*　　*

I cannot bear any more of my aunt's sighs and glances, so instead at dinner I ask her about her plans for her home. She is constantly painting walls and moving furniture around. The effect is always the same – a drab house where a fussy woman lives – but she is pleased to describe the colours she might choose or detail the tables she might commission. I think of Onions, with his book of wallpapers – these two have more in common than they know.

'I am inspired by *The Ruins of Palmyra*,' she announces.

When Jane comes in with the platter of cake, I avoid her eye. Then I avoid Aunt Elizabeth's, too, for the object is as far from appetising as it is possible to be and if she saw me laugh at it as I want to, she might suspect my heart was repaired without God's involvement.

It is a monstrous creation, resembling both a mountain and a lake. Jane has placed little slices of fruit on the central mound, which has a flat top like a plateau and this is surrounded by a roiling sea of unrisen mixture. The egg smell hangs about it like a little cloud. Jane has presented the origins of the world in cake form; you would not be surprised if Adam and Eve emerged from its depths.

'What's this?' My aunt sounds menacing as she regards the culinary Creation.

'The cake you requested.'

'Don't be ridiculous. My cook never prepares it to look like this.'

'I am sorry, Mistress Jaccob.'

My aunt shudders as if she is looking at a rotting corpse. She pauses, then raises weary eyes to Jane. 'Take it away,' she waves her hand, 'I shall not speak to my brother about the appalling waste of ingredients. You may thank me for that. I would say it was a waste of *good* ingredients, but I suspect you have used up the store cupboard for this and I'll wager the eggs are rotten and the flour is full of weevils.'

Jane is weeping. She does not cry prettily. No little tears fall: instead, two streams of yellow snot stream from her nose.

My aunt watches this dispassionately for a while then, when she can take it no longer, she stands up. 'Get out!' She is changing from sparrow to fishwife. 'Stay out of my sight tomorrow, for if I clap eyes on you I may strike you!'

'I have given Jane a half-day holiday,' I announce. 'It would seem fortunately timed.'

Jane's molten flow has not diminished – in fact, my aunt's anger has made it worse. Now she is confused, too.

'I do not deserve . . .' she begins.

'Jane,' I say, 'my giving you a holiday has fortunately coincided with my aunt's desire that you become temporarily invisible.'

'I did not mean—' Aunt Elizabeth realises that while Jane's punishment has been reduced, she may not impose anything else. We cannot be without a cook for two days.

Jane looks from one to the other of us, her misery complete. I doubt she will enjoy her sudden liberty tomorrow, knowing she must face my aunt's wrath thereafter. It is unlikely to be cooled by then. My aunt is almost on fire with fury.

'You and I will call on our neighbours tomorrow, Anne.' My aunt puffs out again with this announcement.

'No, I—' What can I do? The fair recedes like drained water. 'Alas, Aunt, I cannot.'

She frowns. Surely I can stay away from my prayers for one day?

'I fear I am . . . *visited*.' I look down to my stomach with a modest expression.

'Visited?' She sits back in her chair. She weighs up our possible mutual embarrassment at further questioning, but cannot resist it.

'Do you mean . . . a woman's curse?' she whispers.

'Yes,' I whisper too. 'And I am *most* uncomfortable and might do better to rest here.'

My aunt's eyes are veiled with suspicion. She looks me up and down carefully, as if she might see some outward manifestation of my inner trouble. Short of wrestling me to the ground and raising my skirts to inspect me, she'll have to make do with my explanation. I am certain she is extremely tempted by the wrestling notion. I am ready to slap her away if she does.

'Thank you for being so . . . understanding.' I keep my voice in a whisper, thinking it seems to add an authentic note of sorrow.

'Well.' She shakes her little shoulders. 'Well, it can't be helped. It is yet another burden we women must carry.'

I wonder what weight she struggles with, save having to decide between green or blue walls or which bonnet to wear. If she knew that I had given exactly the same excuse to Onions two days ago, she might send for the physic to investigate my prodigious loss.

In lieu of our making plans for tomorrow, and as time hangs heavy before we retire, Aunt Elizabeth decides to read to me from the Bible. She has a flat little voice, until it comes to quoting any speaker, at which point she fairly shouts. This combination means that one minute I am lulled by the monotony of her narration, the next jolted awake, as she impersonates yet another figure.

'*And He took him outside and said: "Now look towards the heavens, and count the stars, if you are able to count them".*' She sits upright, her back as straight as if there were a board behind it. *'Do not fear, Abram. I am a shield to you. And your reward will be very great.'*

'That is a very well chosen passage,' I say, trying not to put my hands to my ears. 'Were it not that you are the wrong sex, I would suggest you might make a fine preacher.'

She simpers. 'I read to the poor of the parish, Anne. A small kindness, but I want to share the Word where I can.'

I imagine the poor preparing for her visits by stuffing their ears with whatever comes to hand. *'Perhaps you would just bring some stale bread for us next time, Mistress Elizabeth,'* they'd say, wincing as she read. *'Nonsense, this is bread for your souls.'* And on she'd go, boring and startling by turns.

I yawn with great exaggeration, stretching my hands above my head. 'I am fatigued, Aunt.'

'What does he say?' She has a sharp little look about her.

'Who, Aunt?'

'The priest. Of course I agree you may not go tomorrow as you are . . . ailing . . . but has he given you anything to commit to memory, to comfort you?'

'He has.' I think of the vicar, on his knees eating broken cake, or reading the heady verses of Donne to himself in his chilly room, longing not for Heaven but Oxford. 'Aunt, as you may imagine I did not recount in detail what had befallen me. And I did not mention Mr Onions by name, either, of course. I do not sit in judgement of him, but would rather Mr Onions came both to his senses and to his rightful conduct in good time, rather than because of any correction.'

'Of course.' She is struggling to follow this logic. 'But it is not *his* soul that concerns us, only the comfort of your own,' she says.

'The vicar suggested I take long, improving walks and consider how Mr Onions' conduct is damaging only to himself.'

'Walks? Rather than kneel in prayer?'

'He is of the opinion that spending time in God's fresh air, observing the good people I see going about their business, and remembering to thank Him for the rich harvest of His gifts to us, might go some way to help.'

This is novel. A man of the cloth who willingly empties his church. Where would she go to show off her new clothes, or to find the poor within easy reach of her patronage, if not to church? 'Then that is what you must do,' she says reluctantly.

'I am indebted to you, for suggesting that I ask for spiritual guidance.'

'Eh?' she bites her lower lip.

'Were it not for you and your wisdom, Aunt,' I go on, 'I might be floundering in a bog of lonely unhappiness. I would not know how to manage my silent suffering. Your suggestion that I go to the church and seek my answers there was inspired!'

She blinks and blushes. She has forgotten it was not her idea. She is like a kitten, mesmerised by a waggling ribbon and pouncing, not seeing the hand that holds it and pulls it out of reach.

'I had been asking Him to help me, of course.' I look upwards. I had better be careful not to give my aunt the idea that she is responsible for every last morsel of my redemption. 'But it seems your clear instruction was, finally, all that I needed.'

She must follow the ribbon for one last twitch.

'Tomorrow, after resting, I shall set out, as he bid me do.' I cannot help smiling. My aunt takes credit for this expression, too.

'I am glad to see you so much improved,' she purrs, admiring her handiwork. 'Praise the Lord.'

Chapter 15

Fub was like a leech at me yesterday afternoon. In my small mirror, I can see bright purple spots where he sucked. Even if he were to bite me hard enough to let blood, I could not be cured of him.

He told me to wear stout shoes today, but the little boots my uncle gave me to ride in are too small now – I squeezed my left foot into one, but it chafed and pinched even before I took a step. Our route to the fair would leave me walking sore and ragged. My mother has pattens, but I don't know where she keeps them and I daren't risk discovery by searching through her things. My soft new shoes will have to do. If my feet were as hard as my heart is to my family, I would not struggle with the ground beneath them at all.

He waits where he said he would. He wears a cord jacket, and when he turns there is a waistcoat underneath. I am suddenly nervous of him, as though his being dressed so smartly undoes our closeness a little. He pulls his clothes about, as unused to their constriction as I am to their appearance. When he sees me, we smile at each other like new acquaintances. He looks to my feet.

'You are wearing dancing shoes, Anne.' He is immediately

disapproving, his awkwardness forgotten. He may as well be in his apron again. 'We don't dance to the fair, do we, we walk.'

It is too late now, isn't it? The entertainments won't wait while I change my shoes.

'Go easy, then,' I say.

He does not reply, but shrugs .

'Then do not consider me at all. It is my feet I walk on, not yours, Fub. You will not hear me complain if you do not mind on my behalf where we step.'

I look carefully at him. His hair still curls at the back but the front stands up in spikes. The change is unnerving. His hand goes to where my eyes stare. 'I chopped at it.' He looks embarrassed. 'The knives were just back from the barracks and I tested one. I thought I needed tidying.'

I don't like to see his newly revealed forehead. I am angry and discomfited that he did not stay as he was. It is like a scratch on polished glass.

In the hush that falls between us we hear a sound, a soft whispered roar sharpened by cries and shouts: it is a great mass of people. It sounds like an army on the move, but instead they are all revellers bent on their task together. They carry a banner of noise, brandished like regiment colours, and it is coloured with drums, pipes, the pierce of flutes and high songs. None is in tune together but it's a great, raucous hymn to holiday.

'Look!' Fub points upwards; the sky is clear and blue. 'For us!' He smiles at me and I catch his humour; he is full of pleasure and good intentions. He takes my hand, laces his fingers through mine and pulls at me, eager now to start our expedition. The day unravels before us like a bolt of cloth. We shall cut shapes from it as we please.

'Where is your money hid, Anne?' Fub speaks low, as if pick-pockets have better hearing than most. Perhaps they do, and that skill aids their fingers. They can hear which is the cotton and which the velvet purse. Wherever they walk, there must be a constant jangling in their ears of all the coins carried near them.

I pat at my stomacher. 'Under here. I would feel any hands going there.' He looks sideways at me and I know we pleasurably imagine our hands going all ways about each other.

'Give it to me, safer that way.' He stops and turns to me. I stop, too.

At once, I am jostled at the shoulder by a man. He holds a small child by the hand and the two of them stare at me as if I have halted the entire fair, not just delayed them by a moment.

'Silly dressy maggit!' says the boy. His voice is high with outrage. He is about eight years old. I look hard at him. He has the brightest red hair, all in tight curls and as broad as a hat on his head. His face beneath is white with pallor, but he stares back at me with proper anger. How quickly these two have melted my mood. I am tempted to frame a reply but I feel Fub's arm round my waist.

He pulls me to him and whispers 'Come here,' and his voice is enough to restore me to better humour.

I bob a tiny curtsey in mock apology at the pair. The fellow lifts his hat, but the boy just glares at me. I should not like to see him grown to a man, the great pale lummock, and heaven help any wife of his – if he's lucky enough to find one and she's daft enough to take him on. What if I pushed him over, kneeled on his chest and pulled out his orange eyelashes till he sweetened? I stand my ground to watch them go. The boy walks backwards for a while to keep me in his sights.

Fub frowns. 'The crowds here are small, Anne, compared to the mêlée we'll soon find. If you are going to take issue with every bump and knock, we'd do better to turn round now'.

'I am unused to it, that is all.' I do not want him to examine my behaviour – I have enough of that order of things where I stay. Wriggling my hand to where I hid it, I feel for the little bag of coins and pull it free. 'Here,' I hand it to him.

He weighs it, looks inside, grins, then swiftly puts it in his pocket. 'Treats from Mr Jaccob!' he shouts. But I shiver to recall going into my father's study to search for money and finding in the drawer of his desk, hidden there, that little lock of my dead brother's hair, tied up with thin black ribbon.

Fub spreads his jacket open and tucks his fingers into the pockets of his waistcoat, leaning back a little. 'Off to Bartholomew's Fair?' he says, speaking as if his cheeks are plugged with wool. I doubt he has ever spoken to my father, but he is unnervingly accurate in his impersonation. 'Then you cannot go empty handed! Take this money for your food and your fun there, and take my daughter too for your other pleasures!'

He grows in his assumed role. He has his head pushed down onto his chest now, to conceal his neck and make his voice gruffer. 'I am *pleased*, no, I am *honoured*, no, I am *beyond any happiness* that you, such a fine, handsome, hard-working young man, should have chosen my scrappy daughter above other women. I was wondering how I might be rid of her. She is schooled a little, I suppose, but skilled? I doubt it. What's that?' He cups one hand to his ear in a parody of deafness. 'Skilled in the bedroom, you say? Then her virtue is lost! Take her away, do what you will with her, while I, a sorrowing parent, do what I can to assuage her shame.'

He staggers about, feigning sobbing, and mimes the production of a mighty handkerchief, large enough to have to pull hand over hand from his pocket like a sail, to mop at his eyes.

'Assuage! That's a fancy word!'

'Thank you misthtreth!' He puts on the voice of a lisping child, sucks at his thumb. We laugh, and my happiness is smooth and sweet as honey.

The crowd builds now, and the swell and sway of it would make it difficult to change course, so we all go together. But then it seems to bend and fall back on one side, and as the shape changes I see why: at the front of the semicircle it forms, tethered to a post by a thick chain, stands a bear.

It is shockingly large, standing taller than the man who keeps guard beside it. Although the chain is so short that the animal cannot move much, the man holds a stick and feints a little with it, provoking the creature to wave his upper paws about. If it weren't for the huge claws that protrude from them, or the sour reek that hangs in the air, it might almost be a man dressed up, so incongruous does the bear seem, so ungainly, his actions a parody of how a beast might move. He turns his mighty head towards me and I can see his little eyes. They are at once bright but broken.

'That'll be the sport soon,' Fub points to two dogs. They are tied up too and while they growl and pull towards their prey, it seems as if both they and the bear are reluctant players at this game. Then one dog barks, then the other and the noise is harsh and loud – there is no mistaking the menace now.

Suddenly the bear roars. Everyone falls back, a collective gasp propelling them away from the sound, till most begin to laugh a little, embarrassed that they feared such a captive threat. But how powerful that roar should be! It should scatter us, dogs and all, to leave the bear in peace. Instead, emboldened, the assembled mass begins to push forward again, testing the limits of safe distance. The two men who keep the animals apart nod to each other, the dogs' owner bends to release them as they pant and choke to be free. The bear opens his maw; great skeins of spittle join his teeth to his jaw. There is sweat on the faces of the men as they prepare for the fray, and the transparent lines of saliva that hang from the dogs' mouths shake and tremble as they growl. Soon all these waters will run together with wet blood.

We are near the front, but I begin to make my way back through the audience, I have no stomach for what comes next. When I watched the calf die, it was a solemn and necessary affair, minutely planned and deftly done. This will be a random tearing and gashing till the beast dies as much from exhaustion as laceration. I can face a swift execution. This will be ugly and prolonged.

'Anne!' Fub tugs at my arm to pull me back. I shake him off. Behind me, the dogs bark excitedly, the bear answers, the crowd shouts and squeals, but I am the only person facing away from the scene, the only one trying to leave. Against the bulk of people pressed tight together, my progress is slow. Until I step on a toe or dig in an elbow to clear my path, no one looks my way; every gaze is magnetised to the action before them. As Fub follows, his passage is punctuated by the same cries of 'Watch out, there!' and 'Mind me!' and various cusses, as mine is.

Two pillars of striped blue and white cloth rise in front of me and stop me in my tracks. Now they move, alternately, with a vibrating step, and I realise they are trousered legs extended to extreme length, twice my height. Looking up, I can make out a body above them and a face that peers at mine. A girl looks down. Her straw-coloured hair is braided and long and she teeters on her stilts and moves her limbs constantly to keep her balance. I cannot see her face clearly, as the sun is behind her and everything rises to a silhouetted point above me, but I think she smiles.

'Anne?' Fub is beside me now, his hair awry and his expression quizzical. He pulls at his jacket, which has ridden up, and smooths his hair back from his forehead. I can only shake my head at him; I cannot begin to explain how little I'd wished to see the bear baited.

'Are you travellers, requiring a passage?' the girl shouts. 'Hold on.' She points to her limbs: 'One to each leg. I am your guide. Watch this! No one gets in my way.'

And we take the billowing cloth as we might hold her hand and follow where she walks; she is our human maypole. People point and clap at us but she is right, they do not stand in front of her, so we get to a clearer place unobstructed and leave go. She waves and bows low at us, her upper body as lithe as her wooden legs are stiff. I watch her stride off with a pang of regret – I would like to be with her longer, my hand holding her clothes like a child clutches his comforter.

'Were you frightened? You watched the slaughter easily, didn't you?' Fub is like a dog at a bone, worrying at me, determined to get an answer.

'Yes. When you and Levener went about your business, I was ready for it. But today, I am afraid of the sight of blood.' This is simpler than explaining that things should die with dignity. I give him information as if I'm paying out rope, thinking Fub can hold only a little at a time.

'Then when we get to the ring, you must stay outside,' he says
'What ring?'

'Thanks to your father's *generosity*,' he sneers at the word,
meaning no gratitude to the man, 'I have enough to enter a
bout.'

'A bout? You mean to box?'

'Indeed, and if I win – *when* I win – you can return what you
took from him. Or keep it for another such outing.'

Oh, I should have stood still when the dogs snapped, I would
like to see him fight! To see him bare-chested, winking at me as
he clambers over the ropes to face his opponent. I can see him
mock the other's appearance, pretending to be afraid when they
square up to him, then knocking them out clean and quick. He
would be the victor, I have no doubt. I could catch the eyes of
any woman watching and signal to them: *He is mine* as they
admire his skill, his strength. But Fub believes that I am suddenly
squeamish and must not watch.

'Have you seen the wheel?' Fub is almost running ahead of
me, excited as a child.

It is a wonderful thing: wooden carriages circle above the
ground and swing from side to side with enjoyable fragility. They
sway like boats at harbour even as we sit down, so that we are
immediately pressed close. I squeal, clutching at Fub's arm. There
are high girlish noises from every direction. In moments, we
rise a good ten feet above the ground. The men turning the
wheel's handle delight in altering the speed, so we lurch from
rushing to crawling; my stomach flips at each spin and we keep
being thrown together in a clumsy embrace. The unbalanced
sisterhood around me cry aloud too. When we're done, I have
to sit on the ground to get my breath back.

'Wait here,' Fub says, leaving me still spinning. He comes back with a posy of flowers, bound together so that you can pin in to your costume. I watch him as he fixes it to my waist, teaching his large fingers to be dainty.

My feelings for him are rich as cream and I am queasy with desire. I want every hair, every follicle, every pore of him. Touching his head lightly, I say: 'How pretty, thank you.'

But I want to bite him till he cries aloud.

'It was not your father's money that bought it,' he says gruffly. The crowds around us blur and fade – even the sky is muted. He is in sharp relief, coloured and vivid. 'We must find food,' he says sniffing the air like a hound. We feast on cold cured meat and hard bread.

*   *   *

Fub holds my hand and walks with a purposeful tread, scanning the crowds about him, till ahead of us there's a white marquee. He cheers: it is his destination. The man sitting there barely looks up, though he takes the money quickly enough. 'And does she want a ticket?' he says, hopefully, nodding towards me.

'She waits outside,' Fub says, though he can hardly be bothered to finish his sentence in his haste to go in.

When he has gone, the man looks down at his coins and rotas without saying anything. It appears that if I am not going to pay him, I am of no interest to him. There is room on the bench beside him, but he does not bid me sit down. I have no wish to stand near this surly fellow. He has a large ganglion on his right wrist, but we are a long way here from any bibles to flatten it.

I circle the tent slowly; it is my lair with my precious cub within. The first time I pass him, the grump looks up briefly.

The next, because he knows it is me from the colour of my dress, he nods without raising his eyes. From inside the tent, I hear the low excited murmur of a gathering crowd. I pace the ground, but it does not make the time go quicker. I should have argued to stay with Fub but I did not, as I feared an altercation might use up some of his strength. It might only be measured out daily. The crowd roar together in gratified harmony at a hard blow landed.

'*Où est votre amour?*' It is the voice of a child, squeezed and thin. A tiny woman stands in front of me. She comes barely to my waist, though her large head accounts for a great deal of her height. She has applied rouge as you would in a dark room, in thick stripes on each cheek, and above her eyes she has stuck silver moons and stars on her skin in a haphazard constellation.

'*Dov'è?*' she smiles, flashing golden teeth. Without warning or preparation, she tips forward onto her hands and walks about on them, her tiny bright red boots held tightly together. Righting herself, she comes up to me.

'German?' I realise that she is quite old for though she is as small as a girl, there are lines and furrows on her face and her expression is distant and a little blank. 'Do you speak German, then? *Wo ist?*'

'I wait for . . .' I begin, but she doesn't listen. She is on her hands once more, springing from one to the other as her skirts fall about her face. On her feet again, she turns two swift pirouettes.

'Your lover is beautiful. Isn't he? *Beau. Bello. Schön.*' With each phrase, she swishes her skirts to and fro. Her fingers are broad and square and short with hardly enough space between to open them. 'And where is he gone?' She is very close to me now and I realise the irises and pupils of her eyes are all one, the colour of milk stirred into water.

'I cannot see,' the little tumbler says, as if I'd spoken. 'But I can tell the future. You will love him, love him, love him – till you do not!' She somersaults, making the ground seem to spring under her.

From inside the tent, another roar. How does he do? Does he fight well?

My companion bends over backwards to touch the earth behind her. How big is the world in her head? She holds one hand to her ear, listening to the noise with an exaggerated concern. With each swell and swoop of sound, she mimes 'Ooh' and 'Aah' and fans the air in front of her face in a pretence of fainting.

I feel suddenly as weary as if I hadn't slept and I sink to the ground between the tent pegs where the thick ropes are tight with tension. The tiny woman lies down beside me and curls up in a tight bundle. I can feel the warmth of her back against my thigh – she is as hard-muscled as a cat. She sucks on her blunt thumb.

The bout must be nearly done – a low rumble of sound gathers pace and strength as the climax approaches. Then we hear wild applause and shouts of congratulation. I imagine Fub on the winner's podium, his arm raised in triumph, his winnings in the other hand.

'Fub!' I shout at him as he staggers from the marquee. A large cut over his eye leaks steady red down his face. He has only his shirt on and he holds his waistcoat and jacket away from him as if they might burn his body. The shirt, too, is coloured with blood, darker here and solid. I had mistaken the shouts of victory, they were not for him.

'Here, this is for you.' The doll woman has disentangled herself from her slumber. She presses a slip of paper into my hand. What does she want? I must mend Fub now. Surely she understands? She must smell his blood even if she cannot see it.

'Your fortune.' She raises her voice on the last syllable, making it sound like a question. She waves both her hands at once, wiggling her stocky fingers at me. *'Au revoir,'* then, *'Auf Wiedersehen, ciao,* farewell the bye.' She scuttles away, with a rolling gait that throws her body from side to side, as if she is at sea on dry land.

I have no time for farewells and Fub scarely pays her heed as she goes. His life blood still flows from his wounds. How should I nurse him? Should I tear my petticoat for a bandage? How should a bandage go? I open the scrap of paper she gave me, to read before I throw it away. I do not need predictions now, I need . . . Oh, what do I need? Fresh water? The physician? The writing is curled and elaborate, with many dashes and bows around it, to make it seem more important. *When you walk through a web,* it says, *look for the spider after.*

'Oh, God, that I had won.' Fub is sinking to the ground. I cannot see his face – does he weep? I kneel by him, ready to do what I can. But I do not know what to do. His shoulders shake a little. I must be brave now, although I feel a little ball of panic beginning to rise. In many a fantasy, I imagined rescuing him from danger, getting his gratitude and relishing the glory of it. The reality is a jagged, terrifying thing.

'Anne, how can you doubt me so?' He is laughing at me, his face bright with pleasure. 'Annie, I won! I beat the bastard, I sent him home with too many bruises to count and a crooked arm for good measure. Here! Here's to victory!' He pulls me to him; we are on the ground together, and when I kiss him I can taste the blood on his cheek, in his mouth. He licks at my neck. 'My salty darling.' Now his tongue is in my ear, tracing patterns that repeat inside me and I close my eyes.

'A pretty sight! Young love!'

This voice is as familiar and unwanted as the taste of bile. I am flayed open as an anatomical drawing. Where was all warm honey now sits ice. My pulse beats very loud in my head. Fub still holds me, his face at my neck, puzzled that I do not respond, insistent that I should.

'Mistress Jaccob, how delightful to see you again!' The speaker continues, as if we were in a parlour. 'And please send my very good wishes to your parents. How *is* your father?'

By now, I am getting to my feet. Smoothing my dress as I rise, patting my wayward hair into place. The favour lies on the ground, the flowers quite bent. Fub grips his arm at my waist, there is fight left in him. But this adversary is old and frayed, his belly too large for actions and his legs too stout to carry him very far or fast. We do not need our fists ready for him, do we, just quick wits.

And here is his face: his smiling mouth benign, his rheumy eyes triumphant.

'Anne. Do you not know your old friend, Dr Edwards?'

Chapter 16

I could not sleep. All night I felt as if I was on the side of a steep, slippery hill where I could get no purchase, and my shoes slid helplessly as I tried to climb. This waking nightmare would not let me go, and when I closed my eyes it was only to stumble again, and lose my footing.

And much as I try to wish them away, the events of the day before insist themselves into all my thoughts, till all I can see is Dr Edwards' face, shining with glee. It blots out everything else like an eclipse.

*   *   *

At first, at the fair, when he called my name and helped me to my feet, there was something almost innocent in his delight at meeting me. Despite his having seen me tumbled on the ground with only my shoes visible, and even though Fub had stood with his arm about me while he greeted me, Dr Edwards had beamed without guile. At first. Then he began to realise, slow as seeping tar, that he had discovered me where I should not be found and in company I would rather keep secret.

'Who's this?' Fub had said, still ready to push the fellow away even if he couldn't take a beating.

'A friend of my father's.'

'An *old* friend of Mr Jaccob's,' Dr Edwards corrected. 'And a companion of yore to this lady.'

Companion! Pah! I could say nothing, except: 'Dr Edwards stayed at our house for a little while, when I was younger.' I stiffen beside Fub and he moves his arm away at last. 'But we have not . . . that is to say, he has not visited for many years.'

'Is it so long?' Dr Edwards looked slyly at me. 'Of course, I see your father abroad in the town from time to time. When I ask after you, he tells me all is well. And recently, of course, much of the talk about you is of *marriage*.' He said the word with a flourish, as the conjuror reveals the rabbit. He looked from one to the other of us, taking his time. 'Is this gentleman paying court to you, Anne?'

'He is a friend. Mr Frederick Warner.'

'*Mr* Warner,' Dr Edwards looked at him carefully. 'Your notion of friendship is progressive. Most of us conduct our friendships entirely upright.'

'Dr Edwards.' I had to rescue us, our little boat was sinking and Dr Edwards was taking away every bucket we might use to bale. 'I am very pleased to see you again. I have often thought fondly of our schoolroom.' My voice was high with panic.

'You were a very able pupil,' he said.

'And you a fine teacher.' I had to keep him on this narrow path; there was a precipice on either side. 'I have missed our lessons.'

If you tickle a dog, each part tenses in turn and shivers with delight, as it offers itself entirely up to your hand. So Dr Edwards submitted to my stroking.

'Perhaps,' I said, 'we could resume our classes. In some small way.' I could not look at Fub. With every utterance, false as it was, I knew he thought I was betraying him.

'I should like that.' Dr Edwards was hoarse with anticipation. 'Your father must be persuaded, of course, that we . . . Shall I—?'

'Let me discuss this with my father,' I said, speaking swiftly to keep him sweet. 'If you recall, he was of the opinion that my education is of no value and so I will have to prepare him carefully if we are to resume.'

'When he told me that you no longer wished to continue our little lessons, I sensed Thomas was not entirely disappointed.' Dr Edwards laughed as if we shared a confidence. 'Although I was extremely saddened.'

He betrayed no memory of the events of that day, when I was a child? Or, if he remembered, did he think that I had forgotten them? He made my gorge rise, and I violently wished him many miles away, or six feet under. I could not let him go to my father with his great news.

'As I was,' I said, demurely.

'May I escort you further?' Dr Edwards offered his arm. What could I do? Whatever he had seen, Fub and I could no longer go on our way with the carefree happiness we'd enjoyed. 'This young gentleman may need to change his clothes.' He indicated Fub's shirt with a dismissive hand.

Fub's shirt was stained, it was true, with the blood of his opponent and the green of the grass where we'd lain. He looked hard at Dr Edwards for, as ever, the man was covered in spots and stains himself. It twists my heart now when I think of his hurt expression as I linked my arm through Dr Edwards', but we could not speak. I could only say 'Later' under my breath in a hurried whisper to him as we left, but I don't know if he heard me. I walked as if on broken glass, each step more agonising the further away I went.

'You can have a little fun, Anne,' Dr Edwards said, patting my hand on his sleeve, 'but you must avoid that rough sort. Practise your kissing, by all means, but only with your peers. I had observed you together for a few moments before I introduced myself, and saw how he pulled you to the ground. Thank goodness I intervened, otherwise you might not have had the means to protect yourself.'

We went back through the fair, and where before everything was enchanting, now it was all poisoned. The colours were vulgar, the people coarse. When we parted, a little way from the house, I told him I would send word of where we should next meet, and he went on his way happily. He was trying to peer past me as we spoke, of course, lest he caught sight of my father and might thus have been able to insinuate himself into the house all the faster.

* * *

I hate Dr Edwards with all my might. I loathe his gristly face and his thick ears. His sour breath and coarse hands are an affront to me. I despise the very clothes he wears and the food he swallows. I begrudge him the space he takes up on the earth. My hatred swells as if my thoughts inflated it, and it would lift me off my feet if I did not hold on to thinking about Fub, to keep me anchored on solid ground.

When I hear the commotion from downstairs, I am frightened it might be Dr Edwards: he might have decided that any small pleasure he might derive from being my teacher would not be as great as the joy in being my informer. I wait for the inevitable call.

It is not him. My parents are come home. I hear the baby's

cry, but it is quickly shushed. There is no conversation, no thump of boxes returned; I cannot make out any of the bustle I might expect after their absence. Are they both here?

My mother is nowhere to be seen, and my father scarcely looks up when I come to him. 'Her mother died,' he announces.

'My grandmother?'

'The day we arrived. A fever.'

'Is my mother sick?' A clutch of panic at my heart.

He frowns. 'No. She mourns. As you would expect. And would have stayed longer at her father's house, but I insisted we return. Buried her yesterday.' He was probably champing at the bit to get back to his London diversions. I expect he offered my mother no comfort, not even a kerchief for her tears. He looks about him, inspecting what might have shifted in his absence. Then at me, to see if he can spot any changes there. 'And have you been on more outings or suchlike with Simeon?'

'Not . . . no.'

'No?' He taps his foot against the floor, waiting for me to explain. I take a deep breath.

'Aunt Elizabeth forbade him to call on me.'

'Pardon?' I have his full attention now. 'What did she do?'

'She told him that he was not to call. I overheard her, and I was horrified, of course, but what could I do?'

'Why would she do such a thing?' he looks away, breathing hard, turning this strange news over.

'I don't like to besmirch her, Father, but I have thought about why she did it, and I consider that her actions might have been precipitated by . . . envy. I am afraid I think she was jealous of his paying me attention.'

He stares at me. 'That cannot be enough reason,' he says,

squinting into the middle distance. I know that he is unable to imagine how she might feel.

I do not waver. 'She told me that it was not fitting for him to take me to entertainments. When I told her that you had expressly instructed her to let him call, she replied that she was mistress in your stead and he and I must do as she ordered.'

My father breathes heavily. I continue: 'She then told me I was in need of her ministrations and she read the Bible aloud to me, most frequently. She ventured it would improve me more than any marriage would.' I look down as if overcome by sadness at the turn of events. Then I raise my eyes to him and whisper, 'She is, after all, a single woman.'

He sits for a while, his expression fixed. Then, as you might witness the dawn come up over the horizon, his anger rises – reaching first his mouth, which sets in a thin line, and then his eyes, which he narrows. It is most diverting to watch. Eventually, just as it seems he is about to explode from his clothes with fury, he gets to his feet. He almost paws the ground. Aunt Elizabeth had better have her wits about her to fend him off. He might have brute strength on his side but her wings aren't clipped and she can fly away. I would very much like to observe the confrontation, but instead I have to stay where I am.

I hear him roaring at her, then her chirping replies: it is only a short exchange. He seems to be leaving no room for her explanation. Then she bustles up the stairs – I can sense her looking for me; she must be almost drilling through the walls with her eyes to seek me out.

*   *   *

When I can no longer hear her ordering coaches and slamming doors and it is safe to leave my room, I go to my mother.

She sits by her bed on a low chair with her hands in her lap. Grace must be ministering to the baby, the crib is empty beside her. She raises her head, but not so that our eyes meet. She is half an orphan now and it has made her even more grey with sorrow.

'Aunt Elizabeth is gone,' I kneel by her. 'I am happy to have you home but I am sad for your loss, Mother.' I look at her hands; she twists them together but doesn't reach for me.

'She did not linger,' she says. 'That is some comfort.'

The world divides, does it not, into those for whom you wish a speedy end and those you want to suffer. My grandmother was a mouse of a woman, she hardly made an impression on the world – if she had walked across a bowl of set cream her footsteps would not have marked it. She did no one any harm. It is right that she was stamped quickly under God's heel. I would not have wished on her any of the several painful, drawn-out ways I have imagined to send Onions and Dr Edwards to their Maker. I may not voice anything of these thoughts to my mother, so I say: 'It is indeed a comfort.'

'I sang to her,' she ventures a small, embarrassed smile, looking at me directly at last. 'Songs that I cannot remember learning. These things are stored in our heads as if we are born already knowing them, aren't they? Like the alphabet or the times tables.'

My memory of my grandmother is vague, as fuzzy as pulled wool. She hardly ever visited nor did we go much to her, though she lived hardly half a day's ride from us. There is a miniature of my grandmother to remember her by but my mother would leave no trace. I look carefully at her, to store her features for when she is gone. Perhaps the baby will grow to resemble her, as I do not. Jealousy stabs like scissors that open their blades in the wound.

'But they must have been songs she taught me, I suppose.' She weeps without wiping away her tears.

'You taught me songs, too,' I say. I have not sung for a long time. There has not been any music at all in the house since I was small and stood by the piano while Dr Edwards played.

'How have you passed the time, Anne?' she puts one hand out to me. It must hardly have any blood in it, it feels so light. 'Did Mr Onions improve with acquaintance?'

'Aunt Elizabeth would not admit him, Mother.' She frowns. 'But I made do with . . . visits.' For a moment, I think she is going to ask where I went but instead she regards me with an amused expression, as if I have confirmed to her something that she has long suspected. She blinks, quickly dismissing her tears and her thoughts.

She talks of the christening and about the baby's new ways, things that are of no interest to me. In my head I go with Fub to the fair once more. When my mother falls silent, it is a moment before I realise she is watching me.

'Have you heard a word?' she asks. 'You are dreaming, Anne.'

'I was distracted, I'm sorry.'

'I was not reporting matters of any consequence.' She smiles. 'These are only small things.' She pauses, considering what she will say next. 'Are you happy, Anne?'

I must look startled, for she continues without waiting for my answer. 'I do not mean on the question of Onions. I would not expect your happiness to blossom there quite yet.' Or ever, I think. 'I expect you think it will not bloom at all,' she says. We catch each other's smile then. 'I am aware that he might not be the husband you would choose but, when the time comes then we can speak of your married life, and I will prepare you as best I can.'

That is not much of a promise to keep. What possible experience can she draw on, except to use her own unhappy example as the one I should not repeat? My father is the rock and Onions is the hard place. Both are covered in festering, slippery weed, too. How could she help me choose between them?

'No, I meant instead to ask if . . . if you are content in the other paths you take. You spend long hours alone, and I hope you find your own company acceptable.'

'I do.'

'Please tell me if anything in particular concerns you.'

What does she want me to say? This is a strange time for a confidence. Shall I speak of Onions' patent revulsion at everything about me, except the convenience of my being a wife to him? Can I tell her that when I sniff at the sleeve of my dress I can smell where Fub's hand was, gripping me as I slid beside him on a fairground wheel? It is a mixture of sweat and leather that I would wear as a perfume if I could.

'No, there is nothing.' Does she know I lie?

She studies me carefully; again it as if she sees me properly for the first time in a long while. 'You cannot open your heart to me, Anne. But I think that is because it is already preoccupied.'

Her words tug at me. I wish that I could confide in her, but I cannot. If I cling to her now I am sure we will both drown.

'I grieve for my grandmother, your mother.' It is true that if I think about it hard enough, her death saddens me. I stare at my mother's face. Try as I might, I cannot see the girl she was. Her younger self is as distant as the horizon to us both.

'I hope that your husband has an interest in many things, so that you can discuss them together.' She says 'husband' with the faintest suspicion of regret. 'I suspect you would find that very satisfying. I know how quickly your mind turns.'

Then do not saddle me with someone like Onions, I think, who has opinions so unbending they might as well be made of steel and no interest in mine.

'I remember how clever you were at your lessons,' she says. I shiver. How odd that she mentions that now, with the newly summoned shade of Dr Edwards materialising ever more strongly. I can almost hear the piano keys sound as if we played together a floor below.

It is not long before my father crashes into another obstacle to household calm and yells his anger. Jane is shouting, too, so I deduce he must have discovered her wasteful attempts at baking. If my father ever feels uncertain in his long-held belief that women are stupid, he only has to wait an instant for some proof to present itself. My mother turns back to her solitary contemplations. She is deaf to the disorder. I almost embrace her, but she seems too fragile to hold.

'*I find my sister has interfered maliciously in every part of this house!*' my father bellows at Jane. '*She had no proper right to take over management of our affairs in this way*.' She is nodding vigorously, her mouth closed tight.

As when a stone is dropped in a pond, so the ripples of my accusations against Aunt Elizabeth have swiftly spread outwards. Each supposed example of her transgressions adds to the growing circle. Before long there will be no occurrence too small – a hen that does not lay or an object found out of place – that the blame is not laid at Aunt Elizabeth's door.

While my father shouts, Jane catches my eye and seems to react oddly to seeing me. I can't be sure; she is so full of twitches it is hard to tell what she intends. I wait till my father tires of this particular exertion and lumbers off, leaving us alone.

'Does he fret about the cake?' I ask.

'He asked if the house had run smoothly. I did not know what to say, Mistress Anne, but he said that she had done very wrong by you and that you had confessed to it, and that I should, too.'

'Well, she is gone. And Onions, too. So you may cook us some good meat tonight and no one will complain.'

To my surprise, something – perhaps the very mention of meat – makes me weep.

Jane looks horrified at my falling tears. 'Oh Mistress, oh Madam.' She stands on her tiptoes to dab at my eyes. She is near enough for me to catch the sweet, cooked pudding scent of her clothes.

'I have caught a cold,' I sniff, reluctant to take her in to my confidence.

'Oh dear,' she bites her lip. 'Can you see the butcher's boy then, or shall I send him away?'

I grab her arm. 'Oh!' She shrieks, then claps her hand over her mouth before I can tell her to be quiet.

'Where is he?' I hiss, close to her ear. Her look says she knows that she was right to suspect my feelings for Fub are not those of a housewife for a shopkeeper. It is too late to care about that. I have vanquished Onions and Aunt Elizabeth and, if I have to, I'll get this woman out of my way too. But for now, I need her to speak. 'Where. Is. He?' I separate the words, giving each a little punch. She jerks her head.

'At the door. As usual.' She matches my whisper, her lips wet.

'He has been waiting. I could not come and find you, not while your father questioned me.' As I leave, she hisses, 'Mistress'!' and saliva sprays from her mouth.

'What is it?'

She lowers her head but keeps her eyes on me. We are conspirators now. I would not have chosen to take Jane in to my confidence – with her pitted cheeks and perspiring forehead, she is an unattractive accomplice – but it can't be helped.

'Mistress,' she says, 'he has brought no basket of meat with him.' Her meaning is clear. She watches my face with her small eyes and stands more still than I have ever seen her do.

When I go to him, I feel nervous and unprepared. He has his hands in his pockets and doesn't take them out to hold me, but waits, defiant, for me to speak. The words I need do not come easily, and I almost choke on trying to explain who Dr Edwards is, and what he means to us. It seems an age till I have told him all I can, and he still only stands there, keeping his distance from me and his thoughts locked up.

'What shall I do?' I say, calm at last and ready for instruction.

'He is an impediment, to be sure,' Fub says carefully, 'if he were a rogue animal, there would be no question about what would happen to him.'

'How would an animal be called rogue?'

'Several ways. If it did not follow the herd, or it destroyed its pen, or it got too savage to be milked easily, or it fought anyone who approached. Not worth the trouble of keeping for any of those.'

'What would happen to it?'

Fub draws his finger across his throat. 'A kindness.' He grins.

'Dr Edwards. Do you think he resembles a beast?'

'If he *was*,' Fub says, casually, 'You'd know what to do. You've seen it happen, after all.'

I imagine Dr Edwards, roped and suspended upside down from a beam with the blade approaching. I don't need reminding of how a knife works. And how swiftly. 'But as it is, he must be dealt with and I can't lead him to Levener's for dispatching.'

'Take Levener's to him, then. Or rather, take from there what it is you need and what you know.'

I look at Fub, waiting for a smile or a look in his eyes to dilute this strong stuff. He doesn't smile.

'Oh,' I say, deliberately playful, 'you would have me slice Dr Edwards up like a little pig, would you? A very clever solution. How would I do it?'

'I have never killed a man,' Fub says, matching my tone. 'But if I did, I wouldn't go for the jugular.'

I think of Dr Edwards' fleshy chin, which almost conceals the neck below. 'Why not? That worked for the calf.'

'It is good for every animal that will not fight you back. But if they can defend themselves, you'd have to get in close and be quick. But there's a great amount of blood pumping here,' he squeezes his thigh, 'and if the next wound was there,' pointing above his knee, 'it'd be all over in no time.'

I am trying to stand still while he tells me this, although I want to dance with glee. It is both the subject matter that thrills me and the sheer joy of learning new information.

Fub laughs at my happiness. 'You like this game,' he says, as if it truly was just that. 'I can almost believe you are really keen to learn.' He begins to lose the intensity that had me spellbound.

'Play again,' I say. I cannot hide my urgency.

'I am the evil butcher!' He speaks with an artificial,

melodramatic depth, loud and too strong. When I don't respond, he lowers his voice. 'Look at all these blades. To slice a little pig, you need a little knife. And little hands . . .' he takes my hands in his, at last, 'little hands like these,' he kisses my palms, first one then the other, 'can only hold little knives, too. There's a perfect match in those two facts.'

I twist my hands in his and hold on to his wrists, spreading my fingers there. It is as if we face each other ready to begin a dance. There is a vibration around me – a low thrum. It is the sound of all the sharp things from every drawer and on every shelf offering themselves to my hand, their shanks already curved to my touch, the blades tingling.

I lean close to him. 'Are not bigger hands more suited?'

'Bigger hands . . .' he measures what he says with care, stroking my wrists with his circling thumbs, ' . . . are better hidden. Two folk walking together are noticed. You should go alone.' He smiles again, as though he only joked. I see his sharp incisors shine. 'You could wind him in. He looked to me to be half hooked already.' His eyebrows raised, he looks enquiringly at me, to see if I've understood. The blades nearby twitch.

'Get him where he needs to be, then . . . leave him there.' Fub squeezes where he stroked. Where would we go?

'I will arrange to meet with him,' I agree, 'but as for the rest . . .'

'What *rest*?' Fub says innocently. 'What you do when you meet is up to you. How your steady hand proceeds and your strong arm acts, I couldn't say.' He raises his hands together in front of him, clasped together as if he prays. 'Will You help her with this business?' he says to the heavens. 'Can You guide her hand in her necessary deed? For You see everything and therefore understand what it is that must be done.'

I tell him to be quiet, not because he blasphemes – I don't care about that – but because my head is so busy with my thoughts.

'One more thing.' Fub's hand are on my shoulders. 'Leave your window wide tonight.'

'Will you speak with me again later?'

He snorts in reply: 'I won't be saying much. If it were words you needed, I'd say them now. But I have an instruction of a sort for you.' He kisses me, quickly. 'Leave your window wide, then, will you?'

As he turns to go, he says, 'You do sleep in the room to the left of the backyard door, don't you? Your window does have a yellow curtain, doesn't it?'

I laugh aloud at his coyness. He could be a little boy, asking for a sweetmeat. But he is not a child and neither am I and we do not plan childish things, do we? 'Climb up there and see. If it isn't the right place, you'll know soon enough.' I must go away from him now. 'I'll be ready for you.' I want to take his hand and put it between my legs. The pulse that beats softly at my wrist, my temple and my neck beats there more strongly. If I don't leave, I will beg him to touch me. As it is, I struggle to stay upright and would crawl away on all fours if I could.

How foolish Dr Edwards had looked, all those years ago, when he bade me keep my hand on him and strove for his release. The old man was dark with lust; there was nothing light about his panting urgency. We two can scarcely move for brightness. Even though I shield my eyes, desire leaves spots before my eyes.

Chapter 17

How slowly the time goes as I wait for the night. Each maddening second hangs like dripping treacle. I look at the clock so often my father notices.

'Do you wish the time away?' He sticks his neck forward and his lower lip protrudes. 'You seem preoccupied with the passing hours.'

I feign a yawn. 'I am weary, I thought it was late and I might sleep soon, but I see it is not yet the hour to retire.'

'Go when you will.' He picks at his teeth with his fork.

'Thank you, then – good night.' But I am reluctant to leave. If time hangs heavy here it will be ten times weightier when I sit by myself in my room, alert to every sound in case he comes. 'Father?' He stops his excavations. 'May I borrow a book, please?'

'A book? Which book?'

'I had not thought of any in particular. Perhaps I could choose one?'

He blows air into his cheeks. 'I hope you do not think I keep any *poetry*.' We are both thinking of the burning book.

'No, not that. But it is a long while since I read anything but the Bible.'

'I doubt I have anything to interest you. My library is mostly concerned with shipping and law. But there may be a novel or two.'

'May I look?' I move to get up, but he stops me. 'No, no, I will inspect the shelves. Wait here.' He leaves the door ajar, I watch him square his shoulders before he goes into his study as if he's about to do battle.

He is gone for some time, and eventually I go to find him. He may have forgotten his purpose, or nodded off. He is sitting in his chair, a book in his hand, reading, and does not hear me come in. I screw up my eyes to see what holds his attention so strongly. *Fanny Hill*, the book announces, *Memoirs of a Woman of* —. I get no further. My father starts as if he heard a gunshot and snaps the book shut.

'Anne!' He puts his palm flat over the book as if it would spring up and denounce him. 'Why do you creep about?'

'I wasn't intending to alarm you, Father.' He looks flushed. What does this book contain? My father's expression is reminiscent of Dr Edwards' watery ardour. He slides the book towards him, then into the drawer beneath, in one fluid movement. It is a good thing he won't look too closely at the drawer's contents. He might notice the wooden box there doesn't rattle any more. 'Dull, very dull,' he says, still awkward. 'Now, what shall I give you?'

He turns to the shelves, running his finger along the spines. He sounds out the names of authors as he touches each book: *Vol-taire, Jon-a-than Swift,'* like a child at a reader. 'Was your volume about the law?' I ask, my tone innocent. I would love to leave with any of those but I know he only teases me and will not offer them. 'Perhaps I should read it, to understand such things better.'

He has his back to me, but I can see him tense with annoyance. 'You know perfectly well it wasn't.' His voice is steady. With every breath, his anger cancels out his discomfort. It is not long before he is back to full strength, then he faces me.

'You are not as clever as you think, Anne,' he says. 'Do not test me. You might have fooled Elizabeth into doing your bidding but Onions will call again at my behest.'

'I know.' I don't want him too vexed. He might lock me up this very evening in a room that isn't mine, then how will Fub climb in? 'I had only meant to tease you. You are only keeping things from me for my own good, I'm sure.'

He bites at the skin inside his mouth, pulling at his cheek with his thumb for more purchase.

'Well,' he breathes the word out, 'I'll choose a book for you at random. And you'd better be grateful for whatever comes to hand.' I nod. 'Or I could take my time and bring it to you later?'

'I would rather you gave me whatever comes to hand,' I say. He chews again, watching me carefully. 'I am only inclined to read a little before I sleep.' Still looking at me, he swings one arm behind him to the nearest shelf and fumbles unseeing at the books till one works free from the others. He peers at the title. '*A Well Ordered Table*. There!' He almost flings the thing, and dust rises from the pages as I take it.

'Good luck with that!' he chuckles. 'It should hasten your slumber, at least. But there are words in it, plenty of 'em, you can't complain about that. You could spend your time putting them into a more interesting order, if there's not much plot.'

I could remind him that he himself found one story very enlivening tonight. I could also say that he must surely have hurried to my mother's bed once upon a time, or slept with his hand on his groin and some girl in his head. But he has tamped down all such feelings as thoroughly as you do when you kill a fire. 'Thank you, Father. And good rest to you.' *Perhaps you could breathe your last tonight?* 'May you dream of pleasant things.' *And may you not ever wake.*

He shoos me away with the back of his hand. 'Yes, yes, to bed.' He will sleep as if his head was full of coal, neither troubled nor rewarded by visions of any sort. He has only put this poor little book in my hands. But I have so much treasure waiting for me that if I were to live for ever, I wouldn't get to the end of it.

Even in my room, I cannot be patient by myself. How should I wait? And where? In this chair, perhaps, though it is low to the ground and so badly stuffed that the horsehair chafes through my clothes. Or on my bed: I try lying there until the coverlet becomes warm and crumpled beneath me and I must straighten it when I rise. I twist the skirt of my dress in my hands to stop them trembling and hold my breath to be sure I hear everything from inside and outside the house. Each creak of the stair makes me jump, and I go several times to the door, pulling it open a little to see that no one is there, then closing it with great caution, chiding the *thunk* of it as the frame meets the panel. I stare into the empty street, willing it full of him. Where is he now? Anxiety has made me clumsy. I spill water when I raise my drinking glass to my mouth and trip over my wooden case. Should I prepare for bed? Can I be sure that he meant he would come? How have I got so foolish and nervous when I am clever and brave in every other circumstance?

A tiny sound – *dink* – on my window. I speed to it, but even before I can lean out, Fub climbs hand over hand up the creeper to reach me. When he stands in my room, I realise I have so often imagined him there that his presence seems false. He is too large, too rough, too real.

'Ha!' He sounds as if he's laughing, but he's just getting his breath back. He wipes his hands where leaves still cling on his jacket, then begins to take it off. I stand transfixed as if I had just conjured him or he was a ghost made flesh. The unpredictable movements as he strains his arms from his sleeves hypnotise me. He sits heavily on the bed then bends over to remove his boots.

'I have been listening so hard for you my head hurts,' I whisper. He looks up, one boot in his hand. He pretends he will drop it and I gasp, looking round as if I am fearful that there is a crowd outside waiting for just such a sound. He pats the bed beside him and I sit there; the mattress bucks and rocks beneath us as he pulls his foot free. We sit side by side. I have my hands clasped in front of me, awkward as a spinster. Fub kneels up, then he swings his legs open, one over the bed and the other around my waist so that he pins me, his legs wide and I between them. It is entirely right that I place my hands where his legs part.

'Little beast,' he says to me, his hands on my thighs. 'Here are your flanks, all plump and sweet.' And then, sliding his hand over my hips to my waist: 'Your rump, your loins. But you need flaying.' He tugs at my ribbons.

'Clothes are foolish! Curse the snake in Eden that put them there!' I laugh as I speak; he stops me with his mouth. We struggle from our garments, half helping, half fighting the cloth and the challenge of sleeves and buttons. And when there is nothing there, his arms replace them and his fingers go all about me. When his hand goes to my breasts, my feet are envious. I slide my hands down his back, all along his spine, rutted with bone like mud ridges in a dry field, to the audacious swell below. His finger is inside me, his thumb circling, and I spill like grain from a bucket. He is panting, still running his race. I laugh at the incongruous size of him, sticking to his stomach and escaping from the springing hair below. All the while, we stifle our noise and whisper like a church congregation during the sermon. He pinches my lips when I yelp, I shove my fingers in his mouth when he opens it to howl.

'Anne,' he says, stopping and looking down at me. I am pinned like wet washing with his peg. 'Till now, I thought the sweetest sound I could ever hear was cows chewing grass. But this is better.' He sways and we listen to the soft suck at the exact place we meet. Then I move and put all thoughts of livestock out of his head.

* * *

As from below the waterline, we surface. We breathe heavily, beached, adjusting to air. There is a fish smell too, as if the tide had just gone out. I half expect to pick shrimps from my hair or find oysters between my toes. The chill in the room raises the hair on my arms and legs and pricks at my flesh. Where Fub's leg lies across mine, it might be dead meat – it is as inert as anything on a butcher's slab. My leg begins to throb with the beginnings of a cramp. I test my strength, trying the muscle in my limb to see if I can pull free. I cannot move. He does not stir. I raise myself as much as I can, on one arm, and whisper 'Fub!' at him, but this only seems to deepen his sleep.

I have been happily turned and held and stroked this past evening (how long were we about this? An hour? Three? I cannot say), but now I am trapped like a prisoner. The pain that begins in my thigh spreads along my calf and upwards to my hips. Perhaps my blood will cease to flow as he unwittingly cauterises my veins and I'll have to hobble or use a wooden stump to get about.

'Fub!' More urgent now and, although he still closes his eyes, he moves and sets me free. At once, an incessant painful tingling, both sharp and dull, courses from my knee to my foot. I have to rub at it hard to soothe it away.

The clock downstairs chimes. How have the others here in the house spent their time tonight? They are all made up of skin and bones as we are, have the same muscles, organs and hair, all as capable as I am of using their bodies for pleasure, but instead they are only flaccid and desiccated and flatulent. Fub's ripe skin gleams in the faint light from the window, where the lamps are still lit. He lies on his back, his arms stretched wide. He reaches from one side of my narrow bed to the other. He is spread out as if he's a map of himself. I examine him carefully. Like an explorer, I stake my claim to his broad shoulders. I am the new owner of his wrists and thighs. I have negotiated the little thickets of hair on his chest and below his belly and got to the clearing to plant my triumphant flag. All his territories are mine now and I will have investigated each one so thoroughly that before too long I'll be able to chart his exact topography blindfold.

I trace the thick line that runs down his neck, where the muscles flex. He raises himself and looks down, examining my body as if I were on the slab. 'Prime flesh?' I say watching him. He brushes my breasts and stomach with his fingertips and touches a thin smear of blood on one thigh. 'Am I hurt?' I ask.

'Are you?' He smiles. 'It's from the raddling stick,' he says. 'Better not let anyone see how many times you were tupped.'

'Fub?' I turn his face to me, holding his cheeks, making him meet my eyes. 'Would you kill for me?'

He pulls his head away from me, like a colt shying from the halter. 'I kill every day, don't I?' He smoothes my hair then gathers it together into a knot at the nape of my neck. 'I kill every day,' he says again. 'Shall I dedicate each death to you, then?'

'Shall I be a butcher, too?' I say lightly, but I want his proper answer.

'Is that what you'd choose to be?' he says. 'It doesn't suit everyone.'

'It would suit me,' I say softly.

He gets up, gathering his strewn clothes. 'Where is my keep-sake?' I say, watching him dress. Now I know what his skin feels like under his britches, how his feet are roughened at the heel inside his boots. 'To remember me by?' he says. He searches all the pockets of his jacket in turn, then brings out a leather purse. When he opens it, something catches the light. 'Fit for purpose,' he says. It is a little knife, the blade is only a thumb-width across and the handle is short. The tip of it is honed to an elongated point. 'It's a dainty one,' Fub turns it in the air, describing a figure of eight. 'I use it for little calves' vells. You need a knife both nimble and sharp for that. Like this one.'

I take the knife from him. I make a tentative stabbing move-ment with it, but falter as I pierce empty air and my arm falls limp.

Fub is buckling his boots. 'You might practise on a cushion, perhaps. It is a hard skill to master at once,' and it's as if he talks about an embroidery stitch that I found difficult. He stops for a moment, and stares at me, his expression solemn. 'It is for playing our games, Anne. A gift, nothing more.'

'You should have tied a ribbon to it, then.' I look at the blade, lying innocent and clean in my hand.

'You don't need ribbons,' he says and climbs out of the window. As I watch him go, I hold the knife above my heart, like a lover's token. Which, after all, it is.

The room is empty without him. The air rushes noisily into the space he left. I lie on the bed; the covers are still warm but there's no comfort in that. I go to my little glass to see if a woman's eyes are different from a girl's. I inspect my face carefully but I would seem to look the same as I did before. Perhaps my pupils are wider, but that may just be because of the darkness of the hour. I have the taste of him in my mouth. It reminds me of chalk and marrowbone.

I thought he had left me satisfied, but I am hungry again. That is another new sensation.

Chapter 18

There are many hours left until I can send word to Dr Edwards. The long reach of the night is a fertile field and I can usefully sow my plans there. I should discover a meeting place for us first, somewhere where we can be unobserved. Sitting bolt upright, I remember a church near the pleasure gardens that stands at the edge where the town gives way to open ground. I shouldn't want to meet at the church itself, where at the very least a random worshipper might spot us, but the empty fields beyond would seem ideal. I will choose some landmark there as our trysting spot! I will mark it for him with a favour! This notion is so enticing that I leap up to dress, almost forgetting how bereft I was a moment since when my lover left. I pull several lengths of ribbon from my dressing chest. They leap and twist in my hands as if they are as excited as I am at their new purpose.

There's a chinking sound as I close the lid. I feel to the bottom of the chest and my fingers close round two pennies. They must have fallen from my stolen haul. I tuck them into my pocket, though I have no plans to spend them.

I am hurrying so quickly across the landing that I do not see her at first, but Grace is there. She is holding the baby, walking to and fro and rocking it in her arms. Everything is in motion to soothe the child.

'Mistress Anne! Can you not sleep either? Your sister cannot settle.' She smiles at the soft blankets she holds. The infant must be awake, for when Grace's eyes meet hers, she mews. A stink of milk and vanilla hangs round them both.

'Now, now,' Grace murmurs, 'don't fret, little one.' She brings the child's face close to hers, then kisses it softly. There must be so few thoughts in either head, they mostly share one: Grace wants the baby sleeping and her little charge asks for nothing else, either. Even for herself, Grace needs very little: a household to live in and a steady wage for her labours. She walks along a straight path while I am negotiating a maze. I am tired, all of a sudden, and in this instant would like nothing more than to be cradled in Grace's arms, while her low voice croons to comfort me. She seems to have forgotten I'm there, she is so intent on pacifying the baby. At last, she succeeds. All is quiet.

'She sleeps, unless I speak too soon,' she whispers, still swaying her arms. 'She's close to waking, though. I think she has a colic. Where do you go?' She has finally noticed that I am dressed for the outside world.

'My head aches. I thought I would walk to clear it.' I think if everyone who knew me swapped their stories with each other, they would surely decide I must be the most beleaguered and chronic invalid, so often do I cite my ill-health to explain my behaviour.

'Be careful where you go,' she advises me like a mother would, despite her position. 'It is hardly light yet.'

'Mind you keep rocking, she stirs.' The baby begins to mewl

again, a weak cry that weaves upwards like a thin trail of smoke from a small fire.

'Would you like to hold her?' Grace offers the blankets to me.

I recoil. 'I most certainly would not.' I relish her surprise. 'I doubt that I shall ever be a mother but, if I am made to be, I shall have enough nurses to mind my children constantly, so that I can be completely free of them.' I look at Grace defiantly, waiting for her shocked response.

Instead, she says, 'You cannot imagine being a mother till you have your own child, that's all. I am the third of nine children. In our house there were always babies around me and I never had to learn their care, it was all I knew from a little girl. It is different for you, Mistress.' She smiles, convinced it is a kindness to explain this to me.

If I let her continue in this vein, she will begin to think I am to be pitied. 'It is your misfortune to have been born in such a crowd, Grace. It obviously left you little time to be taught about anything else. At least you have put your unsolicited learning to good use.'

She looks unhappy at last, her little smile fades. 'I did not intend you to think that,' she says, softly. Then she mutters something else to the baby that I cannot catch, but I suspect it's about me.

'What did you say? Do you address me?' I speak quietly, but she can hear the threat.

'I whispered to your sister that she should stay asleep.' She frowns at the infant, looking as if the child is going to speak out against her. No doubt she will bring the mite up to mistrust me. I would do the same, in her stead.

'Haven't you work to be getting on with, or will you converse all morning? You seem to like the sound of your own voice, but I prefer silence.'

My words hit her hard as a slap. She flinches then blinks. Her features collapse at my unkindness, crumpling from her forehead to her chin. 'Did you read the book that was burned, Mistress?' Her plump lips purse. There is a challenge in her tone. She is standing up to me. We might be children about to slap and pinch each other. 'You needn't say the words aloud, so that'll be a quiet occupation for you.'

I push her backwards. I touch the massy, dense bundle instead of her arms and she stumbles, clutching the banister with one hand, trying to stay upright and not drop the baby. At this sudden jerking movement, it starts and cries.

Before she can consider the folly of her tart manner, she speaks sharply. 'Now look what you've done!'

'How dare you speak like that to me.' She falls silent and looks afraid. I almost wish I could turn on my heel and leave, but I can't ignore her rudeness and she would not expect me to. We cannot retreat from this or undo it. I sigh. 'Go to your room, I shall speak to my father in the morning about what must be done.'

She looks frightened, hugging the sleeping child to her like a shield. 'Please, Mistress. I didn't mean—'

'It doesn't matter what you didn't mean, does it?' I feel as if I walk across a bog, my feet dragging down and my skirts heavy with clinging mud. 'And I'm sorry you must go back to your numerous family. But you were very—'

Grace tilts her head to one side, her chin forward. Her eyes flash with a new thought. 'And perhaps you should tell him about the boy?' She squares her shoulders.

'What boy?' I ask, although there is no doubt who she means.

'I'm sure your father would be interested to hear about your *lessons* at Levener's.' She touches on the word lightly, as if she jumps on to it on tiptoe. Was the whole of London full of watching eyes when I walked there? I hardly looked to left or right each time, so intent on my path and mindful of my feet. But plenty who know me must have seen me, then told another who passed it on. The news would have been back home before I was. How stupid of me to think I was invisible. Even if I could offer a defence or an excuse, I could not predict that my father would not take the word of this servant over mine. Little barbs of fear prick at my skin and beads of sweat pool at my armpits and brow.

'Go to your room, Grace. You're very tired. That baby cries so often that you must hardly know what day it is, or what hour will strike next. I am prepared to overlook your foolish outburst. But if it should happen again, I cannot promise to be so lenient.'

She stands stock still. I suspect she is planning another assault but the baby begins to unspool another tiny cry. She cannot resist the sound for long, it twists and burrows in her ears until it's all she can hear.

Her head bends over the child. Fine twists of yellow hair fall from her cap and the infant's fingers clutch and grab at them. I seize the chance to leave.

There is a cold, sticky wetness at the top of my legs that catches my petticoat and I am puzzled until I remember how it got there. I feel a childish sense of triumph: *This is what the boy means, Grace.* I open the door wide. *This is why I go through the house, silent as a thief, while the others sleep.* I pull it to behind me, careful and slow.

And there is a knife under my pillow, Grace.

Chapter 19

The church is as I pictured it: in the dawn light it is sleepy and quiet and its overgrown graves suggest it is not attended much. Even the path to the door is only one person wide and bordered by bracken. There is a tree with a thin trunk in the meadow beyond, its branches close to the ground. Holding my ribbons, I circle the tree with my arms in a strange embrace and tie a knot at the end, then slide it low so that it's not visible until you are close. I have hardly flattened the grass where I walked through it; it has sprung up again, long and dense. It has not rained in days.

At Dr Edwards' lodgings, I knock for a good long while before anyone answers. A small boy, perhaps nine or ten, his hair tangled at the back of his head in a fuzzy mass like a baby's after sleep, opens a window above me.

'What is it?' His voice is surprisingly deep; if I couldn't see him, I might imagine him twenty years older.

'I have a note for Dr Edwards,' I shout up to him. 'Is he there?'

He frowns, an expression which wrinkles his entire face in pique. 'He sleeps,' he answers, as if that were obvious and I am stupid to even ask. Of course, it is hardly morning. The boy must have only just woken when he heard me. While I have lived through several lifetimes, the rest of the city slept.

'Can you fetch him, then?'

The boy grins. 'Throw up a penny, first.'

Children have got very mercenary, haven't they, although his price is low. How fortuitous that I am armed. I get a coin, then throw it up. My aim is poor and it doesn't reach him, forcing me to scramble where it fell then scrabble in the dirt to retrieve it. The boy leans his forearms on the sill, watching this sport. He seems to regard me as a sorry adult specimen. After four attempts he's able to catch it. He makes a great show of polishing it clean, breathing on it then rubbing it with his shirt several times.

'Dr Edwards you're wanting, is it?' He has the manner of a man as well as the larynx.

'Yes!' I am exasperated by how long this is taking. My little would-be messenger knows this very well. After raising his eyebrows and more shining of his loot, he retreats. I stare at the window where his little head was. He could have played me for a fool, and be a penny up on the deal. But Dr Edwards stands in the doorway, rubbing his eyes and with his sparse, wiry hair curling round his head in a mockery of a halo.

'Anne!' When his vision clears, he sees me and he is delighted. 'Adam said there was a girl, but I didn't think—'

I don't care a fig for his thoughts, so interrupt him. 'Dr Edwards, will you come to the field behind St Helena-at-the-Wall tomorrow?' He begins nodding vigorously even before he has heard me out. 'At this same time,' I say. He pats his waistcoat as if he kept a timepiece there, but the pocket is flat. 'Listen for the church clock tolling,' I tell him. 'When you have counted six chimes, leave your lodgings.' He must get every detail right. 'There is a tree there, not far from the church wall. I have tied a ribbon round it so you'll know it. It is the perfect place . . .' His little eyes are bright; he follows me like a dog with a bone held above him that he must not lose sight of before he jumps to get it. 'It is the perfect place for you to begin teaching again.'

He sways his large head about, I hope he is not curdling his thoughts. 'In the open air?' he asks.

I nod. 'With a tree for shelter,' I say, smiling as though it's a blessing.

'I have a room here, with a desk.' He points up to the window. 'Better than a field, surely.'

'No, we must begin in secret, Dr Edwards. I began to tell my father of our intention, but he is out of sorts at the moment and not in the mood to listen. His humour will improve in time, I'm sure, and he will accede, but I am too impatient to wait!'

'Well . . .' he mulls this over.

My heart beats rapidly; I had not thought he might refuse. 'Do you have some of your wonderful books here, Sir? If you are not prepared to meet me tomorrow, could you at least bring them to me?' I step towards him, letting my hands go to his.

He looks anxiously about. 'I do, Anne.' He grips my hands in his rough mitts and breathes heavily, then runs his tongue along what remains of his upper teeth. 'But your father has been a good friend to me and I would not want to upset him.' All the world fears my father. He puts very little effort into his tyranny and is all the more effective for it. Here is Dr Edwards, gurning with anxiety while he wrestles with his dilemma.

'Oh, Dr Edwards,' I say, my voice trembling with sadness, 'if we are not to recommence our study, then I shall have to ask my father to send me to his sister to occupy me. I am starved of learning. That will have to suffice. I'm sure she has much to impart.'

'No, no,' he says, piqued, 'if we are resourceful, I expect we can steal some hours when you are safely from the house and I have some time to spare. Eventually, your father can be told. Your aunt is a clever woman, I'm sure, with much to teach you. But she may not know the best way, and I certainly do.'

If Dr Edwards had ever clapped eyes on Aunt Elizabeth, he would not consider her a rival. I raise my eyes to him, and then summon every effort to picture my brother, his little chest heaving as he struggled to breathe in his last hours, then hardly rising at all as his life ebbed away. It is an image as vivid as if I saw it an hour ago and, as I intended, it makes me cry. 'Thank you, Sir,' I say through my tears. I make no attempt to catch them. Dr Edwards waves his hands uselessly, he has nothing to offer to dry my cheeks and fans at the air as if that might do it.

'Dear child, of course we must continue.' He must think I am overcome with gratitude. 'Are those tears of happiness?'

I choke my breath out in uneven gasps as if I sob. 'Yes! And relief,' I answer, truthfully. 'Thank you, I will try and be the best pupil you ever had.' *I'm certainly going to be the last.* He bows and with a reluctant, 'Farewell, my dear student,' he goes inside, muttering about which books he'll bring and what instruction I'll get.

Whenever I catch someone's eye, I wonder if they are waiting till I'm out of sight to run ahead and inform on me. It is tiresome to be so suspicious all the time. Only the wide eyes of stray children seem to look at me with natural curiosity. I certainly hope Grace has made herself scarce. Only if Fub were waiting would I want to hurry home. I place him in every room, as if I'm arranging a doll's house. Here he eats; here he sleeps. Through this door he bathes and next to that, he dresses. And everywhere he strokes, kisses, pushes, rubs, paws, caresses, bites or pulls at me. We get at each other in every corridor or hall, in each doorway, on all the steps and sills. My imagination is so clever at depicting these couplings; so clearly do I see them, they might almost have happened. These visions make me ache below – there might be a weight suspended there it pulls so much.

The house still slumbers, tired from its battles and skirmishes, and does not open an eye when I come in.

* * *

By dint of keeping silent and watchful, I move around all that day unobserved. When I hear Jane come from the kitchen, I leave the hall. When she canters into the dining room, I skip upstairs. My father has gone out – his hat is gone from the hook and nuggets of mud, loosened from the soles of his boots, mark the route of his leaving. From the nursery comes the usual constant, steady murmuring – the baby cries, my mother speaks softly and Grace's high chatter is the descant above.

In the late afternoon, on my bed with my eyes closed, I rehearse the next morning's events. I plot each step carefully, as Ariadne laid the string to guide her. I decide exactly how I shall beguile him to think he's about to have a different sort of lesson. I will bind him twice, once with ties and then with desire. I fetch two long measures of silk I belt my dresses with, and practise a knot. Pulling up my skirt and petticoats, I trace where the blood pumps along its course from my thigh to my knee and press lightly where I'd need to pierce to best effect. There is such sweetness to these plans, such harmony, that when it begins to rain and I hear the drops fall on the slates and piping outside, it is as though my thoughts are bursting into song. Jane calls for supper, but I have no appetite and do not go.

The night is solid, an obstacle that I must climb over to get to the next day. In my dream there is a tapping on the window. I know it to be Dr Edwards himself, his knuckles against the glass. Opening the window, I lean down to him, and unlace the front of my nightgown so that he can see me, my bare skin, my breasts. He holds up a jar of honey and begins to pour it over his head, which is annoying and amusing to me, both at once.

When I wake I have to shake myself free, like a dog from water, from the image of his sticky hair and silly gaze. I kneel at the side of my bed and feel under the bolster. Even though the cloth around it is still warm from the heat of my head, my fingers find cold steel. The blade greets me, familiar as if we were old friends. I remember Fub's hand under my skirt, the saltiness of him. 'Wait,' he'd said, the while putting his tongue in my ear, which was incongruous and yet melted me. 'Wait,' as he guided my hand to him and 'Wait,' till he knew I could not, then still saying 'Wait'. My insides squeeze together at the thought of him, and if I did not hold that little sharp knife, I might return to my bed and fill my head with these thoughts and fill myself with my own hands.

The idea of meeting Dr Edwards when the day has scarcely started makes me catch my breath in a little laugh of pleasure; it jumps in my throat, alive as a bird.

Chapter 20

I wrap a shawl round me, over my dress, and hold the knife beneath it, keeping it in front of me with both hands like a prayer book. The scarves! I almost forget, but there they wait and I push them into my pocket, tied underneath my skirt at my waist. They go in deep and lie softly. The house breathes but does not stir as I tiptoe through it. The first rays of the sun through the windows stripe the dull surfaces of tables and walls, but nothing moves. The noise of the key in the door lock is so sudden and loud it startles me, though I think I am prepared for it. I wait, braced for a cry or call of question, but it does not come. The door creaks a little as it opens, but by now I am confident that I can leave unseen. I don't look back as I go down the street, but for a while I feel the gaze of the house on my back, as if every window watches me. Above some of the door-ways a light still flickers – those lit late that now burn low, to no purpose.

On one corner, a tethered dog is being bothered by a shabby boy – he kneels beside it and worries at its ears, speaking non-sense, too close, into them. The animal, flinching, seems puzzled and a little afraid.

'Leave it!' I say, remembering too late that I should not call any attention to myself. The boy turns cloudy eyes to me – I can tell that a large amount of drink has rendered him no sort of witness.

'What? What?' he says, trying to stand, holding an unhelpful wall for support and sliding over to one side.

'Leave that hound and be off with you!' I am bold with something, but it cannot in all honesty be with something too righteous, can it, considering the task I am about. He scurries away, one arm half in and half out of his jacket – the thing is too big for him. The dog and I regard his awkward passage together for a moment, then it settles its head on its paws with a sigh.

'And thank you graciously, too,' I say, feeling aggrieved. For a moment, I'm tempted to kick the cur. But I cannot waste my time or energy on an undeserving animal. I shouldn't even have bothered myself with a boy in a stolen coat.

The sun will not rise high any more this year, and there is too little power in it to dry yesterday's rain. The streets shimmer in a fine mist, out of focus as in a mirage. The point of the knife is real enough; I test its sharpness against my finger. 'Not too long,' Fub had said. 'This knife is a short, pointed one, thick enough to stand the force but not so wide it doesn't pierce.' The little weapon is up to the task, I am sure – only my strength is untested. What if Fub walked with me now, my accomplice? Might we have to dart into doorways to kiss and touch, forgetting the hurrying time? 'It's a job for one, this,' Fub said. Did he? 'Better alone.' Did he say it? Or do I only hear it in my head?

I pass few people and those I do are either sleepy or intent about their business. We are not concerned with each other. There is time in the day for conversation and play, but at this hour we are all separate and silent. I have no doubt he will be there. Dr Edwards was greedy in accepting this, my last invitation to him. I imagine him as he rises, dresses, drinks, eats, farts and walks into the street. He hears the sounds around him and sees the sun rise above as if it will all be the same tomorrow.

When the cobbled streets give way to earth then to fields, I discover there is a small hole in my shoe. Soft-soled, I can already feel each stone and crack, and a puddle wets my foot. Pushing the gate by the church open on to the meadow, there is a strong smell of fox, dense and fibrous. I walk through a web and in trying to rid myself of every last clinging strand, flailing my arms awkwardly, I catch the point of the knife on my palm. It makes me gasp. 'Get used to the feel of skin,' I say aloud. 'There'll be more of that.'

The church glows as the sun begins to catch its shape. Oftentimes it has people in it who make promises about each other's safe-keeping. And I have sat in churches, too, my head bowed – though my mind wandered. I have no thoughts of God and Love. He has let me down and disappointed me too often, and if He *is* in every living thing, as they say, then He finds himself strangely shaped more often than not. As I go to my rendezvous, is He even now wrestling with the Devil over my soul? 'All this and before I have had time to eat!' He yells, while the Devil smiles and points at me: 'She walks with purpose, does she not? I have her, wouldn't you say?' Blasphemy to add to my other crimes!

Now I am both laughing to myself and also reminded that I have the devil's own hunger, too. First, a little work, then I can eat. I am seldom one to forfeit a meal. *'We care for each other. Or not,'* Dr Edwards had told me as we gazed over London's tiny territories. *As ye sew, so shall ye reap*, I think.

In the meadows below a herd of cows wanders, grazing. They are too far away to hear. I amuse myself by holding out one hand flat in front of me and creating the illusion that they roam on my palm. The scudding clouds move swiftly overhead. It is a painting with moving life in it, and I wonder what names these clouds have, what colours an artist might need to re-create the scene. Dr Edwards would have told me. I feel a shaft of pure sorrow. If he had not betrayed me twice over, there would be no meeting under a tree, no sharpened steel. I might be going to him for more schooling now. In the years that have passed, my head would be so full of learning I might have to walk bent over with its weight. I could not help but know the Latin names of the plants, why the wind blows warm as it does today. I could name clouds and colours. I picture Dr Edwards coming towards me laden with books, perhaps with a violin in its case ready for me to play. But in my vision, I skip towards him like a child and I am not that child now and have not been for some time.

*   *   *

Dr Edwards is there but he doesn't look out for me. A flash of anger – should he not be anxious that I may not come? I should rouse him with a furious yell. But I save this feeling as another weapon to use later; I shall need everything in my armoury to drive the knife home. He is reading, as he so often did, and it is only when my shadow falls over him that he looks up. He lets the book drop and it sinks into the wet grass. His hat falls back and he grabs at it, shoving it hard on to his head, then pushes one arm to the ground to try and raise himself. He is not used to getting up from so low down and he flounders like a beetle on its back. I could help, but first I need to hide the knife.

Removing my shawl, I place both weapon and its shield beside me, the one obscuring the other.

'Annie,' his voice is thick with phlegm – he has obviously spoken to no one else yet today. 'This is the tree you meant, then. I had to look carefully for the ribbon; the rain made it shrink.' I pull at his free arm to right him. He is heavy but my blood is rushing hot and gives me strength. Upright, he pats and smoothes his clothing as if to smarten himself before encountering fine company.

'*Quercus robur*. The mighty oak.' He cannot help but tell me this, I think. Such was our habit, for so long. For a moment I am almost fond of him, which will not help me. But then I remember the fair, his hand on my shoulder and how he gloated when he saw Fub's arm circle my waist. He would speak to my father soon enough, he had promised it and would hold firm. Any affection shrivels like a dried grape.

He fishes into the deep pocket of his coat, and produces a linen-wrapped parcel. 'Comestibles,' he smiles. 'No need to go hungry.'

Hunger again! Everything conspires to remind me of my empty stomach. But I have determined that Dr Edwards ate his last meal out of my sight and I have no wish to dine with him. 'Later, Sir. I am not wanting yet,' I say. 'At least, not for food.' I smile suggestively at him and he looks quickly at me, his eyes bright.

He pockets the little package. 'For what then, Anne? For what kind of things does your appetite quicken? I shall do my humble best to inform you as ever.' He tries a little bow, but his stiff back will only allow a small incline of his shoulders. A soft wind stirs, making its way over the meadow like an incoming tide, bending and denting the grass. Above us, the branches sway and twist and the leaves rustle, but autumn has not quite nudged late summer away and they will not fall yet.

'There was a lesson, a very particular subject, that you began to teach me when I was a little girl.'

'Lesson?' he looks a little suspicious and swivels his gaze about him, as if we may not be alone and the meadow might suddenly reveal others who have been hiding in the concealing grasses. 'Which lesson?'

'An important, *enjoyable* lesson, Sir. Which you were well-placed to teach.' I am going about this too quickly, but I cannot get my breath easily – I am choked by his solid presence. I must speed on with my task before I am stifled.

'You showed me,' I say, biting my lip, modest and sweet, 'that men have a need to get with women, for the differences between them make it urgent and right for them to be with each other.'

He seems puzzled, but he surely cannot have forgotten my small hand on him, his sputtering conclusion.

Then he smiles. 'Ah, yes.' A wet sigh. 'Ah, yes. Do you like to think of that, Anne?'

'I do. And I think of it often.' I give him what I hope is a coy smile. We are standing a little apart, but I step a fraction towards him. Enough to hear the wheeze of his outward breath, and to notice two long, wayward hairs that sprout from a mole on his cheek and cross and tangle together as they grow. 'I hoped, when I asked you here, to continue that class, Dr Edwards.' He listens intently. 'I know you saw me with Fu—, with Mr Warner. And you are right to presume that we have knowledge of each other.'

He breathes in and out quickly, as if he goes over a little bump in the road. 'Knowledge?' His mouth twitches. 'Do you mean . . . ?' He leers at me and puts his hands together, circling the thumbs.

'Oh Sir, you understand me, I know you do. He did what he wished and I did not resist. Even though I should have done,' I simper.

Dr Edwards rolls his shoulders in their sockets. I pick at a spot of dirt on my skirt. Then I look up shyly. He is like a fish on the hook, as Fub said he was, but I must reel him in slowly and steadily, otherwise I'll watch him swim off to safe, deep water. A little more bait.

'Fub is a boy, as you have seen, and because of his callous youth and thoughtless haste, I have to tell you that he went about his business carelessly. He could not *perform* for me as I might, perhaps, have liked.' I look sideways at him. At that 'perhaps', dropped like a cherry into cream, Dr Edwards sniffs the air.

'Perform?' he says, his voice thickening.

'Too *quick*, Sir.' I have him now. 'You began a mighty interest in me with your lesson and I had hoped to, oh, *continue to study*,' another coy glance, 'but in Fub, I lacked a good teacher.'

Dr Edwards stares at me. I look closely at him. The years have not been kind: his eyes water and the lids are pinkly puffy; his cheeks sag and his lips are pitted and cracked. Each breath is dragged in to his lungs like coal sacks over rubble. He may not even have the strength or inclination to undertake another 'demonstration'. Moreover, the need may have passed. Much as when we are grown and we chance on a favourite childhood toy but cannot remember the passion that kept that object cherished, so might Dr Edwards look at his bawdy past with affection but from a great distance, considering it irrelevant and even a little dull. If so, this may prove to be a long lesson.

'I am still a teacher,' he smiles, 'and we should continue our

241

lessons, should we not? I cannot have you arrested in your studies in that churlish way. On that particular topic, I am a veritable professor. But I don't see any furnishings. Where shall the schoolroom be?'

'Here!' I say quickly. His eyes do not leave me now and I have his full attention. The pit is dug and in he falls. 'It is early and no one is around, or about to come upon us. The cows will not be herded in for hours, the church has no service today and the priest is about in the parish.' He does not know how sure I am of my facts. He certainly does not know why. 'God's classroom!' I fling my arms theatrically wide to the fields around.

He laughs, and spreads his arms too, taking an unsteady step towards me. I do not want his embrace. I step back too fast. He looks affronted and so I laugh as if we are playing a delicious game.

'To the lesson: remove your jacket, Sir!'

'Are you the teacher now, giving orders? I do not care for this reversal.' But he begins to wrestle his arms from the heavy cloth. He reaches for the collar of his shirt but I stay his hand.

'No, please leave on your shirt, Dr Edwards. I wish this to be *as before*.' I whisper those last two words as if they have great significance for us. I only think it might suggest he was about some other business (pissing or pleasuring) if he's half-dressed when he's discovered. I realise I am already thinking of him as a dead body and I feel that catch of laughter in my throat once again, at knowing how close his end is.

'As before!' He hears my tone as mutual excitement, and he gets to the ground and fumbles with his britches.

My fingers go to my pockets, where the silky scarves are warm and waiting. 'Put your back to the tree, Dr Edwards, I have brought my own contribution.' I bring the scarves out with a flourish I did not intend and he claps his hands with delight.

'Magic?' he cries, 'do you bring magic? My mother always said I could never resist sleight of hand!'

Do not mention your mother, I think. I do not want to know that buried beneath this carapace of ageing flesh and grey, wild hair, there is the ghost of a little boy, all fresh and curious, who looked at the world with those same eyes that regard me now.

'Better than magic. Give me your hands.' I stand behind him then pull his arms together and bind them with the silk. He is wet from the ground and his fingers are slippery. 'So that you may not move . . .' He struggles a little, but only in mock anguish and protestation. 'Soon, you will not want to move,' I say into his ear, which smells of wax and oil.

He giggles, holding his hands together obediently. With the other tie, I circle the tree, then join the two scarves together. Another knot. Then another two more. I pause to admire my handiwork. It has come out better than I'd hoped. Dr Edwards' age and infirmity have contributed more than I could have asked. His legs are stuck straight out in front of him.

He watches me as I reach for the sash of my dress, then undo the little buttons. I am very glad my costume no longer fastens at the back; there are many advantages to my getting older and this one is obvious. I didn't put on a hoop so that is one less thing to remove. When I step out of my dress leaving me only in my petticoats and stays, Dr Edwards blinks rapidly as if to confirm what he can see. I take off one petticoat, but go no further. He makes a small sound, a single high note of exclamation.

I kneel at his feet and pull off his boots. He laughs and kicks his feet out while I do, but only to help me free them. When I go to the buttons at his waist, I gag, but make a small cough to cover it. 'Just a little way!' I say gaily, trying to pull his britches to his knees. I only get them as far as his thighs and it takes an enormous struggle to get them that far, as his skin seems to cling to the material. His upper legs are mottled with so many different colours you'd lose count if you tried to number them. The flesh is lumpy and cold as unkneaded dough. I wish I had brought a bigger knife, my little weapon may only get as far as his marbling fat. Beneath his gut, pale as semolina and almost folded in half, his little man-person sags.

We both regard it solemnly, as if we'd unearthed a mole from its tunnel. It begins to uncurl, a blind creature with its one unseeing eye searching. Dr Edwards looks sadly at this offering, shifting his behind on the wet grass beneath him.

He must be lulled like a baby now, so that he trusts me entirely. There's no other way to do this except the most unsavoury. 'Let's make him stand to attention!' I cry, taking the thing in my hand. The skin there is soft as milk and I can smell cheese, too. It is so difficult to grip it might be a bladder half-full of water, entirely without muscle, and it slips about as if it would escape. I go about my task with such determination that my teeth begin to ache for I'm gritting them with my effort.

Eventually, it sticks out in front. Fub's hard person stands flat against his belly, tempting as a sweetmeat. This is poor pickings. Dr Edwards begins to squirm; he wants to get his hands there himself but the scarves hold.

'Close your eyes!' I hiss.

He obeys with a contented sigh. I watch him while I fetch the knife: his eyes are screwed tight shut, his bare stomach heaves and his member trembles like a newly-hatched chick. This man was once an infant in his cot and all these parts of him were tickled and loved. His every gasp and gurgle was once exclaimed at with joy and recorded with wonder. His inert body will be pawed over again in due course, but only for the information it holds about his death, not with a kind touch.

I sit astride him, putting my shawl round me like an apron. This will be a messy business and I'm fond of this stomacher. His eyes twitch to open, but I put my free hand over them, closing the lids softly.

It is the last gentle thing I do to him. I examine him carefully then push the knife as hard as I can into his leg. There is resistance from flesh and sinew, then bone stops my progress entirely, so I have to turn the handle this way and that until it's in up to the hilt.

For a moment, he stays as still as if he sleeps, then his eyes open so wide I can see a large circle of white gleam around each iris. He bucks beneath me like a horse, but with his arms pinioned behind his back and his legs immobile underneath the full weight of my body, he can do little. He stops moving and his upper body collapses, deflated by shock.

I wriggle backwards a fraction to examine the wound. Already, bright, wondrously red blood pumps like a river in full flood onto the ground beside him. He looks down at this phenomenon dispassionately. 'I feel no pain,' he says, measuring the sensation as if he were his own experiment.

'Good,' I reply, conversationally.

We pause, and look at each other. We might be at the dinner table and a little short of topics to discuss. I clasp the knife's handle to try and pull it free.

'A strange Excalibur!' Dr Edwards remarks.

It takes a great deal more trouble to remove it than it did to insert the thing.

'I cannot help you,' he says, ruefully, watching my efforts. The weapon is sticky from tip to end and I clean it carefully with my shawl. 'You have cut an artery,' he says.

'Or a vein,' I offer, helpfully.

'No, it is the severed artery causes this eruption,' Dr Edwards explains. He smiles weakly. 'You will have a great deal of my blood on you too, as that is the case. You will have to wash after this.'

I look at my hands and the right one is indeed quite drenched. There is no point in trying to wipe myself clean quite yet. 'Your blood reeks,' I say. I inhale to describe the smell to him accurately. 'It is like iron and vinegar mixed.' He nods, as much as he is able – he is always a stickler for accuracy.

The expression on Dr Edwards' face hardly changes as I lift his shirt and thrust the knife into his chest – a little to the left to avoid his breastbone – and he makes no sound. I replace his shirt as carefully as if I tend to a baby's bedclothes. Then I slice into the other leg.

My butchery is more polished this time and the knife cuts obediently. From the waist down, he is scarlet. Blood spreads across his torso like spilled paint. I watch its steady progress with fascination and wonder where to pierce him next.

'That is enough, child,' he says, as though calling a halt to a particularly taxing lesson to the relief of both teacher and pupil.

'Thank goodness it rained,' I say, climbing off him, and I slide my fingers from palm to tip on the wet ground, leaving foaming pink bubbles on the grass.

'Thank goodness,' Dr Edwards agrees. He sounds almost kindly, as if he is worried about my welfare.

Once more we sit in silence. I had imagined he would succumb almost immediately. It really seems rather rude of him to outstay his welcome by so much. Besides waiting for him to leave, there are no distractions here. I should have brought a book. Perhaps he has something interesting with him in his bag?

He splutters a little and I look at him keenly, but he says 'Not yet,' and we resume our contemplation.

'Anne.' He leans his head towards me as far as his tethered and damaged body will allow. 'I want to tell you something.'

I sigh. 'With what purpose?' I ask, petulantly. 'Do you think I am the right person for your confidence?'

'It is something I have never told anyone and I want to die with my conscience clear,' he says.

'I am to be both your executioner and your priest together, then,' I point out. 'That is a novel appointment.'

He closes his eyes and moans. 'Oh, Annie, I am afraid,' he says softly, 'for it hurts now.' He groans again.

'I am hardly your doctor as well,' I say, tartly. 'What is it you wish to say?'

He clears his throat, and draws in his breath as if he were about to give a sermon. The sound is so wet, I think his blood must be leaking into his chest. 'When my sister and I were young, we often played together. She was younger than I . . .' I frown at him; this sounds like the beginning of a long and tedious narrative. His death and I will fight each other, then, to see who ends it first. 'She had a doll she loved very much,' he continues, ignoring my ill-humour. 'She carried it everywhere, it sat beside her at the table and she slept with it in her cot.' Dr Edwards shakes his head sorrowfully.

'One day, when she had slighted me in her childish fashion, I stole it from her and threw it down the well. The shaft was deep, I did not even hear a splash. She cried so hard because it was lost that they confined her to bed. She became ill with a fever not long afterwards and died within the month. I could not tell anyone what I had done, for I was afraid that I had hastened her death.' His eyes fill with tears, large and round as marbles. 'I believed, in fact, that I had caused it. People *do* die of a broken heart, don't they, Anne? I had surely broken hers.' He closes his eyes, and two fat tears race each other down his cheeks.

'They die more effectively from a stabbing.' I get up. My legs are cramped from sitting still for so long and my skirts are saturated with dew and blood. I look down at him: he sags against the tree and keeps his eyes shut.

'Don't you have a proper confession for me?' I stand with my hands on my hips in front of him. 'You have more to feel guilty about than stolen toys, don't you? Why do you think that we are here and you are dying? Must I explain? You are a thief. You stole my childhood from me then confiscated my education. Then you threatened to remove the one person I care for most. Are you sorry now for your crimes?' He doesn't reply.

'Dr Edwards!' I say more loudly. 'Have you an answer for me?' I shake his bare foot to rouse him; his head lolls heavily on his chest. I study him carefully. He looks somehow changed, although outwardly all of his features and limbs and appendages are the same as they were a moment ago. I half expect him to step from behind the tree, as if he'd left a great stuffed dummy of himself here to fool me. I shake his foot again, but more gently now that I know he will not wake.

I am very disappointed and a little cross with both of us that I missed the exact moment of his death. I had meant to watch for it, to observe the light going out and hear the sigh of his last breath. I wanted to see his calf-eye cloud over. Instead, he is just no longer present.

He certainly cannot cooperate in the untying of the bindings and the releasing of his arms, nor can he comment as I arrange the scene. It is all quite hard to do, and I find I miss his gibes as I fumble, trying to conceal the knife under my bodice and keep from getting more of his blood anywhere else on myself. My shawl is thoroughly ruined so I will have to leave it somewhere as I cannot take it home. A pity, it is a nice one. I take off my sodden petticoat and wipe my hands clean where there is still white cotton. Dressing, I keep watch on Dr Edwards' inert body. Just as he enjoyed the removal of my clothes, so I am relishing putting them back on.

The wind carries shouting from somewhere near the church so I stop what I'm doing and scan the meadow. I see no one, but I had better be quick. I have no idea how long we have been here.

When the clock next chimes, I count each stroke to discover the hour. Ten o'clock! Poor Dr Edwards took an age to depart. *'Never mind "poor" Dr Edwards,'* Fub would say. *'Just cause and just effect. You were judge and jury to him, as well as all your other titles. Go carefully when you leave, remove all traces of yourself. Do not be too hasty. It'll take a while till he's missed, anyway.'*

'Be that as it may,' I would reply, *'But I should hurry to put a distance between me and what's left of him before he's discovered.'*

There is a little black cat on the wall when I go through the gate. It yawns and shows all the inside of its pink mouth. It watches me as I bundle the shawl and petticoat into a ball and hide them under leaves and branches. It arches its back as I stroke along its length then nuzzles into my hand, rubbing its soft head against my palm. 'There's one less living thing in the world now,' I tell it, as it purrs and pushes against me all the more. It is quite at ease with this news, for it has killed a mouse or two in its time. A little death or a big one, it's all the same to us two.

As I turn into the street, I hear in the distance a woman's loud, high cry, as piercing as a fox's scream and full of panic. The people near to me stop abruptly in their tracks. There is no mistaking her urgency, and they begin to run towards the sound.

I walk away slowly and with care, my cat-claws sheathed.

Part Three

Other men's crosses are not mine,
Other men's merits cannot save me.'

John Donne, *Sermons* LXXII

Chapter 21

On my way home, I amuse myself with thoughts of how Dr Edwards will never see these streets again or enjoy his ale any more. He won't return to his lodgings, either – all his things lie as he left them and it's to be hoped they're in good order. Someone will have to clear away his clothes and eat up any food he kept. I expect that boy will get in first and take the best stuff.

I imagine Fub hearing the news in different ways. Sometimes it's Levener with the tidings, at other times I tell him first. Or we hear it together, Fub being astonished that Dr Edwards should have been so fortuitously despatched and me pretending to be surprised, too. 'Oh!' I'd say, 'how is that for a coincidence!' I do not know how I keep from shouting my achievement aloud. If I told anyone about Fub's knife, he'd be shackled to me – which is a sweet notion. But as likely hanged with me, too, which is not. I press my lips together to seal my secrets inside.

If I have a different demeanour now that I have stopped the breath in another, no one in the house remarks on it. They all bustle and stomp or creep about exactly as they did before. I change my dress, for although I have inspected every inch of it and found no trace, I feel as if I drip red gore. The blood on the knife is already brown. I wash it tenderly, scraping with my nails to clean the joint where the blade meets the handle.

I throw my window wide and empty the basin. I wish Fub were here now. All I can see is the bare street and the unclimbed vines. I sit back on my bed, twisting the coverlet to keep my hands busy. Perhaps it is for the best if we don't meet today: if I have murder on my breath, he will surely smell it. But I am so lost without him that I wail softly to myself, keening as if he's dead, too.

My stomach growls, empty. I have not eaten for hours and I run to the kitchen and beg Jane for some bread and fruit. 'That's good to see,' Jane says, watching me eat. 'You were so pale yesterday, I'm glad to see you recovered.' I am hungry enough for two. Perhaps I have taken Dr Edwards' appetite as well as his life. Shovelling food into my mouth, I laugh to myself at how incongruous it is that I sit here in this warm kitchen as if nothing has happened.

'Steady!' Jane pats my back: my laughing has made me choke. I shy away, she's the first person to touch me since Dr Edwards and I cannot help but recoil. Is he found? Where did I put the knife?

'Fub did not come today,' Jane says, watching me carefully. 'Levener himself brought our order.'

I look at her stonily. 'Why should I want to know this?'

'You wanted to be kept informed of household matters.' Jane cannot hide a tiny smile of triumph.

'I did,' I say, crossly. 'but who comes and who does not come is a trifling thing.' I should refrain from saying anything further, but Jane is still twitching and I cannot resist asking: 'Do you know why he didn't come himself?'

Jane is so full of her answer that she swells as if she's about to burst. 'Mr Levener said that Fub's cousin Margaret arrived. He told me that Fub is sweet on her. Mr Levener said it was best to leave them together. He said she is very—'

But I cannot hear her any more. I feel as if I am underwater. I am freezing cold, although I'm by the stove and a fire burns in the grate. Jane speaks to me, but her words distort and I cannot make sense of them. *'Beautiful'* . . . *'since they were children'*. . . *'very sweet-natured.'* On she goes, swimming happily while I flounder and sink. I have only one thought: that I must see him, nothing else matters.

'What did Levener bring today?' I ask, struggling to keep my voice level. She gestures to a linen shroud. When I unwrap it, its meaty contents remind me so forcefully of Dr Edwards' punctured thigh that I gasp. 'Not good enough,' I manage. 'I must tell him.'

'What is the matter with it, Mistress?' Jane hurries after me, but I am resolute and outpace her. 'Not good enough,' I mutter. I do not mean the meat.

The ground sticks to my feet, slowing me down. After the rain, the mud and muck combine to make a thick glue. My shoes are overwhelmed with it, making shire-horse hooves of my feet, and it climbs stealthily up my clothing. What would normally take an hour takes two, and by the time I reach Meek Street, I am weary and sore.

If I had dropped from the skies, Fub could not be more surprised to see me. 'Anne!' he cries, before he remembers he should not use my name unless we are alone.

We are not alone. Summoned by my noisy entrance, a girl stands by him. She blinks when she sees me, then curtseys.

255

Underneath my coating of grime, she can see that my dress is good. 'Mistress Jaccob. Can I . . . can we help you?' Fub says.

He looks from one to the other of us. He does not know which way to turn. The girl and I are like spinning tops. He'll have to run hard between the two of us to keep us moving. Who would he catch if we stopped?

'Indeed you can.' I am in no hurry now. 'Your master delivered an inferior cut to us this morning. Do you know why this happened?'

While he searches for an answer, I look at the girl. Her skin is such a pure white, it's as if she carried a lamp in front of her to illuminate her face. Coils of dark hair fall to her shoulders. Her eyes are set apart and open wide. When she smiles at me, the corners of her mouth turn up to describe a neat half-moon, revealing her pearly teeth. She appears wholly delighted with the world about her. If I stood before her holding a basket of kittens, she could not look more entranced.

'Oh,' she breathes, 'Mistress Jaccob. You must have walked a very long way. Can I fetch you some water?' She has a sweet, small voice, like a child's. You would need to be very close to her to catch everything she says and the closer you got, the further into those blue eyes you'd fall, till you were mired in her syrup. 'I have not been outside today myself, but the rain must have made quite a quagmire of the streets.' Her glance falls to my sodden hem.

'No, thank you. I do not mind a bit of mud.' I greatly wish that I stood here in my finest clothes and had a carriage waiting.

'Frederick says I should be carried everywhere, I have such a dislike of dirt!' The way she calls him by his proper name seems to add inches to his waist and years to his age. 'Ever since we were children,' she continues, 'Frederick could always tease me by threatening to get my clothes messy.'

'Perhaps you could bring a fresh order before nightfall?' I speak to him as if she's not there.

'Before nightfall,' Fub nods.

Margaret begins to plait her hair. As she weaves the thick strands, they loop and twist through her fingers, lithe and black as eels.

With much panting, Levener squeezes through the doorway behind her, Bet following him. Margaret moves towards them as if she is on castors. The hem of her dress sways a perfect inch above the floor.

The butcher stands beside her, so close he'll surely baste her with his fat, and slips one broad arm around her waist. 'Mistress Jaccob!' he squeaks. 'Thus you meet my cousin's daughter. Only let loose in the city because Fub will squire her and keep her from harm.' He closes one porcine eye in a wink.

Bet takes up position on the other side of her: they make a daunting triptych. My teeth are on edge. 'Two little buds, ayee,' Bet sings, looking from Fub to Margaret, admiring them. 'And when he's fully apprenticed, they can ripen together!'

A rush of sweet saliva floods till my mouth is full. My stomach drops as if through a trapdoor and my head feels light. I am going to be sick. I must not empty my guts in front of this doll and these puppets. I hurry outside, muttering a curt goodbye as best I can.

Leaning against a wall, out of sight, I bend double and vomit until I'm empty. I ache all over and feel so tired that if I found a bed in the street, I would lie down on it and fall dead asleep.

Wiping my mouth where sour bile clings, I wait till I am steady on my feet before I set off home.

I hear hurrying footsteps behind me as I walk and gather myself close in case a thief follows, then go more quickly until I am running – but the footsteps keep pace. When I feel a hand on my shoulder, I gasp, but only because I know whose hand stops me. Fub has been running, too, he puts his hands flat on his thighs and bends over to catch his breath.

'Anne! You were as fast as a dog after a hare!' He grabs me and pulls me in to a doorway. We must have all our conversations in lintels or porches, apparently. Both of us are breathing fast.

'What should keep me or slow me down?' I am trying to be cold, but my anger bounces away like spilled apples.

'Anne,' he puts his hands on my cheeks and lifts my face, 'take no notice of that stupid chatter. I am my own man and neither Titus nor Bet nor anyone else will decide my life for me.'

'Are you sure, *Frederick*?' I say. 'She is sweet as a pup and twice as silly. Are you sure you would not like that in your bed tonight?'

He goes to kiss me but shrinks away. 'You smell rank!' He looks at me in disgust.

'Thank you for your sympathy, Fub. I was unwell. I think I must have eaten a maggoty loaf. I am quite recovered now. I shall dine heartily tonight.'

'What is this nonsense about poor meat?' Fub looks sideways at me. 'Were you speaking the truth?'

'I wanted to see you, Fub. Jane told me some tale about your cousin. I was . . . I felt . . .'

'Does Jane think we should replace the order, then?' he shakes his head. 'You had better be careful who you involve with all this.'

'*All this*?' I spit. 'We are not "*all this*", Fub.' I want to cry.

He does not look at me. 'Tell Jane you mistook,' he says, serious and angry. 'I cannot have Levener think he mis-sold you a whole side of beef. Or Jane, either. There's too much business in that. That was fine stock and it has swum and run for miles to get here, too.'

'But will you come to me? Tonight?'

He pauses, rubbing his chin. 'I cannot. Not on account of Margaret, Anne.' He sees me flinch.

'Call her *that girl*, Fub. Or, *my cousin*. But do not use her name to me. It sounds too much like an endearment. Why may you not come?'

Fub is chewing his lip, looking at me as if I were an errant child. 'I must dine with the Leveners,' he says, reluctantly.

'With her, then?'

'Marg— yes, she will be there. It is a long-held arrangement. I cannot come—'

'Stay home, then!' I cut him short. Margaret would not put her lily-white hands on a man's person and stroke him upright, would she? Give her a little knife and see what she does with it: she'd pare an orange, not chop up a man. Fub cannot possibly choose her over me. It would be like taking a monastic vow, she'd be so chaste and pure. I almost tell him what I've done, but there'll be plenty of time for that. Let his world spin as it does for a little while longer before I change its trajectory with a few words.

'We can deny ourselves one night,' I say. 'Next time we meet will be all the better for it.' And I put my hand to him.

He laughs. 'You are bold, we are in the street!' He does not move my hand away but pushes where I rub. I let him grow and thicken, then stop abruptly.

'Enough, now.' And I leave him, laughing at his expression. For the second time today, I touch a man and see on his face that dozy acquiescence, that same succumbing ardour. There was no answer from me to Dr Edwards as he wriggled and squirmed; only when Fub grows do I respond. But it turns out that they are much the same in their appetites, those two.

I look at every man I pass with curiosity and my fingers twitch to tease them. I could easily make trees from all their little acorns. There would be a veritable forest for me to walk home through, if I chose.

It is growing dark. If Dr Edwards has not been moved yet, he will become first stiff, then wet with dew. His little parcel of food will get stale then mouldy. Insects will crawl on to him and make new homes for themselves. How very interested he would have been in these events; how much he would have liked to witness his own decay. He was always the eager scholar.

My father is standing in the hall, next to the fireplace. His face is wet and I wonder if he has come in from a rainstorm, although I know I have just walked through dry streets. I realise then that he weeps. His tears have no separate tracks – instead they course in a wide, steady stream like water over a weir. He raises red, swollen eyes at me. He might have been in a fight, so defeated and bruised does he look.

'Oh, Anne,' he wipes his eyes with his bunched fingertips. 'I have to tell you such a sad and terrible thing.'

I run through a list of potential sorrows. There is only one I can think of that might make him weep. The baby must have died. Infants can perish suddenly while they sleep, with no warning or sickening, can't they? To have two threats to my happiness removed on the same day would seem more than serendipity. If that's the case, I must have strange gods on my side. I prepare to sympathise with this loss, to muse on her little soul being now with the angels and suchlike, when he cries: 'Dr Edwards is murdered!' and I have to stifle my disappointment. Of course, this news has already travelled here.

For a moment, I cannot think of the best thing to say. Should I ask how he was killed? Or who found him?

My father looks at me from under his heavy brow, his face wetter than ever. 'My friend,' he mutters through the downpour. 'To be set upon and dispatched while he rested in a meadow. He was not even robbed. What motive could there possibly have been? He was stabbed through the heart a dozen times!'

How altered this information already is. As one person passed it on to another, each must have embellished what they heard to tell a better tale. They'll have him dismembered and disembowelled before another day's done. I stand by my father and pat his arm. The fabric of his coat is so thick I have to repeat the gesture more forcefully twice before he notices.

'He was such a good tutor to you.' My father inclines his head to me and places his paw over my little mitt; he is already larded with sentiment and enjoying his own performance. 'And a dear friend to me.' Dr Edwards would have been surprised by this epithet: my father has never been a man to whisper endearments to the living. 'Any one of us could be so brutally, cruelly dispatched.' He sniffs violently. It is his own end he fears and mourns, not Dr Edwards'.

Jane comes from the kitchen, holding the frill of her blouse to her face as though she fears breathing in the air around the friend of the deceased. 'Terrible, terrible,' is all she can manage, throwing the words to us like corn to chickens, then scurrying away.

'This is indeed most dreadful,' I say, gravely. 'A fearful death. How are they going to catch the man who did it?'

'They think it must have been several men,' my father replies, his eyes drying now as he gets to the business of the law. 'For he would have fought off a single person. He was not a fragile man, after all.'

But, I think, in a curious way when I slid the knife in he did not resist or cry out my name but rather gave himself up to it. That alone was noble of him at the end. In the future, I might set about raising funds to erect a statue in his memory. It would depict Dr Edwards with his trousers at half-mast, holding a book.

'You smile to remember him, that is good.' My father regards me almost kindly. 'It is well to think fondly of him.'

'I shall think of him often,' I say honestly.

'Anne,' my father speaks ponderously, as though saying his last words. Unfortunately, they are not. 'I have spoken to Onions. We have cleared up the misunderstanding. He will call again.'

I do not trust myself to open my mouth the smallest bit. If I were to make any sound, it would be to shriek like a banshee.

My father takes my silence for acquiescence. 'Good, good. Elizabeth is a silly woman. If there is a wrong way of doing things, she'll take it. She was ever thus,' he inclines his head, as though what he tells me is benign. 'I know you are fearful of marriage, but when the time comes . . .'

I leave him while he is still speaking. Let him speculate on my feelings. He will never know what they are, but fearfulness is not on the list of possibilities.

My mother joins us for dinner and we all three sit in silence. My father is wallowing in his grief, indulging each heavy sigh and shake of his head. For once, Jane does not have to suffer his comments and something like peacefulness blankets the room.

I am not calm. How can it be that I decided to take a man's life, then executed him quite neatly all by myself, and yet I cannot choose my own future? I have a fierce headache, so I peck at my food. After my mother has excused herself and while my father pours himself more wine, I bundle a piece of pie into my skirt to have later, when I feel better.

All is still and shuttered and I am eating alone in my room, when the house is almost lifted from its foundations by a scream. Brushing grease from my hands and wiping my mouth, I hurry out on to the landing.

On the floor above stands Jane, in her nightgown. Her shoulders rise and fall with her gasping breath as she sobs and shakes. Grace attempts to comfort her. 'Ssshhh,' she murmurs, tucking Jane's hair into her nightcap as tenderly as you console a wakeful, frightened child.

I pause for a moment, listening for any other sound in the house, but the noise has only woken me. 'What on earth is the matter, Jane?' I ask, climbing the stairs with speed.

She mutters something, pointing into the dark corner of the stairwell.

'What did she say?' I ask Grace, hoping to get more sense from her.

'She says she saw a ghost,' Grace says and both women cling to each other as if the spectre rose again.

'Who would haunt the house? Is it Dr Edwards who has come?

What does he want here?' I look nervously about; perhaps he will write my guilt with his dead hand.

'Dr Edwards?' Grace looks thoroughly bemused. 'I don't know who that is. No, she saw your grandmother, as was recently deceased.'

'She walked out of the wall,' Jane says. 'All pale and wan, she was.'

'Whatever you saw, it was not her ghost, Jane.' I feel my shoulders sink with relief. 'She will have better things to do in the next life than scuttle round trying to frighten you in this one.' I hear Grace laugh quietly.

'Why would you think Dr Edwards would haunt us?' Jane asks me, suddenly brisk. 'He has his own family to visit.' She must imagine the dead with a list of addresses, ticking off each one as they call on them.

'I was thinking of the person most recently gone and so violently taken, that's all. My grandmother lived a good life and died well; her spirit won't be restless. But a murdered man can't be at peace so easily, can he? If anyone was going to roam, it would be him.'

'Come back to bed, Jane.' Grace guides her gently back to the little room they share.

Alone in the darkness, I shudder, though I am not afraid of Dr Edwards in death any more than I was when he was alive.

Chapter 22

My father is to attend Dr Edwards' funeral. Of course, I may not go, but I decide to walk by the graveyard at the hour of his interment, to see how many and what kind of people mark his passing. The air is unseasonably cold; winter seems to be giving autumn short shrift and promises frosts and ice before too long. The mud is rising from the road in hard, thick ridges and I have to clamber over them. Making my way like this is tiring and I have to watch my step constantly lest I slip.

Ahead of me, although similarly struggling with the terrain, a boy walks more briskly. He has on a red waistcoat, wearing it over his jacket as it is much too big for him. Something about the colour and cut of it is familiar. With a start, I realise it belonged to Dr Edwards. He wore it on the day of the fair; I had to walk the long route home beside it after he'd sent Fub packing.

'Oy!' I call to him.

He turns, his little fists up ready for a challenge if needs be. He nods when he sees me. 'Dr Edwards' friend,' he says, in that grown up voice of his. 'Dr Edwards as was. Late of this parish. Did you hear of his awful, terrible fate?'

'It's lucky I did, otherwise you'd be telling me in a strange and jaunty way.'

'I'm not speaking ill of him, only being factual.' He looks at me carefully, as if deciding how to proceed. 'Do you want to come to his lodgings, Mistress? You might like a keepsake, as you knew him well.'

'Is there anything left?' I indicate his garb.

He looks down at it, disdainfully. 'No one else would want this. It's still got his victuals stuck on it. I'm only wearing it to keep me warm from place to place.'

'Have others picked over his belongings?' We fall in step, as much as we can, as we go over all the little hills and dried runnels.

The boy shoots me a knowing glance. 'He did not have visitors. The law has been, to see if his murderer came there and whether they walked out together. But he went off alone. I saw him go.'

'Did he say anything?' Careful now. I must not appear too inquisitive. 'What was his farewell?'

'He only said that it was a good day for a meeting.' The boy jumps from one ridge to another. He is only a child, playing. 'Oof!' he shouts, as he lands hard. 'Then I told *him* that he looked sparky.'

'Sparky?' How long did they converse, this spit of a boy and the victim. Did the boy go with him some of the way while Dr Edwards babbled about books and lessons? About me?

'He was sprightly and in good humour, that's all.' The boy stops, staring at me, that mess of hair at the back of his head caught upright by the chill wind. He looks petulant. 'I am telling all the same answers to you that I told to the law. It seems to me that it doesn't matter much whether he skipped or limped, he went to his death all the same.'

'Quite the little philosopher.' We're at the lodging house now.

Two men stand outside it. They talk to each other and seem uninterested in who comes and goes. Nevertheless, I hesitate, not wanting to be questioned.

'Family friend.' The boy throws his thumb over his shoulder, indicating me. The men stand aside. I don't meet their eyes, but put my hand to my face like a shield.

'Who are those men?' I puff up the stairs behind him; he is taking them two at a time.

'Bailiffs,' he growls. 'Better get through this quick before they follow.'

The room is in disarray. Whether Dr Edwards unsettled everything before he left, or if someone has searched for clues, I cannot tell, but there is not a single tidy spot. A huge swathe of different cloths lies in an untidy heap. I pull some of them apart between finger and thumb with distaste – they certainly do not smell of the laundry. They are items of bedding and clothing all jumbled together. His books and papers are similarly strewn over every surface. I pick up an illustrated page where it lies face up on the table. It is one of the papers he came armed with, that day he sat beside me and took my childish hand to him. It shows a couple playing cards, the lady holding hers to her chest while her suitor spreads his hand out in a fan. If we had just played cards together, Dr Edwards, then you might be coming back to your room soon. And the first thing I'd advise you to do is tidy it.

'Did he do this?' I ask.

The boy shrugs, the corners of his mouth turning down in disapproval. 'He started it. And when the others came to look, they saw how it was and so they did not take much care how they went.' He picks up and drops several items in quick succession.

267

'Leave them!' He jumps at my harsh tone. 'He may not come back for them, but we should still be careful.'

'Bit late for that.' The boy moves a book on the floor with his foot. '*The Memoirs of a Lady of Pleasure* by John Cleland,' he reads aloud awkwardly, giving the 'h' of John a jolt like a cart in a rut and sounding each word so slowly that it's hard to hear the sense of it. He catches my eye and blushes. 'My reading isn't too clever yet.' He is embarrassed about his skill, not the book's content. 'I am – I *was* – still learning.'

'Who was teaching you?' But as I ask, I know the answer.

'Your man Edwards,' he says and suddenly he looks stricken. 'Oh, that's brought it home. Oh, that's really brought it home.' He clears a little space on the floor and sits there. 'You have a look,' he says magnanimously, opening his arms to the room.

'I have no need of that book; we have a copy at home.' I begin to ferret amongst Dr Edwards' possessions. How sad they are without their owner to make sense of their existence. Jotted on a little scrap of paper, in his thick, cramped hand – so dense the 'o's are filled in like full moons – is a list of people he'll never see again. Is this man, 'Jonah', a friend or a scholar? Does 'Evan' know he has died? I am about to pocket it when I realise I should take nothing that might link me to this room and that man. Whatever I remove, should I see anything worth having, must be an object without connection. I touch the things near to me lightly in turn, as if I'm blessing them.

The boy puts a broad-brimmed hat on his head and shrinks his chin to his shoulders, then sways from side to side in an impression of Dr Edwards' rolling gait. 'Where am I?' he says. 'Now I am gone?'

I round on him. 'Did you hear me, boy? I told you that you should not mock the dead.'

He stops his swaying but he doesn't take off the hat. Instead he peeps at me from underneath it as if it's a lady's bonnet. 'Fond of the old fellow, weren't you?' His eyes are in shadow, but I feel his sharp gaze.

'I knew him a little, that's all,' I say sourly. 'I want nothing here. I will leave now.'

'Penny for my trouble?' He holds his hand out. The lines on his palm are stained dark black. If you were to tell him his fortune from reading them, you'd have an easy task. I can tell without looking that his life-line is very short.

'Penny for what trouble? For bringing me to this ragbag room?'

'He said he was meeting you.' The room chills. He has thrown this over me like cold water and I shiver. 'I asked where he was going, with all his books ready, and he said: "I am *reunited*, Adam dear" (that's how he spoke to me), "I am *reunited* with a pupil that I thought most highly of. But I have not had the pleasure of teaching Miss Jaccob for some time".'

'You remember very clearly.' I speak as evenly as I can, though my mind races. 'That is very . . . impressive. Dr Edwards must have been delighted to have you as a pupil, too.' His mouth twists into a small smile. 'Did you . . .' I am almost on tiptoe in anticipation of his answer '. . . *tell* anyone? Dr Edwards and I were most keen to keep our lessons secret.'

The hat lifts. His small eyes gleam. 'Why should they be a secret?'

'We were rehearsing . . . oh!' I pause and dab at my dry eyes, as if tears fall, 'a recitation for my father's birthday. I knew my father loved a particular poem and I knew, too, that Dr Edwards

– he more than anyone else – could teach me to perform it. But of course we should not tell anyone, in case my father heard of it and his surprise was spoiled. Oh, he shall not hear it now! And I will never be able to read it again without . . . sorrow.' My words trail away, brushing the boy like feathers.

He turns all this over in his head, his little brow furrowing with effort. It is quite possible that some folk might skulk around not to do wrong but rather to learn verses, but he's puzzled as to why. 'Queer,' he announces. 'Worth a few pence not to inform those gentlemen, though. They might want to hear this tale from you, mightn't they?'

He has caught my panic; my insouciance has not fooled him.

'You are a most resourceful boy. A most promising boy, too. I hate to think of all Dr Edwards's teaching coming to naught. He spoke so highly of you. He indicated he might raise you, if not exactly as his *son*, then as a *protégé*.' He wriggles uncomfortably, not knowing if that would have been a good thing or a bad one, but not liking to be considered for the role anyhow. 'Perhaps you and I should continue?' I step towards him, holding out my hand.

'I have had enough of all that. I can read sufficient.' He gets to his feet. I want to cling to his knees so that he may not leave. Or get ahead of him and lock him in. But he is a wily snip and knows he has something precious to me. Our paths might not cross again if I do not snare him now.

'I have no money,' I say, not taking my eyes from his face. 'But I should like to reward you, as you suggest. I know where some is kept. A great deal of it, just there for the taking.'

The boy stops as if his path were snagged by brambles. 'Why should you tell me that?' he frowns, 'I am not a common thief that I need to know about hidden coin.'

'It is not fair that Dr Edwards, who might have lived to be your benefactor, should be taken without the opportunity to provide for you.' I step towards him, putting my hands on his shoulders. They are so small my fingers almost meet at his neck.

Again, he wriggles. 'That's heavy,' he protests, ducking out from under my grasp. His cornflower-blue eyes are perfect, almost lidless half circles. In the corner of each there is a dot of yellow crust. No mother wipes his sleep from him, then.

'I am only suggesting that the parish might take care of you.'

'The parish?' he says, suspiciously, as if it were another word for gaol. 'I don't need taking care of. I get pretty far on my own.'

'Of course,' I soothe. It is tricky to find the way in to him, but I will. 'And all I will do is point you to where the money is – it is honest money, given by the folk hereabouts to aid those in need – and you can consider how you might proceed.'

He puts the toe of one shabby boot over the over and stands, twisted and wobbling. 'You talk fancy, like he did. I hope *you* know what you're saying, I'm not sure I follow.' He extends his arms to keep his balance, catching his lower lip in his teeth in concentration. I copy him, crossing my legs as he does and when he sees me he bridles, then laughs when I stumble and fail to keep upright.

'You are better than I at this game,' I say.

'Try this!' he stands on one leg. I do. 'And this!' He leaps on to the other. I oblige. But I cannot hop about all day, for when I have sorted this child, I must see Fub.

Fub! He has been unaccountably out of my thoughts. Now he is returned as swiftly and deeply as darkness at the day's close. Margaret takes shape, too, at first shadowy but becoming more substantial by the moment. I try to shrug her off, but she resists.

Her phantom person is, if anything, more awful than her cor-
poreal form. She clings to him like a creeper and douses us both
in her sweet sticky sap. With a thrill of fear, sharp as if I stood
barefoot on a flint, I realise I cannot see Fub's face clearly. His
brown hair, his mismatched eyes and his wide mouth are all
separate, like cut-outs for a collage, and I am unable to assemble
the whole.

'Mistress?' the boy pokes my side. 'Have you stopped playing?'

'We should not be merry here, it is a shrine of sorts. We must
leave.' I push him by the shoulder and he goes to the door: he
is angry that we don't play more but he's enough of a child to
obey orders. 'Meet me at the side of the house,' I instruct. The
men keeping guard outside should not see us leave together. 'Is
there a door at the back?' He nods. 'Then go out from there.
Let us race to be quickest!'

He leaps to the challenge, but I remain alone for a moment,
regarding Dr Edwards' sorry possessions. I should like to take
a book, for I am starved of them, but there is a pervading
dampness in the air and it occurs to me that they will all begin
to rot soon, like their owner, and that any I took would soon
be pulp.

'You walk so slowly! You are a snail!' Triumphant, the boy
waits. I should have bet him a penny I would win, to keep him
sweet.

I smile at him. 'You are quick in every way,' I tell him. He
smiles back. He hopes that he'll get a better reward than my
words before too long. I let him walk a little behind me, anxious
that no one thinks us close companions. Several times, I have
to wait as he is easily distracted: he kicks stones or watches
laden carriages, challenges himself to hop some of the way or

pretends to hide. I want to grab him roughly, inflicting pain and urging him to keep up with me, but when I look at his head, the tousled hair and his small ears pink with cold, I think that my brother might well have grown to be such a child and so I should be kind to this one, for his last moments.

I do not know when my plan formed, but perhaps after all my long hours calculating how to dispatch Dr Edwards, these things are coming more easily to me. The words of the vicar: *a high tower, a glassless window,*' suggest themselves, as if they are the pages of a book that falls open at a marked spot.

'A church!' the boy looks disappointed at our destination. 'There's no money in 'em.'

'Oh, but there is,' I put my finger to my lips in a pantomime of demanding silence. 'Wait here. I must see if the way is clear.'

He picks up a stone and, taking aim, lobs it at a grave. 'Bullseye!' he cries, delighted, as it hits the target. Poor Amy Croft lying underneath. I hope she's not too disturbed. I leave him to his game.

As ever, no one walks through the churchyard. There is no one about inside either and when I push open his study door – ready with a question about the christening, should I need it – the vicar is not there. A plate of biscuits waits for his return. The empty rows of pews gape and the aisles and arches have an expectancy about them, as if they would all quickly cope with being occupied. Only the altar is calm, the surrounding statues sightless and unquestioning. There are several doors behind, but two are locked. The third leads straight to a winding spiral of steps.

The boy insists on throwing several more stones at the hapless memorials before he deigns to follow me. The tower echoes with our footsteps as we begin climbing the many stairs. The air very quickly feels thin. We walk in silence; there is nothing to discuss.

'Where is the treasure hid?' he says at one point, but my powers of invention are muffled by my exertions so I pretend not to hear him. 'It's too high!' the boy protests, panting, his little chest rising and falling in his exertion.

'Very!' I agree.

'Oh, I cannot go on. I die!' He leans heavily against the wall, clutching himself in mock anguish.

'You need not climb any further, then,' I say, turning as if to go back down. 'That is a shame, for I had tuppence ready for you if you could.'

'I can! I can!' he wheels about and starts to run up the stairs. White plaster lifts from the walls as we pass and once a bee flies at us. No other living thing makes its home here. There are no webs or droppings. In the turret, the wind blows cross ways and cuts the room with cold. Above us, the heavy bells hang silent, their thick, striped ropes secured by hooks on the wall. I am tall enough to see out of the glassless windows, but the boy cannot. He looks about him, more in perturbation than anger.

'Why have you made me come here?' The room is bare, he begins to be suspicious. 'There is nothing hid. There is nothing at all.' He is almost crying.

'I will show you where the money is kept when we descend. I thought you might be interested in the view.' I turn away and look out. Far below, the people are small as insects and wind their way between the buildings and around each other without ever looking up. 'You can see St Paul's,' I say, but I know that won't get him to the window.

'I can see St Paul's on the ground any day,' he says. He seems smaller in here than he did in the streets.

I look out of the window again, then turn back to him, clapping my hand to my mouth. 'Oh!' I say. 'Mercy!'

'What is it?' He perks up, bobbing and jumping to try and see. I look out again and giggle. 'My! In the street!'

'What? What?' He is at my waist, attempting to use me as a ladder.

'There is a man and a woman . . . no, you should not see that!'

'See what?' he comes nearer, his anger and upset are both completely forgotten. 'What do they do?'

'They do in broad daylight what they should be doing in their bed.'

He grins. This is the prize for his mountaineering. 'I know what that means. I want to see it.'

I stand away from the window and wave my hand to him, pointing the way with a florid curl of my hand, like a courtier to a princeling. 'You can try,' I say.

'I cannot reach!' On his tiptoes, he springs as high as he can. 'Lift me up! Lift me up!'

Of course, I do. I put my hands under his little feet and raise him against the sill. His boots are more holes than leather. His clothes smell of musk and beer.

He scrabbles at the wall frantically to get higher. He is waist level to the opening now, halfway to the drop. 'I do not see them. Which way should I look?'

'In front of you.' I lift him higher.

He begins to struggle, seeing the ground below more clearly and more nearly than he wants to. His legs kick where I hold him and his hands flail to get back in, but he is no match for me. His short, hard life has left him ill fed and weak. He is saying something, but as I have no intention of replying, I make no effort to decipher it. Straightening my arms, I thrust him up and through the gap in the bricks. He falls away.

There is a pleasing symmetry in that he leaves the world head first, just as he came in to it. He had little time to cry, but someone on the ground shrieks loudly for him. There might be a commotion beginning afterwards, but it mingles indistinctly with all the other street noises. I would like to see what is happening but I dare not – even if they have never noticed it before, everyone will be looking up at this tower now.

My arms feel newly light without their burden but my hands are black with holding his boots. I spit on them and rub with the underside of my dress, doing my best to get them clean.

I descend the steps – so many of them! – with uncomfortable haste, tripping several times and cursing. Two broken necks in the vicinity would be very unfortunate. Going endlessly round and round in the confined space makes me queasy. There is only one pair of feet coming back down where he and I strode up together and my shoes scuff the stone with a soft *shush*. Eventually, I fling myself into one of the pews, sinking to my knees and clasping my grubby hands in prayer. My heart thumps; the effort of climbing and shoving has taxed me greatly. I am really quite envious of poisoners, who only have to lift a little vial to get their work done.

'Do not let Fub love that girl,' I say to my plaster companions, those several saints. 'How can she be to him what I am? Her button mouth would not open wide and take in his bone to suck at it for the marrow. She would not let his finger go inside her or his tongue either. She would be as solid and smooth below as china.'

Behind me the great door of the church is opened violently, crashing against the wall and shaking its locks and bolts. The vicar runs in, stopping in his tracks when he sees me. His collar is loose and flapping. He wrings his hands. 'Most dreadful!' he exclaims.

I get to my feet. 'Sir, you look as though all the horrors of the world pursue you.'

'Only one, but the worst.' He sinks down. He tries to speak several times, but buries his head in his hands instead. Finally, he turns to me. 'A small boy, no more than ten, I would say, appears to have fallen from the bell tower.'

From my vantage point standing over him, I examine the top of his head. A ring of hair surrounds a patch of pale, bare skin, like a clearing in the forest. As before, when my father wept to tell me of Dr Edwards' departure, I am deliberating what my next sentence should be. I choose: 'Is he dead?'

The vicar looks startled. 'Oh, Mistress Jaccob. The tower is very high. Of course, there is no reason why you should know how far he fell, but suffice it to say he is . . . quite dead.'

'Will he be buried here?' I ask, conversationally. This man was not related to the boy, after all, he should not mind such a practical enquiry.

'I do not even know who he is!' The vicar rises abruptly. 'There is a great deal to be done before anyone can think of funerals.' Who he *was*, I think, but I hold my tongue. 'His family must be found and informed.' The vicar commences his hand-wringing again.

That will take some searching, I imagine. He would appear to have lived a solitary life. Perhaps a few folk might notice that they have not seen him for a while, but they will most likely think it briefly and not even say it aloud to anyone. The waters will close over his head and any ripples fade quickly enough. It will soon be almost as if he were never here.

'Does he lie outside still?'

At this, the vicar gives me a curious glance, as if I were suddenly not the person he thought he had been speaking to. 'He does, poor child. He is covered. With my cloak,' he adds. He continues to look hard at me. 'Did you see him come in?'

The church holds its breath for my answer.

'I did not. I was on my knees. My dear grandmother is recently . . . departed. I came here to pray for her.'

'Yes, of course,' he exhales, reminded of the purpose of the building.

'There were some others here,' I offer. 'But we did not converse.'

He reassembles himself as a man of the church, adjusting his collar and straightening his shoulders. 'I trust you found comfort,' he says, though the unkind world pulls at his sleeve, wanting to question his certainty of God's presence in the face of such unfairness.

'As I always do,' I say, bowing my head. If I am not too late, there is another death and funeral I am interested in.

'I shall see you on the morrow, in happier circumstances.' He extends his arm to me.

As I did before, I shrink away. I am too-reminded of dead flesh by his living hand. Besides, I fear my hasty ablutions have not quite erased the dirt there, so I put my hands in my shawl, out of reach. I had quite forgotten the christening, but I have no interest in it now that I'm reminded. Pretending to bill and coo over that baby would not suit my mood.

*   *   *

Only a few stragglers stand about near the fresh mound of Dr Edwards' grave; my father is not among them. They converse in brisk, loud tones and are making plans for the evening. The reason for their gathering is quite forgotten – they are even turned away from him.

Apart from this robust circle stands a girl. She weeps with her head bowed and her large shoulders heave up and down. I stand beside her – she is of a substantial build and serves as a windbreak as well as a companion. In time, she may question my presence with the customary chitchat of the bereaved, but for now she keeps her face buried as efficiently in her handkerchief as Dr Edwards is concealed underground.

When she eventually acknowledges me, giving me the small, brave smile of shared loss, I see that she is quite the ugliest creature I have seen in a long while. I gasp but, fortunately, her spluttering is loud enough to drown out any other noise. Her skin is florid: dark veins snake in large numbers across her already red face and even her forehead is loudly pink. But had she a porcelain complexion, her features would deny her any chance of beauty. Her eyes are set very close together – only the unusually protruding bridge of her nose keeps them apart. Her thin mouth fights for occupation of her large chin. There are two sharp indentations on either side of her nose, as if her Maker pushed his fingers there while she was still soft.

'He was a good man,' I say, concentrating on the heap of dirt that marks him, to avoid inspecting her further.

'Did you know him well?' She stops crying, mopping her eyes

then pushing the sodden rag up her sleeve. She seems grateful to be able to share her grief.

'For a little while I saw him often. He was my tutor when I was a child.'

'He has, or I should say, he *had*, not had any pupils for a while, I think,' she says, sniffing loudly. 'Latterly, he rather doubted himself. His memory had begun to fail.'

This is a revelation. I think of the boy, his last student, left confident that he could read after only a little tuition. Dr Edwards gave no sign of a man in turmoil. He accepted my invitation to resume our lessons easily enough. If he hesitated, it was surely only in anticipation of my father's wrath. Who is this woman who can speak for Dr Edwards' state of mind?

'And were you a friend to him?' I do not want to look her full in the face when I speak to her. I feel truly sorry she must venture daily in the world with such an affliction, her appearance is so disconcerting.

'More than a friend, I suppose. Although I would have relished his friendship, for he had the most marvellous mind and possessed a rare degree of loyalty. I am his daughter.'

How I keep from expostulating, I do not know. As the snail shell cracks to reveal its viscous contents, so this information spills stickily from her. I stare at the earth where he is buried as if I could summon him to explain himself. I'd like to drag him from his hole and scoop the dirt from his mouth so he could speak. There were better confessions he could have made to me than all that nonsense about dolls, weren't there? Does he leave a widow?

'Where is your mother?' It is best to be bald with the enquiry. I look across to where the other mourners cluster. 'I thought he lived alone.' There was certainly no indication of a woman's hand in his hovel of a room. 'I was only a child when he taught me, but he never mentioned a wife.'

'They were not . . .' she leans in to whisper, ' . . . married.' She pauses to see if I am shocked and I nod to encourage her both that I am not and that she should continue. 'They never even shared a house. My mother told me she had shouted through his open window to tell him that she carried his child, and he yelled back that he would provide for me, in return. With the regular stipend came letters to me and, when I was old enough, I wrote back to him.'

I want to laugh at the naked absence of romance or poetry in the tale. The girl would appear to be of the same years as I. Surely he was reminded of his epistolary child whenever he saw me? However more deserved does Dr Edwards' fate seem now.

'My mother was an unhappy woman. I'm afraid she drank to alleviate her sadness. She died many years ago.' That is more like it. Only a rolling drunkard would lie down easily under him.

I touch her arm in condolence. 'I am sorry you have lost him, then. I am especially saddened by the manner of his death.'

At this she weeps. 'How did you hear of it?' She grabs her kerchief again and turns it over to find a dry corner. 'He must have suffered so!'

'My father told me. They kept company sometimes. He always spoke well of him.' In this instance, the posthumous eulogy my father spoke only once will have to stand for 'often'.

'I have not seen him for many years. His letters were so beautiful, I shall miss them very much! !' She breathes in deeply. 'He would not see me. I think he was ashamed – although whether of himself or of me, I could not say.' She sighs and I cannot tell if she alludes to her bastard state or her physiognomy. There is much to bewail about both. She turns to me with an eager expression. 'Did you call on him frequently? Did he live well?'

I balance her happiness on the palm of my hand, as though I toss a coin. If it lands truth-side up she leaves miserable. The other way is a happy falsehood. I am not given to spontaneous acts of charity, neither is speaking well of Dr Edwards my due, but I wish this unhappy girl no more ill than the world has doled out already.

'I have not encountered Dr – your father – since I was a small child. He was always extremely dapper then. Very smartly turned out, that I do recall.' She smiles happily at this spruce and spry vision of her father. How strangely easy it is to lie. Like a parasite on its host, my falsehoods take their nourishment from being believed and gain more strength.

'He was inspiring,' I say, 'and scarcely a day goes by without me remembering what he taught me.'

'Thank you for coming,' is all she says, but her tears have dried. She turns away from me and regards his grave with solemn zeal.

How little each plot begins to describe their owner. The boy will soon lie under just such a pile of turned earth as Dr Edwards does, with no sign either of his living vigour or size.

Thus dismissed, I can leave. I ought to go home. I have a christening to talk my way out of.

Chapter 23

The streets are strangely emptied, as sometimes happens, as
though everyone but me has been ordered inside by curfew.
Once or twice though, I have the sensation of being observed,
but I will not humour it by turning round. I am happy rifling
in the store cupboard of my head, counting and sorting and
planning.

Dr Edwards and the boy were gone as easily as flicking crumbs
from a sleeve, but Margaret clings as closely as ivy. Do not let
it be that she keeps her grip tight with Fub's help. My nostrils
fill with acrid smoke: someone is burning a rank lump of meat
over a brazier. I still have the stench about me when I get to
Meek Street. I sniff at the cloth of my shawl and, sure enough,
the smell already seems to be woven into the material. The last
time I saw him, Fub was revolted by the reek of me. He won't
be enchanted now, either, will he?

I am still disconcerted by how vague Fub's face is to me when
I try and conjure it. I cannot summon my desire for him either.
It would be easier to recall a dream and they are slippery things.
This is ill-timed, when I have gone so far in removing obstacles
to our being together. With a great effort of will, I succeed in
remembering his fingers going in, thinking of how he licked

them to make their journey easier. Before long I have a pleasant, heavy sensation where they went. I will see his face soon enough, to complete the picture.

I hesitate to go in, lest the Leveners line up inside, stupid as cattle in their pen.

Fub is at the counter, working away at something as he did when I first saw him here. He is alone. I stare at him, wondering why I am not immediately glad to see him. It is as if I carry my feelings in a glass case and I dare not try and touch them, lest it shatters in my hands.

When he sees me, he bursts out laughing. 'You look as angry as if you had a storm cloud over your head while everyone else enjoyed sunshine! You have soot on you.' He gestures to his own nose to show me where I'm smudged. 'My hands are bloody, else I'd wipe your dirty face.' I must have failed, as I had feared, to clean off the grime. He gives me a cloth, already stiff with gore.

'I need water,' I say, 'to do this properly.'

He pauses. Thoughts cross his face like scudding clouds. 'Upstairs,' he says, then he walks from the shop, not looking to see if I follow. I do.

I almost have to duck my head under the lintel of the doorway beyond the slaughter yard. A neat parlour gives way to a tiny hall; anyone passing another here would either have to squeeze in tight or give way. It must be a struggle for that man-mountain Levener to walk through. An assortment of hats hang on hooks on the wall. He must fell them like a scythe winnowing corn, every time he brushes past them. Ahead of us, a narrow, steep flight of steps bends away and out of sight. All these places are diminutive in scale. I do not see one room where I could even stretch my arms wide without almost touching both sides. The walls are bare. Not a single picture, nor an ornament of any sort, breaks their plain surfaces.

Fub himself is too big for the corridor and, when we get to his room, he dwarfs the little cabinet and tiny bed, the only furniture he has. There is not even a glass to see yourself in. He does at least have a jug and basin and he pours some water for me. Rejecting the half-bloodied cloth he offers, I dip the edge of my shawl and moisten my face. Without a mirror, Fub has to reflect back to me whether or not I am successful.

He lets me wipe away at myself a good while before he pronounces: 'Clean!' and I can stop. He stares at me for what seems just as long afterwards, without speaking. I am in no mood to start a conversation.

'Anne,' he begins, but then he stares again. 'There is no one in the house.' He raises his eyebrows at me and gestures, indicating his bed with an extravagant sweep of his arm.

'Are you wooing me?' I say. 'Then I had better warn you that I am not so easy as to lie down just because you pointed to your bed.'

Then he kisses me and proves me wrong – I am very quick to lie down after all. There follows an episode of putting and taking and sighing and moaning, both reassuringly the same, and delightfully different, as before.

* * *

Looking at him afterwards, his face so close I can see the shadows of his lashes on his cheek and the reddened insides of his nose, I am as full as if I'd feasted and I am calm without wanting sleep.

'When we are together always, we shall have a bed as big as France!' I say, happily.

Fub groans and puts one hand over my mouth. 'Shush your chatter,' he says, 'do not spoil this for talk of an impossibility.'

I feel a tiny shard of fear, thin as an icicle and twice as cold, start in my stomach and reach sharply up to my heart. 'Don't say it is impossible,' I chide, but it is too late. He props himself up on one elbow to look at me and his face is as serious as if he had bad news to impart.

'We cannot be together, Anne. You know that.' He softens what he says when he sees my expression. 'I thought you knew. I did not think you were enough of a child to believe in fairy stories. I cannot be your prince just because you kissed me.'

'I love you,' I say, 'that is magic enough.' I wait for him to agree, but instead he sighs. We are players in different scenes, each holding a script the other does not recognise.

'You cannot eat magic.' Fub sounds weary at having to explain. 'Or pay bills with it. Your family would cut you off without a penny and I'd lose my living, that is the truth.'

Can Fub not see how resourceful I am, how I could provide for both of us with my wits? I can prove my love and my cunning.

'Fub,' I say, holding his gaze. 'Dr Edwards is dead.'

He frowns, waiting for an explanation.

'He was murdered. Stabbed to death,' I continue. 'So he cannot inform my father about us. That is one problem less, isn't it?'

'Wait.' Fub sits upright, putting his bare feet on the floor with a heavy slap. He leans his elbows on his thighs and begins rubbing his temples with his fingertips. 'You do not know who killed him, or how or when he died, do you? He may already have spoken about us. Or written it down like a confession.' He circles his fingers on his forehead all the more.

I am not so sure of myself now. Why does he throw these strange ideas like scattered pins in my path? He must need to have it spelled out, to erase all doubt before he can celebrate.

'Fub, I killed him.'

He looks momentarily aghast, as though I'd winded him. Then he gets his breath back and laughs. 'Oh.' He shakes his head, then swallows. 'Anne!' He squeezes my shoulders, as if we were jesting friends. 'You are a doll! I believed you, almost, for a moment.' He works his jaw; he is curious. 'How did he really die, then? Run over by a carriage? Did his heart give out? I would not be surprised, it must have had a great deal of work to do, to get blood round that gross body.'

I thought he would react with glee, that he might swing me up in his arms and call me his clever little darling. Tears of wounded pride spring to my eyes. Looking at him as he describes to himself the possible ways Dr Edwards departed this life, I realise that even if I gave him chapter and verse of my killing, he'd pat my head and say 'Of course!' all the while thinking I was only a mistress of invention. If I added the exit of Adam at my hand to my catalogue, he'd slap his thighs in mirth.

'But you gave me a knife,' I say.

He smiles, still enjoying the joke. 'Oh, that is very good.' He blows air out of his cheeks, regarding me like a performing animal that has just tried a new trick. 'Very good.'

'Perhaps I could prove I did it,' I say,' With another murder.'

'Anne, enough. We are playmates, you and I. We mustn't question the future, we shouldn't ask anything of each other. That way, we can have our *fun*,' he smooths the bedcover as he speaks, 'and nobody suffers.'

'Margaret could suffer,' I say quietly.

Fub flinches as if I'd whipped him. He grabs my wrist. He is not playful any more. 'Stop it!' he says, holding me harder, 'I know that you are young, that you say things you do not mean because you do not know their power. But hear this: I do not love Margaret. I love you. That is how it is for the present. But I cannot love you always and, who knows, I might have to love her in the future.'

I wish I was hard as stone, so that his words would bounce off me. Instead I am soft and porous as moss.

'You cannot ever love her,' I say, my protesting voice high and thin. 'Why do you say that?'

He lets me go, then strokes my arm where he gripped me. 'Anne, don't make me say these things.' He cups my chin with his hand and tilts my face up to him. 'I don't think of the future. I hardly consider two days hence. But this is the truth: Margaret and I weigh equally in the scales. She knows the price of things. She won't bother me with books. My family will take her to their hearts and hearth. Levener will give me a position and so it goes on. You and I cannot be together anywhere where you are known, even if your father gave you money to live on, which he would not. If it isn't Onions, it's somebody else's big house you'll live in and whose large purse you'll spend. You'd quickly tire of going hungry and having no change of clothes. And you'd be wanting your own soft bed after a very short while in this one.' He pats the coarse, hard mattress to demonstrate. *'Margaret could suffer,'* he mimics in a childish treble. 'I don't like to hear you pretending to be evil.' He kisses my forehead. 'When you are wicked underneath me, though, I like it very much! This much!'

He grapples with me and, although I do not resist, I am like a rag doll, flung this way and that. He quits me before the end and I feel his spilling and watch his gurning dispassionately. With a shock as hot as fire, I feel a flash of distaste for all this careless fluid and his awkward limbs. I kiss his mouth and neck till I am blind and deaf to any doubt.

*   *   *

When we lie tangled afterwards, I examine him carefully. I know his broad forehead and his blemished eye very well. If he stuck his arm through a fence and I could not see the rest of him, I would know it was his. If I flew over him, I would be able to pick out the top of his head amongst a crowd of others. But if I was asked if he preferred berries to apples, I could not answer. Neither do I know his childhood fears or his first words. The house where he grew up is a mystery; his favourite toy is unknown. We have never talked of our families, except to mock them to each other for effect. I could not tell you how he decided on his trade or if he chooses summer heat over winter chill. I only know how he likes his mouth kissed and that he wants my fingers on his sack while he finishes.

I will not ask him anything now. He believes he has happily silenced me. But when our time of talking comes, he will be hoarse from answering my questions.

Chapter 24

We speak of nothing much while we dress. Fub whistles as he fastens his clothes and pulls his boots back on; he has put in a good day's work with me and is satisfied. An insistent thought flits and buzzes around my head like a fly: *perhaps one more*, it hisses, *then he'll understand*. He only thinks he cares for Margaret because she still exists – if she is no more, then all his affection must come to me. This seems so simple to me, so clear and so true that I open my mouth to share this with him. But when I look at him, Fub's face is as blank as putty. I must keep all my thoughts to myself. With a thrill of revulsion, sudden as stepping barefoot on a slug, I resent his simple head.

'How goes the rest of your day?' Fub asks conversationally as we negotiate the confined spaces of the house.

'My sister is to be christened,' I say, although I had forgotten it until he spoke.

'And will you say the Lord's Prayer backwards while the priest talks?' he says and rolls his eyes and shakes his head in imitation of someone touched. It makes him look lumpen and solid. I look away.

'You mock my proper hatred of the baby and ignore the reasons why,' I almost whisper in my fury.

He stops his gibbering and looks at me with amusement. 'I know you feel nothing for the child. I am impressed by how steadfast you are in your disinterest.' I am steadfast in my intentions, too, I think. My plans for us are unaltered.

One more, perhaps. I cannot meet his eye in case my excitement shows and he wants to know the cause of it. 'I shall be appropriate at the ceremony,' I say. 'I would not want to keep her out of heaven when her time comes.'

'You are morbid, Annie.' He laughs at me again. 'Do you foretell my end? Imagine me slicing through a vein or crushed under a cow?' I hold him tight in answer. The only death I want for him is simultaneous with my own.

'I shall come to your house tomorrow.' Fub is slipping his heavy apron over his head, his eyes on the meat he needs to joint.

'You won't have to *attend* to your cousin then?' I say.

'No, I will not,' he says, distracted by his task and missing the teasing in my tone. 'I will come in the afternoon.' He picks up the meat with tender care, like a father at his child's crib. 'Make sure you can . . .' he turns it over, holds it to his nose, inhaling, then looks at me at last, fully concentrating on his words, ' . . . supervise.'

'If I have no other calls on my time.'

'Let me take up your time. I will try not to be too quick about it.'

'If you are too fast, I will wait till you are ready again.'

'I am always prepared for you.'

'Are you ready now?'

'You could feel how ready if you come here.'

It is easy for us to talk in this way. When we share a house together, when we are man and wife and a large bed waits upstairs every night, then we can play and jest in this manner all the time. How could I have doubted that he was anything other than everything to me?

I hear Levener's wheezy cough from the slaughterhouse. This is spurs to my flank and I'm off. I know the route home so well now that I am able to think of other things as I walk, so when someone calls my name, I do not take any notice at first. But then 'Miss Jaccob!' called out a second time snakes into my head and scatters my thoughts like startled chickens. I swing round.

Margaret stands there, smiling at me as if we were friends. Her lustrous hair gleams as if it were recently oiled; her white skin shines too.

'Miss Jaccob.' She curtsies, then looks up at me from her bent stance, her eyes glittering bright under her black lashes. 'You visit us again?' If it were not for her clear gaze and even-toothed smile, I might imagine she was making fun of me.

'I do.' She waits for my explanation. Her thoughts stack as neatly as children's bricks, it will be up to me to pull out the lowest and watch them topple. 'I owed Mr Levener an apology. My housekeeper was mistaken in thinking the beef was poor quality.'

'How kind of you to intervene for her.' Once more, I study her for signs of amusement. She is serious. The fates mixed beauty and sweetness in her bowl but omitted wit and humour from the recipe.

'She does not have the words to explain herself.' Poor Jane! By the time I have finished describing her, she might as well be made entirely of dough, so daft will she sound. 'And we value

Mr Levener's business too highly to entrust an explanation to her.'

Margaret will not be versed in the way of dealing with servants, I can say what I like. She smiles again; she has an endless supply of smiles. I think of my little knife, buried under my clothes in the drawer in my room. Its sharp blade could slice at each corner of her mouth and scar her smile onto her face for ever. She would have to grin through every sadness as she'd be rendered unable to look anything but happy for the rest of her life. However long – or short – that span turns out to be.

She pulls her shawl about her, planning to walk away and, as she does, I notice a token threaded on to a thin ribbon and pinned to her dress. 'What is that?' I say, as I snatch at it. I know what it is. It is a button, identical to the one Fub gave me.

'This?' she looks down to where my fingers grip. 'Frederick wanted me to have it. It was from his mother, to remind him of his home.' She puts her hand over mine to detach my fingers; two tiny lines of concern appear between her brows. 'It is worthless.'

'Then you will not mind if I take it.' I tug at it and the ribbon frays and gives.

'Oh!' Margaret whimpers, her hand now closing only on the empty pin. 'Why do you want it?'

My mind races. I regret my impulse; I did not want to betray myself to this creature before I had made my plans for her. I wanted to keep her as happy as a caged bird, swinging to and fro and singing to herself, till I had decided her fate.

'It is the very same as one I lost,' I say. 'Forgive my rude haste, I should have asked properly if I could have it, but I was so relieved to find a match. May I take it?'

Margaret tips her head from side to side as if she lets this idea fly about. It settles. She smiles. 'I am delighted you have found it so unexpectedly,' she sighs, 'although if I am sorry to let it go, it is only because it was precious to Frederick.' I could tell her he has plenty more.

'Margaret.' I take her hands in mine. Her fingers are soft and smooth. Even if they were to spend a long time under water, I suspect the tips would not pucker. She stiffens at this intimacy, pulling her elbows in. 'I need something else from you.' She starts like a cornered deer: perhaps she thinks I want every last item of clothing she stands up in and I'll leave her naked in the street. 'Do not fret,' I say, trying to smile as widely as she had been doing, to reassure her. Holding the expression for longer than a second is tiring and my cheeks begin to ache. I marvel at her stamina. 'What I want you can easily give. There will be no more stolen buttons.' I laugh, but she only looks puzzled at the reference.

'What do you want, Miss Jaccob?'

'A lesson.' What else could I say? Old habits die hard and most people seem to like the idea they can teach me something. 'Do you sing? I expect you have a very fine tone, your speaking voice is so sweet.'

'Oh, I love to sing.' Her hands relax in my grip, softening like dead fish, and I let them go. She looks upwards at the pearly sky with her sapphire eyes. 'But I am not sure I have any skills at music to pass on to you.'

'I do not want a *singing* lesson, Margaret, but rather to learn a particular song. My sister is christened soon and I wish to serenade her.' She sways at this news: it's as if she herself rocks the baby's cradle. 'Teach me your sweetest lullaby. I cannot ask my mother or the nurse without revealing my intention.' The christening will be over and done with by the time I see her again, but she'll never know that.

Margaret glances about her, as though surveying the street for a suitable place to begin.

'Not here,' I say sharply. 'Where do you stay?'

'I have a little room at the top of the house. It is very plain,' she adds nervously, perhaps presuming I need furbelows.

'That is perfect!' I say. 'But we must be alone. I should be embarrassed for anyone else to hear. My voice is only adequate at best.'

She is still wary of me, alternately meeting my gaze and looking quickly away. You might think we were friends if you saw us, for we are standing very close together and only need to speak in low voices to hear each other. I could easily either slap her or stroke her cheek without much effort. The same muscles could move my arms to embrace or to hurt her. It would be such a simple thing to stop her heart. Her thoughts would fade like mist in sunshine.

'When can we meet uninterrupted?' I say. Behind her, I think I see Fub and step even closer in so that she conceals me. The figure moves on; it is not him but someone altogether coarser and stockier. I grunt with relief and she recoils as if my breath were rank.

'Come tomorrow, early. Titus goes to see the cows driven in. Fub will go there, too.'

'And Bet?' I ask. Neither of them must see me. The christening is set for the late afternoon. I will have time to change my dress. I will need to change my dress.

'Bet goes to her sister's,' she shrugs. 'It will be all muck and mooing at the market, won't it? They would not expect me to go.' If she had a few more days alive, which she does not, we would include the visit. It would be diverting to watch her attempt to keep her skirt clean as cattle swirl about her.

'If we are to be alone, leave a hat on your window sill where it can be seen from the street, and I will come in.' She nods, her face solemn with committing the instruction to memory. It occurs to me that all her froth and airiness masks stupidity. 'Do you have such a hat?' I had better spell it out.

'I have a bonnet. It has a blue ribbon, and many small flowers round the crown. Some are like daisies, only without a yellow centre. The colour is more akin to . . .' she wrinkles her nose in thought 'an orange. Quite pale, though. But the flowers are the brightest white. Oh, what colour is the middle exactly?' I am exasperated by hearing her recite the interminable details of her hat. The more she speaks, the more vapid she appears. Fub will be very grateful to me for what I am planning. Two hours in her company would drive him to distraction and a lifetime would be untenable. 'Apricot!' she announces. 'Oh, I love apricots. Do you?'

Is this how friends talk to each other? I am glad I settled so early for my own company; I could only keep this sort of conversation up for a little while before I screamed. I smile. 'Oh, I do!' I agree, matching her tone. 'Especially if they are still warm from the sun when they are picked.' *Prunus armeniaca*, I think, seeing the small fruit cupped in the palm of Dr Edwards' large hand.

'Oh, yes!' She would twirl right around with joy if there were space in the road. If all I needed to do to get her attention was warble about hats and fruit, I might have saved myself some time. Although I fear I might have expired with the effort. It makes me feel heavy to be so light.

'*And sing blow away the morning dew, the dew and the dew. Blow away the morning dew, how sweet the winds do blow.*'

Margaret sings in a high, pure voice. It is surprisingly loud, loud enough for two people passing to stop and listen to her, applauding briefly at the end. She catches their eye and then smiles, catching her bottom lip prettily in her teeth. Both she and her audience are delighted with this display. I clap my own hands together lest I seem dour.

'So!' I cry, to shatter the moment, taking my hammer to her stained glass. 'You sing beautifully. I am very much looking forward to your tuition.' Margaret dimples, a skill I do not have and cannot mirror. She goes on her way, still humming.

*   *   *

I am energetic with my enterprises as I walk home. How best to deal with her?

'Anne Jaccob?' says a child's voice, close by my elbow and, without thinking, I turn straight away and say 'Yes?'

The boy who speaks looks as if he has won a race. He has overtaken me easily, hurling my own name in my path to trip me.

'What do you want?' I say. It is too late to deny being myself. He has only one eye fixed on me, the other iris wanders lazily away to the outer corner. It is hard to know which one to look at.

'Here,' he says, peering closely with his good side at a scrap of paper then thrusting it up to me. He has held it so tightly for so long it is warm and curled. I have to pick it open with my fingernails. *Frederick Warner. Known as Fub*, I read. The writing is thick and black, the vowels filled with ink. Dr Edwards' hand is as familiar as my own. Indeed, I have seen it more. *Cornu aspersum*, it would once have said, or *sum, es, est, sumus, estis, sunt.*

I look round instinctively, as if Dr Edwards were about to step forward and claim his paper. Two thoughts crash in my head as if they fought there: he is dead and he writes Fub's name.

'Where did you get this?' I ask the squinting child.

He does not reply but instead he points across the street. I look at what he sees with his one straight eye. Onions, his oversized coat flapping, waves as though we met each other across a park on a summer's day. He weaves in and out of the other pedestrians, making his way towards me deliberately but without haste. I realise that I have always known I would see him again. We were interrupted in our game of strategies and must now take it up.

Reaching us, he extends a long arm into one deep pocket. He brings out a lace-trimmed kerchief and puts it to his nose. Closing his eyes, he inhales deeply. 'Musk,' he says. 'I have to remind myself that the noxious fumes around me do not represent every fragrance.' The boy and I are an unwilling audience but he looks contentedly to the air above our heads as if we were about to applaud. 'Here, child.' The boy looks sideways at him as Onions hands him a coin. I am trembling and clench my jaw so that he will not notice.

'Are you well?' he says, unable to stop his lips curling in a smile. 'Of course, I can see that you are *recovered* but, alas, that will change as surely and as swiftly as the waxing and waning of the moon, given the nature of your previous indisposition. Will it not?' His voice is rich and dark as wet mud.

The boy, who has not spoken save to christen me, pipes up, 'One more piece, Sir?' and wishes promptly that he had stayed silent. Onions smites him on the head with his many-ringed hand. The glancing blow reverberates like an echo and the boy sways on his feet. A bloom of fresh piss spreads on the front of his thin trousers. Onions closes his eyes and says 'Go,' with such weary menace that the boy cries out before he leaves. I cannot bear to watch his departure. My heart is a little out of place with sorrow for him and I need to right myself. I have no fellow-feeling to spare.

'Ah,' Onions puts his fingertips together. 'You have the note? You know the handwriting, I think?' He looks around. 'It is unfortunate that we must converse in the street like this. But then you have had many intimate conversations in such places, have you not?' He presses his fingers together and the tips whiten. 'So many of your secret doings have, perversely, been conducted in the open air.' He looks at me carefully, like a cobra poised to spit. 'You have been observed,' he says wearily, as though he himself had maintained a continual surveillance. 'The author of that missive, my friend the scholar Thomas Edwards, is dead. Oh!' He puts one index finger to his lips, stroking them with its long nail. 'Oh! You did *know* he had died, didn't you? I am not breaking the news to you, I hope?' He raises his eyebrows and inclines his head in a show of sympathy.

Sometimes you need only add the smallest amount to balance the scales exactly. Now this last piece of information weighs everything even. However unlikely and unpalatable their alliance, Onions and Dr Edwards link arms and block my path.

'My father told me.' To my relief, my voice does not tremble.

He taps the nail against his upper teeth. 'Do you grieve very much for your beloved teacher?'

'My father grieves enough for both of us. I had not seen him for many years.'

'Oh, but you *had*.' He pretends disappointment. 'Anne, do not lie to me,' he sighs, raising his eyes to heaven as if he and God despaired together at my moral failure. 'You read the note. Are you going to deny you know that name?'

I return his stare, blank eye for blank eye.

'I know the name,' I say.

'Thomas was convinced that you and . . . oh, what *is* he called?' He frowns, as if he really cannot remember Fub's name, 'Frederick, is that correct? Yes, Frederick. He thought that you and the butcher's boy, *Frederick,* were planning a future together. One visit to his employers was enough to convince me what a foolish notion that was. He would not own two pence to his name and they'd a pretty bride planned for him, anyway.'

'You went to the Leveners!' I speak too loudly but I cannot help crying out. I wish I could stuff my words back into my mouth.

Onions watches my distress dispassionately. 'The *Leveners*,' he says eventually, as though he might introduce us later. 'I am a little peeved, to tell the truth, that I have had to reveal my hand so soon.' Onions rubs lightly at the base of his throat, his skeletal fingers spread wide. 'You had no doubt hoped to taunt me with what you saw. *Simeon*, you would say, *I know about your boy*. And I was so very much hoping to reply: *'And I know about yours.'* But your father came to see me in such distress that I had to abandon my plan for a drawn out game.' He has made his move. He thinks he has won.

'"Simeon, can you forgive me?" he said.' He mimics my father's guttural tone. 'My sister was mistaken to send you away and I will remonstrate with her.' He imitates the way my father stands as he speaks, precisely catching his habit of looking out from under his eyebrows as though he had a broad brimmed hat squashed low on his head.

'I reassured him that I was not offended. That woman, his sister, is obviously an imbecile and not worth engaging with. 'You tested her honour, Sir!' he parrots, flapping his hands as Elizabeth does.

He had better not begin to describe my mother to me, should he wish to amuse himself further with more mockery of our household. 'I have not told your father of your dalliance, Anne. Merely that I will *consent* to pay you court once again. Suffice it to say, if you give me the smallest cause for my feeling vexed, then . . . I'm afraid I shall be persuaded to confess what I know.' He drops his head for a moment, saddened by the prospect. 'So you would do well not to disturb my fragile equilibrium.'

He glares at a passer-by who comes too close to us and then closes his eyes, as if the sight makes him dizzy and nauseous. He looks at me as though he has me trapped under a glass. 'Do you walk home now, Anne? Or will you try and run to the butcher's to whisper of your being discovered ?' He steps back to let me pass, motioning me to leave. 'I have no need to follow you; do not think that I shall. I never did. The streets are as full as ever of my little spies.'

Of course. Every small boy who ran past me, who crept behind me when I walked or looked down on me from high walls or through windows was in his employ. The world is a pierced screen through which I have been watched by hundreds of pairs of eyes. He has been noting my movements with care and over time, as when you observe mice going in and out of the skirting, the better to choose the place to set the trap.

'I have no plans to elope with that fool Fub,' I say. 'He was an experiment. I wanted to see if I could make someone dote on me and his fawning was instant and abject. It only served to persuade me that I have no need of the affections of men. And I will never let you near me.'

Onions breathes hard through his nose. He moves his tongue in his mouth as if chasing a splinter of bone. 'We are united in our oppositions, aren't we?'

I laugh at both my little wit and his larger discomfort. 'I do not know what you said to my father.' He opens his mouth to speak. 'And I do not wish to,' I continue. 'But I will rail against any union with you as long as I must.'

It is as if a great hand plucks me by the back of my dress and holds me aloft. I look down at us both. Onions is greatly reduced from this vantage point. His miniature person sways and topples like an ant carrying a leaf. What he knows is a burden only to him.

I can squash him with my littlest toe.

'Miss Jaccob.' Onions elongates his neck, then bows in courtly politeness. 'I had hoped you would begin to see that our nuptials might be *beneficial* and *appropriate*, if not a meeting of minds. And there will certainly be no mention of love!' He snorts at the thought. 'But it is of no importance whether you do or do not appreciate my offer. Your recalcitrance presents a challenge, to which I shall rise. Let us create our own unique companionship. Each, as it were, to his own.' He gathers himself upright. 'I am in no hurry. It is your father who may wish to proceed with haste.'

He winds away through the crowds. After I am gone, he will easily bear the humiliation of my absence. He will shed me like a snake his skin and wrap his coils around another. I imagine Fub beside me now, one hand at my waist while the other pats my behind in approval. *'You'll soon be rid of that idiot,'* he says, squeezing me, *'We will be away from here by nightfall. One more!'*

His words in my head are a tonic. I feel as restored as if I had newly bathed. And I have my little task to complete, to which I am greatly looking forward.

Chapter 25

The house bristles with purpose when I arrive home. Someone has severed a small branch of leaves from its tree and placed it, together with a wilting tangle of flowers, into a large vase on the hall table. Lace covers sit awkwardly on the surface of every piece of furniture; they have been kept hidden for so long that they are marked with brown striations of folded storage. A bundle of fresh lavender scents the air with the inappropriate smell of fresh laundry. The coverlet underneath it is already peppered with its tiny fallen flowers.

'Anne!' My mother leans over the banister; she looks relieved to see me. 'I feared you would not be here in time. The vicar comes soon. Are you prepared?'

I can only change my clothes to be ready, not my attitude. I will answer only for my attire. I had wanted to extricate myself with another imagined malady, but she holds my gaze in a way that prevents me leaving. 'In a moment,' I say, climbing the stairs towards her, but she is already gone – doubtless to squash the baby into the christening gown. I had helped dress my brother when he wore it, easing his plump hands through its tight sleeves and laughing at him almost trussed with its starching when I had finished. She calls me to follow but she will have to manage alone this time; I could not promise to be as gentle with my sister's pink skin.

We assemble in the drawing room. The newly scattered cloths flutter up with each arrival. Aunt Elizabeth practically sweeps them away; she comes like a ship in full sail. The feathers on her hat tremble magnificently. She glares at me in greeting. I suspect my answering smile is more of a simper. My father is nervous: having the vicar visit is akin to being examined. His ways of household management will be held up to the light and he himself appraised. He shifts from foot to foot and adjusts his coat several times.

When the vicar comes in, my father and Aunt Elizabeth both stiffen as if a lightning bolt struck them. The vicar beams as though this rigidity was normal. He has a boy with him, dressed in a similar collar and carrying a Bible and a small box, but his face has such a livid rash of pimples that it's hard to notice his calling. He keeps his eyes to the floor, doubtless to avoid any familiar expressions of revulsion in those who look at him.

The entrance of my mother and the baby softens the room, as when you suddenly feel the warm sun on your back. Swaddled in layers of linen, the child's face is almost obscured but her small fists beat the air. Jane and Grace follow, both concentrating on my mother and the infant. They have no proper place here, no task to perform, so they do not know what face to make in our company. I won't indulge them by being friendly. My mother smiles at each of us in turn, probably celebrating that this infant lives another day as much as her welcome to the church.

There's a sudden rapping at the door and when Jane goes to it, she comes back in so swiftly she trips and collides with the blemished boy. They shout together in discomfort then apologise in unison, then both are silenced by my father's cold stare. All this does nothing to distract from the fact that she went to admit Onions. Of course he comes! He has discarded his enveloping coat and is dressed in a ludicrously bright velvet coat with so much lace hanging from his sleeves and at his throat it's as if he has an entire other person underneath his clothes, struggling to escape.

My mother does not react, so preoccupied is she by her child, but she is the only one unaffected. Aunt Elizabeth almost levitates with anger. Jane's distress has coloured her cheeks a livid mauve and the vicar is loudly introducing himself, although there is no need. His curate has flattened himself to the wall, avoiding more collisions, and my father is propelling Onions into the room with a hearty slap on his back. Grace is looking at me and there is a flicker of something like solidarity in her expression, though I do not return it.

'*Simeon!*' my father booms.

'Ssshh . . .' warns my mother, shielding her child from his bluster. Then she looks up properly, first at Onions, next across at my father. 'Oh,' she says, 'Mr Onions, I did not know—'

'Madam,' he cuts her short. 'I am honoured to be a guest at such a propitious occasion. When an infant is baptised, how special and how splendid it is.' He peers at the bundle from a safe distance. 'And to think that soon I shall forever be joined to your family!' He does not look at me, though I am sure he can feel my eyes on his back, for he wriggles and hunches as he speaks.

My father steps forward. He addresses all his remarks to the vicar, rightly thinking this is a safe port of call. 'Sir,' he says, 'my sister is standing godparent for me.' Aunt Elizabeth whinnies in delight. 'And, as my wife comes from a sadly *reduced* family,' he glances at my mother, who is impassive, watching him, 'my friend, Mr Simeon Onions, therefore deputes for her.'

There is such a forceful, simultaneous intake of breath at this that you might imagine there was no air left to breathe in the room afterwards. Without knowing that he does so, the vicar provides a welcome distraction from the consternation by setting out his stall. The boy shakes a length of material loose and lays it across the table, next he takes a small vial of holy water from the box and sets it on top. There is much crossing of themselves and muttering throughout, though it seems to stem from routine not holy observance.

My mother looks aghast, but what can she do? She can hardly clutch the baby to her and run from the room, can she? Jane and Grace look ready to catch her if she falls, at least. I take some small comfort from the incredulous expression on Aunt Elizabeth's face. She opened her eyes wide at the announcement and her mouth fell open, while her hands clutched her cheeks and thus she has remained, as though set in stone. The coffin will have to be modelled to accommodate her pose when she dies.

Onions is preening; he directly faces a large mirror which affords him much opportunity for admiring glances and adjust-ments of his garments. He probably imagines the room newly-papered in a garish design of his choice. I hear a strange thumping in my ears and it is a while before I realise it is my pulsing blood. As quickly as I have identified the sound, so do I feel an immense gathering nausea and my head feels so light I think all matter must have been removed from it. Unaccountably, the floor rushes towards me in a manner which is both mysterious and swift.

When I come to, Grace is kneeling beside me, one hand holding a cold cloth to my head, the other a little glass of water. My mother kneels on the other side and it is her voice I hear, insisting I am safe and will be well. She is not holding the baby and I get to my feet shouting 'Evelyn!' although I did not know I cared where she might be. My father stands at the far end of the room as though my fainting were a female concern and might, in addition, be contagious. Onions sits alone, bored by this new demonstration of my physiology. Aunt Elizabeth steps forward, holding her great niece with such awkwardness it makes me laugh. At least I have unlocked her arms. I'm dizzy again – I have stood up too fast.

'Where is the vicar?' I ask.

'He has gone to the kitchen,' says Grace. 'Jane said she would take him for refreshments while you recovered.' Then he has his daily cake. All is well for him, it seems. I am consumed with the suddenly remembered horror of Onions' threat to me. My cage is closing – unless I am quick, the lock will turn. I must get to Margaret as I promised. I am weak as a kitten. I close my eyes, it is suddenly too wearying to look at the world.

The vicar, summoned to return, comes in wiping his mouth and brushing his hands as he always does. His little acolyte follows suit, adding gazing wistfully at Grace to his repertoire. Even if he were miraculously cured of his pustules in an instant, I doubt she would pay him heed. He is too frail and too nervous, and he quivers where he stands: she would bend him in half like a reed in a gale.

'So,' the vicar begins. My father has not met my eyes once since his speech. Onions likewise has not glanced my way. But now, as if on cue, they both turn in my direction. I think of the helpless bear, held fast by its chains to be bitten and torn. But I am not tied up. I flex my feet in their shoes and feel them move when I wish. I curl my fingers in to a fist and dig my nails in to my palms. I smile winsomely at them both and in an instant they are disarmed, grinning at each other. They think I am so easily won! The tables are turned. I am no captive beast but instead I am the serpent hypnotising its prey. *Do not think*, I hiss to myself, *that I will waste my venom on either of you.*

'We name this child Evelyn Anne,' the vicar says, startling me as effectively as sal volatile held under my nose. I choke on my own spit, but disguise it as a cough.

'For you,' my mother says to me. 'For my treasured daughters, that they will always share a name.'

When my brother died, Jane told me that all my mother's lost children would wait for her in heaven. As they were quite large in number, I imagined my mother burdened for eternity with their care. If anyone thinks that, because I am now mentioned on some godly roster, I will be a heavenly nursemaid too, then they had better have another thought coming.

I nod my head, hoping that this passes for happy acquiescence. Behind the vicar a small spider winches itself slowly down on its strong thread. I watch it intently while the vicar banishes the Devil. He sprinkles water on the baby's head and she mewls in protest. The assembled company are so focussed on these events that no one sees me sidle towards the door. I have no need to explain my leaving; after all I fell to the ground insensible not long ago, didn't I? I am permitted fragility and a desire for air. The hallway seems so delightfully empty that I luxuriate in it for a moment. Then I fetch what I need and leave it where I can easily find it.

As I am sliding back to my place in the gathering, Onions appears beside me like a summoned shade. 'Anne,' he whispers, his wet mouth at my ear, 'we must resume where we left off, must we not?' I try and move but he takes my elbow and holds it too firmly. His fingers are stiff and the long nails prick. 'I will arrange a further outing for us.' He tightens his grip and I bite my lip to avoid crying out. 'She is recovered,' he announces to the assembly, as though we had been discussing my health. 'Such very, very good news. Now we can all turn our full attention to Evelyn, as befits the day. It is hard to turn from one beauty to another, but we must!'

'I have prepared sweetmeats,' Jane rushes to the door and stands like a plump sentry beside it.

'I fear I cannot consume them,' Onions pats the velvet fabric over his stomach, staying his hand to caress himself while he speaks. 'I do not tolerate baked goods. Although I am positive that you will produce the most delicious of all.' Where once she might have reddened with pleasure, Jane now stays immobile. He is the invading army of her fortified domestic terrain. Grace glowers at him too, sergeant to Jane's general. Onions ignores their hostility. 'Madam', he bows to my mother, 'since I shall not join you in happy consumption, I will take my leave to meditate on my rewarding and spiritual role. I shall call soon.'

There is an air of embarrassment when he has gone, as if he left behind a noxious smell. My mother wraps the baby's shawl more tightly about its little form. 'I will take some food,' she says, 'I have eaten very little today.' Jane takes the bundle from her.

'Come, Madam,' Grace says, all three visibly relieved to have their duties and place restored.

'Will you stay, Sir?' my father asks the priest. To my surprise, he refuses.

As he draws level with me, he says: 'We buried the child yesterday evening. The poor boy who fell from the bell tower,' he adds, mistaking my silence for forgetting. 'There was sparse attendance, of course. He sometimes lived in a shared house, with a transient population. Only a few of them attended. And I learned that one of their number was . . .' he leans in, thinking his voice is hushed, but he whispers with great force, 'recently *murdered*!'

This is a word everyone hears. It rises above any hubbub. It has no difficulty reaching the ears of each person in the room, stopping them in their tracks.

'What's that?' says my father.

'Ugh!' is all the boy can manage.

'Alas!' cries Aunt Elizabeth, as though she witnessed it.

The vicar raises himself to his full height, enjoying their attention. 'A little lad died in our churchyard,' he says, 'and it transpired he knew a man that was recently murdered.' Jane and Grace cross themselves, they'll be working up to seeing more ghostly visitors again.

'Who was it?' My father is serious now, walking heavily towards the vicar, scattering the fluttering women nearby. 'Who was it?' he asks again, with more intensity.

'I do not know the victim's name.' The vicar looks nervous now, as if he were a suspect. 'A professor, they told me. Killed in a field for his purse.'

'Dr Edwards.' My father crumples, his head in his hands. 'It must be him they speak of. He was a dear, dear friend.' Sentimental tears well in his eyes. 'And now a child dead, too? These are terrible times.'

'The boy's death was an accident, of course. And I am sorry for the loss of your friend.' The vicar lays a reassuring hand on my father's arm. 'The Lord giveth . . .' He looks upwards and my father's gaze follows momentarily, with reluctance.

'Did they say there were any clues, any more information? Have they any idea who might have done it? What did they tell you?' My father shakes the man's hand away as he speaks, his voice rising with agitation.

The vicar regards this outburst with some distaste. 'Sir,' he says, 'please do not ask these questions of me. I was officiating at a funeral, not conducting an enquiry. It would have been inappropriate of me to press the mourners on these matters. Tantamount to gathering *gossip*. It was mentioned that there had been another death, a savage one. That is all. They vouchsafed nothing more and I did not press them.'

'Of course, of course,' my father mutters, though it is clear he thinks it was an opportunity wasted. His brow stays furrowed as he considers what he's heard. I think I can actually hear the cogs turning in his brain and, sure enough, he turns to me. 'What business is it of hers?' he says, nodding in my direction.

'What? Oh, Mistress Anne was present. That is to say, she was in the church. On the very day the boy died. Quite possibly at the very time.' He shakes his head ruefully. 'The angels could have brushed you with their wings, Miss Jaccob, but instead you were closer to the devil's work.'

'Indeed?' My father still doesn't look at me but I feel the gathering storm. Just as there is a tang of iron in the air before rain falls, so there is lead behind his words. 'You have been in the church a great deal recently, haven't you? Elizabeth!' Aunt

Elizabeth jumps like a startled nag. 'Didn't you tell me Anne had attended church with unusual frequency of late?'

When she realises it is *I* being quizzed and not she, she puts her shoulders back and marches forward. 'Yes, yes,' she agrees. 'When we had our . . . difficulty with Mr Onions . . .' she trails off, she must not offend my father or she'll be cast out again. 'I did tell her that a young woman might do better to spend her time elsewhere, or doing good works, but she was adamant. *"I have led him on, Aunt,"* she said to me, *"It was wicked of me, and I must atone."'*

I once stood at the edge of a high wall and felt a swooping sensation in the pit of my stomach when I looked down. My exhilarating fear dared me to jump or fall. As I listen to Aunt Elizabeth's betrayal, my insides lurch again. *If Fub were here,* I think.

But if Fub were here, he would be of no use to me. He would stand transfixed while my father held the magnet of his authority up to him, then stick fast, unable to move. This is the plain truth and, as ever, the truth is a sorry thing and lets me down. I know I must deal with these tribulations alone.

'Well?' my father's face is close to mine. I could easily count the large open pores on his nose.

'Sir.' The vicar tries to intervene, his tone kindly but ineffectual. 'Your daughter is a clever girl, who—`

'Clever!' my father retorts as if he had called me a bad name: 'I agree that she can find her way from the front to the back of a book, but she isn't clever enough to behave as she should. Her wanton attitude nearly cost her the hand of a good man in marriage, but fortunately,' he strokes his lips, pleased with himself, 'I have the brains to put things right.' He puts his hand on the vicar's back, guiding him out of the room. He has had enough of rhetoric. 'Many people, Sir,' he explains, 'are doubtless as *clever*, too. But you need your native wits about you to get on. Cleverness chases common sense away.'

'I can see where that absence leads, to be sure. As I fear that I myself have no native wit, then I must be content to stay where I am in life.' As he goes, the vicar turns to me and I think I catch him winking, but I cannot be sure. The pitted boy sidles crab-like behind him, bearing the box as if it were a small coffin.

'Come and eat, Anne.' My mother takes my hand. Her action keeps my father at bay. When I turn to her I cannot see her clearly; she seems out of focus and distant.

'My head aches,' I say. 'The room oppresses me still, I must have some air.'

She lets me go. 'Later,' she says.

'Off to church again, eh?' my father shouts after me.

The vicar and his boy are ahead of me on the road; they walk side by side in step. Their heads are close as they speak and then a burst of riotous laughter drives them away from and towards each other several times, the merriment doubling at each meeting.

If I were near enough to send them into the path of a carriage, I would. Or at least under the passage of an emptied pot.

Chapter 26

Carrying a candle under a shawl proves harder than stowing a knife. The beeswax smell climbs into my nostrils and lodges there. At first, I do not mind – it makes a change from horse muck and human sweat – there is something of the church about it and that's pleasant. But soon I find it cloying: it scents my hands and clings to my clothes till, if it were a poison, I'd be dead of it. The fact that I am carrying a large candlestick as well makes my burden all the more awkward.

The shop is dark and shuttered, as Margaret had promised. In the little window at the top, her hat sits in plain view. With a heavy heart, I realise this is the first visit to Levener's where I will not see Fub. In my mind's eye, though, I see him everywhere. He walks jauntily from the slaughterhouse, his hands sticky. I hear him whistling as he sharpens a knife. He sits at the bench to eat, sweeping the crumbs into his palm. He takes the stairs two at a time in front of me as I go to Margaret's room and swings the door wide. '*Here she is,*' he says. '*Make it quick. I will see you soon.*'

Margaret looks up, frightened. 'You didn't knock . . .' She rises from her little chair. 'I thought I would have to guide you here.'

There is no point in explaining how, and how well, I know the house. If you put your ear to the wall, you might still hear us. Fub says I am a noisy girl but I do not know another way to be and he seems loud enough, anyway. This thinking is very distracting. We must lie down together soon or I will have to squeal away on my own. 'I followed my instinct,' I say. 'Are you prepared?'

She nods and smooths her skirts, although they have no creases. When she notices the swollen shape of my shawl, she stares for longer than she should. Her eyes meet mine again and she looks away quickly, as if she caught me naked. She goes towards her chest of drawers.

'Oh, wait. I have brought something for you.'

She turns to see me holding the candle. It is a ten, large enough to last several weeks. 'Wax?' she says, taking it and sniffing the stem. 'How precious. And a candlestick, too,' she says, biting her lip in wonder as I assemble the pair. 'That is what you carried!' she says, as delighted as if we played a guessing game.

'You might like to see it lit,' I say. 'I swear they have a purer flame than tallow.'

'And no stink.' She pauses, looking guilty at having said a vulgar word. 'But we shouldn't light it now, it's not nearly dark yet.'

'I should like you to see it burn. It'll last you a good long while, do not fret, but I want to show you how bright and clear it is. Do you have a tinderbox here?' The ashes in her grate look dry, they are probably several days old.

'By the kitchen range,' she answers reluctantly, disappointed by my insistence. She makes to leave.

'I will go,' I tell her. 'You prepare our music.'

'I have only a few sheets,' she says, embarrassed. 'The best song is only in my head.'

'I will write it down as you sing,' I say. 'I have no talent for remembering. I can use the back of these pages for the purpose.'

The kitchen smells so strongly of meat and fat that I almost have to slice my way in. The aprons hang on their hooks; they are empty of their owners but hold their shape: Levener's swells, dome-like, in the centre, while Fub's is straight. I turn it away from me, stroking the smooth underside where it lies against him. Holding it to my face, I breathe him in. Above me, Margaret practises her hums and trills. The floor is swept clean and dry, there's no sound from the slaughterhouse and the suspended meat hangs still and cold. Empty hooks wait ready and sharp.

I stand behind the counter, pressing my hands flat on the bare wood. 'Six eggs and a belly of pig?' I say to the empty air. 'Fub'll ready that for you.' My voice sounds like a child's would do playing shop. I look down at my splayed fingers; they are pink and soft, the nails tipped white. There'll be grime there soon, dried blood and skeins of fat. Washing my hands over and over will make them red and coarse, the nails will break and the knuckles roughen. 'Fub'll prepare that for you,' I say, loudly. 'Wait here, Fub is coming.'

'Mistress Jaccob?' Margaret calls from upstairs. I had almost forgotten she was there. 'Did somebody come?'

'No,' I shout back. 'I am alone.'

'I thought I heard you speaking.' She comes in to the room, her dress hovering that miraculous distance above the ground. 'There is no fire here,' she says sweetly, as though I am the simple one. 'The kitchen is beyond.' She gestures with the grace of a dancer. I follow her to the range and coax a little flame onto a firelighter. As we climb the stairs, my hand cupped over it, it would be easy to touch it to the hem of her swinging skirt. But then she could run to her room, shut the door and extinguish the flames, sacrificing only her petticoat, so I wait. My hand shakes with the effort of keeping the flame close to me.

'The sheets of music are here,' she holds them up. 'These are two songs, but I have a third that is more suitable for such an occasion.' '*What is so strong as her soft and delicate hand?*' she sings, then breaks off with a nervous cough. The sound of music in the small room makes us unwontedly intimate with each other.

'There!' I light the candle easily, though neither of us trimmed the wick. I put the firelighter in the grate where it splutters and dies in the cold ash.

'Thank you for this gift,' she breathes, and the flame trembles with her exhalation. We regard it silently for a moment, bravely shining into daylight. Margaret raises her limpid eyes to me. 'May I pinch it now?'

'A moment more. Sing to me what you will teach, please.' She frowns, then puts her little white hands together in preparation. 'Wait,' I say. I draw the little curtain across the window. It has a pattern of stars printed on the thin fabric and hardly shuts out the light.

'Sit on your bed,' I tell her. Then, seeing her becoming downcast as she struggles with my commands, I smile and say more softly, 'I will not ask much more of you, Margaret.' I have never said a truer word, have I?

She perches on the very edge of her coverlet, automatically arranging her skirts wide. 'Good,' I say. 'I intend to transcribe the verses, but let me just listen as you sing, so I may become familiar with the song.' The sheaves of paper lie beside her, the tableau is complete.

As she sings, I drop my eyes to the floor so that we do not have to look at each other, but nonetheless her cheeks are bright red by the time she reaches the last verse. She stops, drawing a deep breath as if she'd used it all up. I choose not to applaud – the sound of a single pair of hands clapping might sound cruel. 'My turn,' I say.

'Do you know it already?' she asks.

'To begin,' I say, 'I will hum the tune only, so you can hear if I have that part down pat, then you may say the verses aloud for me to transcribe them.' She seems satisfied with that.

There is a sudden loud rattling of the shutters in the street, then a voice cries 'Levener!' and Margaret and I freeze, listening. 'Shall I tell them he is not here?' she asks, her eyes wide. She is caught between our secret and hard business.

'No,' I whisper, 'they will gather that for themselves.' The banging on the door continues for a while, in case Levener merely dozes in his bed. We stare at each other. Eventually, there is silence.

We seem more alone together than before. Margaret looks inquiringly at me, awaiting my next instruction. It is: 'Close your eyes, I am nervous and do not wish to be observed.'

She does. With her half-moon of dark lashes against her pale skin, the rose in her cheeks fading and her chest rising and falling evenly, she could not look more perfect. It is better to end her like this, I reason, than when she begins to spoil. She opens one eye cautiously, to discover why I am delayed. 'Margaret!' I admonish, and she giggles like a child and squeezes her eyes shut. She wriggles further onto the bed until her back is nearly at the wall.

I begin to hum the tune she taught me and, keeping my eyes fixed on her all the time, I separate the candlestick from the still burning candle. Raising the candlestick as high as I can, I bring it down on her shining hair and pretty head with one strong swing. Just as I end my snatch of song, so she moans and sighs. It is not the duet she planned.

The blow has landed well. Margaret slumps fully against the wall, sitting upright with her eyes closed shut as they were a moment ago but with no sense behind them. Her mouth still curves up in its usual expression of sweet content. Thus far, everything has happened as it should.

I remember the tedious amount of mess when Dr Edwards bled to death from his wounds and wish I could leave now, but I cannot tell if I have hit her hard enough to deny her ever waking again. She groans, a lower note this time and seems about to say something. That decides me. My arms shake with the weight of my weapon in one hand and the unaccustomed effort of keeping the burning candle away from my clothing in the other. I press my feet flat to the floor to steady myself, then rock gently from side to side to build momentum. 'Now,' I say aloud, although I did not mean to speak. The edge of the candlestick, cupped to catch dripping wax, slices as if it had been sharpened for the purpose. It splits her skull with a shocking short clap of splintering bone and then sticks fast a little way in her unthinking brain. With effort, I stand up straight again and pull it free. 'Oh, forgive me,' I say, apologising for the undignified suck as it's released from its gelatinous mooring. I say sorry to her again when I smash it several times on to her hands, first the right and then the left. I have some idea that I must spoil all her perfect features one by one before she burns.

The only sound now is my panting, coarse and quick like an animal after a chase. This is another vulgar noise that would be an affront to her sensibilities if she were still in a position to be upset by such things. She would be mortified, too, by the disarray. How quickly her broken fingers would fly up to tidy and to tend, if they could. Unstopped by either of us, blood streams from her wound and onto her bodice. It already obscures one closed eye and coats the cheek in its path. The smell is salty, dense and strong. Beneath her skin she is no sweeter than anyone else.

I study her carefully. Her chest rises and falls, but the movement is so little that you could leave a porcelain cup balanced there without fear of its falling. There are long intervals between each tiny breath.

In the street, two voices join together as they pass, and there is a sudden shrill of laughter. The sound is so vital and so near that I half expect Margaret to incline her head towards it. She stays drooped in her last pose and does not stir.

Outside the world still turns, but I will stop the clock for her in here. I have more to do. If I left now, if the laceration didn't finish her, she might well live on, though she would be reduced and ugly and with only half a head of hair to tend. That would not suffice. I mean to make her ash, blowing away on the wind of Fub's hot breath as he calls her name to find her. 'Come, Anne,' I say, imitating her soft tone. 'Will you leave me like this?' I shake my head as if she really had enquired and set the candlestick down carefully. All this clouting was just the preparation. It is a bonfire I plan.

The candle flame bends away from its task as I kneel in front of her, a draft insisting it back as I direct it forward. I am the victor, though, and a steady blaze takes hold on the hem of her skirt. I light the pages of music, dropping them quickly when they catch. When I hold the candle to the bed cover, bright dots of flame quickly join together and form a sparkling chain. The fire is eager now for more tinder and I oblige with a touch to her hat: the dry straw crackles and the little flowers pop. Little eddies of air coming from under the door, in at the window and down the chimney encourage the fire's spread. The dryness of its kindling does the rest. Leaning towards her to ignite her hair, I stub my toe hard against the heavy candlestick where I left it on the floor and cry out.

Whether it is my shriek or the cooking of her ankles that rouses her, I do not know but Margaret's one ungummed eye opens. She stares ahead unseeing and brings her hands instinctively to her face. Her bent fingers dangle, useless as twigs held up against swords. She begins to try and to suppress the flames patting ineffectually at her skirt. She is screaming: a high, steady, ugly note made with the same voice that sang so sweetly only moments before. Her mouth opens wide to reveal red teeth.

As much as her battered body will allow, she turns and looks at me. 'Why?' she gasps, her voice thick with her own blood. As if I will answer. I go to the door and a gust of air rushes in as I open it, fanning the flames all the more. She begins to burn like an effigy, her arms stretched wide. 'Anne!' she wails, the only time she's ever said my name. Though she should be tethered to the bed by fire and pain, she begins to rise. The sheets are alight now and the curtains go up in flames. She lumbers towards me, as unsteady as a child learning to walk. She babbles like a baby too. Her progress is so slow it's almost comical. Either the fire or her wound will kill her and they fight to be first. I watch, transfixed, from the doorway, as if I had a bet on the outcome. Her first creator did well with her, but I am proud of her leaking head and stiffening limbs.

With a thrill, I realise that I might soon see the exact moment of her end, a transformation that Dr Edwards with his sudden haste and the boy with his flying absence denied me. I clap my hands together in joy, something which, of course, she can no longer do. She can still point her arms towards me though and as they swing together she is suddenly so close they touch my sleeves. I cough as the smoke thickens, sticking in my throat and pricking my eyes. Her flesh roasts and reeks like any other beast's. If I do not make haste, the fumes will choke and blind me and Margaret will smother me in her blistering embrace.

I dart behind the door, then hold it tightly shut between us. I hear her hands brushing against the wood, she cannot make fists of them any more. Only when there is no sound from her do I realise the handle is getting hot and I let go. There are other noises, though: the shattering of glass and splintering of wood as the fire seeks more fuel. Smoke spirals from underneath the door and out between little cracks in the wood. I had not thought the fire would take hold so greedily once it had done its bidding. I can smell my own singed bonnet where I got too close and my costume is peppered with ash. I creep down the stairs, though the blaze's roar would let me leave safely unheard even if I was wearing my father's heaviest boots.

There are already a few people outside, shouting for help and water and attempting to break down the door. I go through the slaughter room to the stable door beyond. Both bolts are slid shut and I wrestle with each ineffectually in turn, there must be a trick to their opening I do not know. 'I cannot die here,' I say aloud. A plaintive cry answers. A calf, penned in and frightened, senses the conflagration and my panic and kicks against its prison. I crouch down and speak through the slatted wood to where its dark eyes peer back at me. 'We will get out together,' I say, 'neither of us will be roasted today, one carcass is enough.'

One bolt gives, then another and the door opens at last on to the narrow alley. There's a runnel full of red liquid in the middle. This is where the slaughter waste must be sluiced away – it is dyed with animal blood. I let the calf free from its pen. It sniffs, its wide nostrils trembling, and takes only a few tentative steps, scarcely getting itself through the doorway. It fears this new freedom. I push hard at its obstinate rump, then prod it with my toe for encouragement. 'I cannot wait all day for you to leave,' I say. It walks into the alley then begins to trot briskly away. 'Thank *you*,' I mock, dropping a curtsey to its retreating rear.

The sound of shouting is louder now, they must have got into the shop and be searching the rooms.

I find myself in a maze of unfamiliar passages and ginnels. It is beginning to grow dark – great, red streaks stripe the sky. An orange glow marks the place where Levener's still burns. I think I can smell cooking meat in the air but I might be mistaken. I walk in a wide circle, checking my pace so that I do not appear hurried or anxious.

Emerging into the street after what I consider an appropriate interval, during which I sing several verses of Margaret's last song to pass the time, I am surprised to see there are still flames and smoke rising. Little is left of the butcher's. I had thought myself foolish to leave the candle and stick behind, but the fire has obliterated the scene so completely I could have left a signed confession with no fear of discovery. They will scarcely even know that Margaret was there, and her little hat will be all ashes by now, too.

Neighbouring buildings are alight. The concerned occupants have formed a chain along which they pass buckets. Each one's contents lands on the flames with a small hiss, smoke spurts briefly, but the fire burns on. Where is the Dutchman's cart, to begin the extinguishing? There's a flurry of bright cinders in the air and when one lands on my skirt it leaves a grey mark, despite my furious brushing. I am scarred with the song in my head, too. It is stuck as firmly as if it has taken root, and though I try and be rid of it with singing other tunes, it is to no avail.

I turn for home. My heart almost bursts from my chest with a rush of happiness. It is done. The slow cold of approaching autumn nips at my toes and leaks in at my collar and cuffs, but I am as warm as if my bones were molten.

The fire in the hall hearth is small, a tame cat compared to the tiger I unleashed. I hold my hands to it for a moment, more to consider my next plan than for warmth. Above the mantel, I am reflected in the cloudy glass. There is a line of dark spots on my temple and cheeks. I peer at them: they are little marks of ash, so I lean more closely towards my reflection to wipe them away.

'Mistress!' Grace grabs my arm and pulls me back. She points to where the hem of my dress spills over the grate like water. 'You may burn your costume,' she says. 'Take care.'

'How do you do, Grace?' I ask. She is outwardly as milky and sweet as Margaret, though a great deal more sharp within.

'I am well,' she says carefully. Since I threatened her, except for when I fainted and was safely comatose, she has been wary of me: skirting the edges of rooms when I enter them and hugging the banister if we cross on the stairs. If I were her, I should have pushed me into the hearth just now instead of saving me from harm. Margaret melted like a waxen doll, but I suspect there would be a black heart left uncharred in my ashes.

'Are *you* well, Mistress?' Grace is a picture of concern. 'I was afraid for your health when you fainted.'

I feel aggrieved that she saw me so vulnerable and unguarded. 'Oh, I am quite recovered. In fact, I feel as well as I ever did.'

She smiles. 'And the baby sleeps,' she says, as though that will be our next topic. 'She is in the nursery, of course, now that she is named.' She lies in the very same cot where my brother died. The same curtains pull shut around it, the same soft blankets moult. I shiver. As if I'd found a maggot in an apple, a thought worms into my brain, wiggling insistently whichever way I turn. *The baby is in the way,* it murmurs as it slithers, *she is in your way*.

Grace is frowning, looking at the clock face and counting on her fingers. 'She sleeps too long,' she says. 'I must have been dozing too, and forgot the time.' She yawns at the mention of her slumber.

'There was much coming and going today and many visitors; the excitement will have tired her,' I offer helpfully.

'You're right,' she says, looking wary at my explanation – it is all the right facts but the wrong person delivering them.

'I will go to her,' I say. 'I'll soothe her if she grumbles.'

She looks astonished. 'Will you, Mistress? No, I cannot let you do that. I should see to her.'

I seize her arm, holding a handful of her coarse woollen sleeve. She freezes in the act of leaving, torn between her duty and her weariness. 'Yes, yes, I shall do it, you may go, Grace.' I shoo her away. She hesitates for a moment more, waiting to see if I might change my mind, then scampers off. I'll bet she cannot wait to get to Jane with this news.

Babies are not silent when they sleep. Evelyn snorts and snores like a piglet. She stirs at the sound of the door. I pause, holding my breath in case even that sound disturbs her and she is still for a moment, then a floorboard creaks under my foot and the bedclothes rustle as she moves again. 'Hush,' I whisper, but she does not know my voice and begins to whimper. 'Hush,' I say again. On tiptoe, I approach the crib. She cries now, a thin mewl punctuated with drawn gasps. I listen carefully. She cries again and hearing it makes my own breath catch in my throat with panic. This is a new sound: urgent and unhappy.

I creep to the crib and peer in. She has kicked off her covers – her fat legs flail against the air and her mouth is open wide. Her black eyes meet mine and she stops crying as she examines my face. Instinctively, I place my hand on her forehead, to calm and reassure her. She wails again, but there is no power in it: no wonder neither Grace nor my mother come. She burns beneath my fingers. She is so hot that her skin feels dry and crisp as paper. 'Hush,' I tell her, but in her distress she is deaf to any soothing. She is consumed by fever. I slide to the floor beside her crib.

Perhaps I should place a pillow over my sister's face. It would surely be a blessing to us both. We suffer in our different ways simply because she is alive. She will be too weak to struggle much, I would not need to use any force. I lean against the cot's wooden side, my eyelids itching with weariness; I long to close them and sleep. My arms ache where I held the door shut against Margaret's escape and my legs are heavy, too. I haven't the strength to fight even a baby. She sobs and her breath grates. I begin to breathe in and out in time with her rhythm and it is too shallow and quick for comfort. This runt is not a proper adversary and, besides, what is the use of my ending what I didn't start? I may well change my mind in the future, but I have no plans for her tonight.

I sigh to myself, resigned to an act of kindness. 'Now, now,' I say, getting to my feet. 'What's all this fussing?' I lift her hot little body from her bed. 'Come along,' I say, wrapping her shawl around her. On the landing, I call out and the bedroom doors fling open like traps. When my mother sees Evelyn in my arms she smiles, but as she takes her from me, the baby's burning fever scalds her, too.

Chapter 27

Where is Fub? I have rehearsed his discovery of the scene. I have imagined pacing the roads between our houses with a cartographer's eye for detail and still he does not come. Everything is burnt, he has only himself to bring – and I am sure he kept all his coins in his britches for safekeeping, both those that I stole for him and his small earnings.

The doctor fusses about; each aspect of Evelyn's recovery is reported to me now I have seemingly enrolled myself in the sisterhood of concern, and I imitate relief well enough. I think more of my mother's horrified, fearful expression at her baby's peril than I do of the child's welfare – I do not want to see her so unhappy again. She embraced me so hard and for so long when the doctor pronounced the fever subsided, that I can still feel where she held me several hours later and it is a good bruise.

Jane beckons to me as I sit with my hands in my lap, watching the window. 'The butcher's boy is here,' she says. She doesn't call him 'Fub'. She bites her lip in concern, and takes my arm as we go to him. Neither of us pulls away. I like the little warmth of her and the slight pressure.

Fub leans against the door as he did when I first saw him, but that is all that is the same. His eyes are bloodshot and the lower lids sag to reveal a livid inner rim. He is stooped. If you had marked where his head reached on the door frame that little while earlier, you would make a much lower mark now. He holds a hat in his hands and twists it in a miserable circle as he waits. It falls from his grasp when he sees me.

'Anne,' he says, not noticing that he uses my name in front of Jane. It is only the second time he has done so. Then he had fresh sap in him, clattering his hammer and springing to his feet. Now he droops like a flower out of water.

Tears leak from each eye. I have never seen him cry and it makes my arms stick to my sides. I look around for Jane, but she has left us alone, which is uncharacteristically considerate of her. I am disappointed – I want a witness to this terrible exhibition.

'Anne,' he says again, hoarse and low. I go to him and put my head on his chest, though my arms still hang down. I can hear the gurgle of his guts and the steady thump of his heart. He puts his arms around my back. For a moment we stay silent, then I grip my hands in a fist behind his back and squeeze till he splutters. He is saying something into my hair but when I try to lift my head to hear him, he pushes his jaw down to stop me. The top of my skull aches with the pressure. 'Fub!' I protest and pull clean away from him. He looks damaged, as though he had been broken down to his constituent parts and reassembled ineptly. If it weren't for the smell of him and his brown smudged eye, I might think him an impostor.

'Lost, Annie,' he says, and waits for me to speak.

'Tell me what is lost,' I say, wondering where he'll start.

'Levener's place.' His head hangs, he mutters as if he had food in his mouth. 'The trade. Margaret.' With this last word, his voice rises to a faltering treble.

My thoughts gallop like a pack of dogs – I must be careful not to let them bite. 'How are they lost?' I say, as if they might perhaps be roaming in some woods.

'All gone in a fire, Annie. A terrible destruction.'

The dogs nip at my ankles. 'Is Margaret . . . dead?' I must have it confirmed just in case some foolish heroism prevailed. He nods. I hope I am not smiling. His manner suggests that I do not. The butcher's shop will leave a great cavity like a pulled tooth. I had not given any thought to how the Leveners might deal with this gaping wound. I expect Titus will shrink with grief and it will be a great sorrow to him that he cannot conserve his own useful fat. Bet's mournful 'Ayees' will deafen everyone for miles around.

Suddenly, I remember the little dogs, squirming blindly under their mother. 'The puppies!' I say, and I begin to cry.

Fub stares at me oddly, as though my tears run black. 'You weep for *them*?' he says, incredulous.

'They would have burned where they were,' I say, picturing them huddling together against an enemy they could not understand.

Fub frowns. 'You did not shed tears for Margaret, did you? Your heart is a strange thing: stone cold on one side and melted on the other.' *She built her own pyre, that one*, I think.

'They were innocent,' I say.

I wish I had not. Fub says the word over and over, along with 'Margaret' and 'the good-hearted Leveners' and suchlike. This interlude must finish soon. I wish I could go away and get on with something useful, returning when he's done.

'I'll have to go back to my family now,' Fub says. 'I have nothing. No bed, no lodging, no work. Titus and Bet stay with her sister, but there is no room for me there.' He looks away to some point in the distance as though he watched the disaster still unfolding.

'Another employer would take you. Will you not stay? ' I say in a whisper. I know the answer he will give, which made it easy to ask.

'Annie, I must go home.' He is still looking away. Then he turns to me and draws in his breath, looking nervous, as if he's about to make a difficult speech.

'Perhaps you would come with me? There are families you could work for, in service, till I am able to get a house for us.' I have no answer for that. I realise that I never did. 'It smoulders still,' he says, because I do not speak.

'The fire took hold quickly, did it not, and the cart was much delayed.' I am thinking of the bright orange sky.

'It was,' he agrees.

'When it did come, it was of no use then? The Leveners probably hadn't the insurance mark displayed, so the men wouldn't put their hoses to it.'

He looks at me with sudden appraisal. 'How did you know? I never told you that.'

I shrug. 'I am only guessing from what you say. If it is still going, then it can't have had water sprayed.' He continues to stare. 'I know very little of fires,' I finish, plaintively.

The room is pregnant with silence.

'You know very little of fires,' he repeats, quietly. 'What *do* you know of, Anne?'

He is an amateur mathematician, adding up numbers incorrectly in his head. I go nearer. He flinches, but I kiss him, flicking my tongue into the corners of his mouth and finishing with a nip. 'I know of *that*,' I say. 'And this.' I go to his britches, but he stops my hand.

'Enough.' He leans against the wall, looking sullen. 'What did you think would happen?' he says. 'That we could keep our secrets together?'

'Yours are so small you could hide them under your tongue with your mouth open. My secrets are big enough to choke me if I even try to speak of them.' I stand with my hands on my hips, challenging him to fight back.

He picks at a hang of skin on his thumb. 'You are childish,' he says, sounding like a little boy himself. 'It is what children do, Anne,' he explains, patiently. 'They claim random actions as their own planning. You must have thought me foolish to believe you capable of such things. Or as wicked as you would like to seem.'

'I did not think you the former. I hoped you had a modicum of the latter.'

'Eh?' He stretches his arms upwards then folds them behind his head. We might be in sunshine in an open field with him resting by a tree. He still has the expression of a superior wearily examining a junior, trying to cajole me into an apology. 'Did you think I would come running to you with a knapsack, grab you by the hand and shout: "Come! Nothing stands in our way now! We shall run away together".'

Now, that's a beguiling picture. What would he have brought? Enough food for the journey and a stout blanket? He'd have to have bought them on the way here, otherwise he could only offer me a bag full of cinders. But I could carry provisions, instead. I look about the kitchen to see what I might take. I am hungry already.

'No answer, then?' he persists. I examine him. His torn jacket flaps open, his shirt is flecked with soot. He has no knapsack. Dr Edwards peers through the window, waving. Margaret perches on the kitchen table, taking care her dress doesn't spoil. The boy stands in the sink, ready to jump down. They are waiting to see what I will do.

A crevasse opens between the two of us. It gets wider and deeper. I feel the ground tremble. Fub seems small and foolish on the other side, asking 'What, Annie?' and 'How?', though the earth gapes before him. I taste his mouth on mine. If I had known it was a farewell kiss, I'd have sucked harder. If he pushed me to the ground with my skirts up, would I let him poke? If he guided my fingers to his person, would I stroke him? I cannot remember why I ever thought that was a good idea.

'Why are you smiling, Anne?' says Fub. I did not know I was, of course. 'Do you feel any sorrow for what has happened? Have you ever known grief?'

How dare he ask me that? Oh, when I mourned my brother a great sadness hung about me, but it was like a garment that didn't suit any season, it made me either too hot or too cold. I shrugged it off. I do not want such covering any more, I am happy in my bare skin. On the high shelf above Fub's head stands a row of jars filled with red fruit. Jane has labelled them in her big, looped hand. He could not read them if his life depended on it. I cannot love him to save him, either.

Fub looks at me with sudden malice. 'I have taught you some tricks, at least. I have been useful to you, haven't I? But I cannot say what you have taught me, except to be wary.' He shrinks as he speaks – he will have to leave by a mousehole soon. He turns to leave, picking his sorry hat from the floor where it fell.

'Wait,' I say. I delve into my pocket, then show him what I've found. 'The little button you gave me. Your mother's precious gift.' I hold it out to him. 'You can give it to your next girl.'

He snorts. 'I shall be keeping away from female company. You filled me up, then you emptied me. I'm useless now.' I say nothing. 'You don't want a keepsake, Anne? A reminder of me?' he says, though he takes it.

He scattered them too widely. They are devalued. I remember Margaret with her pinned token. I open my mouth to tell him I took it from her, but he seems reduced enough.

We have become acquaintances who must go about our business. If I wore a hat myself I would tip it to him. I hold out my hand. He laughs and takes it, then turns my palm up. 'No ash clings, at least,' he says. 'I should bid you take care, but it is others who must mind out.' His fingers are calloused. There is a wart coming near his nose. He is both the sweetest and the worst thing I ever saw.

'Anne?' My mother calls. He lets go of my hand and in the time that it takes me to turn to answer her, he is gone. The fallen leaves eddy in small circles where he walked, then settle in light heaps.

'Anne,' she stands in the hall. 'You were a long time at the door.'

' Levener, the butcher, has lost his place in a fire. He sent his boy to say.'

She raises her eyebrows. 'Unfortunate for him. But I shall leave Jane to appoint a successor. One butcher seems much like another to me.'

'As long as there's meat on the table,' I say, imagining a row of Fubs, all identical as soldiers.

'Onions comes tomorrow,' my mother says, moving an ornament on the mantel to no great effect. She turns to me. 'Shall you be here to receive him?'

'Is it my decision?' I reply, wondering why she asks.

She strokes her neck with her long fingers. 'I will be here,' she says, 'but then, I have no choice.' She steps close to me, her breath smells of almonds. 'Will you be here?' she says again. Her eyes are amber. She holds my arms, leaning towards me, studying me intently, then takes a strand of my hair and winds it gently round her fingers. We might both be girls of twenty together, confidantes in a boudoir. 'You have a choice. Go to your room,' she says and I see tears in her eyes. Was this what Jane had meant when she compared us?

'Do not cry,' I tell her, for I am not sure why she weeps.

'Take this,' she says and gives me her shawl, warm as a puppy from her wearing it.

Chapter 28

There is a little purse on the bed; it is from my mother's trousseau and embroidered with her initials. Even before I pick it up, I can see it bulges with coins. I will go in the clothes I wear now and leave everything else behind. I take down Donne's verses from the shelf. The cover still smells of smoke. That will be a useful *aide-mémoire* of my achievements, then. Perhaps I should leave something for my mother? When Keziah emptied my careful curation I did not set about replacing the artefacts. I contented myself with storing an invisible hoard of my thoughts and plans. There is only one precious thing of mine that she might treasure, too. I push my hand into the drawer of my closet and feel for what I know is there, keeping my eyes closed as if I am blindfolded. My fingers find the lock of my brother's hair – it has already begun to coarsen and is dry to the touch. Even after so short a time since I tied it, the ribbon frays.

She hardly needs a reminder of such a loss and even if she sends me away herself, I am soon gone altogether from her, too. This tiny emblem represents only a double sadness. Placing it on my lap, I untie the knot and the gathered hair falls apart into separate strands. Slowly at first, then with more speed, I brush

336

and flick and sweep them away from my skirt, though some stubbornly resist and cling.

As if I am seeing it for the first time, and because it will be the last, I take careful stock of the room. *Honour thy father and thy mother*, the sampler still instructs. At least I am half successful in the execution of that motto. Just as Fub shrank before me, so now I grow too large for the place; the small bed is doll-sized and only a fairy could store clothes in the dresser. I'd have to crouch to make use of the mirror, so I shall leave unseen. I saw myself reflected well in my mother's eyes, that should suffice.

I will smell her marzipan scent on the shawl till I am many miles hence. Tucking the purse into my pocket, I put my finger to my lips. 'Keep my secrets,' I whisper, closing the door.

Jane is crossing the hallway below, one hand to her apron, twisting its bow to the back, the other holding a jug. I wait till she has bustled away. I have told enough lies for a while and Jane would die of the truth. I don't want her death on my conscience. None of the others are, after all.

To the east lies the butcher's ruin. Fub slouches westwards. The Jacobites claim the northlands, but here is the south for my fresh path. I have to resist the temptation to break into a run – I want to be hurling down the streets with my arms spread wide. Instead, I walk slowly and carefully, casting my eyes down with appropriate modesty.

'Unne.' I recognise the flattened vowel. No one else says my name as 'Unne'. But I hardly recognise him. The little Scotsman's face is vastly swollen, his jaw so disfigured that one side hangs down, exposing teeth. Above his bruised cheeks, his eyes are screwed up, as if he views the world against a bright light. 'Now, girl,' he says when he sees me blanch, 'the other fellows look worse than I do.' He tries to smile, but only one side of his mouth lifts. 'Walk alongside me.' He says, taking my arm. I am stiff with horror, but he propels me gently till I soften.

'I thought I might go home, till I was set upon.' He limps, too, and drags my elbow down at each alternate step. We will not get very far together. He could not take me to Meek Street now.

'Are there worse injuries I cannot see?' I ask.

He snorts. 'I think my outward appearance is a fair reflection of the chaos underneath. Ribs broken. My ankle is snapped. I cannot eat for my stomach recoils and my throat closes.' He points to each place as he lists them, and I notice that his finger is bent, too. 'I think they left me to die. But that's taking longer than expected.' We walk a few weary steps more.

'Do you want me to take you to a doctor?'

He snorts again in answer. 'It is too late for that. I can't be patched up now. You can give them my corpse for their practising. What remains, anyway.' His voice trembles but not with self-pity, only effort. 'So, Mistress Anne, how flows the river for you? Do you sink or swim?'

I smile. 'I am dry,' I say.

'Not even a little flask of love?'

'Not even that. I spat out the last of it.'

'Have you had your fill?'

'I have. I was drunk with it, but I am sober now.' I remember Fub, sitting on his hard bed and holding out his arms to me. Let him clap them together over empty air. 'We cannot walk much farther together. Where shall I leave you?'

'I do not much mind. Just somewhere where discovering my

dead body will not frighten anyone unduly.' I would take him home and leave him to sleep towards his ugly death in my bed, if I were not so set on my course. 'You walk with purpose, Anne,' he says, as if in answer to my thoughts. 'Where do you go?'

I would tell if I knew. Any secret is safe with him now: he will take it to his grave very soon. This confessor would not offer me forgiveness or redemption, for the world affords him neither.

'South.' That is the whole truth anyway.

'Ah, South. To sunshine and warm nights, eh?'

'Away from here.' Fub is very small now, I could easily swill him down a drain. 'Love is not like water. I think it was a splinter lodged inside me. A rich pus built up around it and expelled it.'

He laughs, a great guttural hack that forms sputum. He spits. 'I fear I have not the strength to debate that. You think love a sharp thing. Do you want to get pricked again?'

My little claws twitch. I think that I could easily play with love like a cat with a mouse, but I would rather fight an equal adversary. 'Only if I choose to.'

'If you have to choose, then you won't feel love. It is not a thing to be picked up and put down at will.' We have come to an alley; at the far end is an archway with a glimpse of trees beyond. It seems a decent enough place to be his last. 'Leave me here,' he says, without discussion.

I settle him against a doorway. 'How much is a burial?' I ask.

'Ten shillings or so,' he says. He sees me frown. 'More if you feed the mourners,' he adds. We smile at each other. There will be no one at the service except the vicar, so that's a saving. I am loath to part with so much but I cannot condemn him to a pauper's grave. I count the money out, then look him over to see a possible hiding place for it.

'Where can it go so that only the undertaker will find it?'

'I am tempted to give an answer unsuited to your lady's ears,' he laughs, but then winces as even this hurts him. 'It can go into my boot.' I make for his crippled foot and he cries out: 'No!' with a force that shocks us both.

I pull at the other leg as carefully as I can, not least because the boot itself is so flimsy that it threatens to fall apart in my hands before the task is done. It comes off to reveal more hole than stocking, so I push the money as far into the toe as I can and wrangle it back on to him. He cannot help; he has no strength to push against my hands. I am reminded of Dr Edwards' limp form when I arranged him – at least I can make this man look decent for his discovery.

I settle his beret on his head and straighten his felted coat. He closes his eyes for longer and longer intervals. I recognise death pushing against an easily opened door to claim him. *Here's another one for you, Sir*, I think, *and this one comes of his own accord*. What useful notes Death and I could exchange about our methods: I am in thrall to his efficiency and he must envy me my invention. We will be companions again before too long.

'God speed,' the man hisses. Saliva bubbles at his gaping jaw. Artists lie about our last moments, painting them decorous and noble. The daintily speared leak only drops of blood and the elderly drift into a peaceful sleep. It is no wonder that they depict it thus, the truth is so much uglier. From what I've seen, Death come with suppuration, protestation and no grace. It makes a great deal of noise, too, and this man's last breaths are loud, spluttering coughs and squeaks. There is a strange odour coming off him: he is already rotting.

It would be hypocritical to bless him, but unkind not to speak. 'Go to your mother,' I say.

In a heartbeat – mine alone, for he has none now – I take back the coins from his boot.

If you saw me from above, you might almost be able to see little fleshy wings sprouting on my back, so quickly do I move. My feet hardly touch the ground and I do not bother to watch where I walk, for I fear no obstacles in my path. Behind me, everything is caught up, as if in a fisherman's net. And just as bright fish dart amongst the unwanted oily cloths and driftwood of a catch, so things that I cared for gleam and flash for a moment. Then they are lost to view with the flotsam and jetsam in the fast-moving tide.

I face the sun, feeling my heavy money in my pocket and my light heart empty.

Acknowledgements

Huge thanks to the following people who have helped and supported me in all sorts of ways. They include my friends Fanny Blake and Melanie Cantor; my early champions Sarah Hall and Paul Burston; my agent Gordon Wise; my publisher and editor Lisa Highton; my early anonymous readers and my copy editor Sara Kinsella; the lovely team at Two Roads: Rosie Gailer, Ben Gutcher, Ross Fraser, Kate Brunt, Alasdair Oliver, Amanda Jones, Federico Andornino and Ilse Scheepers; Timorous Beasties for the jacket art; Mark 'Vole' Samuelson; The Worshipful Company of Butchers; Erin Kelly and Anna Davis; my CB Class of '14.

And my love and gratitude to my darlings – my children Sophie, Jackson and Martha and my husband, John (who will smile because, in the nicest possible way, he always knew this was coming).

I am also indebted to the multitudes, past and present, whose behaviour, sayings and lives give me an amazing and constant insight into human behaviour: that's why I was staring.

Author's Notes

When I was a little girl, at school, I loved history. Which is to say: I loved hearing about the Olden Days and the funny people, frozen in time and odd clothes in the pages of my text books, who lurched from war to probably another war with some religious or civil uprisings in between. I loved it because it was also about stories and who doesn't love them? I remember hearing about the awful conditions in Days of Yore – child labour and repression and high rates of infant mortality, that sort of thing – and thinking, they must have felt different from us. Something must have protected them, in their hearts and minds, from the privations and grief people suffered routinely on their way to central heating and the NHS.

Then I read Mary Shelley's account of the death of her infant daughter. It was, of course, as harrowing and vivid as any mother's account would be: Mary Shelley had not grown a carapace of stoicism to protect her from life's sorrows, her generation had not somehow mutated and adapted to grief. She might as well have been any contemporary mother, coping with tragedy. She might have been me. In other words, history is us.

I have always been drawn to personal ephemera and documents. It probably stems, in part, from daily diary keeping from the age of ten to my mid-teens. I grew up in the sixties and seventies, decades when the world was experiencing seismic changes and major events. I was, too, it's just that mine were things like the eleven plus exam and boyfriends. History was happening alongside my important, busy life and I barely nodded in its direction. I love reading letters and diaries from past times that describe little triumphs and forgotten upsets, moments of humour or food consumed, knowing that big stuff was happening but not necessarily alluded to. Without social history, it's all just Acts and Tracts.

When Anne Jaccob, my heroine, arrived in my head (apologies for a pseud's corner 'writerly' phrase, but that's what it felt like), there were a number of reasons why I wanted her London to look, feel, sound and smell different from mine. I was fascinated by the idea that, three hundred years ago, an undereducated young woman with a smart mind and febrile imagination would have very little to go on when it came to making sense of, and dealing with, her world. She'd have hardly any conversation with anyone, there'd be precious little communication with her peer group and the impositions of her rank and gender meant that she'd have to find a way of coping with what happened to her . . . and that way turned out to be highly unusual and idiosyncratic.

I love the look and what I imagine to be the atmosphere of Georgian London. Pleasingly, in most areas, you don't have to look very hard to catch glimpses of it today and I thoroughly enjoyed finding my way around Anne's city. But I have to admit I chose 1763 specifically because nothing much happened. Of course, if you were a horticulturalist, the arrival of the rhodo-dendron was quite something. The Treaty of Paris ended the Seven Year/French and Indian War (and France ceded Canada to Great Britain) which probably affected a few lives. But, on the whole, it was a peaceable time. No big skirmishes, no religious difficulties of note and everyone seemed to like their new, young King George Third. Although my adolescent ability to prioritise my doings over World Events amuses me, I can see that if I'd written about Anne's activities in another year and had ignored a sizeable chunk of important history, it would have taken some explaining.

Boswell met Dr Johnson, though, in that year. *That's* big news.

London, December 2015

About the Author

Janet Ellis trained as an actress at the Central School of Speech and Drama. She is best known for presenting *Blue Peter* and contributes to numerous radio and TV programmes.

She recently graduated from the Curtis Brown creative writing school. *The Butcher's Hook* is her first novel.

twitter.com/missjanetellis

TWO ROADS

Stories . . . voices . . . places . . . lives

We hope you enjoyed *The Butcher's Hook*. If you'd like to know more about this book or any other title on our list, please go to
www.tworoadsbooks.com

For news on forthcoming Two Roads titles, please sign up for our newsletter

enquiries@tworoadsbooks.com

TwoRoadsBooks